Trouble in Seattle

PIKE PLACE VIEWED IN 1930 FROM FIRST AVE.

TROUBLE IN SEATTLE

Lea Macquarrie

CHB Media, Publisher

ISBN 9798885897556

LIBRARY OF CONGRESS CONTROL NUMBER: 2022950105

CHB MEDIA, PUBLISHER

(386) 690-9295
chbmedia@gmail.com
www.chbbooks.com

First Edition
Printed in the USA

Cover art by Kathy Raines

Book design, CHB Media

For Marilyn,

and for my native city and spiritual home, Seattle

Authors' Note

Although this novel takes place in Seattle during the 1930's, this is a work of fiction. Persons and events in this novel have no past or present existence outside of the author's imagination.

Book One

THE RAILS

IN A DESOLATE MONTANA RAILROAD YARD just before sunrise on a cold windy morning in 1931, a destitute middle-aged white man and shivering Indian girl huddled together beside a small campfire. The girl carried bedrolls consisting of tightly rolled army blankets, the man a full pack with food, clothing, and cooking utensils. Everything they could not carry with them they had either sold or were leaving behind. The man, Jack Vogel, at age forty-two was starting over in life. Starting what exactly he didn't know.

He had spent over a decade working the Cat Creek oil fields bordering the Crow reservation. Now they were about to join the nomads of the Great Depression and waited to hop a freight to Seattle where Jack hoped to find his brother and work in a shipyard or lumber mill.

He clutched his checkered lumberjack jacket under which he wore several flannel shirts with wool pants. A black stocking cap was pulled down low on his ears. His backpack was stocked with supplies for their journey and, having been advised a boxcar door once closed couldn't be opened again except from the outside, he carried a crowbar to prop the boxcar door and keep it from closing. He'd sold all his other tools.

The girl, Juanita Rose, his daughter, had turned fourteen years of age a week earlier. He should not have brought her. Her hands were dirty and her face was smudged with soot from their fire, she was cold and probably hungry. He wished he were a better father. In this, as in everything else he undertook in life, he was a failure. He was a failed ranch hand, failed railroad worker, failed logger, failed father, husband and breadwinner, failed human being. He was going to change that. Get work in Seattle though his brother Frank. Purchase Juanita some nice new clean clothes; get her in a good school. Provide for her as a father should.

She held her hands and fingers close as possible to the fire's dying coals without burning them. She had no gloves. Her teeth chattered so hard he could hear them.

"It's so cold," she said. "When does the train come, Papa?"

"Soon, Juanita."

But he didn't know.

He spat on the ground and pulled his coat around him tightly.

"Will it be warm on the train?"

"I doubt it, honey. Not in a boxcar. But it'll be warmer than this."

"We can still turn around and go back, Papa."

"Go back to what? We have been evicted from our home, Juanita. Any furniture I couldn't sell is probably out in the street by now. I sold our tools, our truck, Misty and anything I could to raise money for Seattle."

Misty was her horse and he probably shouldn't have mentioned her. His daughter was still crying about losing Misty late last night and he had promised the mare had gone to folks who would love and care for her while knowing she would end up being butchered and eaten.

"There's no future for us in Cat Creek, Juanita. No future at all."

"For me there is. There's school."

"You were a notorious truant. You skipped more than you went."

"I can't argue it, though I regret it."

He had raised Juanita best he could manage with no mother but it was nowhere near good enough. She could hunt, fish, rope, and handle an axe or saw as well as anyone in Cat Creek, but could

Lea Macquarrie

barely read or write. She was a tomboy and a discipline problem in school, from which she had been suspended many times for fighting and for truancy. At home she was different, a true helpmate, good about her chores, with a sweet disposition most of the time.

They squatted on the semi-frozen ground where a few remaining clumps of frosted weeds clung to the earth. The area around them was flat and cleared of trees, but clumps of frozen bushes provided partial concealment from other squatters and the yardman's shack. Far down the tracks were as many as a dozen widely scattered campfires around which men waited for the incoming freight. He had deliberately camped away from them. Most men were good, but you had to watch out for the bad ones, especially when traveling with a young girl—and with their life's savings in his boot. Hopefully he and Juanita might have a boxcar to themselves. How exactly, he didn't know. He had never jumped freight before, though he had repaired track across much of Montana and Idaho.

More men kept arriving. They looked like shadows, ghosts in the darkness stumbling out of the brush as if drawn by the fires. To avoid drawing unwanted company he had deliberately kept their own fire minimally kindled, but with the result it had been too small to effectively warm them. At best it allowed them to warm their hands.

"I am going to miss Aunt Vi," said Juanita.

Vi meaning Elvira, his sister-in-law, who had been briefly married to his rambling-man womanizing big brother Frank. The plan had been originally for Vi to keep Juanita till he found work in Seattle and could send back a train ticket purchased with his first paycheck. Juanita might then travel train like a real passenger instead of a tramp but no, she threw a tantrum and threatened to hop freight to Seattle on her own if he wouldn't take her with him. He knew her to be obstinate and spiteful enough to follow up on it, too. What frightened him most about Juanita was her fearlessness.

"I know you'll miss her. I will too. Vi was my best friend and as close you ever had to a mother. Don't worry though, we'll send for her when we're settled. You'll see. You, me, Frank, Vi, we're all going to live together in a big house with anybody in the family we can find and round up."

"Vi won't come. You'll never get her out of that shack in the woods."

"She'll come. Especially when she sees the fancy big house we are going to live in. Frank said he already had several in mind. We're going to get the whole family together. You'll see."

"She said she'd shoot Frank between the eyes if she ever saw him again."

He watched her remove the gold and silver locket from her neck and stroke its smooth surface between her fingers, rubbing it as if her mother was inside of it and it were a magical charm which might conjure her to life. She flipped open the tiny metal clasp holding its face closed and lifted the lid to look inside, and there was her Mother. Who she never knew. Alma, his dear Alma who died when Juanita was still so young the poor girl was bereft of even her memory.

The locket bore the inscription, *For J Vogel, love Alma.*

She snapped it closed again and replaced it securely around her neck and said, "Tell me about her. Anything that comes to mind. I don't care if you've told me before."

"It hurts but in a way I can't explain your inquiries bring her back to me and I welcome her memory. She was cheerful, Juanita. Happy, high spirited and full of joy. She loved to dance, have fun. Her laugh made everyone around her happy. Around the house she wore my cotton pants and shirts like you and a red bandana around her head but when she dressed up to go dancing she became a different person. She wore red nail polish and lipstick and a red dress and looked pretty. Smelled pretty too. She liked to sing at home when doing chores and if there was a local band that would let her, on stage. She didn't sing all that well but there was a sweetness to her voice. She looked nice in whatever she chose to wear, even in an old hand-me-down dress. Your mother had shinny jet black hair like you. I watched her brush it a hundred times every night. Sometimes I brushed it for her but mostly I didn't because I loved to watch her do it. Everyone loved her, but me most of all."

It was, he knew, mildly fabricated for her benefit. All but the part about how much he loved her. Her mother had been a problem on the reservation and later in the town of Cat Creek itself. Excessive drinking, fighting. But there was a side to her she saved for those she loved. He had not healed from her loss, even after all these years.

"Read Uncle Frank's letter again," said Juanita.

He carefully unfolded it. Frank had mailed it to him from Seattle months earlier. It was wrinkled and smudged but still legible. Elvira had read the letter aloud so many times for his benefit he had just about memorized it. He couldn't actually read but was trying to learn. He had studied it so hard by now he was able to recognize the words. Near as he could remember, here is what the letter had to say.

It's a worker's paradise here, Jack. There's shipbuilding at Bethlehem Steel here in Seattle, lumber mills are hiring in Everett and Marysville and if you like working outdoors there's work on fishing boats. All you have to do is walk around the waterfront and say you're looking to hire onto a crew. East of the mountains there's abundant agricultural work. We'll find something for you, no need to worry. It's been our mutual dream for a long time to get what's left of our family back together under one roof, and this is the right time and place to do it, Jack.

The remainder of the letter mostly warned him of the dangers of hopping a freight. Jack chose not to read it aloud to Juanita.

If you can't get into a boxcar before the train leaves the yard, run alongside and grab on from the front of the car, not the back where you can be swung around like a rag doll and thrown under the wheels. Don't pick a car hauling steel, iron, or any load that shifts. Dress Juanita as a boy and keep her female identity secret. Maybe cut her hair or tuck it under a longshoreman's or newsboy hat. Stuff some rolled up stockings in her underwear near her privates.

You can find me at the Seattle Unemployed Citizens office or the Socialist Club on Yesler Way. Can't wait till we're all living together in a big house. There are plenty here empty.

He rolled a Bull Durham and lighted it with a wooden match and threw the match into the dying fire. Morning light was beginning to seep through the darkness. Shapes of trees and bushes not seen in the night became faintly visible in the approaching dawn.

"You know Daddy, mother had an offer to be in the movies."

"That would be news to me. I never heard that."

"Yeah. Aunt Vi told me about it. Seems this producer, some kind of Hollywood bigshot, well, he drives into the reservation looking for a location to shoot a western and sees mother hanging laundry. She's so pretty they do a screen test. They want to put her in the movies, but she got sick before they started production of the picture. Vi says she would have been a big star."

He doubted Elvira said any such thing. Juanita's mind was made up her mother had been some kind of beauty queen movie star type, which she was not.

"Wasn't she the most beautiful woman you had ever imagined? Did you think you were dreaming when you first danced with her?"

Jack shifted on the hard ground and said, "She was a good-looking woman in her youth. Not as pretty as you, maybe, but good looking. You're right about dancing though. From the first time I danced with her I knew we belonged together."

"Was she fat?"

"A little plump before she got sick maybe, but I wouldn't say fat."

"Will I be fat?"

"Who knows, Juanita? I doubt it. Not at the rate we're eating."

"So many of the women on the Reservation are fat. I probably will be too."

"You're of German descent. Like me."

"Yeah but I'm Indian too, like my mother."

"Your mother was a breed. She wasn't full blooded. We don't know her family history. We do know about my side of the family. Unskilled German immigrants who worked like beasts in factories from dawn to dusk. As hard as it was for them it was harder for Indians. It's why I moved us off the rez into the town of Cat Creek proper. Anyway, we're leaving Indian country for good now, Juanita."

"Won't there be Indians in Seattle?"

"I don't know. Probably."

He did not encourage further discussion. He had taken her off the reservation into the adjacent town of Cat Creek so that she could have a better opportunity in life. He had wanted a better school for her there but she had become a schoolhouse problem and, they said, a troublemaker.

They saw dawn approach before feeling the warmth of the sun, which rose in an almost imperceptible ascent over the distant white peaks of snowcapped mountains. In another hour or so, when the sun was all the way up, it would be at least another twenty degrees warmer, maybe more. The morning sun, hazy and blurry initially, became an immense ball of orange fire spilling light over the distant snow-capped mountains but the air remained cold. It was because of the wind, thought Jack. It blew down from the mountains as frosty, harsh, and mean as the land they were squatting on. It would be good to leave Montana but they would have to go right through those mountains to do it. Maybe take a day and night to get completely on the other side. The mountains were much farther away than they looked. The plains could be deceptive in that way.

"I'm sorry Mother died so young," said Juanita.

"So am I, honey."

"It's strange. I don't remember her, but I dream about her. Aunt Vi said she didn't even know Mom was sick until it was too late."

"None of us did, honey. I reckon it was just her time."

"But she died so young."

"Yes."

"Then how could it be her time?"

Jack shrugged and put his cigarette out on his boot.

"I'm only a man, honey. I don't know why things are the way they are."

* * *

It had taken them a full day to reach the Northern Pacific rail yard in Helena, which was in the opposite direction of both Cat Creek and Seattle but the closest railyard where they could catch on to a western bound train to Seattle. There was full morning light now. The yard watchman limped out of the yardman's shack and hesitated on the wooden steps as if not entirely wakened from a deep sleep. He unzipped his pants and urinated in the dirt, zipped up and lighted his pipe. He led his leashed watchdogs along the tracks but seemed to deliberately stay away from trespassers.

It seemed to Jack the train should be in by now. Men who claimed to have wide prior experience had earlier told him where to catch on, what to look out for and how to get to the closest major rail yard and make his connection. Among these advisors were many of his Cat Creek neighbors, but they didn't always agree. Frank had said in his letters that the Helena yard bulls were tramp-friendly. Most he talked to agreed and said he needed a northwest-ward bound Union Pacific train with flags hung on the engine car. The flag had to have a red ball in the center of a white background. Otherwise he could end up on a local making every whistle stop between here and nowhere and take forever to get there.

He heard the train before seeing it, the nose of its blackened engine car appearing first, then its lengthy column of wooden box-cars. It chugged slowly to a sputtering halt, trailing a plume of black smoke, its low hanging cloud of steam hugging the greasy stained earth below its iron wheels. An engineer climbed down from the engine car, scratched his balls and spat in the dirt and walked slowly across the field to the watchman's shack. Tramps were gathering their belongings in preparation to board open boxcars.

The watchman opened the main gates to the yard. A half dozen previously concealed trucks and sedans came from behind the distant tree line and high brush to charge full throttle through the gates, raising great clouds of dust. Yardbulls were swinging nightsticks, cursing and shouting, leaping out of the previously concealed vehicles. Jack heard the dull thump of hard wood against bone, the cries of surprise, anger and pain from fleeing men. Snarling yard dogs chased after them, leaping and taking some down. A few men mauled by dogs were screaming. Other men were down and being kicked hard by railroad yard bulls before being dragged outside of the gates.

Either times had changed or Frank had been wrong about the yard being tramp friendly. He and Juanita jogged the length of the train, then along a rock-strewn edge of a sandy incline where loose gravel made it difficult to maintain a footing. They had gone about a hundred yards when he stumbled, tripped and fell, landing hard on a large sharp rock embedded in the dirt. He felt a trickle of blood down his leg. He managed to get up, limping along the embankment until they were out of sight. Winded, he slumped down on the dirt behind some stunted shrubbery to catch his breath and rolled up his pants to examine his injured knee. He knew it would slow him down.

He was breathing hard when he said, "We're all right, Juanita. Don't be afraid."

"I'm not afraid, Papa"

His knee throbbed.

"Goddamn," he whispered.

He rarely swore around his daughter and wished he hadn't, but he was frightened, angry, confused and dumbfounded. It wasn't supposed to be like this. He'd planned to simply walk the length of the train until finding a well-sealed, preferably empty boxcar. Jumping a moving train was a dangerous proposition even for the experienced vagrant and it now seemed their only chance if they were going to get to Seattle and Frank. If you didn't get it right you could lose your legs or get mangled and killed. Jack had once witnessed it with his own eyes when he was repairing track outside of Great Falls and it was a terrible thing to see.

He led them further along the tracks to a vacated industrial work site where sand and gravel had been bulldozed into tall mounds of sand. From the crest of the gravel pile they had an advantageous view of the entire area but were far enough the yardmen to be safe from harm. He wiped the perspiration from his eyes and assessed their position. He estimated them to be about two hundred yards from the train's engine car, which would be moving maybe up to thirty-five miles per hour by the time it reached them. Even if a man could jump into a boxcar moving at that speed it would be like taking a nosedive from a tall tree into a lake that had dried up. Probably break an arm at least.

Fifty yards from where they perched the tracks made an extreme sharp turn. Jack knew from his days working the rails the train would have to slow up there. With a running start aided by the slope of the gravel pile, they had a shot. He did a few bends, testing his injured knee. Hell, he could make it easy enough; the steepness of the gravel pile would assist in the descent. The timing was the thing. The timing had to be perfect.

He regarded Juanita solemnly and said, "Now honey, I seen you run before. You're fast, I know that. I've seen you catch roosters and jackrabbits with your bare hands. But I know you're tired too, and you've got to get over it for just a little longer. You're going to have to run as fast as your legs can carry you, as fast as they *ever* carried you. This is important, Juanita. Do you understand me? I mean it now. Otherwise, you could get hurt. Hurt bad, I mean. We are going to have to outrun this train but we'll have the advantage of a head start when it starts to slow on the curve. When I say go we'll charge down this gravel pile as fast as we can. When I'm inside a boxcar I'll reach down and pull you in. When I do, make sure you keep your knees and feet high and don't let them get sucked under. If you feel that happening, push yourself away as far as you can. It's your only chance. "

The train approached so slowly it seemed not quite up the task. Jack's spirits rose with the probability of an easy hop after all. They began collecting their gear and securing their packs. They charged down the gravel slope, he with the heavy pack on his back, she ahead of him by at least ten yards. He was breathing hard, but smiling: No worry about Juanita keeping up, she ran like a deer. Lady Luck was with them too, because the train was moving so slowly around the bend they would be able to climb into an open boxcar easily.

The weight of his pack accelerated his decline down the gravel pile but the momentum turned against him. The steepness of the gravel pile propelled him downhill faster than he could manage. He felt himself sliding on the surface of the gravel as if waterskiing over a waterfall, felt himself slipping on loose gravel in a slow motion sequence of losing his balance and falling into the sand. There was gravel in his mouth and he was sliding face down on his stomach. The loose gravel was like sandpaper on his face; he tasted sand in his mouth and reflexively spat, gagging and trying not to swallow it. It was thick in his hair and in his ears.

The crowbar, loosened from his pack, appeared within view

and he managed to grab it just in time as it slid away from him.

It was the crowbar that saved him. He plunged it as deeply as he could manage into the ground and came to a sliding stop mere inches away from death. He felt the rush of warm air beneath the train wheels. The tracks themselves smelled like a blacksmith's heated metal. He rolled away instinctively, tasting dirt in his mouth, his heart pounding. The train was making a sharp turn. Juanita was nowhere in sight. He thought he might hear her calling to him. At first he thought he might be imagining it because her voice was so small and distant but then he saw her, far down the tracks, leaning out of an open boxcar, waving her arms from the boxcar door opening. Then she was gone. She disappeared around the bend and then he saw her no more, only the tail end of the last few remaining boxcars and caboose, and then they too were gone.

There was no hope of catching up but he ran as if chasing a miracle, alternately running and limping, breathing hard, his line of sight blurry with sweat and tears. When he rounded the bend he caught sight of the train again. It had stopped. A landslide from one of the gravel pits had buried the tracks in spillage. Men were finishing the task of shoving gravel off the tracks.

He was alongside the train when it began moving again. Juanita was leaning out of a boxcar and calling to him but he couldn't make out her words over the creak of wooden boxcars and shriek of train wheels against the tracks. She leaned out of the boxcar so far he was afraid she would lose her balance and fall out. When he was beside her he was afraid to grab onto her hand for fear of pulling her out and under the wheels. He grabbed hold of the boxcar's rusty iron railing with the last of his remaining strength, pulled himself up and collapsed inside. There he hugged Juanita so hard she later said she couldn't breathe and thought she might faint.

* * *

Jack's nostrils were filled with the dust and soot that circulated through the boxcar, and he was having difficulty breathing. When he breathed through his nostrils, there seemed no passage and hardly enough oxygen to fill his lungs. When he breathed with his mouth he tasted dirt. It was warmer in the car than it had been during the night, and he hoped it would soon be warm enough for some fresh air. When he opened the boxcar door the air was crisp, but the wind from the motion of the train continued to circulate dust. Alma would have had it all swept out. Made a home of it. Hung curtains and pictures on the walls. He watched the countryside as they wound through a succession of sparsely populated townships and forlorn ranch towns with peaked church steeples, water towers and grain storage silos. Mostly there was unpopulated land. Fields of hops and corn stalks danced in the wind. It was getting warmer now. Sometimes children waved to them along the tracks. Barking dogs chased after them. The train picked up speed and soon there were no more farms or ranches or centers of population at all, just prairie, flatland and the mountains beyond.

The rocking of the train and the sound of its iron wheels on the tracks were sleep inducing but the dirty floorboards were hard. Juanita sat close beside him at the open boxcar door, leaning outward and pointing. The wind whistled so loudly she had to shout over it, her silky raven black hair blowing wildly around her face. When she turned from the view out of the boxcar to face him, Jack thought she looked wild, as Indian as he had ever seen her. It startled him to see it.

He pulled her back from the open boxcar door, gripped her arms and said, "Not so close, Juanita. It's dangerous. You could fall out."

She pulled away from him and said, "Don't you recognize it, Daddy?"

"What?"

There was nothing but the empty expanse of mesa he hoped to be finally getting away from.

"It's the reservation, Daddy."

Since they had had to travel East to get to the rail yard it was possible but how would anyone know it from any other god-forsaken place out here? He had spent a decade on the border of the reservation but nevertheless, when walking out of Cat Creek into the countryside wilderness, he'd had to take care not to get lost, especially on the far side of the reservation where Elvira lived. Everything out there blended and looked alike. But if his daughter said it was the reservation they were looking at she was probably right. To him a tree was a tree but to her they were people. She knew the size and shape of each hill as if it were a relative, the markings of woodpeckers on pine or the bend of a certain spruce, the shades of colors the sun made on the leaves in the woods at certain times of day, the specific unique call of individual creeks that flowed down from the mountains and the distinctive odors of pine pitch, sap and Douglas Fir whether green and standing or cut and burning. She recognized landmarks where he saw nothing and she remembered them like human faces. He figured it was an Indian thing, born into her, but there was no future in it. None at all. Not in the land, not in being an Indian. He was glad to be finally taking her out of it into something better.

* * *

Awake and hungry while her father slept, Juanita tried to stop thinking about the beef jerky in their pack. Their food and water were to be rationed but was within easy reach and an irresistible temptation. She quietly unhinged the pack and opened it, her dirty fingers furtively probing inside for what she might steal. She felt some tinned canned goods of no use to her, then the sticks of venison jerky. She removed three from the pack and ate them in the darkness, chewing as quietly and secretively as she could manage.

When finished she wiped her mouth and felt ashamed. She tasted the residue of salted venison, as repugnant to her now as the taste of blood. She spat on the wooden floorboards but the taste wouldn't go away, and she was thirsty now too. She watched the moonlight flash through the slats of the boxcar and felt the chill of night. The sky was jeweled with the soft blue glitter of millions of brilliant stars. Moonlight reflected softly on hills of snow. Except for the sound of wind and the train, the night was mostly silent, the train a lullaby rocking her to sleep. From somewhere within the darkness she heard the plaintive cry of a wolf.

* * *

Jack woke uncertain of the time of day or how long he had slept. He looked at his pocket watch but he had forgotten to wind it and it had stopped. It was early morning and cold. The boxcar door was closed all the way to the crowbar but golden light between the wooden slats made a slanted grid on the walls and dusty floorboards. Juanita slept. She wore two pairs of pants and long johns, a cap and shirt and thick sweater. With her hair pinned tight and tucked under her kit cap pulled down to her ears she might have been mistaken for a slightly plump adolescent boy. Underneath the bulk of outerwear she was bone thin.

Later he opened the boxcar door slightly, gazing outward upon a swiftly moving river carrying floating chunks of melting ice. The slate blue sky was clear and the sun felt warm on his face. He had no idea of where they were but figured they were coming down out of the mountains now because the pressure in his ears was diminishing. The train followed the bends of the river. He rolled a Bull Durham and smoked at the open door. It had become bright and sunny. Behind him, along the row of open boxcars, tramps sat with their legs hanging out while taking in the fresh air. All across the country men were out of work, riding the rails, uprooted from jobs and families, and nobody from the lowest field hand on the farm to the men in suits to the man himself in Washington knew what to do about it, except maybe the Communists, who probably didn't know more than anybody else but at least had some ideas about it. Now there was this new guy, Roosevelt, who was talking about a New Deal.

His brother Frank, a veteran labor organizer who fought for workers in cities across America, had tried to explain to him what the Communists were talking about. Frank had been wanted for inciting a riot at the time and passing through on the run. His head wrapped in dirty bandages after a beating during a steelworker's strike in Allentown, Frank said this was the thanks he got after fighting for his country in the trenches of Europe and then in the streets at home for worker's rights. Anyway, the basic argument of Marxism, the way Frank explained it then, was capitalism wouldn't work because individual greed for wealth would eventually lead to

Lea Macquarrie

overproduction, which in turn would drive down the wage, devalue the worker and ultimately result in lower wages and unsafe labor practices by profiteering owners even worse than now.

Frank said something else too, something that worried Jack and caused him to wonder if taking Juanita so far from the reservation was the right thing to do. Frank said if you wanted to see Communism at work, all you had to do was study life on the reservation where everyone shared, and the emphasis was not on individual ownership but on community. But Frank had lost Jack a little on that one. No one on the reservation had much of anything to share, and what little they did have consisted largely of handouts from the government.

* * *

They shared a can of Dinty Moore beef stew, eating it right out of the can, passing a common spoon. The rye bread he'd baked for their travels was so stale he didn't dare try. Not with his teeth he didn't. Juanita gnawed at it and it sounded like she was trying to eat gravel.

He was going to make all this up to her. When they got to Seattle and reunited with Frank, they were going to eat good and healthy. He'd make sure she had milk like a growing girl should, and in Seattle there would be apples free for the picking and rivers filled with fresh salmon so plentiful you could reach in and take one with your bare hands.

But what if it didn't work out for them? When had it ever, for him? He tried to hide it from Juanita but he was worried and afraid. She had no idea. She trusted him. He watched her sleep, dressed in her torn denim trousers at least two sizes too big cinched with a rope belt so tight it was a wonder she could breathe, holes in the baggy knees, cuffs ragged and shredded it wasn't fair because she was a pretty girl and couldn't show it. She didn't even know it.

He remembered how at Wilson's Drugs in town she'd browse the magazine rack and show him glossy pictures featuring movie stars and society page women wearing high-heeled shoes with stylish skirts and nylon stockings and silk blouses, clothing unsuitable for the harsh climate and lifestyle of Cat Creek. She poked fun at these women in the magazines, mocking them as false and silly but even then he suspected she might like to see herself differently, if only out of curiosity, and he knew, while she did not, that if her hair were styled, her fingernails properly manicured, her teeth professionally cleaned and maintained, she would be pretty. Prettier than Alma, maybe as pretty as the women she made fun of in the magazines she held in her hands far too long to be genuinely disinterested.

Well, what was a man to do, a widower like himself raising six kids with no mother? His older kids might have helped but no, they left Cat Creek at the earliest opportunity and he couldn't blame them. Nor could he blame an unattached woman who might otherwise take an interest in him for not wanting to take on his brood of kids. Alma had three when he married her and then three by his seed. Highly sexed, some said. A whore, said a few, but she wasn't and those were fighting words. She loved him, but she was sick with the alcoholism and sometimes when she drank showed bad judgment and woke up in a bed not her own. When she sobered up, she felt worse about it than he did.

He didn't know where most of his kids were today. Gone. Flown away like migrating birds. Better off without him, just as Juanita would have been better off left with Elvira. Back in his working days the kids often had to look after each other or stay with Elvira while he was off working somewhere. Now there was no work. But he'd work in Seattle, by God. Get Juanita some new clothes, get her back in school. Bring her up right. She wiped her dirty mouth and smiled, and it made him feel worse than he already did.

"I'm sorry about this," he said. "You were right. We never should have left Montana and should have stayed with Elvira."

"No, Daddy, I'm glad you took me with you. I'm glad to get out of Cat Creek. I've never been anywhere else, Daddy. I've never really been *anywhere*. I want to experience what it's like in a city. What other people's lives are like, people different from me. What it's like to be in one of those tall buildings I've seen pictures of in school. I'd like to not dress like a boy. Maybe have a boyfriend. I've never had a boyfriend, Daddy."

"Well, I can name a few who tried to kiss you but you punched them in the mouth."

"Because I didn't like those boys and didn't want them to kiss me. I want a nice clean boy like the ones I see in the magazines. I don't like the boys in Cat Creek. Maybe I'll find a boy I like in Seattle. But you know what I really want? More than anything? I want to learn to read. Not skipping around looking for words I recognize like I do now but like other people read."

"You've never said this before, Juanita. You keep skipping school."

"I fell too far behind. I felt stupid there. And the teachers ignored me except when I was getting into trouble."

They huddled together in the broken lighting and listened to the train and the hard wind whistling alongside their boxcar. The crowbar was wedged to prevent the boxcar door from sliding shut and locking, but the resulting gap let in cold air. They shivered under their blankets, resembling survivors of an arctic expedition gone wrong.

That night they woke to the cessation of motion. The train was stopped and hissing and tramps were shouting. He groped for the flashlight, turned the switch and followed the beam in the darkness to the boxcar door. At first he thought a bear was crawling into it. He was relieved to see instead a bearded man attempting to climb aboard. The man carried a sawed-off two by four, which he used to prop the door. The path of light provided by the flashlight illuminated hundreds of dancing dust motes imitating snowfall.

The man who boarded flopped in their midst like a dying fish thrown on a dock. The rank stench of his body odor and sour clothing caused Juanita to cover her face with her sleeve. Jack figured they probably didn't smell much better, but this man stank of alcohol.

He tucked Juanita's long ponytail under her newsboy cap and whispered for her to adjust the wad of stockings in her jeans.

"Welcome aboard," he said. "My name is Jack Vogel and this here is my son Juan. He don't talk much but he's a good boy. What's your name?"

The man smiled widely, displaying a full set of gleaming white teeth and said, "Shane McLane's the name and international brotherhood's my game. Pleased to meet you."

"Well, same here," replied Jack.

There was something about the folksy way he talked that sounded forced somehow, or if not forced exactly, learned from observation and practice instead of part of his upbringing.

"Tell you what though, Jack Vogel. I'm so hungry I could eat a skunk. Haven't eaten since breakfast yesterday. Do you have anything to offer a fellow hobo?"

"Not much, but you're welcome to share what we've got."

"Well, I'd be much obliged and grateful to you. "

Jack studied the man in the beam of the flashlight. He wore baggy torn dungarees and a buttoned flannel shirt over a white tee shirt turned gray where it was visible at the throat. He looked destitute, more so than them even, except the man's boots looked new and might have cost as much as fifty dollars. Maybe more. They were the kind of boots he had wanted all his life and could never afford, hand stitched riding boots from the look of them, suitable for hard work but also for fancy events when required. He shone the light and tossed the man an apple and the man squinted and all but closed his eyes, his bearded face ghoulish in the stream of light. He held up his hands to catch the apple but missed, and he scampered after it on his hands and knees. He ate the apple, core and all, spat out some seeds and said, "Do you mind pointing that light in another direction."

"Of course, "said Jack. "I apologize."

Jack could only wish the remaining teeth he still had were adequate to the task of masticating an apple core. He considered this newcomer's incongruous full set of choppers, his fancy boots. He placed the flashlight on the floor next to their pack, which provided a path of light in their passenger's direction, but not into his face.

"No apology needed, Jack. We're going to be traveling together for a while and I expect we'll all be good friends by the time we get where we're going. You there, Juan. You okay? You'd probably prefer to be left alone with your dad. I'm sorry to intrude on a family situation, but it can't be helped. You know the saying. Beggars can't be choosers and all that. But I'll be no trouble. You'll see. We are going to get along just fine. "

He pointed to Jack's pack and said, "Hey, Jack, excuse me for askin', but do you happened to have any wine or bootleg gin in that pack?"

"No, we don't drink."

"No? First hobo I ever met who didn't. I don't understand a man who doesn't have need of drink. Especially in these times. Against your religion or something? You Mormon, maybe?"

"No it's nothing like that. I used to drink, but my wife had a problem with the alcohol, so I swore it off."

"I can't help but notice your boy has some bread there. Think you could spare some?"

"Hell, it's so stale it's hardly edible but you're welcome, sure."

Jack tossed the man the remainder of the bread and his Swiss Army knife to slice it. The man sawed off a large section and gnawed at it like dog with a bone. Afterwards he tossed what little remained of it back to Jack and put the Swiss Army knife in his pants pocket.

"That's my knife," said Jack.

"It sure is. My mistake. Here you go."

* * *

The man slept through the night and much of the next morning. All through the night he kept scratching himself. He was peppered with mosquito and bug bites. In the morning Jack was able to see him clearly in the daylight. His stocking hat had come off in his sleep and Jack saw his balding scalp was covered with sores. His nose had obviously been broken in the past. His knuckles were raw and partly scabbed over. Jack figured him to be in his late thirties or early forties, but who could say, under all that dirt? The man's face was so black with soot he couldn't even be sure what color the man was. His features were Caucasian though, not Negro, not Indian.

Later the man woke displaying his improbably perfect white teeth while flashing his broad friendly smile and saying, "Good morning, Vogels."

His voice was hoarse and to Jack sounded as if he was having trouble getting the words out.

He then began coughing. Jack thought the man was going to die he coughed so hard. He spat up a huge gob of phlegm so thick they heard it splatter on the wooden floorboards.

Jack said, "You all right, Mister?"

"I cough most mornings, and not much after. That plus I haven't had any tobacco in a while and my lungs are mad at me, haw haw haw."

Jack found the laughter theatrical and fake. As was his smile, which Jack thought well intended but insincere. And his boots, like his teeth, did not seem to belong to a man hoboing.

The man broke into song, his delivery boisterous and resonant, the lyrics sung with feeling.

They used to tell me I was building a dream
With peace and glory ahead
Why should I be standing in line
Just waiting for bread?
Once I built a railroad, I made it run
Made it race against time
Once I built a railroad, now it's done
Brother, can you spare a dime?

He sang two more verses. Juanita applauded, obviously delighted with this turn of events. She'd loved music almost from birth, Jack remembered. Alma sang to her when she had been in her infancy, and later, after her mother was gone, she used to sit on her Uncle Frank's knee and listen to him play the banjo and sing Joe Hill IWW songs.

"That was a nice way to wake up, Shane. Thank you."

"It's a good song. Speaks the truth."

"Yes, one of my brother's favorites. He used to sing it often."

"So what's for breakfast, Jack?"

Jack tossed him some venison jerky and an orange, which the man ate while breathing hard, smacking his lips and making guttural noises of pleasure.

"Mighty kind of you, Jack."

Lea Macquarrie

He smiled widely, but with his mouth only and not with his eyes, with no expression of warmth or friendship in his smile. His blue eyes were beautiful but ice cold. They were the eyes of a man who was sizing you up, speculating on what he might take from you. Jack didn't like to prejudge but he'd seen men with eyes like these when working on ranches, in the oil fields, the Montana forests and railways. Men who displayed no warmth, always calculating and without a desire or need for friendship, men who made trouble, cheated at cards, stole what they could and moved on.

* * *

Shane, if that was even his real name, turned out to be a big talker. When he wasn't talking, which was most of the time, he exercised. He often did both, counting off fifty morning pushups and a hundred sit-ups and yakking through them all.

"Be always strong in mind and body, that's my motto. How about you, boy? Have to keep in shape young man. You do pushups? Let's see your arms, boy. Show me your muscles."

Juanita found a far corner of the boxcar and squatted on the floor without answering.

"He's shy," said Jack. "Not much for talking."

"It's no concern of mine. Seems like a nice enough kid. So where you headed, Jack?"

"Seattle."

"I'm going to Yakima myself. That's in Eastern Washington. From there if you go west over the Cascade mountain range you're in Seattle. How long you been catching on?"

"I'm not sure I get your meaning."

"Riding the rails. Catching onto a freight."

"This is our first time."

"Well, it can be dangerous but otherwise not a bad way to travel. Personally, I like it. You meet a lot of interesting people. People who share what we got no matter how little. That's the way we are. Comrades all the way. Brothers."

He directed his attention back to Juanita and said, "Must be exciting for you, young man. First time riding the rails and all."

Juanita sat quietly, staring at her boots and avoiding eye contact.

Jack said, "Where do you think we are now, Mr. Wayne?"

"Probably still in Montana somewhere. Maybe eastern Idaho. Hard to say. But call me Shane. No need for formalities here. So what's your line, Jack? What kind of work did you do before you took to tramping?"

"Just about everything. Anything I could, mostly."

"Well, that's me too. You name it, I done it. Now we're here brought by fate and politics. Brothers, like I said. You a political man, Jack?"

"Not really. My older brother was, but he was smarter than me. Got himself educated and went in the military. Served in the war in Europe."

"Well, there's still a war going on, Jack. War between the poor and the rich who want to keep them poor. Between labor and management. War for worker's rights, *rights* mind you, not hand-outs but basic rights. Fair pay and safe conditions for an international brotherhood of workers. That's who we are and what we want."

"Now you sound like my brother Frank."

They could no longer hear each other. The train whistle obliterated all else. Jack saw the man's lips moving but heard nothing. He felt the train cut its speed, passing through a small town or the industrial outskirts of a city. The cry of the train whistle was a sad country song evoking memories of heartsick nights listening and worrying about where Alma might be and when or if she would be coming home. And later, when she was gone, the haunting whistle of the fast moving Great Northern freight passing every night at 3 AM a hundred yards from their shack seemed to mimic her voice as if calling to him from the great insurmountable lonely divide that separates the living from the dead.

The train rocked hard to the left and caused him to stagger, adjusting his balance.

"Wait a minute, Jack. Wait just a doggone minute here! Holy mackerel! Did you say Frank? Frank Vogel the union organizer is your brother?"

"The very same. Do you know him?"

"Well not exactly but I know *of* him. Most of us riding the rails do. Your brother is kind of famous. I'd always hoped I'd run into him one of these days and figured eventually I would, somewhere on these tracks. Might still, someday."

"He's in Seattle. That's where I'm going. He's going to find me work. Find a place for Juan and me to live."

"Well, I'll be damned, Jack. It's a small world, as they say. And any friend of Frank Vogel's is a friend of mine. Kin is even better. It's an honor."

He offered his hand for Jack to shake but when Jack took it his own hand felt small in comparison and the man's unnecessarily harsh grip suggested they were not sealing a bond of comradeship so much as competing in an unacknowledged show of strength. McLane won the contest easily. Jack's hand and fingers were caught inside the man's iron grip as if in a bear trap and his hand throbbed painfully when the man released it. Jack did his best not to show it, smiling and saying nothing.

The man returned his smile but it was different this time. Jack saw it, the gratified smile of a competitor who had just won a small victory.

* * *

The train descended switchbacks leading out of the mountains and when it leveled out the terrain outside the open boxcar door began to change from shadowed verdant forest to desert sunlight, mesquite and tumbleweed. The temperature soared. Heat waves rippled over the barren horizon.

Jack rummaged through his pack inventorying their food supply. He hadn't figured on sharing, and they would arrive in Seattle with very little food if any. He McLane's cold blue eyes watching him as he counted cans of beans and sticks of jerky, bars of soap and miscellaneous articles he had hastily added when leaving Cat Creek.

"What all do you have in that pack, Jack."

"Nowhere near as much as I need and that's for sure."

Enormous boulders simmered in the glaring sunlight. The

boxcar became a mobile oven. Even with the door open to a strong breeze sweat dripped down their necks and backs. Their passenger complained about it plenty, saying they were stingy with the rationed water. The train stopped for no apparent reason they could discern. Shane called it a whistle stop and said there would be two dispersed blasts of its whistle again before it began moving again. Here they could relieve themselves. Juanita said she had no need. Shane, frowning, shook his head and said, "You sure, boy?"

Both Jack and Shane jumped off the train and joined a horizontal column of urinating men. When they returned to the boxcar Juanita announced she had to go after all.

"Be quick about it," said Shane. "I can tell by the sound of the engine this train is getting ready to go."

Juanita jumped off the train, Jack watching as she wandered off, disappearing behind some boulders. He imagined her bladder was about to explode after holding in all day.

The stilled train made the boxcar even hotter than before. The men stripped down to their underwear for relief from the heat. Juanita, having returned, wore the jockey shorts stuffed with stockings and kept her chest covered with a tee shirt. The train began moving again. Shane stepped out of his boxers and stood bare naked.

"Have some decency and cover yourself," said Jack.

"Why? You never seen a naked man before?"

"It's not anything I want to see," said Jack.

"Then don't look."

"Mister, if you want to share our food and water you put some shorts on right this minute."

McLane smiled and stepped into his boxer shorts and dropped suddenly to the wooden boxcar floorboards and began counting off pushups in cadence. *One hut two hut three hut hut hut.* He slapped his hands together on the huts.

He stopped at fifty and said, "Got to keep active, Jack. You should join me, Juan. You too Jack. A man's got to stay fit. You look kind of soft, you know? Not like your brother Frank."

"I thought you didn't know my brother."

"Only by reputation. A man of strength is what they say. A

fighting man. A man you want at your side when fighting scabs."

And with this he began a tediously long political speech more suited for a soapbox than a boxcar, detailing his personal history of heroic deeds fighting for workers' rights in just about every state in the union. There was, apparently, no stopping him, not even after Jack and Juanita lay down on their blankets and were sleeping.

* * *

Their view was into a desert wasteland without as much as a buzzard, rattlesnake or jackrabbit in sight. Jack and Juanita sat side by side at the open boxcar door, their feet dangling over the side. The noisy warm breeze whooshing in their ears and blowing across their faces gave little relief from the heat but provided the ability to talk outside of their sleeping interloper's range of hearing.

"I'm sick of listening to him," whispered Juanita. "He even talks in his sleep."

"He's a nuisance but harmless. Anyway what do you want me to do about it? Kick him off? We don't own this boxcar. We got no right. We're here together like it or not. We just got to get along."

"When you aren't looking he watches me. I don't like the way he does it."

"Yeah, I noticed that too. What did I tell you about wearing just a tee shirt on top, Juanita? You need to wear one of those flannel shirts I packed. I know it's hot in here, but you're showing a little of your femaleness."

"Breasts? You think?"

"A little bit maybe, yes."

"I never thought I wanted them but now I think maybe I do. I'm getting tired of being a boy."

"You're not a boy, Juanita Rose. You never were."

"I'm a tomboy. I think I would like to be different. I want boys to see me different. Not as someone to roughhouse with but someone to treat ladylike. I wish Aunt Elvira was here. If not Vi then at least someone female. All I've seen since we left home is men. It's like someone rounded up all the women like horses and corralled them somewhere out of sight."

"When we get to Seattle you can have girlfriends and make all the girl talk you want."

"When though? When do we get there?"

"Those mountains yesterday were probably the last of Montana. I don't know if we are in Western Idaho or Eastern Washington. Wherever it is we are we're on the move and getting closer. We just got to be patient."

He turned and saw their uninvited passenger on his knees foraging through their pack. He looked up from a stick of half chewed jerky held in his fist, his mouth full but still smiling, always smiling.

"You out of them apples, Jack? I couldn't find any in here. You're not hiding them, are you?"

"Shane I thought I told you this before. Pretty sure I did, in fact. We're willing to share what we got but we're rationing our food. You're welcome to eat when we eat but not whenever you want."

"Your brother never taught you? Tramp code is share and share alike."

"Well then fine with me, Mister, what do you have to share?"

"Not a thing and that's the point. You're supposed to help a brother out."

"We've been sharing everything we got."

"Maybe, maybe not. I'll bet you got a cash grubstake in your boot."

"I don't, but it's none of your business."

"Yeah, I thought so. Why else would you sleep with your boots on?"

He smiled again, but with the same cold expression in his eyes.

Jack made Pork n' Beans warmed with Canned Heat, over the scowling protests of their passenger, who wanted to drink it for its alcohol content.

"This canned heat isn't for drinking but for cooking," said Jack.

"In my opinion it's a damn waste. We could eat them beans cold."

* * *

The moon leaked through the wooden slats of the boxcar, dividing it into horizontal patches of shadow and light. Light

Lea Macquarrie

from the half open box car door pooled on the floorboards as if accidentally spilled there but most of the boxcar was in darkness. Somewhere in this darkness, Juanita was calling to him. Her voice sounded strangled. He squinted and saw in a flickering patch of light that she was trapped. Shane McLane held her in a chokehold. Her bare feet were not touching the floorboards and she was kicking and fighting for a foothold like someone being hanged. She opened her mouth in a scream but no sound came out because the man's right arm was pressed so hard around her throat. Jack saw it happening. The more she tried to escape his grip the more her windpipe was cut off and the more she gasped and choked.

He moved in with his fists held in fighting position the way Frank had taught him but the man lifted her higher and said, "Back off. I could easily snap her neck, Jack. It would be no trouble at all."

He plunged a free hand into the front of her jeans, emerged with the roll of stockings from her underpants and said, "You lied to me, Jack, told me she was a boy. Why did you do that? Do you see now what you made me do? I don't want to hurt her at all but I will if you don't do as I say."

Juanita was able to make noises now but they were made un-intelligible by the pressure of the man's arm pressing on her neck and Adam's apple.

"Put her down, Mister. Why are you doing this? What do you want?"

The man lowered her so that feet were touching the floor-boards again but did not release his grip or in any way lessen his power over her. She bit his hand hard and when he removed it from her mouth shouted, "Let me go." Her voice was hoarse and wounded; she did not sound like herself at all.

"Shut up, girlie. You want me to stuff these dirty socks I pulled out of your crotch into your mouth? Because I will. You know I will."

He again increased the pressure on her throat. She could no longer speak.

"I want you to sit down, Jack. Right here right now."

Jack squatted on his knees but the man shook his head no.

"No, not on your knees, Jack. On your butt with your legs stretched out in front of you. Take off your boots."

"You want my old nasty boots? Why? Yours are better."

"You know why, Jack Vogel. Do as I say."

As slowly as he might convincingly manage, pretending his foot might be swollen and stuck inside he said, "I got a bit of the gout, Shane. I don't think it's going to come off."

"Then your kid here dies while you watch."

"It's only a boot, Shane. Not worth killing for."

He removed it and said, "I don't know why you want this boot, but here it is."

"Turn it upside down and shake it hard. Get over in the light where I can see."

Some sand and a few pebbles escaped, but nothing more.

"Take off the other boot, Vogel. I know you got a bankroll in there. Why else would you sleep with your boots on?"

Jack heard Juanita gagging in strangulation and knew he had no choice. He reluctantly removed the second boot but it was more than a boot. It was their future. It was their hope for a better life. It was end of their dream of Seattle and reunion with his brother Frank. Greenbacks fluttered from his boot like dying moths.

"So you lied about the money too. Looks like you have plenty enough to share. But don't get the wrong idea, I'm not sharing. Pick up those greenbacks and count them off to me one by one, Jack."

Jack counted out three hundred dollars in ten and twenty dollar bills, the product of a life's savings and the sale of all they had of value plus a small loan from Elvira who couldn't afford it.

"Put the money in the pack and toss it over. Don't leave a single damn bill, you hear? Okay, good Jack, I'm glad I'm not going to have to hurt your daughter here. I have what I want and as soon as this train slows down I'll be taking my leave of you. I won't be continuing on to Yakima so don't bother to look for me there. You'll never see me again."

Shane tossed Juanita away. Jack heard her land hard. He hur-

Lea Macquarrie

ried to her side, knelt and said, "Are you hurt, Juanita?"

He saw only trapped anger and fierceness in her eyes, no fear. She waved him off and said, "No, but it doesn't matter right now. He's done with me. You need to protect yourself now."

"Smart girl," said Shane. "She's right."

She crawled as far from them as possible to huddle in a dark shadow of the boxcar.

"Mister, do you intend to leave us with nothing? What happened to all your big talk of share and share alike, the international brotherhood of men, working men united in a common cause? Were they just words, with no belief behind them?"

"Well, Jack, see, it's like this. If you had been honest with me instead of lying, if you'd shared the way you should have, I'd have left you half. But you did lie. So this is basically your fault, you see. And I don't consider you a brother at all. You're selfish. I came on board with nothing at all when I boarded. Not a jacket, not even a blanket. You should have cared, Jack. You didn't and now I don't either."

"What I saw when you came on board was a man wearing a fifty dollar pair of boots that I couldn't afford no matter how hard or long I worked for them. Like new, the soles and heels hardly worn. A man with all his teeth. I don't think you are a working man at all. I don't think you're a hobo either. Not a real one. I think you are a liar and a thief. I think you're riding the rails and living the way you do by choice, not out of a lack of choice like me and Juanita here. From the start something about you never did add up. So I'm not the only one who lied. You lied too. And now I'm going to have to fight you for what is mine. You leave me no choice."

"Well, come on then, Jack, if you think you must; I respect that but you're going to get hurt and you won't get your money back."

"Maybe not but I have to try. You are leaving us with nothing, only the clothing we have on our backs."

"All right then, Jack. Come on then."

The train rocked hard to the left and Jack assumed his fighting stance for balance. He had fought men before, some bigger than him, mostly men in Cat Creek who thought they could take advantage of Alma because of her drinking problem, but never a man of this size. His opponent had the advantage in height, reach, weight and probably just plain meanness, with massive fists that looked like catcher's mitts. Jack raised his much smaller fists, took a tentative step forward and was hit hard in the face without getting close enough to throw a punch of his own. He staggered two awkward steps backward from the impact, felt his legs weaken and then wobbled as if he might fall, but recovered his balance. He stepped backward, he hoped out of harm's way, and prepared himself for another exchange of fisticuffs.

He would not be able to defeat this man with brute strength; instead, he was going to have to outthink him. He would box him, dance around him and fight him defensively the way Frank had once taught him how to take on a larger man. He raised his fists this time not in a striking position but defensively, his arms ready to jab or punch whenever an opportunity arose but otherwise held close to his face in defense. He waded into the fight, his arms and fists held high to protect his face and successfully deflected a blow to his head. His adversary responded by punching him in the ribs with a blow that doubled him up. It felt like he had been hit by a baseball bat. He fell to his knees, the wind knocked out him. The pain was excruciating, worse than when he had been hit in the face. It weakened him and left him unable to get up, gasping for breath. Shane did not persist but stood over him, his stance wide, his enormous fists clenched. Groaning, Jack struggled to his feet.

"Don't come back at me, Jack. You'll only get hurt again. Worse next time."

Jack assumed a fighting position and said, "I don't want to but I have to. I have a young girl I'm responsible for."

Shane punched him in the head, more of warning tap than an actual blow, but the man was so strong and his hands so big Jack was knocked backward and nearly fell from the impact. To his shame, he found himself with tears in his eyes. He wiped them away with the back of his hand.

"What's this? Frank Vogel's kid brother crying in a fight?"

But his fists were still clenched and he wasn't finished.

"I'm not crying from the fighting, Mister whoever you are. It's more than that. It's my daughter, our future in Seattle and what I'd hoped for us."

Jack suddenly landed a hard a punch when his opponent was unprepared and not expecting it and knew immediately from the sound of its impact and the pain in his fist it had been a good one. Maybe as good as he had in him. His opponent staggered backwards on wobbly legs. He fought for his balance, recovered it and wiped his bloody nose and smiled, genuinely this time, as if surprised and mildly pleased.

"Good for you, Jack. You many have even broke my nose. Not that it hasn't been broken plenty of times before."

"We don't have to do this you know."

"Well, maybe not but here we are doing it."

The next punch landed on Jack's mouth and he collapsed to the deck where he curled himself into as tight a ball as possible and spat blood, waiting for the man's kicks, but they never came. He commanded himself to his knees but couldn't get up. He shook violently and spat blood to the floorboards. He thought he might have had some teeth knocked out but when he felt around in his mouth, they were all there, though one was loosened. His hands were swollen and knuckles ached. He tried to rise and groped for an absent handhold. Juanita cringed in a dark corner, as far from them as possible. Jack could hear her whimpering.

"Don't hurt my Daddy," she cried. "Please."

"Don't try to get up," said Shane to Jack.

"I have to, Shane. Don't you understand yet? I have to."

"I'll hurt you bad, Jack. Real bad. I don't want to have to do that but I will."

"Whatever you do to me won't be as bad as if I let you steal our future without a fight. I'm sorry, Shane, but I have to finish this."

He tried to get up and continue the fight but could not manage it and remained on his knees.

Shane laughed as if Jack had just told a hilarious joke. Jack, who assumed he was about to receive an ass beating like he had never before had the misfortune to experience in his life, failed to see what was so funny. The man's laughter filled all four corners of the boxcar.

"Well now I have heard everything, Jack Vogel. I tell a man I am going to hurt him bad and don't want to and he apologizes to me for the necessity of it? Says he sorry he has to let me beat him up? Haw haw haw, Jack, you can't fight for shit but your spunk would make your brother proud."

Jack, dazed from the blows to his head, felt a felt a wet splatter across his face. He looked up at the giant before him and saw him teetering uncertainly. Then the giant fell to his knees; Goliath slain by David. Twitching. He heard what sounded like a homerun being hit out of a ballpark and then another. By now he was drenched in whatever had splattered him before. The man fell forward, his head in Jack's lap, which became so wet he wondered if he had pissed himself. In the moonlight he saw Juanita standing behind the fallen giant, a crowbar in her fist dripping blood down the hand that clutched it.

Jack took it from her. She held it in her fist so tightly he had to pry her fingers apart. He wiped it clean with his bandana and said, "Juanita, what in God's name have you done? I fear this man is dead. Get the flashlight, quickly."

Blood pooled under the man's head. There was much of it, making a trickle across the floorboards in the direction of the boxcar door. Shane's face was barely recognizable. One side of his head was caved in. His nose was pushed against his face and his left eye was not where it was supposed to be.

"My God, Juanita."

She said nothing, just stood there trembling. He shone the light on her and saw her face was painted with blood. There was gore in her hair and on her face.

"You were crying, Daddy. You're crying now. You don't have to anymore. It's over.'

"It's *not* over, Juanita. Now it will never be over. We're worse off now than if we had let him take our money. And we were negotiating. I think he was coming around."

For a moment he thought he was in a dream. He gazed out the boxcar door where the night was clear. Moonlight shone softly on scrub pine and sandy low hills. The moonlight made the dying man's face even more grotesque. He was no longer a person. Half his face was missing.

He saw numerous scattered stars out of the boxcar frame and wished he could be among them, somewhere up there with Alma, wherever she might be. A man was dead by their daughter's hand. Now he was dragging the man by his ankles to the boxcar door. The man's demolished face left a streak of gore on the wooden floorboards.

"We can't be found here with him, Juanita. As much as it troubles me to do it, we have to get him out of here. We'll have to push him out somewhere he won't be seen by a brake man or the man in the caboose."

He watched the passing landscape outside, waiting for a culvert, ravine, or tall brush. Juanita was crying and he didn't know what to say to her. The boxcar became suddenly enveloped in blackness without a trace of moonlight coming through the slats or door. They were in a tunnel.

"There won't be a better place, Juanita. "

Jack rolled the man out of the train like a dead dog and that might have been the end of him except Jack figured you didn't rid yourself of a man by killing him. Instead you were bound to him for the rest of your life.

PIER 91, SEATTLE

WALTER MCCABE STOOD BEFORE THE salt-pitted windows of his Seattle office at the end of Pier 91 to contemplate the decline of the ramshackle waterfront neighborhood he loved and was so invested in. His office, a wind- battered aluminum rectangle on the third and uppermost floor of a storage unit accessible by an iron stairwell, was not one might expect of a successful shipping magnate, which in fact he no longer was and in honest retrospect may never have been. Furnished with his grand roll top desk, a worn leather couch, metal and oak file cabinets and wooden chairs, it possessed a small corner sink and closet-sized toilet but personal flourishes were few and consisted mostly of glass framed paintings of ships at sea. The massive desk, imported from Italy, was like a fortress and probably worth a year's rent. A photo of his wife was placed face down on its surface so he might drink in peace without her frowning disapproval.

A red brick street ran parallel to the docks where inoperative freighters waited to be loaded. His single ship, leased and in need of a crew and cargo, measured 400 feet and could carry 6000 gross tons at a speed of 10 knots with a cargo of at least 8000 tons, which was below its optimal 14 knots when new. Now it was idle, waiting union arbitration of a strike. Behind the piers and docks, destitute men and women prowled the red brick streets and foraged the alleys, picking through trash cans or glumly hanging around bread lines and day-labor employment agency blackboards.

Present and most prominent among those gathered in his office were King County Sheriff Gus Gustafson, Robert "Bobby" Stone, and Michael M. Drake. All of the men present were members of *The Waterfront Improvement Commission* and were assembled to discuss the future of industrial waterfront development in Seattle generally and the problem of Hooverville specifically. The meeting was taking place just a few days before Jack Vogel and his daughter arrived in Seattle, and would be the last such meeting Walter Mc-Cabe would attend.

Three months earlier, in cooperation with the King County Fire Department, with an edict from the Public Health Department, a citizen's militia supervised by the Seattle Police Department had flushed out and evacuated the Hooverville inhabitants and afterwards burned the settlement to the ground. McCabe watched the dispossessed men of Hooverville return to rebuild their shantytown utilizing materials salvaged from docks, railroads, and dumpsters. Tin and tar paper and packing crates and whatever they could lay their hands on. Scrap materials others found useless.

Located on the site of what was once the Skinner and Eddy shipyard, Hooverville had since expanded to four hundred shacks at last count. It seemed a new shack was going up every day. Mc-Cabe imagined what the men might accomplish with real building materials, hot food, and a paycheck every week. He admired these men's fortitude and will and had come to believe they shared the enterprising spirit of the founding fathers who had rebuilt Seattle after the great fire of 1889.

Bobby Stone stood beside him at the window.

"Look at them," he sneered,

Stone oversaw the King Street Public Railroad Station and held a seat on the board of the City of Seattle Transportation Department and had extensive real estate holdings. He owned, in partnership with Mike Drake, numerous speakeasies, whorehouses, and gambling operations all across the city. Back in the days when it paid to unload and transport freight, Stone had overseen docking operations for the Port of Seattle. Drake had been briefly a police officer but had been caught in a prostitution and gambling scandal and made to resign. Seattle politics being what they were, he was now, among other things, a prominent member of the Chamber of Commerce. Both Mike Drake and Bobby Stone were mortgage bond officers with holdings in investment trusts.

"More every day," said McCabe.

Ole Olafson, who had been silent during most of the meeting, took a puff off his cigar. Gesturing with it in the direction of the window he said, "The Republic of the Penniless. It's a damn shame."

McCabe agreed. Those men needed warm clothing, blankets, hot meals and proper sanitation but Olafson wasn't going to do anything about it. No one would go against Drake, Stone, or Gustafson. The three of them had too much influence and too much power. Not to mention they had too much damaging information none would want reported in Seattle newspapers.

Stone turned away from the window and said, "They've brought nothing but disease and pestilence. I can't stand to look at them. Scurrying around the docks like an infestation of wharf rats."

"They're not rats," objected McCabe. "They're men same as us. That's the shame and the pity of it."

"They're ruining the image of our city," said Stone. "They've taken over the waterfront and made it ugly as a municipal dump. In fact, that's what it is now. A dump for human garbage."

"Quit calling them that. That's part of the problem. That whole attitude. Those men down there are if anything in the spirit of the Denny Party forefathers who built Seattle on the banks of Alkai Point with nothing but a few saws and axes."

"The Denny Party knew how to build. They had skills. What do these men have?"

"The crabs," said Drake. "TB and VD."

"The place is a germ factory," said Stone. "It's only a matter of time before a serious outbreak of disease spreads to the rest of the city."

"Well if you're so concerned for their hygiene why not help clean the place up," asked McCabe rhetorically. "We could give vaccinations, test for TB, set up a bunker of hot showers and a dozen or so hygienic privies. We could delouse those who need it, provide haircuts, dispense clean clothing, boots, issue soap and toilet paper. Let's not forget this depression is going to be temporary. We just need to see it through and outlast it. When it's over, they'll get jobs and move on."

Gustafson said, "How would we finance something like that, Mac? Where would the money come from?" Gustafson was Seattle's sheriff. McCabe thought him to be a better man than Mike Drake or Bobby Stone but not by all that much.

"Damn it, men. We don't want to make their lives easier. We don't want to make them comfortable. We want them to move out of Hooverville and return the waterfront to investors who want to improve it." This was from Stone.

Eric Woziak glanced at his pocket watch and snapped it closed. Unlike Drake and Stone, he had no known ties to organized crime. McCabe was the oldest among them by two decades and had been a Commission member long before Stone and Drake changed its mission from protecting and improving the waterfront to fattening their personal bank accounts.

"What concerns me," said Woziak, is that the men might claim squatter's rights. I've met with my attorneys regarding this, and they warned me the men of Hooverville might have a legal claim."

"We can't let that happen, men. When this Depression finally ends, and it will, believe me, that land is going to be worth a lot of money. Enough to make all of us rich."

McCabe stood with his back turned and hands clasped behind him while gazing toward the northernmost edge of Skid Row and the dilapidated indigent shacks firmly established on the once thriving but now abandoned shipyard. Stone was right they had taken over the waterfront. The shacks, which had begun in a confined area on the tide flats south of Yesler Way, now extended to cover most of the view from his widow. Investors wanted the squatters removed, but what to do with them? There was plenty of empty housing in the city, but people couldn't pay rent and were being evicted.

"Well they've got to go, period. They're hurting Seattle's reputation from coast to coast. There was even an article about us in the

New York Times. Did you know we have the biggest Hooverville in the nation? Do you know what that article was titled? *Seattle's Shame.*"

McCabe scoffed. "Let New Yorkers concern themselves with New York and mind their own damn business. They're the ones that ought to be ashamed. New York elitists and Wall Street speculators are to blame for bringing this down on us in the first place. "

"Why are we even talking about New York? We're supposed to be talking about our problem here in Seattle. I don't know why you're arguing with us, Mac. I thought we were together on this."

"Together on what, exactly?"

"The removal of these interlopers. They're outsiders and don't belong here."

"Then neither do you. I'm probably the only born and bred Seattle native in this room. The rest of you all came from somewhere else just like them."

"Yeah, but we contribute to the city. They just take from it."

"What? What are they taking? Our garbage, our scrap?"

"I say we burn it down," said Drake. "There's all kinds of vice, corruption and disease down there. They're having orgies and corrupting the youth."

McCabe scoffed and said, "That's hogwash, Drake. What you have in Hooverville are honest unemployed working men trying to survive some hard times. They aren't breaking any laws and they aren't hurting anybody."

"They're breeding like rats down there."

"That's nonsense. There's few women in Hooverville and you'd have to look twice to recognize them as female."

"They're whores," said Drake. "Ugly as sin and willing to put out for a swallow of bootleg gin."

Drake, tall and lean with a broad forehead, wide flat nose and small black eyes, had a minor speech impediment and spoke with a slight whistle. Recently divorced, he was living with and engaged to a burlesque dancer but was known to solicit boys on First Avenue and around Pioneer Square.

"That's completely false, Drake. And you're no one to complain about whores. You are presently living with one."

"She's an exotic dancer and that's out of line, Mac."

"Men, men," interjected Sheriff Gustafson. "Take it easy. This is a meeting, not a brawl."

"I apologize," said McCabe. "I should not have said that."

"One thing I think we can all agree on," said Gustafson, "is Hooverville has to go."

"Who says we all agree on that?" asked McCabe. "I don't agree with it. The only problem with these men is they don't have work and that isn't their fault."

"Well," said Stone, "it isn't our fault either."

No one knew for certain exactly how many business interests Stone had in Seattle or how far his influence ranged but it was rumored to reach all the way to the state capital in Olympia where it was speculated he might be groomed as a candidate in a future campaign for state representative.

"Hooverville is contributing to the depression and prolonging it," he said. "Those men down there don't even want to work. They're just bums. Meanwhile Hooverville is spreading from its present location into the rest of the waterfront and it's bad for business."

"What business?" asked Olafson rhetorically.

"They're not bums," objected McCabe.

"Then what are they? They're not workers, not contributors."

"They're workers without jobs. Loggers, firefighters, brakemen, miners, fishermen, cooks."

Drake gestured out the window and said, "We're making this into a bigger problem than it has to be. We could solve this problem in one night with two five-man teams carrying gasoline cans under the cover of darkness. Presto, problem solved."

"Yeah, if it would stop raining long enough to get a fire started."

"Hell, they'd just rebuild again like they're doing now."

"Hire some local thugs to go down there with baseball bats, tire chains and lead pipes."

"That won't stop them. We need to torch the place. Torch it

and pave it over. Get some men to stand guard and run off any interlopers who might return."

Sheriff Gustafson shook his head and said, "Look, I agree the place is a health hazard and a damn nuisance but arson, that's a serious matter. Dangerous, illegal and liable to provoke another confrontation with the *Unemployed Citizen's League* and the revolutionists. We've tried getting them out before and what did we get? A riot that got out of hand and ensuing litigation ending in their favor. McCabe may be right. We may just have to live with Hooverville as part of the Depression."

McCabe gazed out the window across the choppy waters of Puget Sound toward the sea where, beyond the whitecaps of the Sound, his son Chester was sailing home on the S.S. Piersal. McCabe had been years preparing him for taking over the business but the boy objected, saying a life at sea, or even in the office was not for him, insisting he wanted no part of such a life. That he would then turn around and sail for another line was an offense beyond his pardon. The boy had turned his back on his family and rejected his birthright. It seemed deliberate and personal and he didn't understand it. Outside, it was raining gently on the piers and pattering on the gray water below. Hundreds of small whitecaps moved restlessly across the surface of the sound. The gray smoke of cook fires hovered over Hooverville Flats. McCabe listened silently to the conversation in the room and could hardly believe what he was hearing. Arson was an option that should never even be considered but here they all were, talking openly about it as if it were a solution.

"I will not tolerate a discussion of arson in my office," said McCabe. "It's out of the question. I won't abide by it."

"You never objected last time we burned them out."

"Because it was with an edict from the Police Department and approval by the Fire Marshall with forewarning to and evacuation of the inhabitants. What you men are talking about is a criminal arson and I won't be any part of it. If Hooverville burns, I'm going report you to Fire Marshall Petrovitch. He's a personal friend and can't be bought like some of Seattle's other officials."

He glanced at Sheriff Gustafson accusatorily.

Opening his attaché case, Stone said, "You know, we don't need you McCabe. If you don't want to support our decisions and policies we have the option of voting you off the commission altogether.

"You won't have to. I'm ashamed of what this commission has become. And I'm ashamed of all of you. Meanwhile, as far as I'm concerned, the subject of arson is closed and this meeting is over. Now you can all get the hell out of my office, and if you have any thoughts of sending a team of thugs to quiet me like you did Frank Vogel remember as Commission secretary I've been taking minutes of all our meetings and there's enough in them to indict you all on criminal charges. Now get the hell out of my office."

Stone slammed close the attaché case in anger. The last to leave, he hesitated at the door, attaché case in hand, McCabe's illegally imported Canadian whiskey on his breath. At six feet three, he towered over McCabe, a stout man twenty years his elder.

"We're going to do what's best for Seattle with or without your approval, Mac. If you aren't with us then we at least expect you to stay out of our way."

* * *

The meeting moved to a neighborhood restaurant across the bridge in Fremont. Arriving in separate cars Stone, Drake, and Gustafson took a booth in the rear of the restaurant's spacious dining area. Order pad in hand, a shapely waitress with a friendly smile approached their booth. She wore her sandy blonde hair in a ponytail, her oversized waitress uniform and apron failing to conceal her ample bust. The men ordered coffee and asked for menus, which she placed before them on the table. When she returned with the coffee she prepared to take their orders.

"Have you gentlemen decided what you would like to eat?"

"I'd like to eat you," said Drake. He reached for her apron to pull her into his lap but she was already backing away.

"Sorry," she said, "but I'm not for sale."

"Who said anything about paying?"

Sheriff Gustafson ordered a hamburger and potatoes, Drake a steak, Stone apple pie with a wedge of cheddar cheese. The men's somber voices, cautiously low in volume, were occasionally broken up by the clatter of silverware and banging of pots and pans in the back kitchen.

"Looks like Seattle has a problem other than Hooverville," said Stone.

"Meaning what, exactly?"

"Obstacles to progress. Enemies of the Seattle waterfront."

"I don't follow you."

"I'm talking about McCabe."

"He's harmless," said Gustafson. "You yourself said we don't need him. Build your city without him."

"He's harmless now but could be trouble later. And we're not talking about building but excavating. Hooverville is in our way and it has to go. Mike is right. We can have it bulldozed and afterwards post a goon squad to guard it."

"We've been over that," said Gustafson. "Permits would be initially denied. We'd have to appeal and litigation would go on indefinitely. Even if we did get permission and bulldozed the shacks the residents of Hooverville and attorneys for the Unemployed Citizen's League would sue the city. They're more organized than you might think."

"Hooverville is a tinderbox. Accidents happen. Set it afire and blame it on faulty woodstoves or jimmied electrics," said Drake.

"I can't endorse that, Mike. Fires by their nature are uncontrollable. You can't predict them. People could get hurt."

Stone said, "We aren't asking for your endorsement, Sheriff Gustafson. Or for your permission for that matter."

"What then? Surely you don't think I'm going to condone arson."

"Why not? We can burn it down and charge and convict a Hooverville scapegoat."

"No," said Sheriff Gustafson. "It's out of my jurisdiction. The fire marshal would lead the investigation, not me. I'm sorry men but I can't take part in this. I shouldn't even be having this discussion with you. You heard what McCabe said. He's right about the new fire marshal. The man's a fanatic for safety and can't be bought."

In the early days Gustafson, Drake and Stone had been friends, sharing fishing trips to Coeur d'Alene, deer hunting in Montana and season ticket seats at Huskies home games. Both had gotten married around the same time. When Gustafson had first been elected Sheriff, Drake had attended his swearing-in ceremony. Drake himself had briefly been on the City Council before becoming the subject of a scandal causing his dismissal, afterwards going into business. Business being a polite word for racketeering.

The waitress came with their food and more coffee. The men changed the subject to football until she was out of earshot.

"Gustafson said, "There remains the matter of the Chief's monthly payment."

"Why do we pay him at all," objected Drake. "He doesn't do anything for us."

"He's the Chief of Police, Mike. We pay him to look the other way and not interfere."

Stone opened his valise and removed two manila envelopes, one for the chief that was marked with the letter C, the other for Gustafson himself.

Stone said, "You owe us whatever favor we ask or request we might make, Gus. We financed your campaign. We have an election coming up. Don't forget, we can just as easily support an opponent. But of course, we don't want to do that."

"I believe I have paid you in full for whatever you think I owe you. My dry squads have allowed you to run your speakeasies freely and close down independents that refuse to pay you a percentage of their profits."

"Sure, because you and your troops have been taking a cut of the action. Suppose the *Seattle Times* got hold of that. You can imagine."

"Are you blackmailing me?"

"I wouldn't put it that way, Gus."

Gustafson said, "What about you, Mike? Have you forgotten those pedophilia charges I got dropped?'

"They were bogus to begin with. How was I to know the boy's age?"

"You could have asked."

"I did. He said he was twenty."

"He was underage, and you knew it. He didn't look a day over twelve. I doubt he even had any pubic hair. He was destitute, and you took advantage of him, Mike."

"The boy may have been young, but he was no victim. He was a paid prostitute with a butthole as big and round as a truck tire and sloppy inside as a grease pit. It's a wonder I didn't fall in and hurt myself. "

"There was a lot of blood, Mike. The boy's rectum had to be surgically reconstructed."

"Hey, what's a guy to do? Is it my fault God endowed me with an extraordinary enormous dick? "

Gustafson, repulsed, picked up the envelopes of cash, paid his tab at the checkout counter and returned to his police car parked in front. He opened the briefcase on the front seat, inserted the two envelopes and closed it. He drove to the precinct, retrieved the envelope marked with the letter C and took it to the Chief's office. The chief accepted it with a nod of acknowledgment and locked it in his desk drawer. Not a word passed between the two men.

Lea Macquarrie

PALENTINE AVENUE

WALTER MCCABE FOLDED HIS UMBRELLA and got behind the wheel of his beloved 1931 Hudson four-door sedan, an automobile so battle-worthy it might be capable of sustaining a landmine because sometimes, damn it, Seattle drivers were all over the road, vying for position as if they were in some kind of competition and they had damn well best get out of his way. Not that he was an aggressive driver, he followed the rules of the road, was a courteous, civil and law abiding responsible citizen, but he remained steadfastly unyielding to those less deferential than himself.

His Hudson was built to sustain whatever might get in its way and had the battle scars and dents to show for it. He loved this car and everything about it, from the solid reassuring sound of its door thudding closed to the roar of its eight-cylinder engine after turning the key. To fools who bragged up their wretched Ford and Chevrolet death traps he unapologetically scoffed. Not only was his Hudson built like a tank, it could outrun and out outmaneuver its rival manufacturers on the road and off. The windshield wipers were too slow, however, with the result that cascading rivulets of rainwater gushing down his windshield distorted the landscape and transformed buildings into aqueous hallucinatory streetscapes, as if the city were under water and he was piloting a submarine.

He pulled out, almost missing a stack of barrels piled by the dock, but not quite. The front fender hit the outside edge and the barrels went flying off like bowling pins, most of them into the Sound, but one landed on his hood where it had been previously dented from when he had once hit a tree and a limb had fallen on it. He drove to the high chain link fence, stopped and got out to unlock the gate but the Hudson, left in neutral, inched forward without him, almost pinning him. He jumped out of the way at the last second. The Hudson rammed the gate, but the gate held it. He hurried back behind the driver's seat and applied the emergency brake, then got out and opened the gate and drove through. Once on the main road it was a matter mostly of avoiding nitwits with no business behind a wheel. Fortunately his superior driving skills enabled him to avoid near collisions not his fault. He drove over the Freemont Bridge, turned on Phinney Avenue and passed Woodlawn Park and drove down the steep incline to his estate on Palentine Avenue. .

His house was a monster perched on a rock, an emblem of a once prosperous family in decline. The McCabe home was larger than any other on the hill, dwarfing its neighbors and casting a shadow over houses that abutted it. A four story giant, it was considered an eyesore in the neighborhood but was none the less an impressive sight, majestically regal with large bay windows facing the street on the ground floor and rectangular dormer windows on the second and third floors and spacious slanted attic. The house was in need of painting and repair, its surface bubbly with flaking paint, its windows so dirty it was hard to see out, with visible wood rot on the eaves and missing shingles on the porch roof, the yard gone to weed, lawn so high it could no longer be cut with a lawn mower, but nevertheless possessing a proud aloof majesty despite its obvious neglect, which was precisely why neighbors whispered it was such a shame and embarrassment.

But if the grass and weeds overtook most of the unkempt yard, if bushes, shrubbery, and limbs strangled the several steep winding flights of granite steps to the front porch, he had greater concerns. He had his failing import-export business on Pier 91 to protect and an inclination to sequester himself in the office as much as possible. Besides, it gave him perverse pleasure to annoy his complaining

Lea Macquarrie

neighbors who should mind their own damn business and stay out of his, and he had better things to do with his money than squander it on costly unimportant appearances.

The house was Cora's project and one gone bad. Cora had been mismanaging the estate, squandering their savings, burning their dinners and allowing junk to accumulate for as long as he could remember. He had married her knowing her eccentricities and left her do as she wished so long as she kept out of his business and his marriage was the least of it because the whole damn country had gone to hell.

There was no driveway, the house occupied an imposing perch too steep to allow for one, but parking was available curbside on the street below. He stashed his flask in the glove compartment, exited the Hudson and stood in the street craning his neck to look up to his monstrous atrocity hulking far above. Bay windows glared at him accusatorily as if angry for not having been washed in years. McCabe sighed and began climbing the moss covered stone steps. Fortunately there was a substantial handrail, because the steps were not only steep but slippery with squishy moss and wet leaves. One day he would no longer be able to make this climb, and then what? Well, the way his shipping business was going lately, maybe he'd move down into Hooverville with the rest of the bums. At least he could drink down there without having to hide it from Cora.

He opened the front door to the parlor where, as always, the hallway was strewn with accumulated mail and newspapers dropped through the mail slot, dangerous as hell underfoot. The closest Cora ever seemed to get in removing the mess was to kick it out of her way in the process of clearing a pathway. Whether from stubbornness or curiosity he had determined to wait her out in disposing of the accumulation. His business mail was delivered to his office, so this was mostly unimportant circulars, newspapers and magazines.

Great cumulous clouds of black smoke drifted from the kitchen. That, of course, would be dinner burning. Cora burned everything. She sometimes sat in the first-floor library and forgot she was even cooking until their lungs filled with smoke and eyes began to water.

He lingered outside the kitchen, sadly watching her futile attempt to clear the smoke with her hands while failing to turn down the flame under a burning pan on the stovetop. She had a cigarette in her left hand while another burned a windowsill. A third smoldered in an ashtray on the kitchen table. She always had three or four going at once that she forgot about soon after lighting. The woman was an outrageous fire hazard. One day she would kill them all.

He entered the kitchen to turn down the flame on the stove.

"What's cooking," he inquired? "Or should I more accurately inquire, what's burning?"

A skillet held a slab of violated meat that might be pork, pot roast, lamb, or perhaps one of his old rain boots. It was hard to guess and didn't matter because whatever it turned out to be it would be the same as always: flavorless and burned beyond recognition. A pot of potatoes on the stove had boiled to the degree they had disintegrated and were near to liquefying. She would serve these too, along with overcooked boiled carrots, which she seemed always to forget he loathed and invariably refused.

"Dinner will be served soon," she said. "It's almost ready."

Almost ready?

Cora cooked worse than he played the piano, but when she kissed him on the cheek all was forgiven. He loved her still, after thirty-five years of marriage, always had, from the first time he saw her at the Nile Temple dance hall. She had been a raven- haired beauty then and was now an older version of that beauty. She had the same thoughtful brown eyes suggestive of depth of character, the same narrow pretty face, soft full lips and perfect nose that seemed to beg for the touch of his lips on its bridge. Her hair, braided into a crown on top of her head, was silver now, and she had lost a couple of inches in height. She wore loose unflattering house dresses far too often, with nylons rolled up to the knee, but sometimes surprised him by dressing for dinner. Not tonight though.

"Call me when dinner is served," he said. "I'm going to go play the piano."

"Oh, no," she despaired. "Do you have to?"

He went down the hall to the music room, its bay windows giving a glimpse of Ballard Bay and Puget Sound. He lifted the piano bench cover, removed a pint of Canadian Club and took a deep, long drink. Cora would call him to dinner almost as soon as he began playing. He was certain of it. Meanwhile Rachmaninoff on the stand awaited his brutal desecration. The piece was to be played pianissimo with great subtlety, but he pounded the keys with guts and fury. He knew he was a terrible pianist but let no one tell him. He played the only way he knew, in defiance of all good taste, sensitivity, and musicality. He played with a vengeance.

And so he began.

"Dinner," called Cora.

Of course.

He arrived at the formal dining room to find their linen-covered table set with sterling silver platters, cutlery and serving spoons, crystal glassware and china plates and cups. One thing about Cora, maybe she couldn't cook worth a damn, but she set a pretty table. He pulled up a chair across from her and inhaled steaming overcooked vegetables and mysterious meat of unidentifiable origin. .

"Let me guess. I suspect a pot roast."

"I think it might be. I can't remember. It might be stewing beef."

God, what he wouldn't give for a decent pot roast. She used to make it perfectly.

Cora smiled and picked up the silver ladle from the bowl of boiled potatoes.

"Here," she said, "let me serve you."

She scooped up the potatoes, but they broke apart on the ladle when she served them. Tepid vegetable water spilled across his plate. Frowning, he watched her serve boiled carrots cut into wedges and mixed with the potatoes. He watched her saw at the blackened, mutilated slab of mystery meat with a large carving knife. She was having a great deal of difficulty managing it. A strand of her braided silver hair had loosened and was dangling in the gravy.

Finally she managed to cut a piece and place it on his platter.

He took a tentative bite. Five minutes later he was still chewing it. His jaw began to ache from the effort.

"How is it?" asked Cora.

"A tad overcooked perhaps, but exquisitely presented."

He gave up on whatever it was he had been chewing and discreetly placed it within his folded napkin.

"But you didn't marry me for my cooking did you now, Walter dear?"

"I did not. Though back in the day you cooked as well as anyone."

"But that's not why you chose me."

"No."

"You chose me because I was so good looking and such a graceful dancer didn't you, Walter."

"Yes. That and for your pretty, sweet, melodious voice. But why did you ever agree, Cora?"

"Agree to what?"

"To marry me."

"I felt sorry for you. Such a grumpy, unhappy man."

"Yes, well, that hasn't changed much, I'm afraid."

"Walter?"

"Yes, Cora?"

"I think I can't do this any longer."

"What? You can't be my wife any longer? Then I will jump out the window to my death."

"No, Walter dear, the windows have been painted closed for years, remember?"

"Foiled again, my dear."

"I'm serious, Walter. I can't keep this up. I try, I really do, but I keep forgetting what I am doing. I may have ruined this meal, and it's a shame when so many are hungry."

"I agree."

"And the house. It's gone to rubbish, Walter. Haven't you noticed?"

"I have."

"I need some help with the cooking and cleaning. It certainly

Lea Macquarrie

shouldn't be difficult to find someone who needs a place to live in exchange for regular meals, a roof over their head and a small salary, don't you agree?"

"Well, we will see", he replied. "Perhaps. Let me think it over."

But he did not want strangers living his house.

His mind was made up on the subject.

RAIL YARD, EVERETT WASHINGTON

THE VOGEL'S WATCHED WHAT SEEMED like the entire tramp population leap off the stalled train. He and Juanita stayed behind while the other tramps gathered their gear from where they had thrown it before wandering off toward scattered distant city buildings on the outskirts of what Jack was not sure was Seattle and would later learn was Everett. The train, its engines cut, gave no promise of proceeding anywhere anytime soon. When it seemed to Jack safe to leave without being seen, they tossed their bedrolls and packs off the boxcar and dropped to the ground. Blood stained their clothing. It was early morning, and sunlight was just beginning to break through the low lying cloud cover. It was raining lightly. Juanita had gore in her hair. They crouched alongside vacated parked trains and boxcars, Jack making sure they were out of sight. It horrified him to see her bloodstained face. He thought she looked like an Apache warrior who had participated in the killing of a wagon team of westward pioneers. He pulled her along the tracks but would not speak to her or even look at her directly.

The dream and promise of Seattle was as dead as the man she had killed. She had destroyed it when picking up that crowbar. It would have been better if the man had taken their money and skedaddled unharmed. There was no future for them now other than flight from justice and truth, of lies and evasion and a terrible burden of secrecy ending in eventual, inevitable captivity. Juanita had done this to them and he didn't know if he could forgive her. He didn't know what to say to her, how to be with her now that she had stolen his dream of a better life in Seattle. He dared not even look at her. He hid his face from her for fear his eyes might reveal what he was thinking about her. She seemed to avoid eye contact with him as well.

He was ashamed of these thoughts, but could not stop them. What kind of man was he, to think this way? He was her father. He was supposed to love her unconditionally. He did love her, of course he loved her, but he wanted to punish her severely, both for her own good and his personal satisfaction.

Crying, she said, "Are you mad at me, Daddy?"

"No," he lied.

It was the first word he had spoken to her since leaving the train. She had been crying from the moment they had disposed of the body and he was glad of it. He wanted her to be crying. She had killed a man. She said it was to protect him but it was more than that. It was her temper. Elvira had warned him of it, but he had been a fool. He'd figured she would grow out of it.

They were out of the rail yard now and walking the tracks alongside what he knew was Puget Sound. Thoughts crashed around in his head like the whitecaps breaking on the jagged shoreline. He kept seeing the pulverized face of the man his daughter had killed. He wanted to vomit but his stomach was empty.

The tracks led them along the Sound, but instead of the city of Seattle they were entering wilderness. They eventually came to a succession of three abandoned sawmills in the center of a vast empty wet parking lot. There were no cars present, and the mills appeared to be shut down. At one he found what he was looking for, a water spigot.

He shoved her head under the spigot, knelt and scrubbed her hair with a bar of soap from their pack. The water that cascaded down her back became pink with residual blood. It made him nauseous to touch the gore in her hair. There were clumps of organic matter congealed like glue he could not dislodge and he began gagging and retching in the attempt to do so. He removed his Swiss

Army knife and pulled back a fistful of her hair to cut out globs of brain matter with its scissors but her hair resisted the inadequate scissor blades, which were made for cutting paper or thread. He snapped the scissors close and extracted a knife blade with his thumbnail. The knife was dull and would not cut evenly. He had to hack and saw at the gore like old leather. There was no other way. Her gore encrusted hair came off in shredded, uneven strands. She was crying and trembling and saying over and over no Daddy no, not my hair, please. Another Indian thing, the long raven black hair she was so proud of. He hacked it away. Her body shook so violently with her sobbing he thought her bones might break inside of her.

And then he was crying as well. This was his daughter. How dare he judge her? She was barely fourteen years old, just a frightened little girl inside. He was the one who should be judged. It was his fault; he knew it was his fault. *He* was the guilty one. He had brought her along on this ill-fated, god-forsaken dream of Seattle. His dream, not hers.

He unrolled one of the blankets they carried, wrapped it around her trembling frame and held her close to him, peppering her with little kisses. He kissed her soft wet cheek and the salty tears in her eyes, saying over and over again it was not her fault, that he was to blame if anyone, that he loved her, would always love her and protect her and he was sorry, so sorry, he was just afraid, for both of them. He felt her violent shaking subside to a tremble, her little gasps slowly diminishing, and then she was kissing him, kissing his neck and burying her face in his shoulder and saying I love you Daddy, I love you so much, I'm sorry, I'm sorry, I'm sorry. They sat there together until cried out. He would have stayed with her like this longer had he not begun to sensibly worry about being discovered. They had to move on. Both changed into clothing from their pack. Their soiled clothing was beyond salvaging so he placed it in a pile and tried to light it but at most it smoldered. The drizzling Seattle weather kept it from burning.

Wait for me here," he said.

"You'll come back, won't you Daddy? You won't leave me here?"

"Never. Not in the flesh and not in my heart. I'm sorry I lost my temper with you, Juanita. I shouldn't have cut your hair the way I did."

"Why did you, Daddy. I loved my long hair, you knew that."

"It was a meanness in me. But I was afraid of what we had done. And when we tried to wash away the blood some of the man's brains were lodged in your hair and I couldn't pick it out. It had dried and congealed there. It sickened me. I'm sorry I did this to you, Juanita."

But he wondered if in his anger and grief he had meant to cut away her Indian identity, a fierceness she had inherited from her mother. He shouldered his pack and left her on the railroad tracks and wandered off into the dense forest beyond. About fifty yards into the thick underbrush he knelt on the mossy ground and dug a pit with the crowbar. Birds perched on the limbs of trees sang to him. He was where he most liked to be, alone in the woods, at one with Nature. His heart swelled at the recognition of so much beauty, so much death. He wished he could stay here, free of his past, a hermit in the forest. It was as close to God as a man could get. Much closer than in a church, which was phony. He placed the soiled bloody clothing and the crowbar in the pit and covered it with dirt, pine needles and leaves.

He hiked back though the underbrush to the tracks and found Juanita crying again.

"What's wrong, Juanita?"

But there was so much wrong the question was ludicrous. Everything was wrong. They had murdered a man, were homeless, exhausted, and headed toward an unknown future that might include a life in prison.

"My locket," she sobbed. "It's gone.

Her locket, all Juanita had of the mother she never really knew. You're sure you don't have it?"

"Of course I'm sure. I didn't take it off, Daddy. It *came* off."

"Did it come off when I was cutting your hair? It's got to be around here, Juanita, maybe under leaves and dirt."

"I think I lost it on the train."

"Why do you say this?"

"I remember the man choking me and the chain digging into my neck. Then it wasn't anymore. I think maybe it broke and fell off."

He imagined inspectors finding the bloody gore streaked boxcar and then the locket, with its inscription, and finally the corpse.

"Let's hope not or we are in deep trouble."

They walked between two sets of railroad tracks, dense forest on one side and the shore on the other. His daughter did not speak to him and he did not encourage it. It was raining lightly again; it seemed to do so in intervals, as if on a timer set for twenty minutes on and twenty minutes off.

Men paid for their crimes, one way or another. Women too. They were judged if not by man's law, by God's. No one got away with anything. No one went unpunished. Their victim's body would eventually be found. It was inevitable. There would be no question of how he had died. The man's wounds would shout murder.

"What are you thinking, Daddy?"

"I wish we hadn't come. I wish I'd never left Montana.

"I ruined it for us, didn't I daddy?"

"It's my fault, Juanita. I'm the one who put us on that train. What happened, what you did, I'm to blame. I shoulda known it was too dangerous for a young girl."

His words were all he had to give her right now. There was no turning back from what they had done and he didn't know how to comfort her. They were going to Hell he couldn't get them out. Seagulls swooped along the beach, gliding in the gray dawn, pecking in the sand for edibles.

They walked without speaking, listening to the sea wash over the rocky embankment, the gentle rain falling between the limbs of drenched pine, Fir and Evergreen.

Finally he said, "Why did you have to keep hitting him, Juanita? He was finished with the first strike of the crowbar."

"I was afraid, Daddy."

"I'm more afraid now."

The words strangled his throat. He felt them throbbing there like the ocean alongside them. Mist and drifting fog hung low and close to the dark saltwater slapping the rocks. Rain pocked the ocean. The dense forest on the opposite the tracks seemed alive with moving shadows. Trees watched them silently, their limbs dripping beads of rain to the mossy ground. The lighting seemed somehow spooky, unpredictably shinning bright one moment and then vanishing inexplicably into the woods, back and forth, leaving its shadows on the tracks. .

"What was that?"

"What?"

"In the woods, Daddy. I heard something. What was it?"

"I don't know. Maybe a deer."

"What about bears?"

"What about them? "

"Do you think they might live in these woods?"

Jack shrugged and wiped rain from his eyes. In a flash behind his eyelids he saw the image of a bear-like man climbing into a boxcar.

"They might eat us", said Juanita."

"Not likely. The way we smell, they'd probably take one whiff and go running back into the woods."

Waves pounded hard, crashing against the rocky embankment below. No one walked the beach; no one was on the tracks. It was too wet and cold. Islands vanished and reappeared in the mist and from time they heard the motor of a fishing boat in the dense fog. They humped with their packs along the railroad tracks, Jack relieved to glimpse the peak of the snow-capped Mt. Rainer through the cloud cover. The sight of it confirmed his belief they were walking in the right direction toward Seattle. Weak with fatigue, they trudged along on tired hurting feet. They began to see houses scattered on the hillsides, some with smokestacks in use. The houses were few and far apart from one another, the first they had seen in over an hour.

"We are getting close to somewhere," said Jack. "I don't know where but somewhere maybe near Seattle."

Shivering sea hawks and pigeons with folded wings stared at them curiously, as if wondering what foolishness had caused them to be here, on these tracks exposed to the elements. Why didn't they seek shelter? Why didn't they hide under the trees? The rain lightened and then stopped and the sun came out and Mount Baker and the Olympic Mountain Range appeared on the land mass across the sound.

They walked in the sun, their steaming clothing sticking to them. Later they came around a bend to a railroad crossing where a two-lane road led to steep hills scattered with wood frame houses within thick verdant forest. A pier some fifty yards long with a bait and tackle shop held aloft by barnacle encrusted pilings appeared. Slippery underfoot, the pier was heavily spattered with gray and white seagull droppings. Some of the wooden planks creaked under their feet as they trudged the slick worn planks to the bait and tackle shop, a weather- beaten single-room shack with windows so smudged with salt spray they couldn't see inside.

A bell over the door rang behind them when they entered. Jack gratefully received the warmth of the shack's interior where a woodstove burned in a corner. Juanita lingered behind him near the door. There was a haphazard display of fishing line, lures and casters. Fishing poles were stacked in the corner opposite the woodstove. The room reeked of fish. He had not eaten since the killing but the stink of fish combined with the imagery of the killing and remembrance of picking gore out of Juanita's hair suppressed his appetite and made him nauseous. The proprietor, an enormous jowly bald man reading a True Detective magazine, looked up from his stool behind the counter. He wore blue overalls with only an undershirt. The overalls were spattered with what looked like seagull shit. He put the magazine down, the limp flesh under his huge arms dangling like wash on a clothesline.

"Good morning, strangers. Cold and damp out there this morning, isn't it? At least it's finally stopped raining for a spell. Nice and sunny now. In another hour it'll be raining again. You're welcome to dry out by the woodstove."

Pausing midsentence to catch his breath, the wheezing proprietor coughed into his clenched fist. He stared long and inquisitively at Juanita.

"You know what they say about the weather around here. If

you don't like it, wait an hour." He spat a wad of chewing tobacco into a metal pail and said, "You plan on doing some fishing?"

"Not today," said Jack. "I was wondering if you had some fresh water to spare." They had emptied their canteens earlier, and both were thirsty.

"Do you have anything to eat here? Maybe a hot dog or sandwich or something?"

"Not unless you like salmon eggs."

"I'm not hungry," said Juanita.

He suspected she felt as he did. He watched her exit the bait shack to stand on the wooden pier looking out to sea, where it was clearing.

"There's a spigot out back. Help yourself so long as you don't take too much. This ain't no bath house, after all."

"No, we just want drinking water."

"That's fine. You new around here? I never seen you before."

"We're from Montana. Pulled up stake and came here to find work."

"Well my advice is turn around and go back to Montana. There damn sure ain't no work around here."

"Hard to believe, what with all the lumber mills and all."

"Oh, we got plenty enough lumber mills. Problem is most of them are closed. The ones that aren't have laid off half their workers."

"We'll be all right, Juanita and me. My brother lives in Seattle and is well known with a lot of friends. He'll find some work for me."

"Well, I hope you're right and maybe you are at that, but Seattle's tough, what with the Depression and all. Keep on walking those tracks and eventually you'll come into Hooverville, maybe the biggest hobo camp in the country. Then you'll see. You got one thing going for you though, you're white. I don't know about this girl you got with you, though."

"What about her? She's my daughter."

"She's an Indian, isn't she?"

Jack was slow to answer.

"Barely," he said. "Maybe a quarter on her mother's side."

"I thought so. She seems like a nice girl. Quiet, polite and well behaved."

If you only knew, thought Jack. About both of us.

"Indians have it toughest. Worse than the colored, maybe. People in these parts don't like em, don't respect em. Too many of them are bums. Especially in Seattle. They drink themselves into a stupor and pass out on the sidewalks so you have to step over them. Your daughter could pass for something else though, maybe Italian or something, and if you want my advice she should. Anyway, water's out back. Help yourself."

Jack thanked the man and went for water.

He worried about what the man had said about Indians. Back home in Cat Creek, Indians were common and anyway it didn't matter so much what you were, so long as you were a good worker. Of course it was hard to show you were a good worker when there was no work to be had. And he had to admit, probably you had a better shot at getting work if you were white.

And his daughter was more white than Indian. It wasn't fair to discriminate against her for the little bit of Indian blood she had. He'd get her into a good Seattle school, get her a proper education. Maybe when she was grown she might become a schoolteacher herself maybe, a nurse or social worker, someone who mattered, a person who might help others in some significant way.

But would it exonerate them from what they had done? Would they then be less deserving of punitive retribution and justice, either God's or man's? It wouldn't be justice for the man they had killed. He would still be dead. He knelt at the spigot and drank from it and filled their canteen. They walked in silence, Jack thoughtful as they trekked along the railroad tracks.

"Juanita, the man you killed was on his knees with the first strike of the crowbar. It was too dark to see clearly but I distinctly heard three maybe four strikes of the crowbar. He was done for with the first strike."

"You keep saying that. It all happened so fast, Daddy. It was like I was in a dream or something. I remember when I snapped out of it I was surprised at what I had done. It was like someone else did it, not me. It still feels that way, like I'm two people and the other person did it."

"But it wasn't someone else, Juanita. *You* did this. A man is dead because of what you did. For all we know he might have a little girl your age somewhere waiting for him to come home. Maybe they're in Yakima right now as we speak, happily anticipating a joyous reunion. We should probably remember that."

"He was a bully and a thief, Daddy. A hurtful man."

"And now he's gone and we're here with what we did. You are not to speak of it to anyone. We can't trust anyone with this, I don't care who it is. That's how people are caught and sent to prison. Going to prison won't get this man's life back. We have to move on from this Juanita. We are going to have to live the rest of our lives keeping a terrible secret."

"All right, Daddy. I can keep a secret. Don't worry."

"Don't worry? Are you serious? Is that even possible?"

"You'll find work, Daddy, we'll get a big house, Uncle Frank will come live with us, maybe even Elvira."

"I'm not so sure anymore, Juanita. But I agree we have to make this move to Seattle count. There's something else, too. I've been thinking about this. When we get there, if anybody asks if you're Indian, tell them you are Italian."

"But I'm not. I'm Crow like Mama. I'm not ashamed of it. "

"And I'm not saying you should be. But your Mother was only half and that makes you only a quarter so you don't have to hang on to it and maybe shouldn't if you want to get ahead in Seattle. Just do it, Juanita. From now on you're Italian."

They came to a small little township with yet another railroad crossing, this one with a pier and ferry landing. The white ferry against the dark sea seemed a creature out of myth. Juanita said it looked like a castle rising out of the sea. Jack told her it was a ferryboat that carried automobiles but Juanita would not believe it so they waited for it to dock and watched the cars unload and drive along the town's single street up a steep incline flanked with towering Evergreens, Spruce, and Douglas Fir. A sea hawk glided in graceful slow concentric circles, swooping down toward the surface of the sound and diving for salmon.

Jack refilled their canteens from a drinking fountain at the ferry landing while Juanita waited. Watching the majestic white ferry against the dark blue sea while kneeling at the spigot, he remembered how Frank, when he came home from the war, said he sometimes had unwelcomed mental glimpses into his past experience of killing men with a bayonet, but mostly he'd put it behind him. Frank said vivid memories of killing came up unpredictably at odd and unexpected times, but were rare and of brief duration, but Frank had tossed and turned restlessly in his sleep and sometimes woke everyone with his screaming. Nobody in the family talked about it, but Frank came back from the war changed. He wouldn't talk to anyone, not even Elvira, about the war and the things he had done there.

It was raining again. Dampness permeated everything. Here rain was not an unrelenting downpour like at home, but a suspended drizzle permeating the very atmosphere she breathed. Whitecaps broke and crashed audibly against the rocky shore, sending high wet plumes of cold morning spray into the misty air. Juanita shivered in the spray of salty wet wind on her face. She had never in her life seen a seascape, never before heard the sound of breaking waves or watched the flight of seagulls or inhaled the ocean reek of salty kelp and seaweed. It was a dream, and she was memorizing everything, the strange shapes scattered along the beach, organisms she had never before seen or imagined as if they did not belong to this planet, gnarled driftwood and bizarre jellyfish, barnacles, seaweed and strange quivering translucent organisms both living and dead, unimaginable, reeking.

An hour later they staggered into a hobo encampment so congested with shacks it might have been mistaken for Seattle itself if not for the city skyline visible behind it. They slogged along its muddy entanglement of puddle-strewn pathways, passing a haphazard conglomeration of tar paper and plywood shacks, some barely standing, others more substantial with more than one floor. Scrawny barking mutt dogs rummaged in refuse heaps. Shabby un-

Lea Macquarrie

shaven men out in the drizzle in front of their shacks gathered scrap or were cooking in pots over small cook fires sheltered from the rain by sheets of tin or tarp. A few of these men said hello, others merely nodded. Most paid them no mind. Raindrops pattered down into puddles as they traversed the wet muddy grounds. A surprising number of women were present but no children at all. They sloshed across a muddy field and then through another sprawl of shacks and then saw the red brick buildings of Seattle proper on the hills above them.

They crossed a set of tracks and began to climb the steep rickety wooden stairs to 1st Avenue and the city itself. The stairway had so many steps and wrapped around so many times Juanita stopped counting halfway up. Her father had to stop more than once to catch his breath. They rested, looking down at grey merchant ships docked at misty piers below. The steep wooden staircase shifted slightly in the wind, the planks under their feet creaking under their weight. The stairwell railing protecting them from falling was wobbly and of questionable safety.

Walking along First Avenue she saw girls her own age and many boys, some cute with warm blue eyes. Many of the boys wore shabby suits with vests and neckties like the adults. Their fedora hats looked comical on boys so young. She wondered if they had girlfriends, if they went to movies and maybe kissed in the balcony. Maybe here in Seattle she would meet such a boy, and he would come to her house with flowers or candy. He would take her to an afternoon matinee and share popcorn and Coca-Cola and afterwards they would walk through the park and maybe sit holding hands on a park bench and kiss.

Other boys were ragamuffins needing haircuts and wearing hand-me-downs like home in Cat Creek. Many sold newspapers or worked at makeshift shoeshine stands. Some wandered in and out of traffic soliciting handouts. There was traffic unlike she had ever imagined, loud automobiles, electric trolleys and construction. It was impossible to hear what her father was saying to her. Noise was all around them in the streets and buildings, in the air they breathed. People walking too fast, talking too loud. Trolleys with shrieking brakes, honking automobiles, newsboys shouting on the corners, music everywhere, tattoo parlors, dubious speakeasies without names, alcoves where men in suits perched reading newspapers on tall stools while men at their feet made rhythms with the snap of shoeshine rags. It was confusion, chaos, sensory overload. It diminished intrusive thoughts of the man on the train, whom she had killed, though she could not remember striking the blow that had caused his death, and it was as if someone other than herself had done it. She was supposed to be sorry even if the man was a liar and a thief and maybe worse who had wanted to hurt her father and steal their life savings.

She hesitated at a large display window of a department store where three beautiful white mannequins wore high fashion dresses like those she saw in the magazines on the rack at *Wilson's Drug Store* at home. She imagined herself wearing such a dress, especially the one with glittering sequins woven into it. It was a dress made for a princess but not for an Indian warrior princess. Not for a girl who killed. Not for her.

She saw her refection in the plate glass, her hair chopped close to the scalp in patches where her father had butchered it, her muddy lace-up boots tied with mismatching strips of rawhide, her pants torn and ragged at the cuffs, holes in the elbows of her jacket. The way she looked she didn't even deserve a boyfriend forget about the so-called knight in shining armor everybody talked about. She tried to imagine herself as a woman of glamour with styled hair and nice clothes, an educated woman who could read, who was not ragged, an educated woman who had not killed a man.

Her father pulled her along storefronts so large whole families could live in them they were so spacious. They passed theatres showing triple features, saloons and restaurants. Sailors milled around the entrances to shabby burlesque theatres with the facades of palaces. Loitering dance hall girls wore slinky garments that flattered their shapely figures under their fur coats. She envied them.

Jack held his daughter's hand tightly when passing through a neighborhood of boarded up storefronts. Native Indian tramps slept openly on the sidewalk with whites and Negroes. Some clutched their heads in both hands as if their heads might otherwise fall off. Others sat in door wells with their knees drawn up around them, hugging themselves as if they believed no one else ever would. This was likely the famous Skid Row he had heard about and it was mostly displaced native Indians.

Frank was right. Indians were a conquered nation. The reservation was a concentration camp subsisting on government handouts. To leave it for the city was worse. The city turned men into drunks who alternated sleeping in flophouses or in city jails. He and Frank had talked about it at length. Jack knew it firsthand. He'd seen his children leave the reservation to set out in search of a better life. And what had become of them? One had been killed in a car wreck, one vanished, another had gone to prison and another come back to the reservation as a thief, drunk, wife batterer and ex-convict. And now Juanita with blood on her hands and a darkness inside of her. He feared for her. He loved her. He hated what she had done.

They waded through hundreds of strutting pigeons gathered near the Pioneer Square totem pole. Their fatigue and the awkwardness of their packs made it difficult not to stumble. The street scene was enough to keep them off balance. It didn't help that so many here were drunk and staggering. Juanita seemed to be near to sleepwalking.

He found the hillside Hotel Lee on a quiet street outside of the perimeter, safer for a girl her age than those around the more affordable hotels surrounding Pioneer Square. They trudged its wet concrete steps and wearily entered the warm hotel lobby. Jack inquired at the desk with an elderly bowing Chinaman with a long white beard who was wearing what looked like a ceremonial robe of some kind. The Chinaman regarded them skeptically.

"Sir, I know we look ragged and dirty, but we traveled a long way. We clean up good, and will be no trouble."

Jack had by now transferred his money from his boot and carried a roll in his pocket. He carried no identification. He peeled off the amount for three weeks rent, figuring it might take that long to find Frank and get a job. The rate was higher than at the hotels in Pioneer Square, but affordable. The Chinaman was so stooped and thin Jack thought he could hear the rattling bones of the man's brittle skeleton as he led them up three flights of stairs to their room. Juanita later told him the Chinaman's beard was so long she was afraid he might trip over it and tumble down the stairwell. A worn carpeted hallway smelling of cigarettes and mildew on the third floor led to their room, which he found to be cramped but warm and vaguely welcoming, with pleasant comfortable furniture and a window with a view to downtown Chinatown and the King Street Train Station. It had a small desk, bookcase, and a framed rainy landscape Jack presumed to be Chinese hung on the wall behind the bed. He was shown a closet sized bathroom in which the sink and bath were clean, the toilet artificially fragrant with clean towels on hooks and soap in the soap dishes on the sink. The bed supplied more than enough room for the two of them. Juanita bounced up and down on it approvingly. He plopped down on it, exhausted and wanting nothing more than a long nap but when he closed his eyes he didn't like what he saw and was made to wonder if he would ever again sleep peacefully.

Maybe he should just give up, go to the police and confess.

He rose, stood at the window and watched the blinking reflection of the hotel's neon sign mirrored on the wet pavement. It was still raining. It hadn't stopped since they'd arrived. Much as he hated to go out in it they were both hungry with nothing to eat, so he reluctantly put on his coat and hat to go out. Juanita looked so young and vulnerable on the bed it frightened him to be the one responsible for her care. How was a man to protect a young daughter from this world and all its unforeseen dangers? He wondered if she was having intrusive thoughts and memories of the killing same as him. He would ask her later.

He found a small neighborhood grocery next to a closed St. Vincent de Paul thrift store. The store was poorly stocked, with empty shelf space. There was no milk at all. He bought some bread and bologna and returned to their room to find Juanita bathed and wearing one of his wrinkled white shirts way too big for her. The contrast of her dark skin against his white shirt made her look even darker and more Indian. He pulled down the window shade. Later, after dinner when she was asleep, he carefully removed his most recent letter from his brother Frank from his vest pocket and unfolded it and sat in a chair by the window with the letter in his lap, its pages reflecting the light of the blinking neon sign outside the window. To merely see Frank's handwriting was itself reassuring. The plan had always been to find his brother Frank. Frank would know what to do. He always had.

Early the next morning he and Juanita sloshed along a steep city street awash with rivulets of cascading rainwater. The view down the hill to the buildings of Seattle was gray and dismal. Pigeons around their feet moved away without being stepped on only at the last possible instant. Far down the hill there was a gray glimpse of Puget Sound.

"Does it ever stop raining in this city?"

Juanita didn't answer. Her mouth was grim, as if biting down on something with a disagreeable taste. She was in one of her moods. Same as her mother. It made him angry. The unlevel wet sidewalk and steepness of the hill made it slippery underfoot. He tried to grab onto her arm for support but she shook it off and was walking too fast for him to keep up.

How easy it would be to slip into an alley and vanish. Move on from here to Alaska. Hitch a ride on a fishing boat or just stick out his thumb. She'd be better off without him anyway. But of course he couldn't leave her. He hated himself for even thinking this.

PIONEER SQUARE

TWO MEN WEARING SHABBY RAINCOATS and wide brimmed fedoras were passing a bottle wrapped in a brown paper bag behind the Pioneer Square Branch of the *Unemployed Citizens' League* when Jack arrived. One of the men was trying to smoke under a leaky umbrella. The other had a full red beard from which tiny beads of glistening rainwater dripped in the manner of a washcloth someone had wrung. They offered Jack a nip but he politely declined. He entered a small bright rectangular room with low ceilings and cheap metal folding chairs in a waiting area occupied by three desultory men not sitting together. He had expected an office with rows of rows of desks and ringing telephones and the clacking of typewriters. Here there was mostly empty space and the pervasive odor of stale tobacco. On a rickety card table were scattered pamphlets, magazines, handbills and periodicals, most of them appearing to be socialist or communist, with photos of demonstrating workers in picket lines. Behind a wooden desk where the room divided, a worker sat making notes while interviewing an older man with crutches who gesticulated with exaggerated hand motions when speaking.

Beside the clerk a woman was typing. A battered gray file cabinet was behind them both. The man behind the desk tore a page from the notebook and handed it over to the man being interviewed, who put it in his jacket pocket, gathered his crutches and hobbled out. Jack hurried up to the desk and took the man's vacated seat.

The official behind the desk looked up from the notebook he had been writing in and said, "You have to take a number and wait your turn."

"How do I get one of these numbers?"

"On the table just past the door where you came in."

It was cold in the room. He saw radiators in the corner, but there was no heat of any kind. He buttoned his jacket. A man in a chair a row ahead of him was shivering. The man wore a thin white shirt and no jacket and Jack thought him too thin; he looked sick and troubled. There were so many kinds of trouble. So many ways to die. Life was perilous, fragile, tenuous and uncertain. No one was safe from it. He heard his number called and approached the desk.

The official behind it wore a pin-striped suit, tie and vest, his jacket thrown over the back of his chair. He was balding, with a high forehead and a handlebar moustache similar to his own but more neatly trimmed. His ruminative dark brown eyes and worried facial expression gave the impression here was a thoughtful man of emotional depth and understanding. He wore a name tag identifying him as Randall Blenman.

He rose from behind the desk, shook Jack's hand and said, "I don't think I have seen you in here before. I'm Randy."

"I'm new to Seattle. Just got in as a matter of fact."

"From?"

"Came here by way of California," said Jack.

It seemed to him prudent not to disclose he had come through Montana, Idaho and eastern Washington, where a man lay dead somewhere on the railroad tracks. "I'm trying to find my brother and he said I might check here. His name is Frank Vogel and I'm his brother Jack. Do you know how I might find him?"

"I'm afraid so. He's in the big house, Jack."

"Is this big house near here?"

" No, it's in Walla Walla."

"Well, do you have an address? He's going to find me work."

"I doubt that, Mr. Vogel, unless the work involves making license plates. He's in the Walla Walla State Penitentiary. He robbed a bank, Mr. Vogel. Well, they say he did. We don't believe it. We believe he was framed. This was several months ago. He'd been trying to unionize the Weyerhaeuser lumber mills, Bethlehem Steel plant, and the Sailor's Friend Hospital. He had a lot of enemies. A month before the so-called robbery, three hired thugs attacked him with baseball bats and broke him up pretty good. Your brother is tough though, and put one of them in the hospital."

"My brother fought in the Golden Gloves when he was in the Army."

"I'm not surprised. He beat one of them up pretty bad, but it was three against one. They told Frank to get out of Seattle and to never show his face here again. He went right back to organizing and making trouble."

It was not difficult for him to imagine his brother in jail; he knew his brother had been locked up many times on any number of charges including vagrancy, inciting a riot, illegal assembly, even petty theft, but in *jail*, never in a penitentiary. His brother might be a petty thief and man who made trouble, but he was no bank robber.

Blenman opened the desk drawer and retrieved a crumpled package of Chesterfields. A cigarette came out of the pack misshapen and wrinkled and Jack watched him straightened it between his thumb and index finger.

"You want one, Jack?"

"Store bought? Sure. I don't get offered one of those too often. Mostly self-rolled Bull Durham."

Blenman lighted it for him when Jack had it between his lips. Jack saw the man was staring at him with a peculiar expression he did not understand and said, "What?"

"You seem different from your brother. I mean no offense but maybe not the fighting man your brother was. There are things about Seattle you need to understand. It's caught in the grip of some bad men who had it in for your brother early on. Your brother was considered a nuisance and troublemaker to most of them, including the King County sheriff, Gus Gustafson. Get in their way, make trouble for them, and you are going to have a fight on your hands you didn't expect, don't want, and can't win."

Blenman tapped his ash on the edge of the planter on his desk and said, "Your brother was represented by an attorney provided by the *Socialist Center* but didn't have a prayer, if you believe in prayer, which I most certainly do not, because what kind of God would allow this kind of injustice? Anyway, if you're from out of town you have to know the legal system is fixed here in Seattle, Mr. Vogel. The entire police department is neck deep in vice and corruption, and the city government is complicit. I know this is bad news, and I'm sorry to be the one to pass it on."

"I've got to see my brother, Mr. Blenman. Where is this Walla Walla State Penitentiary?"

Jack became aware more men had entered the building. Several of the folding chairs were now occupied. Blenman extinguished his cigarette carefully, saving the remainder for later and Jack did the same, putting the butt in his shirt pocket.

"It's about two hundred and fifty miles from here. Do you have transportation?"

"Transportation would put a big dent in my savings I can't afford. I have a young daughter in my care. I need a job, Mister Blenman."

"Who doesn't?"

"You don't. You have a job."

"I'm an unpaid volunteer here, Mr. Vogel."

"Well can you help me find work or not?"

"Do you even know what it is we do here, Mr. Vogel, who we are?"

"No, I can't say that I do."

"Take this pamphlet and read it thoroughly. It will give you information regarding the services we provide."

"I'm ashamed to have to say it but I'm not much for reading and writing."

"You're illiterate?"

"I'm ashamed to say so but mostly yes."

"Would you like to change that?"

"Of course."

The telephone rang and the typist picked up. Jack heard her soprano voice and lost track of his conversation with Blenman. When his attention returned Blenman was offering reading lessons.

"We have a number of unemployed teachers who would exchange reading lessons for the performance of odd jobs, especially if you have electrical or automotive repair and maintenance skills. That's the kind of thing we do here. We bring people together in a barter economy."

"Well I'll keep it in mind, but first I have to see my brother. "

"We might be able to assist you with that, Mr. Vogel, if in exchange, you would do some work for us. Not paying work you understand, we can't provide that, but in exchange for a ride to the Walla Walla state penitentiary. Can you be here tomorrow morning say, around eight o'clock?"

"Well I need a real job but it's a deal. You can count on me. Eight o'clock."

"We'll provide coffee and maybe some donuts and a little fresh fruit to eat upon arrival," said Blenman. He rose and shook his hand and called the next client, who flopped into the chair Jack had just vacated.

He left the building and walked to the Saint Vincent de Paul where he found a stylish black dress for Juanita in the women's section. It had the V neck she had admired in the magazines she studied, and seemed to him modern in style. He hoped the purchase might ease some of the loss and shame she felt about her hair. He bought raincoats for them both and carried the purchases in a paper bag up the hill to the Hotel Lee and found Juanita at the dresser mirror trying to fix the hair he had butchered. He should not have done that to her, and would never again.

"I bought you some fancy clothing like in the magazines. If you don't like it, we can take it back and exchange it. There's a Chinese Laundromat down the hill, too. We can wash and dry there."

Juanita held the black dress against her figure while looking into the mirror with a worried, doubtful expression. She turned away from the mirror and said, "I like it but do you think I look like a little girl playing dress-up in this? "

"No, Juanita, I think it suits you."

"I like it; I just hope I can get away with it. These old work boots look stupid with this dress, though."

"With all this rain, I think boots are best. Come on, Juanita, I'm taking you to breakfast."

Wearing the raincoats, they walked down the hill to a neighborhood diner, its warm dry interior aromatic with steaming coffee and sizzling bacon. They hung up their raincoats and took a booth with a window view to the rainy street and splurged on coffee, potatoes, bacon and eggs and thick slices of toast. Men with folded newspapers occupied stools at the counter. The air was thick with cigarette smoke and bacon frying, and there was music on the radio. The rain rippling down the windowpane gave the streetscape a wavering appearance. Automobiles sloshing on the wet street were washed clean. The warm diner comforted them.

Jack watched Juanita puncture her fried eggs with her fork and sop up the spilled yolk with her toast, apparently enjoying her breakfast. The bacon fat and runny egg yolk reminded him of the slaughter she had perpetrated. The idea of going to the police and confessing again nagged at him. Maybe if they turned themselves in the court would show a leniency. He didn't know what to do. He couldn't stop turning it over and over again, a penny flipped from a high cliff. Heads or tails? If only Vi were here. If only Alma had not died. If only he had not left Cat Creek to follow his brother, who he admired more than any man he knew. If only he had insisted on going alone to Seattle, if only Juanita had stayed behind with Vi. If only Alma had lived. If only if only if only.

The barbershop was two blocks from the diner. One of the three barbers was a woman and that's who Jack chose for Juanita. He watched her lather and shave a man with a straight razor and trim his hair and beard. Jack afterwards motioned Juanita forward to the vacated barber chair and told her to sit still while her hair was styled.

The woman barber, whose name tag read Myrna, had enormous breasts that made Jack wonder how she could get close enough to a patron to effectively cut his hair. She wore pants instead of a skirt or dress and a man's white shirt covered by an apron. She was broad shouldered and had a gruff, vaguely masculine demeanor that made Jack wonder. The barber chair in which Juanita sat revolved, and Myrna spun her couple of times, examining her hair from different angles.

"Who did this to you," she said to Juanita.

"My Dad."

The barber shot Jack a dirty look and said, "Were you mad at her? Punishing her for something?"

That truth hit him hard. "She had lice," he replied. The only thing other than the truth he could think of. "We tried everything to get rid of them. Her hair was too long and I had to cut it. Can you fix it?"

"What you've done? Hell no, I can't fix it. Nobody can fix this. I'm no miracle worker. Can't put the hair back where you took it off. To make it look right I'd have to cut it even shorter so it can grow back in an equal length. You'll have to come back later when it's grown an inch or two. Then I might be able to do something with it."

Juanita stared at herself in the barber's mirror and wept.

"I'm a freak," she sobbed. "You can put me to work in the freak tent at the Helena state fair where people will pay to gawk and laugh at me."

The barber patted her shoulder sympathetically and said, "Now now, don't you cry, honey. Myrna Jones has an idea and I think I have just what you need."

She left her station for a room out of sight in back and returned with a navy blue beret. She placed it at a cocked angle on Juanita's head and appraised her in the mirror, turning the stool slowly so Juanita could see herself from different viewpoints.

"Now that's what I call glamorous," said the barber. "You look both interesting and pretty. Not many people have both attributes; it's usually one or the other. Me for example, nobody would ever call me pretty but when I get dressed up I look smart and interesting, like someone you might want to know. Let's get some lipstick on you."

Lea Macquarrie

The barber retrieved some lipstick from her purse and applied it to Juanita's lips and said, "Perfect. If I was a man, I would want to kiss you but would be afraid to because I'd think I wasn't good enough. You look very smart and European."

"Italian?"

"French."

"I'm supposed to look like an Italian."

"You're too pretty for that. Italian women have moustaches. Comes from eating too many tomatoes."

A small radio on a table with magazines was playing *Brother Can You Spare a Dime*. The song sent Jack time traveling back to the shack in Montana where his brother used to sing and play the banjo and from there to the boxcar and the man who called himself Shane, who Jack believed sang well enough to make a career of it had his life not been abruptly taken by this smiling girl in the beret who seemed, day by day, to become less familiar to him, less his daughter and more a person he did not know.

"What do I owe you," he said.

"Well, the lipstick is a gift from me to Juanita here. You can pay me for my time and the beret. How's a dollar sound?"

Jack was in a hurry to get away from the song and the memory it provoked. He dug urgently in his pockets for a dollar and paid. He took Juanita's hand and saw their images reflected in a window as they hurried away, a man with his daughter wearing a French beret. Fugitives who had killed a man.

THE UNEMPLOYED CITIZEN'S LEAGUE

JACK INFORMED JUANITA OF HIS NEED to spend the day working for the Unemployed Citizen's League. He gave her lunch money, told her to bring him the change and said she could walk to the diner at the bottom of the hill but to wander no farther and to return immediately. She was to stay in her room and not gallivant all through the hotel. It wasn't safe.

"Keep your door locked at all times," he said.

He arrived at the Unemployed Citizen's League on time and knocked on the door but the man who answered said, "We don't open until nine o'clock."

The man had a friendly jowly face, cleanly shaven. He wore his hair with a part in the middle. He looked like he might be somewhere near the age of his brother Frank.

"Mr. Blenman asked me to meet him here this morning at eight," said Jack. "Said he had some work for me."

The man behind the door opened it wider and said, "Oh, hey there. You must be Frank Vogel's kid brother they told me about. Come on in. I'm Bud Waterson. I'll be working with you today. You ever done this before?"

"I don't even know what it is I'm supposed to be doing."

"Well come on in and I'll explain to you. We're all in the back."

Jack followed him down a narrow hallway to an interior room with a dozen folding chairs, mostly occupied. There were no women present and the men were dressed for hard dirty work. Some had rain slicks over their laps, most wore hats. Jack glanced around for Mr. Blenman; he did not appear to be present. The men present ranged in age from those approximating his own to a few in their probable late teens who needed haircuts and baths and had the rough demeanor of the kind of boys he would keep Juanita away from. Waterson, obviously in charge, stood before the assembly.

"How many of you," he asked, "have done this before?"

His voice was authoritative without being overbearing or bossy; it was a voice that inspired confidence. Jack could imagine him leading a platoon during the war. But the man hadn't said yet what it was they were going to be doing. Whatever it was, if it would get him to his big brother, he was willing. Frank was Mr. Fixit. He'd know what to do, how to make a go of it in Seattle. With Frank's contacts, he'd get steady work and have a place all set up for him when he got out of prison. Frank would know how help him hide from the law too. Frank knew everything and was successful at everything he tried. It was why he knew his brother never robbed any damn bank. If his brother had robbed a bank, he wouldn't have been caught. He would have gotten away with it. That's the way Frank was. That's who he was. He always knew what to do and he always did everything right.

"Some of you," continued Waterson, "might think of the work we are about to perform as stealing. We prefer to think of it as re-distributing. It's true we'll be hauling away furniture that doesn't belong to us, but neither does it belong to the banks and landlords who have evicted the true owners. They are the greater thieves."

No way could he be participating in any crimes. He couldn't chance it. Suppose he was arrested and taken away, Juanita left with nowhere to go and without ever knowing what had happened to him. He probably shouldn't even have given his real name.

"Our work today will benefit unemployed citizens in dire need," said Waterson. "I'm sure you have seen the empty houses on every block while families go homeless. Our mission is to help evicted families who have been put out in the street with their furniture and personal belongs. We file an illegal eviction suit against the landlord, then place the homeless tenants in a vacant house. Sometimes we put them right back in the house from which they have been evicted and change the locks. We won't be doing much of that today though. Today we will be collecting furniture that belonged to evicted tenants and left on the street."

Jack had heard enough. He rose from the folding chair and said, "I can't be breaking the law. Can't take that chance. I have a young daughter I'm responsible for."

"And you don't have to, Jack. But let me explain. In all the time we have been redistributing not once has one of our men been arrested. Police mostly just drive on by. If they do stop they just tell us to move on. It's debatable whether or not the furniture we take belongs to the landlords in lieu of back rent as they claim, and most don't want it anyway. Ends up going to the city dump, and where is the logic in that? Most of the people we service have not even been legally evicted. Never brought to civic court, not even an eviction notice filed. We work with the landlords toward a solution. What use to them is an empty house they can't rent out? We get the families back inside, then contact the landlord and come up with some kind of solution. Sometimes an extension is granted just to save the hassle of having to deal with League attorneys litigating what turns out to be an illegal eviction, and sometimes they grant an extension in exchange for the security of having residents protecting the property from vandalism."

Waterson blew his nose in a white handkerchief, put it back in his pocket and said, "Excuse me. Darn rain has left me with a cold. Nose is so red I could guide Santa's sleigh." He laughed at his joke but no one laughed with him. Jack wondered if they were not laughing because they were as skeptical as he was.

"Men, some of you may know Frank Vogel. Some of you who don't may know *of* him. Today we have his kid brother with us, Jack Vogel. Welcome aboard, Jack."

"Welcome," the men chorused.

"Your brother was a good man," said another.

"He got a bum rap."

"Sure did."

Lea Macquarrie

"Good to have you with us, Jack."

Men clapped him on the back. Jack was near to blushing with pride but conflicted. How was he going to get out of this? If he didn't go along, word might get back to Frank in prison, who would be disappointed, maybe even a little ashamed of him, a possibility Jack could hardly bear.

Why couldn't he be more like his brother? Frank was fearlessly committed in word and deed to his beliefs while he, Jack, couldn't even say for sure what his own beliefs even were. He was not like Frank at all. He was fearful, maybe even using Juanita right now as an excuse to walk out on this. He'd fought the man on the train bravely, but had to be rescued by a fourteen year old girl. And now this decision to make. Whether to take on this chore and make his brother proud or take the coward's way out and make him ashamed. Frank always did say you had to take chances in life. Jack watched a tiny gray mouse scurry into a hole in the wall. Waterson was still talking.

"It rained hard yesterday and much of what we collect will be soaked and maybe beyond salvaging. If we have room we'll take wet mattresses to our warehouse and try to dry them out. When and if they become suitable, we'll take them down to Hooverville. Furniture goes to our warehouse for later distribution to vacated houses where we place homeless families who have been evicted. We're not salvaging for scrap. We want things people need and can use. That means furniture, appliances, dinnerware, pots and pans, utensils. Let's take abandoned toys as well. Tricycles, sporting equipment, toy soldiers, girl's dolls and dollhouses. Can you imagine how happy it would make some of these poor kids to receive something like that? It would be worth going to jail just to see the smiles on their faces."

No it wouldn't, thought Jack. Nice to see the kid's smile, but not if the price for seeing it was a jail sentence. Not with an unsolved murder and a lost locket with the Vogel name on it in a blood stained boxcar.

"But we're not going to jail, don't you worry about that. When we come across a recently evicted home with furniture in the street, we move fast. Most of the time we're onto the next one before the landlord even knows we were there. And don't worry about any neighborhood witnesses either. You'll find they are on our side. Sometimes they even come out and help us. Now, is there anyone here who wants to opt out on this today? What about you, Jack, you with us?"

"I'm with you in spirit, but I don't know. You say you have been doing this for over a year with no one getting arrested. What if I'm the one guy who does get arrested? Been having some pretty bad luck lately."

"Won't happen, Jack. You'll see."

There was a shuffling of feet and the sound of metal chairs scraping as men rose gathering their jackets and rain gear. Jack knew none of these men, though many spoke to him and all seemed talkative and excited. Men crowded into the narrow hallway two abreast and he felt himself pulled along.

Bud Waterson took hold of his sleeve and said, "You come with me, Jack."

"Where we going?"

"Pier 91 on the waterfront. The dock is leased by a man name of Walt McCabe who has given us permission to use it as a staging operation. Interesting guy, McCabe. He was initially against the League and aligned with a group of crooked politicians who hired goon squads to run us out of town, but he's on our side now. Where's your raincoat?"

"Didn't need it. It was sunny out when I left the hotel. Looks like it's going to be a nice day."

"Hell, Jack, didn't anybody tell you? The weather here in Seattle changes faster than a fickle woman changes her mind. When you see sunshine here, it's probably going to rain."

Waterson had a hand on his arm, leading him along. Arrows of hidden sunlight broke through the gray clouds. Traffic flowed past them. Waterson ignored traffic lights and angry drivers braking to avoid them.

Walter McCabe was much older than Jack had expected. He carried an umbrella and wore glasses and a black raincoat and fedora and rubber boots. He unlocked the chain link fence and opened the gate and the men filed in. A dozen or more automobiles and several trucks were parked along the pier. The men mingled around in small groups, smoking and waiting, for what Jack did not know. He saw a few of them passing a flask, McCabe partaking. Jack stood off by himself while Waterson went from vehicle to vehicle. McCabe made rounds, talking with men he seemed to know.

"If the police pick you up or you get beat by a goon squad, keep McCabe out of it," said a bystander.

"I was told there would be no police," said Jack. "And what's this about goon squads?"

"Nobody told you? Why do you think we're carrying baseball bats? You think they're for a friendly game of sandlot baseball? Think again."

"Let's move," said Waterson to the group.

He was led to a pickup truck driven by a bearded man introduced as Orvin, who wore blue denim overalls and a longshoreman's stocking hat and leather gloves. The three of them crammed into the front seat. Theirs was the lead vehicle in the caravan and the driver obviously knew where they were going and the way to get there. Jack did not. They drove over a steel bridge to Freemont, which was mostly beat hotels and rundown rooming houses, and then down to the Greenwood residential area, their caravan of vehicles following.

Waterson pointed out the many vacant houses they passed. On every block there was at least one house with furniture on the sidewalk. Jack wondered why they were not stopping for it.

"It's been out there too long," said Waterson. "Anything worth taking is gone, and the rest is damaged. We have scouts who tell us about recent evictions, where the pickings are better."

"Your brother got a raw deal," the driver said. "I was truly sorry to see it. But he was careless sometimes too. Maybe a bit cocky and a little too fearless for his own good. He had a lot of friends, but also a lot of enemies. The mistake your brother made union organizing was not in pissing off management, though he succeeded in getting himself beat up pretty bad by their goon squads, but in pissing off the police."

"I don't believe my brother robbed any bank," said Jack.

"Most people don't. But he made an enemy in Sherriff Gus Gustafson. That's what he went to prison for, not for robbing a bank."

He pulled over to a curb and double parked beside a Ford four-door sedan.

"We're here," he said.

A family of four stood outside their vehicle. A tall man wearing a railroad man's cap clamped an unlighted pipe between his teeth while his frazzled wife, wearing a large yellow rain hat, water repellant coat and rubber boots, stood with two children, a boy and girl who might have been fraternal twins, also in raingear. Waterson explained that the family, who gave their names as the Smiths, had only been five dollars behind on their rent when they were threatened with eviction. Mister Smith managed to borrow the five dollars, but was informed when paying the back rent that he owed another two dollar late fee. Mr. Smith didn't have it and couldn't get it. A day later they were evicted and a crew came in and moved their belongings to the street. The eviction was illegal, but the family was locked out.

"So what did the landlord achieve by evicting them," asked Waterson rhetorically. "Nothing. It's unlikely he'll be able to rent this place out. It will just sit empty. Neighborhood kids will throw rocks through the windows. The landlord will have to board it up to protect it from the rain. From a profit standpoint, he'll end up wishing he'd worked something out with the family and not evicted them."

The wife was pale and skinnier than a woman should be, in Jack's opinion, and looked sickly. She cradled a bundled infant in her long thin arms. A girl who looked about four or five years old held a curly-headed raggedy Ann doll dressed in an apron while her brother stood slightly beyond them, performing loop de loops with his Duncan Yo-Yo. The entire group was surrounded by wet furniture. Waterson explained the family had camped here to guard it from theft. Jack peered in the windows of their Ford and saw a tangle of blankets, rumpled clothing, coloring books and stuffed animals.

Lea Macquarrie

Another car pulled up and Waterford ran to greet it. Jack thought the man who exited looked like he might have lived a hard long life but the man's gait was surprisingly limber and sprightly. He wore baggy gray wool pants and a sweatshirt, and on his belt was a key ring that held so many keys Jack wondered how he managed to identify specific ones. This was obviously the locksmith.

"Don't you worry," he said to the family. "I'll have you back in here in no time." He knelt at the front door and began manipulating the locks. He removed them entirely from the door and began replacing them with his own.

"I can't believe this is legal," said Jack.

"It's not, Jack. The furniture is nothing, probably the equivalent of rag picking and not even technically theft, but this here is trespassing and grounds for a breaking and entering charge. Your brother warned us about it. That's why we have to work fast. But you know what else is not legal, Jack? This eviction. It never went through civil court. One morning a half dozen goons showed up, evicted them and took their belongings to the street. Nothing legal about that, either."

"You folks can go back in now," said the locksmith to the family. He handed the keys to the new locks to the man with the pipe.

"Let's start moving this furniture back in," said Waterson to the men.

A dining room table was returned, six chairs, and several wooden crates of dishes and cookware. Mr. Smith unloaded his Ford and brought in more items. The adult bed had been without a mattress since bedbugs were discovered a month earlier, and was left on the curb. Mr. Smith mentioned their intention to sleep on blankets on the floor, adding that at least now they would not be cramped in their old Ford, and could stretch out and get a good night's sleep.

Jack watched the street for the approach of a police car. Behind the house was a fence and vacant lot. He calculated leaping the fence, the route he would take escaping between houses, crouching and hiding behind hedges and bushes, finding a street on the bus line and jumping the first one that passed.

Mrs. Smith, clearly worried and skeptical, approached Waterson and said, "So what has been accomplished here? They'll just evict us again. "

"We're going to file a complaint with the housing authority and make the landlord file a legal eviction notice. That will buy you six weeks. Meanwhile we'll see if we can convince the landlord it's in his best interest to let you stay. Worst case scenario there's plenty of empty houses we can move you into. At least you'll have your furniture."

When they returned to the car Jack said, "I can't be working with you if what we are doing is illegal. I don't care how many times you done it without anyone getting arrested. I am responsible for a dependent fourteen year old girl in my care."

"Don't worry, Jack. This was our last relocation job. From here we just pick up abandoned furniture. Nothing illegal about it."

They moved on to the next block and the next, loading furniture and other abandoned articles into the caravan of trucks and automobiles, and by noon there was no room in their vehicles for more, so they drove to a warehouse leased to the *Seattle Tenants Coalition* where they unloaded it. They ate salmon sandwiches and smoked tobacco, and after an hour rest were back at it.

They worked all afternoon. The locksmith was no longer with them. Mostly the abandoned goods belonging to evicted tenants had been already pilfered, much of it by neighbors. Articles that might have been of value were mostly already sold or traded off. What remained was mostly trash. At one such house Jack was pleased to find, under a pile of broken chairs, wet bedding, books and clothing, a first base catcher's glove, soaking wet but the leather still good. He imagined the smile it would put on a boy's face when receiving the glove.

Waterson said the furniture they collected would be redistributed free of charge to those in need. Often those receiving these articles repaid the Unemployed Citizen's League in labor such as carpentry, electrical or automotive skills on behalf of unemployed citizens seeking League assistance. Those who benefited from the volunteer labor in turn donated their time and whatever skills they might have to offer. Even unskilled labor was needed, such as shopping for infirmed tenants, cooking meals for the elderly, or in a few cases performing childcare services on the rare occasion the head of a household unexpectedly found work and had to leave unsupervised children when on the job. In this way, Waterson explained, a concentric circle of helping was expanded and perpetuated.

Late in the afternoon it began raining hard, and Jack was soaked through. His hands were stinging from lifting furniture without the benefit of gloves. He opened his palms to the gray sky and let the rain fall into them, and the cool rain soothed them. He cupped his palms and tasted some of the coolest, freshest water he'd had since leaving Montana. Rainwater soaked his hair and ran down his face. He licked it away from his grateful lips, raised his head and opened his mouth to swallow as much as he might collect.

They worked all afternoon, rain or no rain, and Jack didn't mind other than his neck was sore from looking back and forth so much for police or goons. When they were done for the day the caravan drove to a warehouse in an industrial neighborhood and unloaded their gear, then returned to the office where the workers assembled in the League's waiting area. Blenman, dressed in his three piece suit after a day behind the desk, applauded them when they entered.

He assembled his troops, made coffee, and passed around donuts.

Men congregated holding cups of hot coffee until gradually the crowd dwindled and only Jack and Blenman were left. Jack's mouth was dry, and it was the only thing about him that was. His soaked clothing dripped to the linoleum. He looked forward to a hot bath.

Blenman opened a file drawer and pulled out a bottle of *4 Roses* whiskey and said, "Now why on Earth would anyone leave this behind, Jack? Brand name, expensive, probably smuggled in from Canada. Must have been some fishwife angry at her hard drinking husband. I have a habit of answering my own questions, as you can see."

He took a drink from the bottle, handed it to Jack and said, "Cheers."

"Thank you, but I don't drink," said Jack. "I used to but no more. Not in years."

"Well then, Jack, what can I do for you?"

"You mentioned getting me passage to Walla Walla. That's why I came along today despite my better judgment."

"Oh yes. I'd forgotten. Fair enough. I know you worked hard today in unpleasant conditions. Where are you staying Jack?"

"Do you know the Hotel Lee?"

"Don't tell me you are staying there."

"Why not? It's comfortable and reasonably priced."

"It's Chinatown, Jack. And it's owned by Mr. Lee. Do you know who he is?"

"He's a Chinaman, is all I know."

"He's much more than that."

"What's that supposed to mean?"

"He's not just a Chinaman, he's *the* Chinaman. You have a lot to learn about Seattle. Just be careful of who you trust. I'll call the hotel with the travel details when I have them and leave a message. Shouldn't be long, Jack."

"Thank you."

"Give my regards to your brother when you see him. Let him know none of us believe he did it."

HOTEL LEE

AS HE WALKED BACK TO THE HOTEL, Jack rehearsed an imaginary conversation with Juanita in preparation for the real one he dreaded, feared, and expected to quickly escalate into a full scale argument. He was going to Walla Walla to see his brother but he was not taking her with him and he was going to have to tell her. The excursion to the penitentiary and back would probably take two days and he only hoped she could manage to go that long without killing anyone.

His sarcasm displeased him and of course he didn't mean it, but truth was he didn't know what to expect from his daughter anymore. He could no longer trust his own perception of her, much less predict her behavior. Their shared experience in the boxcar en route to Seattle would forever be the dividing line where their lives had changed inalterably and could not be changed back.

Seattle in his opinion was beautiful on a sunny day, but full days of sustained sunshine were yet to be experienced. The weather here was generally abysmal, the city not at all what he had expected, just another frontier town like one might see at home in Montana but on a much grander scale. He wondered what had drawn people here, why they had stayed. Maybe because for them it was the end of the line. From Seattle there was nowhere to run, no more western expansion, only the confrontation with the Pacific Ocean. From here one either turned around and went back to where they had come from or turned north for the Canadian wilderness and Alaskan frontier. He could not in honesty say Alaska was not a temptation. No one would find them there, and he knew how to live off the land.

People passed him without so much as a nod; they were clothed in the resignation which had become, over the years, as familiar to them in this climate as the shoes on their feet. The rain owned this land, feeding its forests and replenishing the many lakes and channels and the frigid waters of Puget Sound. Rain pinged around him in a maddeningly persistent litany of monotonous wet drumbeats. Rain pattered in puddles that had formed in the gutters where debris floated like leaves in a stream. There was no point to hurrying because there was no hope of not getting wet. He sloshed his way up the hill as if traversing a shallow but swiftly running trout stream so swift was the runoff. Pigeons strutted around miserably. His lower legs were wet, his stockings drenched, his shoes squishy.

He found Mr. Lee in the library/recreation room. A wooden table supporting a large Victrola phonograph was playing some strange Chinese music. Seated in a high backed leather chair, Mr. Lee held a book aloft, and Jack recognized that the title was not printed in Chinese. It made him ashamed a Chinaman could read a book written in a foreign language while he couldn't even read a book written in American.

Chinamen with whom he had worked laying track across Montana and Idaho did not much mingle with whites, but he found them to be hard working family men like himself. Those without family or whose families were far away in a Chinese province Jack could neither pronounce nor imagine shouldered an almost visible cloak of sadness that isolated them. Jack did not solicit their friendship. They were peculiar and did not seem to want the friendship they probably needed most.

Mr. Lee bowed, his palms pressed together and fingers held aloft as if in prayer. Mr. Lee bowed to everyone, even to Juanita, who was thrilled by it. His white goat-like beard and silver braid suggested a man in the twilight years of his life but Jack believed he discerned a youthful twinkle in the man's eyes. Jack returned Mr. Lee's bow and then got directly to the point.

"I have no right to ask you this, Mr. Lee, but you are looking at a man who needs help and has few options."

Mr. Lee tweaked his beard between his index finger and thumb and said, "I am sorry, Mr. Vogel, but I cannot loan you money or advance you rent."

"No, no, nothing like that. I have a family emergency requiring me to travel to Walla Walla for a few days where my brother is in a hospital. I need someone to keep an eye on Juanita while I'm gone and I was going to ask if you might watch out for her. Because you Chinese understand the importance of family, I thought you might understand and be sympathetic."

Mr. Lee remained silent for much longer than Jack would have liked. The twinkle was no longer in his eyes. He looked thoughtful and dubious. Finally he shook his head and said, "Children and young adults in your culture are not raised to respect or obey their elders."

Jack remembered how Chinese children in the railroad work camps demonstrated an almost reverent respect for their elders, their obedience not limited to their immediate families, but to all elders.

"I cannot assume responsibility for your daughter, Mr. Vogel. What you are asking of me is impossible."

"I wouldn't expect you to be responsible for her behavior, Mr. Lee. What I'm asking is whether you might provide meals and make yourself available to her if she comes to you with an unexpected problem or need. I don't intend to be gone longer than a day or two and I would pay you generously for your trouble."

Jack reached into his pants pocket and emerged with a roll of bills wrapped in cellophane. The bills were slightly damp. Jack was alarmed to see the roll further shrunken. There was less than he thought. He would have to get some work as soon as he returned from visiting Frank, who would give him tips on where to look. He counted out twenty dollars for Mr. Lee and said, "Would this be enough to change your mind?"

Again Mr. Lee was silent. He glanced to his wife, who nodded her assent.

Mr. Lee said another ten dollars would be required and Jack paid him.

He found Juanita perched in their room's single armchair, her legs crossed, a paperback book in her lap. The index finger of her left hand moved across the open page from left to right tracing the words on the page. She wore wool pants he had never seen before and a white blouse under a sky blue sweater. Her beret was slanted at a jaunty angle and she wore the lipstick given to her by the woman at the barber shop - more of it than Jack liked to see on a girl her age. She looked up at him briefly and then went back to her book.

"What do you have there, Juanita?"

"A novel."

She held the book for him to see, its cover a lurid illustration of a woman kissing an Indian brave with war paint on his arms and shirtless chest. A white palomino with black spots bowed its head to drink from the river behind them.

"Where did you get this, Juanita?"

"There's a whole library downstairs. Mostly paperback westerns. That's what Mr. Lee likes."

"But why do you even have this book? What's the point?"

"Mr. Lee recommended it. It's one of his favorites."

"No, that's not what I mean. Why would you take the book when you can't even read?"

"How else am I going to learn? Are *you* going to teach me?"

He heard the sarcasm in her voice loud and clear. The sweater clung to her chest in a manner he disapproved of. A red jacket was slung across her knees. He had never seen it before.

"Where did you get the new clothing, Juanita? Did you steal it?"

"Why would you even ask that?"

"Because I had to pay Wilson's Drugs for the magazines you stole."

"That was the only time and it was over two years ago. I bought these clothes second hand with the money you gave me for lunch."

"The money I gave you was not for spending on things we don't need. I told you to spend what you needed for lunch but to bring me the change. Now you tell me you spent everything I gave you and you didn't even have lunch?"

"I had lunch with Mr. and Mrs. Lee."

"That was disobedient of you, Juanita. I told you to buy lunch and otherwise stay in your room."

Jack watched her submerge herself in the chair as if it might be a hidden passage to a secret room he could not enter. She lifted the jacket from her knees and draped it around herself, a magical vestment deflecting his accusatory questioning.

"Your uncle Frank is in a hospital in Walla Walla, Washington, Juanita. I've made arrangements with an organization willing to pay for my transportation there. It's important to us both that I go."

"Is Uncle Frank going to be okay?"

"I think so."

"When do we leave and how long will we be away, Daddy?"

"It's not like that, Juanita. I can't take you with me. I'm sorry, but the people paying for my transportation won't pay for yours. You know it's important for us to save what little money we have left until we're settled and I have a job. I'll only be gone two days at most. Maybe even get back the same day. Mr. Lee has agreed to provide your meals and to look after you."

For a quick moment she frightened him; her beautiful brown eyes turned fierce; he felt her anger.

"You're not going to come back for me," she hissed. "Something will happen to you. Maybe that's what you want. An excuse to leave me."

"What? Of course I'm not going to leave you, Juanita. I can't believe you even thought that."

"You don't love me anymore because of what happened. You don't want to be my father anymore."

"That's not true, Juanita."

"Why is it so important to see Uncle Frank now, why not wait until we're settled?"

"Because Frank knows Seattle. He can give me tips on where to find work."

"You're lying," she said, and Jack saw the fierceness in her eyes again. "Why can't you go out on your own and look for work?"

It was a legitimate question pinning him to a lie. He would ask Frank about job prospects and seek his advice regarding what had happened on the train sure, but the truth was he missed his brother and longed for him with a need beyond his understanding.

Meanwhile he was exhausted with the memory of the killing flickering through his mind day and night. When he closed his eyes to rest, he saw a movie of the killing on the inside of his eyelids. He was afraid of his urge to confess and get it over with. Only Frank provided the safe opportunity to unburden himself of the terrible secret he was carrying. Frank was the only one he trusted.

"Where is this Walla Walla anyway? And what's the matter with Uncle Frank?"

He heard the mistrust in her voice.

"I'm not sure about Frank. I heard it was pretty serious. They said he would probably recover, but it would be a long illness. Walla Walla is south of here, almost on the Oregon border from what I'm told."

"Isn't Oregon near California?"

"I believe so."

"Then we could keep on going, try California. Get out the rain, finally."

"We just got to Seattle, Juanita. This is where Frank said we could get a new start. You want to leave already?"

"You'll probably keep going if that isn't your plan already. I know you want to leave me."

"Don't be silly, Juanita. I would never do that."

"Sometimes people do what we least expect. Sometimes what happens is a surprise even to them."

"You're too young to think such things."

"What happened in the boxcar wasn't predicted or planned."

She was smart enough to frighten him sometimes. And he wasn't certain he didn't want to leave her. He only knew he couldn't, wouldn't, not even while mention of California conjured seductive visions of landscapes where the sun was always shining and where it was always warm and pleasant and where, if necessary, one could live in an agreeable climate all year long without having to endure the snow and ice of Montana winters or the incessant rain of Seattle. There was agricultural work in California, he'd heard. He wondered what it might be like working on his hands and knees between rows of asparagus, loading the stalks into wicker baskets and taking them to be weighed at the paymaster station. He imagined standing on the rung of a ladder while harvesting oranges, the warm sun pleasantly bearing down on his bare back, maybe taking an orange and peeling it, squeezing it and sucking the juice, feeling the juice run down his bare chest and stomach. He'd have to grow gills if he were to stay here in Seattle.

"You'll be fine, Juanita. I'll leave you a little money but don't spend it on clothes. Mr. Lee will feed you. I'll be gone two days at the most."

"I don't believe you. You won't be back. You think you will, but you won't. I hate you Daddy."

"I know you don't mean that, Juanita, but it still hurts to hear you say it."

"You've brought me nothing but trouble and you lied to me. You brought me here, made me think it would be better here, that you would get me in a good school, that Frank would be with us and Elvira too, all of us living together in a big house. All these promises you made, only to leave me here."

"That's not really true or fair, Juanita. I tried to get you to stay behind with Vi and you wouldn't hear of it."

"And now you are leaving me. I'll never see you again."

She lifted the book like a shield, hid her face behind it, and glared at him hatefully when he took it from her hands.

THE WALLS

JACK WAS SURPRISED WHEN THE DENTED 1933 two door Ford coupe arrived for him at the hotel. He had expected a roomier more comfortable vehicle suitable for long distance passengers, not this cramped, unwashed specimen of dubious reliability showing evidence of prior wreckage. The owner of this vehicle, one Emory Evans, was an unemployed carpenter visiting his cousin. Because of his lanky height and thin frame he was also known as Stringbean, or just Bean. Evans maintained that his cousin, initially convicted of petty theft, should never had been confined within a maximum security and would instead be in a minimum security facility had he not skipped bail and failed to appear in court on his sentencing date. Instead his cousin had vanished into the isolation of the drenched Olympic Rain Forest for six months until, driven half mad with rain and solitude, he made the mistake of drinking too much in the only town within reach of his campsite, where he was arrested and charged with drunk and disorderly. His fugitive status was subsequently discovered and he was charged, in addition to his original crime, with Flight to Avoid Prosecution, which automatically meant maximum security time.

Their female passenger was one Helen Costa who wore sunglasses and in Jack's opinion too much jewelry and perfume and who was not overly friendly when they arrived at her rented house in Ballard Bay. She initially refused to give her first name and insisted on being formally addressed as Miss Costa. She complained she was unable to ride in the back seat and needed a front seat view out of the windshield and was subject to otherwise vomit, if riding in back.

Emory pulled the front seat forward allowing Jack to squeeze in the back. Because the dented passenger-side door would not open, Emory had to get out for Miss Costa to enter on the driver's side and scoot over. She said she was visiting her ex-husband with a parole hearing a month away but in Jack's opinion something about her story didn't add up. Not that he cared, or even wanted to know. She was a woman who talked with gestures, her arms and hands rattling annoyingly with all the damn bracelets she wore. What did she think; she was some kind of gypsy? He was cramped and uncomfortable and overcome with the odor of her perfume, which was making him slightly nauseous. Or maybe it was her hair that stunk. He remembered Alma once using some stinky concoction supposed to bleach her hair and all it had done was turn it orange. He asked Miss Costa if she could roll down her window but she complained it would muss up her hair which was a shade he remembered Alma called platinum blonde. Alma said Jean Harlow and Carole Lombard were women who wore this color. Miss Costa rummaged through her purse and then opened a small bottle of nail polish. She opened the glove box door, extended her long fingers and pressed them down on its surface and began to paint her fingernails.

"Hey," she complained. "Can't you drive a little more carefully?"

"This ain't no beauty salon, Miss Costa. I'm driving the best I can but the road is bumpy."

He had to agree Emory was a terrible driver. Meanwhile a protruding spring in the ripped back seat cushioning seemed persistently intent on pursing his asshole. He was eager to trade places with Evans who, clasping the wheel with both hands as if it might get away from him, was yawning. Miss Costa did not drive. Said it made her sick with nerves. You don't want me to drive, she said. I might kill us all.

Jack took the wheel. Found some country music on the radio and thought about his brother, the most admirable man he ever knew. Five years without seeing him. Hard to imagine him locked up. *He* was the criminal, the fugitive on the run from what he had done. They had locked up the wrong brother.

The Seattle skyline out the back window became incrementally smaller, shrinking until it was no longer visible. They had changed direction now, driving southeast instead of due south. An hour later they were in dense mountainous forests. An extended series of switchbacks descended into a valley of high grassland where sheep and goats grazed.

They were on a country road when he felt the steering wheel shake violently and the Ford coupe veer hard to the right. He slowed without applying undue pressure to the brakes, a flat tire slapping audibly against on the road. He pulled off and opened the driver's side door and motioned Miss Costa out of the vehicle. She futilely pushed at the passenger side door which would not budge and finally gave up and slid across the front seat to exit on the driver's side. Emory, who had been sleeping in the back seat, followed.

"You got a jack and a spare, Emory?"

"In the rumble seat."

The rumble seat was dirty from the spare, which looked none too good. He began the process of changing the tire while the others watched. He loosened the lug nuts from the damaged tire, one of them stubbornly resisting but finally yielding. He turned them part way and began jacking the Ford to a height sufficient to remove and replace the tire.

He held the tire iron in preparation to finish removing the lugs and replace the tire. It was warm breezy day. The pastoral setting reminded him of how much happier he was in the country. He was not the sort of man who thrived in a city. He was one who belonged to nature, who would always prefer walking or riding horseback to driving. There were no other vehicles on the two lane country road. He heard the drone of cicadas and a hum of flies and bees. There was a confluence of competing scents from vivid wildflowers, manure, tar, sun-baked road, alfalfa and sage. From the uppermost rail of a wooden three-rail fence, a dozen silent black crows watched him work.

He squatted beside the car in a trancelike reverie, no longer attending to the flat tire, lost in memory of the Montana plains, the farms of his youth, his boyhood. He remembered Frank taking him trapping, hunting and hiking, instilling in him a love of nature and teaching him survival skills. Frank, his big brother who he loved so much, who was now incarcerated for a crime he did not commit. A horsefly buzzed around his face persistently as if it wanted to take up residence in his ear. He swatted it away. He rose, stretched his legs, squatted and returned to his task, remembering his purpose, Frank waiting for him down in Walla Walla, wherever that turned out to be. Maybe there was work there. He and Juanita could move down there, get themselves a place, visit Frank every week.

Emory and Helen Costa stood smoking and watching him work. Jack was only vaguely aware of them when Emory said, "Hey, Frank, you awake? You gonna change that tire or not?"

He'd been somewhere else. He looked down at his hands smeared with grease and the grease became blood and it was not a lug wrench he was holding but a crowbar. He'd just pried it out of Juanita's clenched bloody fist. He flung the tire iron away from him as if having discovered it was a rattlesnake he was holding.

"Jack? You all right? You looked scared, like you were seeing a ghost or something."

"Naw, Bean. Just daydreaming is all."

"Look on your face was a little scary, Jack."

"I was thinking about rattlesnakes is all, how they sometimes appear without your notice."

He walked down the road to retrieve the jack and finished removing the lug nuts. He removed the flat tire and tossed it aside and replaced it with the spare. He lifted the flat tire and dropped it into the rumble seat, tossed in the jack and lug wrench and closed the seat. Everyone piled back into the Ford again, Emory into the back seat, then Miss Costa sliding past the steering wheel to the window seat. He drove a flat dusty two-lane country road, passing a mailbox and farmhouse every five to ten miles. Unpaved dirt side roads led to three story wood frame farmhouses surrounded by vast fields of fenced farmland, most with grain silos and barns and livestock. Jack saw work horses and mules, Holstein cows, pigs, and free range chickens.

The beauty of the countryside left him unprepared for the sudden appearance of high concrete walls topped with concertina wire and guard towers. Miss Costa, who had visited many times before, wiped her glasses with a silk handkerchief and said, "It's always a shock isn't it? It's even worse inside. The prisoners call it The Walls."

The unlighted lenses of searchlights on guard towers reflected sunlight and were like predatory eyes watching them. A uniformed guard at the gate directed them to a visitor's parking area. From there they were escorted beyond a second set of gates, this one taking them inside the high concrete walls of the prison itself.

At a holding section bearing a sign reading *Visitor Processing Center* their identification and visitation forms were scrutinized. Orientation was delivered by a guard with a strong voice, weak chin and narrowed mistrustful eyes. A can of snuff was partly visible in his shirt pocket.

"Visiting an inmate in the state penitentiary is a privilege, not a right. It is a privilege we can revoke at any time without need for explanation or justification if protocols and rules of conduct are not strictly adhered to."

He began a monotonic reading of rules and procedures. Afterwards they were subjected to a pat-down body search. Jack understood the need, but in his opinion the guards were treating visitors with no more respect, consideration, or basic human kindness than their prisoners. Their attitudes seemed to convey that they regarded visitors no differently than the criminals they locked up. Maybe it was a matter of guilt by association. If you were related to a criminal, had a close friend who was a criminal or did business with a criminal, then you were probably one yourself. In his case they were right. They just didn't know it.

Everyone was issued a locker provided for personal items forbidden beyond the visitor orientation area. Wallets, loose cash, car keys, pens, metal combs and other personal items were held securely

Lea Macquarrie

in the lockers. A metal lockbox fixed to the wall contained the locker keys, the key numbers recorded in a ledger. A guard responsible for their dispensation and safe-keeping sat yawning on a stool next to the lock box. It occurred to Jack how easy it would be to plant incriminating articles in his locker. He wouldn't put it past them. That the system was crooked was evidenced by his brother having been framed.

Miss Costa was taken somewhere separately and he didn't know where Emory had gone. Just so long as they didn't leave without him he didn't much care but the idea of being left alone locked up in here made him shiver. The narrow corridors were rank with too many men confined in prolonged close proximity. He couldn't imagine his brother Frank in such a place.

The guard escorting him from Processing to the visiting area was the first official to speak to him in a manner bordering on friendliness. He seemed to have no motive or secondary agenda when he said, "Are you visiting Frank Vogel?"

Jack was certain that he already knew this but replied, "Yes, I'm his brother."

"He's a good man," said the guard.

He was happy to hear this but not altogether surprised. His brother seemed to make friends wherever he went. Problem was, he made enemies too, often in equal or greater number. Noise exploded from the cell blocks where prisoners were caged. He couldn't imagine living in such conditions. A man would be unable to hear himself think. Following the guard down yet another long colorless corridor, he wondered how one ever found ones way around in this maze? What if he got lost? What if he couldn't find his way out? He heard the clatter of keys in locks, the clang of metal doors opening and closing.

The guard removed a mortise key from the ring on his belt and unlocked a metal door containing a window opening to another door with a smaller window, through which he would view his brother. There would be no clasping of hands, no familial hugs. No shoulder punches or elbow bumps, hugs or pat on the back. He would be talking through a window to his brother in an adjoining room.

He worried what Frank might look like when they brought him in. God only knew what they may have done to him in here. Would his brother be manacled, with chains around his legs necessitating he take the very smallest of steps? A broken man, limping and shuffling, bone thin, stoop shouldered, unshaven with haunted eyes, neurological twitches and a tremor? It would break his heart to see Frank with the fight beaten out of him, his will shattered, submissive as a beaten dog. He resolved not to cry when they brought Frank in.

He needn't have worried. What he saw through the little windowpane in the door when a guard let his brother into the prisoner's visiting room was the same old Frank. Same broad shoulders and thick neck, his familiar bearing suggestive of a military background. He wore glasses and had some streaks of gray in his hair that was new but retained the handlebar moustache.

Frank sat on the bench under the window and displayed his characteristic big grin as if they were meeting in a friendly pool hall instead of a prison. The best big brother a man could hope for. There wasn't a prison made that could break him. Probably not even one that could hold him. It wouldn't surprise him if Frank escaped. It would be just like him to try. Now that Frank was close up, Jack could discern a faint purple ring around his left eye.

"How the hell are you, Jackie?"

Jack automatically felt the distance of years fall away when hearing himself addressed by the nickname of his youth.

"What do you mean how am I, Frank? You're the one wearing a jailbird suit."

"Yeah, I noticed that."

"Did you really rob a bank?"

"Bank robbery under certain circumstances is an act of retribution and justice. Bankers are the real thieves, Jack. Think of all the money they have stolen from investors who trusted them with their life's savings. I have to respect a bank robber like Pretty Boy Floyd, the way he'd rob banks and destroy mortgage notes. He saved a lot of farmers from foreclosure."

"Some of the guards seem to respect you, I noticed."

"Yeah, but the administration hates me. I've been organizing, encouraging the guards to unionize."

"I see you got a bit of a shiner there, Frank."

"Yeah, it's just about gone but if you look close you can still see it. One of the cons attacked me because I'm an outspoken soapbox communist and he took offense saying it was Un-American. Poor guy is still in the infirmary. It was self-defense on my part, but I probably hurt him more than I needed."

"Well did you or didn't you?"

"Did I what?"

"Did you rob a bank?"

"I thought I answered that. I'll tell you this though. I would admire a bank robber motivated by philanthropy."

"Always with the big words. What is philanthropy?"

"Caring about and helping them. It's like altruism."

"I don't know that word either."

"You need to get yourself a dictionary, Jack. I always did say you needed to practice your reading."

"You used to twist my arm until I cried. That was my reading lesson from you."

"Well, it was the only way I could get you to practice."

"Words on a page just look like a jumble to me, Frank, unless I hold the page up to a mirror. They say I'm word blind."

"The word is dyslexic Jack. It makes reading difficult but it can be overcome."

"How are they treating you here, Frank?"

"Pretty much like a prisoner convicted of felony bank robbery."

"Which you didn't do. You didn't, did you?"

"You're still on that? That's what you ask me about after all these years? Is that what you think, that I'm bank robber who deserves to be locked up?"

"Well, no, but…."

"Well then, there you go, Jackie."

Again the big smile. His brother had been winning people over with that smile for as long as he could remember.

"You look like you have lost quite a bit of weight, Jack."

"Well, I haven't been eating so good. Food scarcity and all."

"There is no true food scarcity, little brother. The government is using food scarcity as a control system. We have millions of fish in the Columbia River, Puget Sound and in the ocean channel but nobody has money to buy it's so it's not profitable to unload the catch. Not that there is much of a fishing industry anymore. I've seen boats rot at their docks because it didn't pay the men ran who them to make a run. Meanwhile on the other side of the Cascades fruit ripens on the vine in Eastern Washington orchards and lies rotting on the ground because it isn't profitable to ship it over the mountains into Seattle. No one is buying. Farms are foreclosing and milk is thrown out like dirty dishwater. Bankers hold notes on the farms and fishing boats and they'd rather throw food away than distribute it at a loss. It's the American Way, Jackie. Capitalism of the Damned. Your democracy at work. What are you doing here anyway, Jackie?"

Jack frowned at the absurdity of the question. It puzzled him. He scratched his head and said, "Well what kind of stupid question is that anyway, Professor Smarty Pants from Cat Creek. I came to see you. Why do you think?"

"No, no, not here in the prison. I mean what are you doing here in Washington State?"

"I came to find work in Seattle the way you told me."

"No, no, no, I told you to forget about Seattle and stay in Cat Creek. Didn't you get my letters?"

"Your letters are *why* I came to Seattle. You told me about work in the shipyards, lumber plants, in the fishing industry and agricultural jobs. You said to come and we'd get our family back together, we'd all live together in a big house. I came like you said and Juanita came with me."

"No, I mean the other letters. The later ones I sent saying the depression had changed everything and to stay put. I wrote three or four. You didn't get them?"

"No."

"Then I apologize. Our mail is read coming in and going out. If the censors see something they don't like, even something trivial about how the prison food is lousy, for instance, they don't black it out, they just toss out the whole letter without telling us. We wait for a reply that never comes and don't know why. I'm sorry, Jackie. Our dream of living in Seattle in a big house is probably not going to work out. Attorneys from the *League of Seattle Socialists* have filed an appeal but I'm not optimistic."

"Won't you come up for parole? We can wait. We can still do this."

"Brother, I'm not waiting for parole board lackeys to decide my future or dictate the terms of my freedom. Damn, Jackie, it's good to see you. I've missed the family since they locked me up. Does Elvira ask about me? I sent her a letter but she never answered it."

"She says she misses you." It was a lie for his brother's benefit, whom still had feelings for her. She'd miss him with her shotgun and poor aim but that was about all.

"I wish you had brought Juanita. Why didn't you? Is she all right?"

"I left her in a hotel in Seattle."

"You left a teenage girl alone in hotel in Seattle? What were you thinking, Jackie? Seattle is not Cat Creek. A girl can get in all kinds of trouble left alone in Seattle. "

"She's already in trouble, Jack. So am I. The worst kind of trouble. Trouble so bad I don't want to say it aloud. It's another reason I'm here. I need your help."

"What kind of trouble are you in, exactly?"

"The worse kind, Frank. Worse trouble than you by far. Is it safe to talk in here?"

"Talk softly, Jack. Put your mouth right up to the window and whisper."

Jack whispered into the glass and began telling his brother his trouble.

"Jesus Christ, Frank, not that softly. I can't even hear you."

He backed up, started over and began his account of hopping the freight, how Juanita had outrun him and was first to catch on and how the train had almost taken her away from him before he could climb on. He told his brother a man who called himself Shane McLane who claimed to be IWW climbed aboard.

"He said he knew of you, that he fought alongside Wobblies during IWW demonstrations and strikes."

"Never heard of him and that's a name I wouldn't forget. Sounds phony to me."

Jack went on to tell Frank of how the man, friendly in the beginning, became increasingly agitated, demanding, and hostile. Then he told of the attempted robbery, beginning with the fistfight.

"The guy was built like a truck, Frank. Tall, with arms so long it was hard for me to get close enough for my fists to reach him. When he hit me, I couldn't believe it was with his fists; I thought he must have been holding a weapon of some kind, but no it was just his fists. That's how hard the guy hit me. I tried to fight him defensively the way you showed me, protecting my face, but he hit me in the stomach so hard it brought me to my knees. I got up though, even got a in a good punch that had him licking blood off his mouth. Might of even broke his nose. He just shook it off though."

"So what happened, Jackie? What did you do? Did you let him take your money?"

"I couldn't. I basically told him he was going to have to kill me or beat me unconscious. We started fighting again, but it was different from before. It was like he still intended to take my money but he no longer wanted to really hurt me."

"Sounds like you might have won his respect, Jack."

"Maybe. I could tell he wasn't hitting me as hard as before, but enough to let me know I couldn't win. But I meant to fight him to the end, Frank. I couldn't let him have that money. It was everything we had. Juanita and I had nowhere to go back to. We'd been evicted, sold all our furniture, my tools, Juanita's horse, anything we could."

"So what happened?"

"I don't know if it's safe to say it here, Frank."

Jack dialed down his volume, a whisper hiding in the shadow

of another whisper. He leaned into the window so far he could see his breath on its surface and said, "Juanita killed the man with a crowbar. When the train entered a tunnel, we tossed him out."

Jack expected Frank's facial expression would convey the shock of what he had just heard; that his jaw would tighten, the muscles in his face tense or maybe his eyes widen in surprise or narrow in calculation but Frank received the information as if it were no more significant than talk about the weather.

He stroked his moustache thoughtfully and said, "You shouldn't have told me. You shouldn't tell anyone, not even me. You have to live with this for the rest of your life without sharing it with anyone under any circumstances."

"We'll never get away with it, Frank. I'm thinking of going to the police and confessing. I'd say I did it, not Juanita, plead self defense. I won't let Juanita go to prison."

"Neither one of you has to go to prison, Jack. Not if you're careful. If you don't talk they'll never catch you."

"The boxcar was filthy with blood and gore. They will know something happened there. They'll find the body on the tracks. They might even have the locket Juanita used to wear. It had a photo of Alma inside and was inscribed for *J. Vogel*. Surely you remember how Juanita was rarely without it around her neck. She lost it and its possible it was left in the boxcar."

"Don't ever confess to a damn thing, Jackie. So someone has the locket. So what? That's circumstantial evidence at best. It's possible the matter won't even be investigated. Just another bum killed along the tracks."

"There's more. After it happened, I told Juanita that she had ruined any hope of making a life in Seattle like we had planned. I told her it was her fault, as if I was in no way responsible. I made her think I hated her for it. And the whole time, Frank, it was my responsibility. She's just a child. It was my fault. I should never have taken her on the road with me. I should have left her with Elvira. I was mean to her, Frank. I pushed her to her knees and cut her hair almost to the scalp. Later I apologized and tried to explain I did it because I was afraid and that's the truth, Frank, I *was* afraid, for both of us. But somehow I caused her to believe I didn't love her anymore. When I left her in the hotel and told her I was coming here to see you she said she knew I would never come back, that she would never see me again because I didn't love her or want to be her father anymore. She was crying when she said it."

Frank's eyes gave nothing away.

"Juanita is a smart girl. Was she right about that?"

"Of course not. I'm heading back to her as soon as I leave here."

"Yeah, but do you still love her?"

"Of course I do. She's more important to me than anything. More now than ever because I got her into this mess. I've never been the father she deserved, Frank, and I feel shame for the ways I have failed her."

"Jack, you have blamed yourself for Alma's alcoholism, for Juanita's troubles in school, even for the breakup between me and Elvira. We all make mistakes but sometimes troubles come to us that are not of our own making. Do you think you are responsible for the conditions that made you desperate enough to hop a freight in the first place? You're a victim of a control system, Jack. We all are. Anyway, you know Juanita loves you so make her know you love her back. My final advice is to take her home to Cat Creek. You don't belong in Seattle."

The guard who had escorted him into the visitor's room returned and tapped the door with his Billy club.

"Visiting hour is over. Time's up."

"Goodbye, Jackie. They're giving the room to another con."

Jack watched him leave and returned to Visitor Processing where he retrieved his personal items. In the visitor parking lot outside he stared at the formidable walls and gave thanks he was outside. It seemed to him a greater crime to lock a human being away in such a place than to rob a bank, which his brother had never even done in the first place. He could not imagine a life within those walls. He was not like his brother, who was unbreakable in mind, body, and spirit. He did not know if he could survive it, or if he would even want to. But it was far worse to imagine such a fate for Juanita.

MR. LEE

JUANITA WOKE IN THE HOTEL LIBRARY to find Mr. Lee in a chair directly across from her. He was no more than three feet distant and staring at her intently. She gasped at the surprise of seeing him there. She did not remember falling asleep, only the embrace of the luxuriously cushioned library chair and the crackle of the fire in the fireplace beside her, the light rain gently tapping at the windows. Mr. Lee's intensely focused stare did not seem to express disapproval or approval as much as inquisitiveness. He wore the usual black tunic with a mandarin collar and matching black baggy pants. His white hair flowed from under a black skull cap with a round black button on top. Juanita thought his eyes had the effect of being half closed when they were not. His patchy white beard was thin and scraggly and his wrinkled face was like granite eroded by a mountain river in a distant exotic land.

"I do hope I did not wake you," he said. "If so I apologize, but I am trying to understand something about your father."

Mr. Lee bent and placed another log on the fire, which caught immediately, flames licking the stone sides of the fireplace.

"I don't think we have ever had an American family here. We are Chinese. We once had an Occidental woman and child for one week, but never learned their circumstances. Nor did we inquire. It would not have been respectful to do so. It would be disrespectful to both yourself and your father as well to inquire into your circumstances, which is why I have not done so. But I cannot help noticing certain things. Your book, for example, is always turned to the same page. May I ask you why this is so?"

"I don't read, Mr. Lee, but I'm trying to learn. I look at words and try to figure out what they say. For example, this one, buffalo. I broke it down into three sounds buff-a-lo and figured out it meant buffalo. Arrow was another one. My goal is to be able to read every word on an entire page. I'm trying to educate myself, Mr. Lee. My Uncle Frank did that, and he's the smartest most informed man I know."

"But why aren't you doing this in school like other children?"

"I want to go to school, but my father hasn't found one for me."

"Then he should. You see, this is something else I do not understand. In our culture, we would never leave a young girl in the care of strangers. Family, close friends of family sometimes if necessary yes, but never strangers. I don't know why your father would do this. Perhaps this is common among American families, but I will say this, I wish it were otherwise. I wish your father had not left, that he was here watching after you and you were in school."

"That makes two of us, Mr. Lee."

The fire flickered and snapped, discharging a live ember to the wooden planks just short of where the carpet began. Mr. Lee quickly picked it up with his bare fingers and tossed it back.

"Ouch," he said, smiling.

"That must hurt, Mr. Lee."

"Only briefly."

He added a log of oak to the fire and said, "You are a child and not responsible for your circumstances. Your father on the other hand is. I believe your father might be doing you a disservice."

"The thought has occurred to me as well, Mr. Lee. Especially lately."

Which was true. She was angry with him, not only for leaving her, but for bringing her here to Seattle. Yes she had insisted on coming but he was the father and could have said no. He could have left her with Elvira and then sent for her when he had a job and a permanent place to live. Her father was a good man with a good heart, everybody said so, and she knew he loved her, but she was beginning to see him in a way she had not before. He seemed sad and unlucky and unable to implement any of his plans. Nothing ever worked out for him, and she didn't know if she should let him make decisions for her anymore. It didn't seem fair that she was supposed to follow his lead just because he was her father. What if his decisions for them were always the wrong ones?

Mr. Lee frowned and stroked his long beard.

"When your father returns, I will speak with him. He has a duty to you he must honor. The book you are trying to read is one of my favorites. I like American Westerns because they are similar to books about Chinese warriors. If you wish, I will help you to read it. Meanwhile, I am curious. Do you know how to play Hop Ching Checkers?"

"No, I'm sorry. What is it?"

"It is a board game. Some refer to it as Chinese Checkers but it is not a Chinese game. Mah Jong is the Chinese game, but it takes four people to play. I believe this game originated in Germany under a different name. Would you like to learn?"

He set up the board, explained the rules of the game, and played three games, winning them all. Afterwards Mr. Lee, who had been mostly silent except when explaining the game, then said, "May I ask you one further question? Who is responsible for cutting for your hair?"

"My father."

"But why? How had you offended him?"

"I killed a man with a crowbar," replied Juanita.

There was no way to take the words back. She couldn't explain to herself why she had spoken them except out of defiance against her father. Mr. Lee was staring at her expectantly as if awaiting explanation. His expression conveyed he was speculating on what she had said to him. He seemed to be making up his mind.

He smiled very faintly and said, "Of course I don't believe what you told me Juanita Vogel, but I wonder why you would say something so peculiar. Perhaps you can explain to me."

Mrs. Lee rescued her at exactly that moment. She carried a tray containing a teapot and three round cups without handles, a plate of almond cookies and a yellow rose. Juanita had not actually seen or observed her entrance. One rarely did. Mrs. Lee did not visually or audibly make her presence known; rather she just appeared, as if materializing out of invisibility. She didn't think Mrs. Lee heard her remark to Mr. Lee about the crowbar though.

"Miss Vogel here has just uttered the most remarkable and peculiar sentence about a past deed. Of course I don't believe it, but it is so strange one wonders why she would speak such a thing."

"She is only a child, dear. Perhaps it is her imagination at work. Perhaps she will one day be a writer. She is always reading, is she not?"

Mrs. Lee wore her long hair in an elaborate braided configuration unlike any she had seen on the braided women in Cat Creek. She donned yet another of her many silk robes, this one adorned with a formation of white doves over a shimmering blue lake. Juanita never failed to compliment them. Mrs. Lee had once explained she wore slippers and traditional robes to please her husband, but Chinese women today were generally much more modernized and Americanized. She described herself and her husband as traditionalists. Her eyes almost always hid a distant amusement, as if she possessed slightly humorous information about life others did not. Placing the tray on the table, she bowed and said, "This rose is for you, Miss Vogel."

When she spoke, it was like singing. Juanita could not remember a voice so sweet.

She accepted the rose but didn't know what to do with it. Was she supposed to wear it? Pin it to her sweater? Dance with it in her teeth? Is that what Italians did? She set the rose back on the tray and thanked her. Mr. Lee fingered his long white beard; his gaze penetrating as he scrutinized her intently.

She pointed at the game board and said to Mrs. Lee, "Your husband refuses to let me win."

"He is both fiercely competitive and a bad sport."

"Not so," interrupted Mr. Lee. "Do not believe her."

"Sometimes," said Mrs. Lee, "when I win at Mah Jong, he gets angry with me."

"My Uncle Frank once gave me a large book of famous paintings and photographs. That's what it's like looking at your robes. Like looking at art. At beauty itself."

"I have many. Perhaps too many. I have over the years compiled what has turned out to be an unintentional collection. I will show you. Follow me, Juanita. Bring the rose with you, dear. I have an idea for it." To her husband she said, "I will return Juanita to you shortly and you can then continue to bully her over your board game."

She felt the warmth of Mrs. Lee's tiny hand as they left and entered the hallway. Her gratitude to Mrs. Lee was immeasurable. For now at least it was possible she was free of Mr. Lee's inquest but she was going to have come up with an explanation for the crowbar remark and as of yet had none. But at least Mr. Lee had said he did not believe her. That was something. She dutifully followed Mrs. Lee's diminutive inaudible footsteps. Mrs. Lee wore silk slippers on feet so tiny they may have belonged to an infant.

Mrs. Lee led her along a hallway to another area of the house unknown to her. They entered a large opulently furnished room where incense burned in hanging golden globes the size of softballs. The floor and walls displayed carpets with faded designs and colors she imagined had once been as vibrant as Mrs. Lee's robe. She heard exotic music playing on a radio. It was music unlike anything she had ever heard before, a stringed instrument of some kind but not at all similar to Uncle Frank's banjo and by comparison out of tune. A woman's voice began to accompany the stringed instrument and was even more atonal. Mrs. Lee sang along in quiet unison, humming softly, almost as if unaware of doing so. Juanita was familiar with incense but not this scent. At home they had burned white sage and sometimes cedar chips, but here the scent was much sweeter.

Mrs. Lee guided her into an adjoining feminine room with high ceilings and silk drapery. Prominent in the room was a large bed with four tall bedposts that almost reached the ceiling and from which a blue silk canopy decorated with white doves was hung. Comfortable wingback chairs were at opposite corners of the room and small tables with jade vases and stained glass lamps were nearby. Paintings of Chinese landscapes hung on the walls and a small love seat was situated in front of a mirrored dresser on which were small jars of various creams and lotions, delicate perfume bottles, pearl handled hairbrushes and hand mirrors. Mrs. Lee lifted a bottle with an attached spray and misted them both. Juanita felt the mist on her neck and smiled, surprised by the gesture and pleased to carry a woman's scent for the first time in her life. Had her mother worn perfume? Aunt Elvira didn't but maybe should have. Elvira smelled of hard work and body odor.

She studied Mrs. Lee's face in the mirror and thought Mrs. Lee seemed to carry within her a secret about happiness. Her dark brown eyes were minimally slanted, their large round pupils dark brown and moist. Her lips expressed the hint of a smile as if amused by private thoughts she was not prepared to share. Juanita saw her own face in the mirror and quickly looked away, embarrassed by her ugly hair. She quickly tried to fix it, mussing it up into some kind of style, maybe French like the woman in the barber shop had suggested, but it didn't work and she gave up and wished she had worn her beret.

A large wardrobe made from a species of wood Mrs. Lee called Teak took up an entire wall. Juanita knew wood as well as anyone, but not this oily golden brown variety unlike any in her experience. The three doors to the wardrobe were opened with brass tiger-shaped handles. The doors themselves were designed with carved tigers and birds cut deep into the wood. There must have been as many as fifty robes inside. Mrs. Lee removed three and laid them out across the bed.

"Which do you prefer?" she inquired.

Juanita had no difficulty, her hands lighting on a black silk robe with red and green birds sewn along its sleeves and pockets. Yellow and light blue butterflies decorated its cuffs and sleeves. A brilliant green peacock encompassed the garment's entire backside.

"This one then, will be yours, Juanita. I want you to have it. "

"I can have this?"

"You may."

"You would do this for me, Mrs. Lee? Give me such a beautiful gift?"

"I have much enjoyed having young female company, and as I have said I have too many of these gowns. You may either wear it or put it on display."

"Oh, I want to wear it."

"I think you will look lovely in it.

"May I wear it now?"

"If you wish. We are near the same size and I suspect it will fit you without need of alteration."

Juanita removed her jeans, sweatshirt and boots and slipped into the robe, which fastened from the side.

"It fits you well," said Mrs. Lee. "I knew it would. Here, let me pin the rose to it. Do you see how the yellow rose compliments it?"

Juanita looked into the mirror and saw not the scalped waif who had entered this room, but a pretty young woman who had been transformed by it. She had never thought of herself as pretty before. She paced back and forth in front of the full length mirror, stealing sideways glances.

Mrs. Lee escorted her to another large room, this one containing a throne-like high-backed chair in a space as large as the library lounging area but with even more books, many oversized and bound with leather covers in both Chinese and English. Juanita ran her fingers over the spines, imagining what stories or information the books might contain.

Juanita examined a book containing pictures of Chinese warriors.

"My husband is fascinated with warfare, but I disapprove of his interest. I am Confucian and value education and harmony above warfare or conquest. My husband however does not share my abhorrence of warfare, unfortunately."

A large glass cabinet displayed a collection of a dozen large swords, axes, and spears. The blades of the swords were polished to such sheen that they were like mirrors. She estimated them to be at least three feet in length and so heavy they would probably have to be wielded with both hands. They both fascinated and terrified her.

"My husband collects these. He is, or was, a master of them. Some are centuries old and very valuable. They are very heavy. I can barely lift one over my head. My husband manipulates them as if they were as light and harmless as a bath towel, swinging them over his head, against his hips and behind him so quickly the eye loses track and sees only a blur of motion. A strike delivered anywhere results in a severed limb at the least."

"Was he a warrior of some kind?"

"He used to practice martial arts. To this day I do not understand why anyone would refer to the practice as an art, but he said it placed him in a harmonious relationship with power. He performs a sword ritual every morning. Sometimes he uses the swords in combat with an imaginary opponent. In the old days, tournaments were held."

"With swords? Weren't people killed? Dismembered?"

She tried to imagine it. She remembered the chickens she'd had to kill for supper back in Cat Creek, horrified at witnessing her first decapitation, how the headless animal ran around the yard spurting a geyser of blood from its neck. Was its brain still alive? Was it still thinking? Could it see its decapitated head on the blood soaked earth? She had killed many chickens at home. Forcibly held their heads to a stump and raised the hatchet over them as they squawked and fluttered and fought to escape as if they knew what awaited them. She had also killed a human being, an enemy who intended harm, for whom she had no more sympathy than for the chickens she killed. Living in the country where there were wolves, coyotes, poisonous snakes, floods and brush fires, it was nature's way. Nature was cruel. So were some people.

Mrs. Lee said, "In tournaments today sword combat is prohibited. Participants are rated for form, not for combat. We deny those who falsely accuse the Chinese community of promoting unsanctioned fights to the death in arenas kept highly secret. My husband has been accused of being a promoter, but he assures me otherwise. But tell me, my dear, is it true you killed a man?"

The question caused her to audibly gasp. She pressed both palms against her heart as if to quiet it and said, "Thank you for this beautiful robe, Mrs. Lee. I will always treasure it. I believe Mr. Lee is waiting for me to finish the game we are playing. Please excuse me."

She gathered her clothing and closed the door behind her. Wearing the robe, she passed through the lobby clutching her old clothing bundled her arms as if it were an unwanted child she was taking to an orphanage. Her hands shook and she dropped the boots she carried and stooped to pick them up. Her breathing felt shallow, as if her inhalations were met with resistance.

The lobby chairs were occupied by the usual Asian men wearing black suits, white dress shirts and ties. Many held briefcases in their laps. What might they think, watching her pass, she an occidental dressed like a Chinese? Who could be certain with these Asians? She could not understand them; they gave away nothing of what they might be thinking or feeling. Mrs. Lee was an intelligent woman, not easily fooled. She tried to remember Mrs. Lee's tone when she had asked about the killing. Had it been accusatory or merely inquisitive? She had no intention of going back upstairs and joining Mr. Lee at the game board as she had told Mrs. Lee. They were playing a different game now, a game of truth and consequences putting her at risk. She had made a careless move she could not take back.

She hurried upstairs to her room and locked the door. All she could do now was wait. Either the police would arrive to arrest her or she would be summoned to Mr. Lee and have to explain. Mr. Lee had a way of looking right into her when she spoke, as if deciphering a secret language she did not understand or know she was speaking. All her secrets exposed to his scrutiny.

She hurried from the bed for the toilet. She fell to her knees over the toilet bowl and waited. Nothing came up and she wished it would. The salty taste in her mouth was like blood. Finally it came, and she shuddered as it splashed into the bowl. She waited, knowing there was more. Another wave followed and then it was over. She flushed it down and wiped her mouth at the sink, staring at her reflection in the little mirror over the medicine cabinet. Her face was shiny and speckled with droplets of perspiration. She filled the sink with lukewarm water and submerged a washcloth in its depths. She scrubbed her face and eyes as if the soft damp cloth might wipe away her fears. She felt its warmth behind her closed eyelids, on her cheeks and lips. The warm water ran down her neck. She wrung out the washcloth and replaced it and dried her face and neck with a soft towel from the rack. There was a foul taste in her mouth. She spread a generous amount of baking soda on her brush and scrubbed her teeth, in no hurry to spit the liquid from her mouth. She filled her mouth with water from the glass on the shelf but did not swallow. She swirled the liquid in her mouth until the foul taste was gone and then spat it out into the sink.

She stood at the bureau mirror. She had hips and small breasts she had not had a year ago. On the rez there were girls her age who were already young mothers. She was pretty, worthy of the robe Mrs. Lee had given her. She hugged it tightly against her body. She hated her hair. Someone was tapping lightly on the door.

The young Asian clerk who normally worked the desk stood in the hallway. He looked her up and down and frowned as if disapproving of her Chinese robe.

He bowed and said, "Mr. Lee requests your presence in his chambers."

"I'm not feeling well," she replied. I've just brushed my teeth and I'm going to bed."

"One does not say no to Mr. Lee unless you are Mrs. Lee, which you are clearly not. Mr. Lee is not a man to be refused. He is man of great prestige and influence. One does not offend Mr. Lee by refusing to honor his invitation. Come with me. You follow."

Descending the stairs, numerous unconvincing possibilities of explanations for her crowbar remark came to mind and were immediately rejected as unconvincing. Downstairs, the clerk motioned her inside in a spacious room furnished with many small flags and framed maps of China and its provinces. An enormous thick rug was underfoot. Mr. Lee sat enthroned where the rug ended.

Lea Macquarrie

"The carpet upon which you stand is old, not Chinese, but Tibetan. The pattern is called a Mandala."

She did not want to look up to meet Mr. Lee's eyes. She stole a glance briefly to his regal posture seated at his throne, but not to his face. He sat perfectly erect, his hands grasping the raised mahogany arms of his high-backed chair carved into the shape of dragons. Mr. Lee's eyes, when she dared to look, were accusatory and judgmental. This was going to be an interrogation and she didn't know if she could lie to him while meeting his eyes.

"Look at me," he said.

He wore his usual black tunic and matching trousers, his beard braided into knots and beaded. Across his lap was a thick blanket though it was not cold in the room. He locked his eyes on her and, staring at her without so much as blinking while slowly, almost ritualistically removing the blanket. A large gleaming sword was then in his lap. Her breath retreated inside of her and refused to come out and she thought she might be having an asthma attack because she couldn't get another breath inside of her. Mr. Lee raised the sword from his lap and ran a cloth over its gleaming blade and then returned it to his lap and covered it again with the blanket. She was having difficulty swallowing. Again, as in the room earlier, she experienced nausea and the taste of blood, bile and fear.

Mr. Lee twirled his braided white beard between his thumb and index finger while scrutinizing her. Mr. Lee would decide her fate. Not her father, not the police, not any God above but Mr. Lee. Again he uncovered the sword. He wiped the blade with the blanket and rose from the throne and stood holding it at shoulder level with both hands.

"Do you like it, Miss Vogel?"

"It frightens me."

"It should. It is a lethal weapon of war. I believe you also may at one time have held a lethal weapon in your hands. Those men you saw seated outside are waiting, one by one, to be called to my chambers so they may have the honor to stand where you are now. Why, you may ask? They seek my favor, my counsel, my wisdom. You do not, but I give it anyway, because you are young and don't know you need it or how to ask for it. You mentioned earlier a weapon I was unfamiliar with. What was it you said? A crowbar? I did not know this weapon. I had to look it up in the dictionary. It is common tool sold in a hardware store. It is not an honorable weapon like a sword but I believe you spoke the truth. I believe in your hands it was a weapon. I believe you spoke the truth when you said you killed a man. I believe this because I *recognized* it in you.

"The outcome of two adversaries locked in mortal combat is determined by skill, but also by fate. There is great honor in this. One trusts in the transformative power of the process. But the man who dies by a common hardware store tool is deprived of an honorable death. He does not die honorably in combat, but is murdered."

He stepped down from the throne and unlocked the cabinet displaying his weapons and removed a large dagger encased within a sheath encrusted with small red and green jewels. He locked the case with the small key he wore around his neck, returned to his chair and presented the dagger to her and said, "This is a proper weapon for a woman."

She accepted it tentatively, running her fingers along the jewels encrusted in its sheath. She tentatively removed the knife, hearing and feeling it slide out from its bejeweled case.

"It's almost like a miniature sword," she observed. "It's beautiful."

Mr. Lee took it from her and said, "Perhaps, in addition to my wife's gowns, you would like to have this, but I have no intention of giving it to you. You haven't the discipline to own such a weapon."

"I wouldn't think of accepting it, Mr. Lee."

"And yet you have no difficulty in accepting my wife's ceremonial robe."

"I'm sorry if I have offended you, Mr. Lee. I will return the gown."

"You should never have accepted it. "

"I promise to return it."

"She won't let you. To offer it back would be an insult to her. You should learn that some things cannot be undone, Miss Vogel. Think on this. It is an important lesson."

Lea Macquarrie

"I am sorry, Mr. Lee."

"Regret changes nothing important. What has been done has been done. Your father failed in his responsibility to teach you how to act honorably. He allowed you to become who you are."

"And who am I, Mr. Lee? Sometimes I don't know myself."

"You are a foolish girl who does not understand how much trouble she is in."

WALLA WALLA

FRANK WAS RIGHT. He should never have Juanita behind. It was yet another in a long line of mistakes, and he could see more mistakes lined up behind this one like failed men in a breadline. When would it stop? When would he get smart and start making the right decisions? Meanwhile his daughter was left alone in the care of a Chinaman neither friend or family, and who could guess what trouble she may have gotten into. His palms sweated and he had a headache. It was late in the afternoon and the high prison walls were washed with slowly diminishing light. He smoked and craned his stiff neck looking up at the guard tower gun turrets and rotating spotlights. It worried him Frank might try to escape this fortress. Be just like him. One more thing to worry about.

His heartbeat felt to him irregular, like it was beating too hard and too fast like his body was another kind of prison and his heart inside was trying to escape and run away. He fingered the diminishing roll of cash in his pocket again, rubbing it between his thumb and index finger, but it felt thin and he was afraid to count it. He returned to the visitor parking lot but couldn't remember where exactly they had parked and the lot was filled almost to capacity. He strode the length and width of the lot systematically between rows of parked cars. He wished he could walk backward into the past beyond the day he had jumped the freight that had changed his life forever from bad to worse. He found Emory at the car in the parking lot but not Miss Costa.

"I was wondering where the hell you were," said Emory. "Thought maybe they'd decided to keep you." He smiled, showing a row of stained, crooked teeth.

"Where is Miss Costa," asked Jack. "We're supposed to be on our way back. I don't intend to wait much longer. "

"I don't know where she is but don't even think about leaving without her. She's the one who financed this trip. I don't know about you but I don't have enough cash for gasoline to get us back without her." Emory sat himself on the hood of the car and rolled a cigarette, his skinny long legs hanging off the fender. He spat on the pavement and said, "How did it go with your brother in there?"

"It was hurtful to see him locked up like a criminal. Much as it did my heart good to see him again, part of me wishes I had never come."

"I'd like to say you get used to it but you don't. Only family I have left is locked up in there. Breaks my heart."

Jack was about to reply when he saw Helen Costa. Her blonde hair was loose to her shoulders and she was wearing the dark glasses. She fumbled in her purse for a cigarette, lighted it and then sauntered through the parking lot to their vehicle.

"Something's come up," she said. "I'm going to have stay another night and leave tomorrow afternoon."

"That's impossible, "said Jack. "I have a little girl I have to get back to."

"Then get back to her. I'm not preventing you." She took a drag off the cigarette and blew smoke into the air as if punctuating the end of a declarative sentence.

"I came along with the understanding we'd be gone two days at most," said Jack. "Maybe even get back the same day. I'm sorry, Miss Costa, but we are going to have to leave you."

Emory shook his head and said, "You paying for the gas, Jack?"

They dropped Miss Costa at a moderately priced midtown hotel where she paid for a room and said, "Pick me up tomorrow morning by ten to take me back to the prison. I'll need a couple of hours there and then we can be on our way." The wind had picked up and she hugged herself, turned and walked the steps leading to the hotel entrance. She turned one last time and waved.

Jack drove them to the Salvation Army where he inquired at the desk for a place to sleep. The clerk said they were full but there was a mission two blocks away where indigents sometimes slept in the basement. They walked to the mission but there too it was filled to capacity. By now it was turning dark and getting colder by the minute.

Back at the car Emory said, "I guess this is where we room for the night, Jack. You can have the front seat and I'll take the back."

"Why do you get the back seat?"

"Because it's my car."

"You know, Bean, there's a sharp wire coming out the seat cushion. That thing will be up your ass before nightfall."

"I'll put my coat over it."

"I don't suppose anyone thought to pack any blankets."

"I sure as hell don't have one, do you?"

Jack shivered through the night, sleeping fitfully, pulling his jacket around him repeatedly but never enough to warm him properly. He positioned and repositioned himself to get comfortable, never succeeding enough to sleep deeply. Now and then he heard footsteps outside the vehicle. There was very little automobile traffic heard on the street. Mostly he heard Emory snoring and wondered how the man could sleep in such circumstances. The man was thin enough to have room to move horizontally but his folded long legs had to be cramped. Jack heard him repeatedly adjusting his legs through the night, his feet bumping the doorframe. Finally they both fell asleep. .

A hammering on the window awakened him. He sat up, rubbed his eyes and then rubbed the window and tried to look out but there was condensation on the window and it was foggy and someone was shining a light in his eyes. He wiped the window and saw a policeman held him in a flashlight beam. The policeman tapped the flashlight on the window and commanded they roll it down. Jack complied.

"You know we lock up vagrants in this town," said the policeman.

Jack fought back what tasted like fear if fear had a taste. But he was going to have act natural and not show it. He was going to have lie and get good at it because he was going to be doing a lot of it from now on.

"Right now it's so cold jail doesn't sound half so bad," said Jack, "but we aren't vagrants. We came to visit relations in the penitentiary but the hotel was full and so was the Salvation Army and the Mission. We plan to be there for visiting hours tomorrow and then you will never see us again."

"I don't want to see you now," said policeman. "Move this vehicle on out of here. You can park somewhere out near the prison. Pull off the road or something but if I see you in town again I'll have you locked up."

"Fair enough, officer. You won't see us again."

This would be his life now, this always looking over his shoulder for police, preparing his lies in the event of being questioned. He was going to have to make up a whole new past for himself. Change his name, his history, anything that might relate him to a certain locket somewhere along the railroad tracks in Idaho or eastern Washington. He wished he had thought to get details from Frank about where to obtain false identification. Another mistake. He had to stop making them.

"I was sure my brother was innocent," said Jack as he drove, "but now I'm not so sure."

"Why is that Jack?"

"He didn't deny it. He talked about bank robbery as if it were a political act. A good deed, like he thought he was Robin Hood."

They drove out of town and were back raising dust on an unpaved road in farm country. He again considered being locked up for a minor offense such as vagrancy and whether the name J. Vogel might be listed on an interstate search of some kind. He pulled off onto the shoulder of the road, then dipped the Ford into the ditch alongside it, his tires spewing dirt and pebbles as the vehicle spun out. He extinguished the headlights and drove into the depths of a dark cornfield, the leaves of high cornstalks slapping against the side of the car and across the windshield like shirt sleeves worn by a legion of scarecrows. He turned off the engine and lay down on the front seat, his feet below the steering wheel and head against the passenger side door. Behind him was a narrow path of crushed corn stalks.

"Just one question," said Emory in the back seat. "How in hell do you expect us to find our way out of here, Jack? You never heard of a corn maze before?"

"Listen, that policeman threatened to lock us up for vagrancy, Bean. Here we're concealed from the road. This is no maze, Bean. I can back out the way I came. If that doesn't work, I'll just make a U turn and gun it."

"Well, I hope so."

Jack worried whether he had made a mistake in giving his name at the prison. Wouldn't there be a record of a Jack Vogel having visited a prisoner? He wondered if visitation records were shared outside of the prison and thought to ask Bean.

"Bean?"

But there was no answer. Bean was asleep. Jack rested in the safety of the corn that concealed them. He closed his eyes and may have briefly dozed. When he next opened his eyes and looked out moonlight was illuminating tall corn stalks that were like sentient beings watching over them. He let himself drift, and then he was dreaming. He was back in Seattle after an unspecified absence during which he had been lost in the fog. In the dream he was running hard, panting and wheezing, his ribcage aching, his heart pounding so hard it hurt. He found himself swimming the fog was so thick. He stroked his arms and kicked his feet like a man with fins doing a frog kick. He swam in the fog to the Hotel Lee and the fog lifted and he was walking on solid ground. The steps to the hotel entrance seemed to multiply under his feet. There were too many and he didn't seem to be making progress. He could hear Juanita calling for him from the upper floors. He followed the sound of her voice up the stairs and down the surrealistically elongated hallway to their room. He could hear her crying but the door was locked. He kicked the door where the lock met the jamb and it flew open. A man sat on the bed waiting for him. He was smoking a cigarette

Lea Macquarrie

and his face was a mask of gore, one side of it unrecognizable, an eyeball hanging by a strand. There was blood on the walls, window shade, and bedspread.

He woke with a scream that startled Emory awake.

"What? Jack?"

"It's nothing. Go back to sleep."

He had an urgent need to urinate. He stepped out of the car and stood in a field of golden liquid moonlight leaking into a field of gently swaying corn stalks. It encompassed his entire view and felt no more real than the dream he had wakened from, the remnants of which seemed important but beyond his recall. He unzipped his pants and urinated, the sound of his stream hitting the ground the only intrusion on the morning silence. He was about to zip up when a brilliantly colored butterfly emerged from the corn stalks and lighted on his hand. It seemed somehow, in a way he did not understand, to have chosen him deliberately. He turned his hand over and the butterfly rose brightly into the air but then returned and settled on his palm and looked at him. He shooed it away, and it flew off into the cornfield.

The sun rose slowly and the field of golden yellow corn became even brighter. He was not absolutely sure he was not still dreaming. He kept thinking about the butterfly and how nothing seemed real, not even the corn. It was as if he was seeing through Alma's vision instead of his own. Alma was always looking for coincidences, signals, omens and messenger spirits he mostly didn't believe in. He briefly wondered if the butterfly that had landed on his hand had been sent from her. He was not prone to metaphysical speculations but she had told him often if she were to die before him she would send him signs and signals. It was her way.

He began brushing corn leaves from the hood and windshield of the car, coughing in the dust it raised as he swept at it with his arms. Dust stung his eyes and clogged his nostrils. He got back behind the wheel and started the Ford, made a U turn and gunned the motor. The Ford shot into the culvert, spitting dirt under its wheels on its way out. It fishtailed sideways and took up both lanes of the road.

Emory sat up in the back seat and said, "What the hell are you trying do, Jack, kill us?"

"I had to accelerate to get us out of the ditch, Bean."

"Yeah, but what if there had been a car coming."

"Well, then we would have had an accident probably. But I rolled down the window and listened for cars before I pulled us out. All I heard was the wind through the corn stalks."

"Well, it was risky but I have to admit you're a better driver than I am. I can't hardly see more than ten feet."

"Bean, have you ever had had a premonition?"

"Have I ever had a what?"

"It's a word my brother taught me. It's a feeling in your mind, without any rational explanation or evidence to support it, that something important and probably bad is about to happen. Last night I had this dream about my daughter but, oh, never mind, Bean, forget it. I don't understand it myself."

He drove to Helen Costa's hotel. Her room smelled of coffee and cigarettes and some kind of perfume that made him sneeze. He saw she wore freshly applied lipstick and makeup but was otherwise not ready.

"You're early," she said.

"I'm not early," replied Jack. "You're late."

"Where is Emory?"

"In the car."

She wore only a silk slip through which he could faintly see the outline of her bra and the elastic of her panties. There was no exhibitionism or flirtation in this at all as far as Jack could discern, and he was grateful to her for that at least. She dressed quickly in a smart black skirt and matching jacket.

Jack said, "We were supposed to be getting out of here yesterday. That was the agreement. We're going today. Now in fact. If you don't want to come that's up to you. I'll personally pay for the gas to get us back without you."

She sat facing her bureau mirror and began brushing her hair in short, hurried angry strokes.

"If that's the way you want it, okay Jack. Good luck to you and no hard feelings. But if you take me to the walls and give me just one hour there, maybe two at the most, we can be out of here and I'll cover the gasoline expenses as agreed."

"One hour," agreed Jack.

He sat on the hotel room bed and watched her pack. She hardly glanced at him. Truth was he never much liked her and liked her less by the day. She finished packing her small suitcase and he carried it for her and put it in the back seat of the Ford next to Emory. They drove her to the prison and let her out of the Ford.

"We need gas," Emory said to her. "We'll drive back into town and fill her up and come back for you."

She gave them both dirty looks and peeled off several bills and dropped them through the open window.

"Don't you guys dare leave me here," she said.

Jack drove into the sleepy town of Walla Walla. He pulled into a forlorn little single pump gas station just inside the city limits and got out of the car. He leaned in the open window and said to Bean, "If she's not ready when we get back, we're leaving without her."

"No we're not, Jack. She's the reason we're on this trip. It wouldn't have happened without her."

"Fill her up," said Jack to the attendant.

He washed his hands and face in the gas station restroom, which was dirty and had a foul odor. The gasoline attendant was washing the windshield when he returned to the driver's seat. In the rear view mirror he saw a police car pull in. He heard the thud of the police car door closing, then saw the police officer's polished black boots below the chassis as he stepped out of the police car. He could not see the policeman's eyes behind the sunglasses but the man's mouth was grim. Jack felt his hands tremble and his mouth go so dry.

"I thought I told you boys to get out of town," said the policeman.

"We're going, sir. Gassing up right now and then we are out your life."

"Be quick about it."

Jack drove back the way they had come, on a narrow country

road bordered by fields of hops, corn, barley and wheat, wondering again if this would be his life now, if the mere sight of a policeman would immobilize him with fear. The morning sun was already high and fierce and shone brilliantly on the concrete parking lot where Helen Costa was already waiting. Her eyes were swollen and red with crying. Jack had to exit the vehicle to let her slide behind the steering wheel to the passenger side window. Emory leaned over the front seat trying to find out what had happened to make her cry, but she refused to talk about it and ignored his attempt to console her with his ineffective platitudes.

Lea Macquarrie

HOTEL LEE

THE ROAD SEEMED TO END at the descending sun, which looked like it might be located at the end of the world. Soft afternoon light muted the fields of wheat and barley. He had been a fool to trust Mr. Lee with Juanita. Chinatown was said to be a dangerous enclave of Tongs fighting over territory. Or so he'd heard, mostly from railroad workers who didn't like Orientals. But it was more than that. He was losing Juanita in a way he had not foreseen and did not understand. Maybe that was what the butterfly in Alma's language had been trying to impart. Your little girl is a butterfly. You can briefly hold her in your hand, but then she flies away and is gone.

The sun died below the cornfields, its wounded light spilling across the valley. He turned on the headlights when night fell, pushing the Ford to its limit. Helen Costa wadded up her jacket and used it as a pillow again the passenger side window. Emory was still talking from the back seat but much more softly now as if knowing no one listened, the words strung farther apart until their pauses elongated into silence. Jack turned on the radio and stared at the path his headlights made.

They were in the mountains, climbing switchbacks. There was no traffic and little remaining light. At the summit an hour later Emory woke and said he had to urinate and for Jack to pull over to the side of the road. Jack complied and joined him in the woods, where both relieved their bladders. Jack walked across the road to a viewing point and stood in the darkness, looking out across the valley below. There was little ground light and the star-jeweled sky above him reminded him of the sky at home. He returned to the Ford, taking the back seat this time, intending to sleep. Emory took the wheel but the engine would not turn over no matter how many times it was cranked.

"Sounds like it's not getting enough spark," said Jack. "Do you have a flashlight?"

"In the glove box."

Jack got out with the flashlight, removed a toolbox from the rumble seat and lifted the hood. After about ten minutes he said, "Try it now."

Emory cranked the engine, which started at the first attempt.

"What did you do out there," he inquired when Jack had returned.

"I removed the starter switch from the starter. It wasn't hard to do. Just four screws to remove. Then I disconnected the battery cable from the starter switch. The brass piece in the switch and the contact on the starter needed to be cleaned. Dirt was keeping it from passing enough current to turn the starter."

"Damn, Jack, glad you were along. You definitely have some skills there."

"I know more about tractors than I do cars."

Jack fell asleep while Emory drove and when he woke they were passing through a country town with lights in the windows.

"Where are we," asked Jack.

"City of Yakima."

"Stop the car, Bean. I think I'm going to be sick."

He stood by the side of the road, repelling waves of nausea. He retched forth a small amount of bile; they had eaten little. He wiped his mouth, spat and went back to the car and climbed in the back seat and closed his eyes and did not speak again until they were outside of Seattle.

It was turning light when Emmett dropped him off at the

hotel. Juanita was not in her room. The bed was made, the coverlets pulled tight at the corners the way he had taught her. The towels in the bathroom were neatly folded over their hangars and there was a full pitcher of water on the nightstand but it looked as if no one had slept in the bed during his entire absence. He hurried downstairs to the desk clerk, who was placing mail in slots.

"Have you seen my daughter?"

The clerk opened the wooden half gate separating the lobby from the interior of the building an escorted him down a long hallway through a laundry room containing hand cranked washing machines where damp sheets hung on a clothesline, then through a door into another long hallway ending at a massive brass framed wooden door carved with Asian emblems. The clerk tapped what sounded like a code on the door, which was opened by Mrs. Lee. She shooed the clerk away with a peculiar motion of her hand as if she might be releasing a locust. Or, thought Jack, a butterfly. He was led into a parlor furnished with luxuriant cushioned chairs, a sofa, end tables and bookshelves. A radio played softly. Mrs. Lee, her back to him, talked with her hands as they walked. Come, they said, come, come. He followed her to a large room where a fire burned in the stone fireplace. Seated at a table were Mr. Lee and a teenaged Chinese girl wearing a black silk robe decorated with flowers and birds. The table held a bowl of cherries, a plate of cookies, a board game, and a pot of tea. Mr. Lee wore black trousers and a black collarless jacket contrasting with his snow white beard. He stood in acknowledgment when Jack entered but did not bow.

The girl smiled at him and said, "Hi, Daddy. We're playing Chinese Checkers. Mrs. Lee made cookies."

He watched her rise from her chair and bow politely in the exact manner of Mr. Lee. What did she think, she was Chinese now? And where did she get the robe?

Mr. Lee said, "Perhaps we should talk, Mr. Vogel. Juanita, please give your father and I some privacy."

His daughter responded obediently, her long silk Chinese gown whispering secrets in its passing. But what was the meaning of this? She was not Chinese and this was not her family. When they were alone Mr. Lee poured them tea and gestured for him to sit at the table.

"Your daughter made a very peculiar statement, Mr. Vogel. She said she killed a man with a crowbar. My wife and I both heard it. It was a very peculiar and curious thing to say, don't you agree, Mr. Vogel?"

Jack briefly wondered if Mr. Lee could hear his heart pounding.

"I do," he replied with difficulty, "and it's not the first time she has told such tales. She has told people she was adopted, that she was kidnapped, that she can read minds, all kinds of crazy things. She even said she was an Indian princess when everybody knows she's Italian. I don't know why she does it, but you can be sure I will talk to her about it."

"I am hesitant to pry into a family matter, Mr. Vogel, but honor requires me to inquire as to why you do not have this young lady in school. She is unable to read and suffers shame because of it."

"Well, I intend to enroll her once we're settled."

"And when do you suppose that will be, Mr. Vogel? Do you intend to stay on?"

"Yes, I do. Soon as I get some work I'll pay whatever I owe."

"There is a school near here, Mr. Vogel. I hope you will enroll your daughter soon. I hope you will also provide clothing more appropriate to the wet Seattle climate."

"I intend to provide for all her needs, Mr. Lee. It's why we came to Seattle in the first place."

"I am pleased to hear this, Mr. Vogel. There remains however the unresolved issue of payment of rent."

"Is it due?"

"It is overdue, Mr. Vogel. Not by much, but we do not credit rooms or permit an accumulation of debt."

"That is not a problem, Mr. Lee. I will be able to pay you very soon. Today. Now if you wish."

But it was a problem. He knew fingering the roll in his pocket the money he had saved was running out and he didn't know how he would raise more if he didn't find work. He paid what he owed and said, "Now if you will excuse me, I would like to return to my daughter."

He found her in their room, seated in the armchair by the window, an oversized leather-bound book that looked heavy taking up most of her lap. The delicate embroidered birds on the sleeve of her Chinese robe gave the appearance of rising up her arm in flight as she stretched and yawned. She glanced at him briefly from her book, an expression he could not determine to be resignation or boredom flitting across her impassive face.

"You told them, Juanita."

She went back to her book and it infuriated him. How to deal with this reckless, disobedient child? She with a book in her lap she can't even read and wearing that silly robe suitable for some kind of Chinese Empress when she was just a dirt poor Indian girl from Cat Creek, Montana. She had to have known the danger she had placed them in. And he loathed this game of exhibitionistic posturing with the book on her lap she couldn't read, the French beret and now some kind of Chinese concoction he didn't understand.

"We had a trust, Juanita. You put us both in danger."

"That makes us even, Dad. I put you in danger when I talked to Mr. Lee and you put me in danger when you put me on that goddamned freight car."

"It was not my idea to bring you and watch your language."

"It's only cussing, Daddy. The trouble we're in you're worried about cussing?"

She turned a page in the book without looking at him.

"I'm not worried about it exactly, but I do care about it. I'm still your father and you are under my care."

"Yes, and that's just the problem."

"What's that supposed to mean?"

She looked up from the opened book and met his eyes and said, "Mr. Lee says you have failed in your responsibility to me. Mr. Lee says I'd do better on my own. At the very least you should have me in school. He says you never should have brought me here, taken me away from my home and everyone I knew to leave me with strangers. You should have known better, Dad. You're supposed to be the parent and you're not. But it's okay because you taught me not to need one anymore. I'm growing up, not a kid anymore."

"You're old enough to have killed a man. Old enough to go to prison for it. Hand over that damn book, Juanita. You can't read so it's a lie. It's make-believe fantasy no different than when you were a little girl pretending to be Hiawatha. You're too old for it. If you really want to learn to read, get a children's book and study it."

Damn Chinese finches were rising up the sleeve again. She slammed the book closed so hard he could hear it curse him.

"Give it to me, Juanita. Right now."

She handed it over and there were more birds in flight. Looked like the whole damn robe was about to fly off and take her with it. He opened the book and found himself staring at partially naked women. Their breasts were dark and round with even darker nipples. He stared maybe a little longer than he should and said, "You're looking at pornography?"

"It's an art book, Dad. "

"This is art? Women with bare breasts? Women suckling?"

"It's Paul Gauguin, Dad. He's a famous artist."

"Well put it away. I don't want you looking at it. And take that damn robe off. We are not Chinese and we are not royalty. We are dirt poor working class folk from the Montana oil fields and that's all we will ever be. And there is nothing wrong with that, Juanita. What matters is to be true to our word. You said you would not share our secret. You broke our trust. Oh and by the way ditch that phony French beret too. You're not French either."

"No and neither am I Italian. I'm Crow and we both know it. You want me to ditch the beret? Fine but only if you give me my hair back. That's why I wear it, to conceal what you did to me. What you have never apologized for."

"I haven't? Then I am sorry, Juanita. I say this sincerely. I should not have done that."

"No you shouldn't have. Sometimes I wish you weren't my father."

He was familiar with her flares of anger but not this deliberate cruelty. He remembered the old playground taunt, sticks and stones

Lea Macquarrie

may break my bones but words will never hurt me. If only that were true. One healed from broken bones but how did one rebound and recover from words such as these? Didn't she know how deeply she was hurting him, how sad he felt right now? He was reminded of Alma's stinging, incomprehensible meanness when angry. How she made hurtful accusations that could not be undone. He had blamed the alcohol but maybe it was more than that. Maybe it was as much a part of who she was as much as her usual sweet disposition when not drinking.

"That's a terrible, hurtful thing to say, Juanita."

"You left me. I thought I'd never see you again. I was frightened and cried myself to sleep at night."

"I'm sorry, Juanita. I promise I will never leave you again."

"Your promises are worthless. You mean well, but you don't follow through. Mr. Lee would never break a promise. He is a man of honor."

"Who says? Him, probably. You're too easily fooled, Juanita. You hardly know him."

"I know him well enough."

"No. You don't. I'm suspicious of him. I should not have left you with him."

"Then why did you, if you don't trust him."

"I had little choice. It was important that I see Frank."

"Then you should have taken me with you. Is his illness serious?"

"He is going to be laid up for quite some time."

"That's too bad. For him and for us. "

"Frank's tough. He'll pull through."

"I wish you were more like him."

"So do I, sometimes."

"But you're not."

No, thought Jack, and if you knew where Frank really was maybe you wouldn't be wishing I was.

"Mr. Lee says I'm going to end up as parent and you the child, that I'll be taking care of you instead of the other way around. Mr. Lee says I'm old enough to make my own decisions about my life."

"Mr. Lee, Mr. Lee, Mr. Lee. I'm sick of hearing about him. You have forgotten what is most important in life."

"Which is?"

"Family. Mr. Lee does not love you like I do. He never will. He's a Chinaman. You're not Chinese. You and I are family. You, me, Frank, Elvira, our friends back home. Right or wrong, you're the reason I came to Seattle, Juanita. I did it for you. I wanted to give us a better life, a better future."

"You're crying! Please, stop it. You're frightening me."

He hadn't realized it, but yes, so he was. He went to her, stumbled in his haste to reach her, fell on his knees before her, his strangled words trapped in his throat.

"Of course I'm crying. Why don't you just take a crowbar to my head and beat me with it like you did to the man on the train? It would be less hurtful."

"That's why you hate me, isn't it, Daddy. Because of the crowbar."

"Is that what you think? That I hate you? You're wrong, Juanita. I love you more than anything. Don't you know that? Mr. Lee will never love you like I do. I love you more than my own life. I would go to prison or die for you if necessary."

"But you're always trying to get away from me. You didn't want to bring me to Seattle, and then you wouldn't take me with you to visit Uncle Frank in the hospital."

"He's not in a hospital, Juanita."

"He's not?

"He's in prison. I went to Walla Walla to see him in prison."

"What did he do to get sent there?"

"Nothing probably but they convicted him of bank robbery."

"But why did you lie and tell me he was in the hospital?"

"I shouldn't have. I don't know why I did."

"And I don't know why I said what I did to Mr. Lee. I knew it was wrong as soon I said it but I couldn't take it back."

"We can't change what is past, Juanita. I won't pretend what you did on the train hasn't come between us. We've both been hurt by it. But we can't let it turn us against one another. Now more than ever we have to be strong and stick together."

"All right, Daddy, but only because I want to. Not because you are telling me to. From now on I make my own decisions."

"Agreed, Juanita. Just don't stop loving me is all I ask."

Finally she rose from the chair and sank down next to him on the floor and hugged him. His heart was still hurting from her words, but it was his duty to be understanding and forgiving.

But he resented her attachment to Mr. Lee and his wife. Every afternoon she took tea and played chess or Chinese checkers with them. Now she had taken up eating dinner with them, with the result she had developed a fondness for Chinese food. She described it to him but it sounded to him like mostly rice or noodles, from what he understood. She went twirling through the hotel bowing to all and wearing that ridiculous Kimono and it galled him maybe more than it should.

They were behind in their rent. Mr. Lee had initially been charitable, but as weeks continued with only partial payments made toward their accumulating principal, it became impossible to overlook that the debt would likely never be paid in full, but only further accumulate. He walked the streets dutifully every day looking for work but there was nothing to be had other than the rare day job. Jack knew their benefactor's generous hospitality was becoming burdensome and their unpaid residency problematic for them all. Mr. Lee could no longer altogether conceal his diminished confidence in eventual payment of owed back rent so when the time came Jack had no choice but to accept the bad news he had long known was coming.

"I'm sorry," said Mr. Lee, "but you will have to leave. Today. I've rented your room to another party."

Mr. Lee abruptly turned his back and made a phone call. Jack waited for him to finish the call, which was in Chinese, but afterwards Mr. Lee motioned for him to be silent and shook his head no. There would be no further discussion.

He sold blood at the Seaman's Friend Hospital and received

five dollars and a glass of orange juice, a delicacy he savored. He'd never given blood before and didn't like needles but it was easy money and nothing to fear, as it turned out. But it was nowhere near enough to pay the rent.

"How often can I do this?" he asked. "Can I come back tomorrow?"

"No, no. Once a month."

Well hooray, thought Jack sarcastically. Steady work at last.

He splurged on a tin of Prince Albert tobacco and a lonely breakfast in a nameless diner where oatmeal was five cents plain, a dime with cream and sugar. Juanita was still taking lunches with the Lee family.

So now what were they going to do? Go home somehow? Cat Creek was as jobless as Seattle but at least they had some friends and family there and that was as good as money. But how was he supposed to get there? He wasn't about to hop another freight, not unless he could send Juanita first as a legitimate paying passenger. And how was he going to manage that? Meanwhile he was going to have tell her they were about to be evicted and it broke his heart. He finished his coffee and looked out the window at the tramps he was about to join and swallowed hard, knowing he would soon be one of them again. He paid up and left, ashamed and resolute.

Back at the hotel, he was astonished to see an adult version of his daughter, as if he had awakened after ten years to find she had become a young woman while he slept. She wore a knee length skirt and sweater, hiking boots, and an insouciantly slanted beret instead of the robe. Maybe the robe was just a passing phase she had grown out of. He hoped so. She smiled at him, her left shoulder raised in a manner suggestive of a question mark.

"Something wrong, Daddy?"

"Yes but I'll tell you when we get to our room, Juanita."

He glanced around their room, sad to know they were leaving it. He'd miss that bed, easily the best he'd ever slept in though both he and Juanita had been troubled with nightmares. No more hot bathes here either, after coming home soaked and chilled to the bone by the Seattle rain. He glanced to the electric hotplate on the counter that he'd used to warm their modest leftovers, or make tiger toast and sometimes eggs, donated by the Unemployed Citizen's League in exchange for carpentry work. He couldn't imagine a way to take the hotplate with them. It would be too cumbersome in his backpack. There was no food anyway. Just a jar of peanut butter mostly scraped out. But without the hotplate how would he be able to provide warm meals should the opportunity arise? There would be no way to heat a can of soup and forget about frying a couple of slices of bacon or an egg. He wasn't sure he would even be able to take their coffeepot.

"We have to pack, Juanita. We've been evicted for non-payment of rent."

"But I thought that was why we had left Cat Creek? Because we had been evicted from our house there."

"Well now we've been evicted here too."

"So where are we going to go?"

"I don't know yet."

"Well that's just perfect, isn't it? You say we have to leave and you don't even know where it is we are going. What next? I don't know how much longer I can live like this, Daddy. If not for Mr. Lee's rice and noodles, I'd starve. I'm hungry almost all the time, and I'm so sick of nothing but Washington apples I don't even want to look at one. I want some trout or venison or Elvira's fried chicken like at home. My stomach hurts from emptiness even when it's full of noodles. And it's raining outside. It's always raining outside."

"I'm sorry for it, Juanita."

"I know you are Dad, you're always sorry but your being sorry doesn't help; it doesn't change anything."

She rose from the bed, turned her back to him and released the window shade. It shot up quickly in a tight cylinder from the bottom of the window ledge to the top of the frame, ending with a sound like a slap across the face.

"Come here," she said from the window. "Look at this."

"What?"

He stepped to the window and looked out. Rainwater poured

down the window. Visibility was distorted and it sounded as if pebbles were being thrown against it.

"Are you telling me we are going out in that?"

"I'm telling you we can't stay here, Juanita."

"I want us to be together, Daddy, but not like this. Not homeless in the rain."

"I'll find us another place, Juanita. I sold some blood today and have some money. Not enough to stay here but we won't be homeless and we'll be together. "

"That's what I always thought I wanted, Dad, to be together, but not like this. I can't live like this."

"We have no choice, Juanita. Our room is rented."

"Maybe for you there isn't a choice, but for me there is. I'll stay on with the Lee's."

"They won't keep you, Juanita."

"Yes they will. I'm part of the family now. You'll see."

"Well meanwhile pack your belongings, Juanita. Don't take more than you can carry. Leave the rest."

Jack tugged at the stubbornly resistant bureau drawer, yanked it out and turned it upside down over the bed.

"Take only what we need and can fit in our packs. You have to choose."

She held a tight fitting sweater she knew he disapproved of and said, "I'm taking this."

Jack heard the defiance in her voice, as if daring him to object. She held a pair of boy's boxer underpants and said, "I'm ditching these. All of them. I'm not a boy and I'm not a tomboy anymore either. I need panties like other girls. And I'm taking my Chinese robe. It's the most important piece of clothing I own and is a precious gift from Mrs. Lee. Not that I'm going with you. I'm merely moving downstairs to the servant's quarters. I will be staying here with the Lee's. I'm part of the family now. Mr. Lee will get me in school like you should have."

Wearing their packs, they entered the lobby where men waited for an audience with Mr. Lee as usual, each man perfectly still and silent wearing neatly pressed black suits and white shirts, their backs straight and eyes fixed straight ahead on the wall as if watching a drama unfold there. Juanita dropped her pack, approached the desk clerk and said, "I want to see Mr. Lee."

"So do these men," said the clerk, nodding toward the seated visitors.

Mr. Lee came out from behind the door that separated the office from the servant quarters. He held the long slender pipe he sometimes smoked during their checkers games.

"Is it true, Mr. Lee? My father says we are being evicted."

Mr. Lee's expression was impassionate and his tone neutral as he said, "Yes, this is the unfortunate truth of the matter."

"I don't want to leave, Mr. Lee. I want to stay with you and Mrs. Lee until dad finds a job. I'd help in the kitchen and with cleaning or whatever you might need in return a small room with a bed in the servant quarters."

Mr. Lee glanced to Jack as if for assistance with a situation beyond his understanding, comfort zone, or past experience.

"I'm sorry, Juanita, but you belong with your father."

"But you said he wasn't doing right by me."

"I will not so much as discuss the possibility. Please leave the premises. Your room has been rented. This is not a place for a young girl and you do not belong here."

Juanita dropped to her knees and began furiously rummaging through her pack until she found what she was looking for. It was the robe. She yanked it out of the pack, rolled it up into a ball, and tossed it at Mr. Lee who stood staring at it where it lay crumpled on the floor like something she had just killed. She gave it a final kick and followed her father out the front door.

THE STREET

THEY HESITATED INDECISIVELY ON THE HOTEL landing, the wind in their faces and the overhead canopy snapping violently. The rain came down hard as they descended the steps and began walking away from the hotel, their cumbersome waterlogged backpacks becoming immediately soaked and made heavier with rainwater. They were hiking down the steep hill toward the Skid Row waterfront. The wind blew rain in their wet faces as they stumbled ahead uncertainly, sloshing through puddles, their wet socks slipping inside their boots.

Jack thought it hardly seemed possible, but the rain came pouring down even more forcefully and they were not so much walking as wading through an ankle deep stream. He and Juanita took high steps but their shoes and pants cuffs were already sopping wet. Jack heard thunder, then saw the first of several jagged lightning bolts. Not a single pedestrian was to be seen on the streets around them.

"We've got to find shelter," he said.

He led them to a covered trolley stop where they sat miserably on a bench and waited for the rain to subside. Jack wanted to smoke but his tobacco and cigarette papers were saturated. They didn't have so much as a destination in mind.

When a trolley pulled to the stop Juanita rose to board but Jack did not.

"Let's get on, Daddy. I want to get out of this rain."

"I'm sorry Juanita, but we can't afford it."

"We don't even have money for trolley fare?"

"We do, but not to merely get out of the rain. We don't have money to squander on anything we can't absolutely do without."

Automobiles sloshed through the flooded streets. The trolley conductor pulled out into traffic without them, cars splashing dirty cold puddle water over the curb and on their feet and ankles. The two of them sat quietly while the rain continued. Jack figured it couldn't go on raining this way much longer. They'd wait it out in the trolley alcove together until it stopped.

Neither of them spoke until finally Jack said, "I'm worried that you think your locket might have been left on the train."

"It's worse than that. That man had his hands around my neck. I remember the chain was hurting me and then it didn't anymore. It's possible the chain broke and the locket came off. I think the man who was choking me might have had it in his fist."

Jack remembered wanting only to be rid of the man's mutilated face where he didn't have to look at it, the man's corpse disposed of as soon as possible. He hadn't thought to search the man's pockets or fists.

On the other hand if the locket was found on the dead man's person it didn't necessarily follow that the owner of the locket was a murder. He could say he had pawned the locket for needed cash. That it was stolen. No, no, none of this would work. They were going to be caught, go to prison. Did Washington State have the death penalty? How were the executions carried out? Firing squad? Hanging?

"Where are we going next, Papa?"

He had no idea. The way their luck was going, probably to prison.

They wandered down to Pioneer Square where men gave tips regarding cheap transient hotels where they might rent by the night. They ended up in a Skid Row rectangular room with dirty windows and three dozen cots occupied by a transient population of some twenty or thirty men, many of whom did not believe Jack and Juanita were father and daughter.

The clerk stared quizzically at Juanita and said, "Indian girl?"

"Italian," said Jack.

They shared a mattress in a small area separated from others by chicken wire. Men made comments like, "Got yourself a piece of that Indian tail there, Jack? Some of that wild red meat?"

"She's Italian and I'm her father," he replied.

"Sure, Jack, sure."

She told him there were men present who when they looked at her made her uncomfortable, and men whose eyes made her afraid. Jack told her to keep away from all men but warned her about one in particular. They stayed there five days.

Their mornings were taken with hunting redeemable scrap and standing in food lines. They slept in the missions along Skid Row but as non-residents of the State of Washington, Jack was told they were not eligible for state assistance. Some took pity on them and bent the rules, but there weren't enough Missions to accommodate everyone in need. Sometimes they were willing to take Juanita but not Jack. Always the relief agencies gave the same advice.

"Take your daughter back to her family in Montana," they said.

"Do it," said Juanita. "Please. I'd gladly be eating cornmeal hush puppies with Aunt Vi back on the reservation. Anything is better than hunting through dumpsters for food and walking the streets begging missions for a place to sleep for a night. I can't keep on like this. I'm hungry all the time. I never seem to dry out from this rain. I'm frightened."

He'd happily take his daughter home to Cat Creek even if he had to hop a freight to do it but he had no money for supplies and the word on the street was that railyard no trespassing policy enforcement had tightened. Yard dicks were said to have become mean as junkyard dogs. Both Jack and Juanita were living on apples and not much else.

They spent long afternoons seeking shelter from the rain in the Public Library.

"Surrounded by all these books I can't read," said Juanita.

"It's my fault," said Jack. "I should have made sure you did your homework, punished you for skipping school and made you go when you faked being sick."

"It wasn't your fault, Dad. Don't blame yourself. I had an opportunity to learn and instead I just wasted it. Sure the teachers were mean and the school was like a jail cell, but I should have done it. Other kids did and I should have too."

Following a rumor of work, he walked hours in the rain to the Bethlehem Steel Plant in West Seattle only to find hundreds of other destitute wet men already in line. Not today, try tomorrow. He looked for work in shipyards, lumber mills and canning factories, at the loading platforms at the Pike Place Public Market, in skid row kitchens and the Saint Vincent de Paul.

Day labor jobs were scarce and you had to be in the right place at the right time to have a chance at getting one. Men gathered behind the gates of warehouses and manufacturing plants, hoping to be chosen. When picked for a day job he was grateful, knowing he was taking a day's wage from another man who needed it just as much as he did but his work, when he was lucky enough to get any, always was in an unskilled capacity. If only he could get a chance to finally show his skills, which included carpentry, plumbing, electrical, automotive. He could make running a railroad forklift look like a kid riding a tricycle, cut tight interloping figure eights with a tractor, juggle chainsaws like a sideshow carnival performer, knew how to rig dynamite to safely detonate explosives, how to rebuild automobile and truck engines, logging, ranching, lumberjacking, he'd done it all. But no one needed these skills. There was nowhere to apply them.

Three days a week he checked in at *The Unemployed Citizen's League*. Both Mr. Blenman and Waterson were long gone. It seemed whenever he came in the office was staffed by different persons. Dropping the name Frank Vogel no longer helped. Maybe when you went to prison, people eventually forgot about you. He wondered who might visit him if he got sent to prison. Maybe Elvira. Frank was already there and Juanita would probably be locked away somewhere in a prison cell too. Then again, maybe he wouldn't get a prison sentence at all but instead an execution date. They'd take him out in the yard and put the rope around his neck and let him drop. Photographers would take pictures. Heirlooms for a future family album. Some future. Some Family. Frank the bank robber and Jack and Juanita the murderers. He took a number and a seat in a folding metal chair and waited to be called. He might have dozed.

A man behind him said, "They're calling your number."

He took the vacant chair at the staff worker's desk. A rectangular plaque on his desk identified the man as Phillip Clarkston. Jack repeated what he had said many times before in this office.

"My brother is Frank Vogel. If the name means nothing to you, it should. He used to work with you guys back when it was a lot more dangerous than it is now. Anyway, I need to get my daughter out of Seattle. I'd like to leave too. My daughter and I want to go home to Cat Creek, Montana."

"I don't see how we can help you with that, Mr. Vogel."

"Call me Jack. The League got me to Walla Walla once before, to see my brother."

"I'm glad to hear that, Jack, but Montana? It's unlikely. We don't have anyone heading East to Montana, Idaho, or even much to Eastern Washington right now. Icy snow covered roads and all. Too cold for at least three more months. But you never know, Jack. Keep in touch. Keep us updated on how to reach you."

"You people have said this just about every time I've come in."

"Sorry. Not much else we can do. The daughter you mention. How old is she?

"She's sixteen," lied Jack. He wasn't sure why he lied. It seemed ever since the killing anyone even slightly resembling an authority figure was threatening to him.

"Then we might have something after all."

"Whatever it is, I'll take it."

"The job isn't for you, Mr. Vogel. Earlier this morning a woman contacted the office for a live-in domestic help with cooking, shopping and cleaning. We here at the League know this woman and her husband and they are fine people of impeccable reputation. Your daughter would have her own room and I can assure you that she would be treated fairly. Payment would consist of free meals and a weekly cash stipend. What's your daughter's name?"

"Juanita Rose Vogel. She's Italian on her mother's side."

"Do you think she might have an interest in something like this?"

Jack would have liked to be able to truthfully say no, she would not. That she would rather stay with him. Rather be homeless and hungry than separated from him. Once he might have been able to truthfully say this, but no more.

"I'd like this opportunity for her," said Jack.

"She would have to be clean, Mr. Vogel. She can't look like a runaway or a delinquent if you get my meaning."

"We haven't had washing facilities."

"Do you have money to pay for a shower at the YWCA? "

"I don't have any money at all, Mr. Clarkston."

"We will advance you a YWCA voucher. It's important to make a good first impression. Remember, there's nothing final. This is a trial posting. The house is on Palentine Avenue and is under the supervision of a Mrs. Cora McCabe who will board your daughter for a week and then make a decision."

Clarkston removed a notebook from his desk drawer and wrote an address in blue ink from a fountain pen.

"I'll contact Mrs. McCabe and let her know you are coming. It's best you take her there and introduce her personally. I don't want the McCabe's to think she has been on her own. Having a father gives her an advantage."

"Not in her case it doesn't."

"Well of course it does, Jack. A girl needs her father. I'll give you trolley tickets. You will need to take the Phinney trolley, get off at the second Woodlawn Park stop and walk down the hill to Palentine Avenue from there."

They rode the Phinney Way trolley early the next morning, Juanita showered and in clean clothes. Jack knew he was dirty and smelled bad and was ashamed. The conductor called the Woodland Park stop and they stepped off into a fog so dense they could not see their feet when walking through it. Jack compared the written address he carried with street signs as they trudged down the hill and found a sign for Palentine Avenue.

They found the McCabe house easily. Moss squished under their shoes as they ascended the steep walkway. Jack felt his weakened legs give. He hung to the iron railing before proceeding. When they reached the massive front porch he struck the lion-faced brass knocker on the immense wooden door. Hungry and tired as he may have been, he still managed to feel a thrill of vicarious happiness for his daughter. Showered and scrubbed clean, she looked much like a younger version of Alma, minus the hair of course. She was modestly dressed in a black skirt and white blouse and carried a large bag with her clothing. She had Alma's features, Alma's coloring.

"There'll be *food* in there," he promised. "Rich people's food. And they will pay you, Juanita. You can save your money and get a train ticket back to Cat Creek if that's what you want. But remember this. Don't ever mention anything that might tie us to that train. And don't go telling these people you are Crow. If they ask say you are Italian or if you don't like that, tell them you are from France or Spain or something. No, not Spain, they might think you are Mexican. Stick with Italian. That's not as good as British or Scottish, but you can't pass and Italian is better than Indian for sure. And be sure to use your middle name, Rose. That sounds more Italian than Juanita."

She clutched his sleeve with what seemed to him like the grasp of a drowning person.

"But what about you, Daddy? When will I see you? How will we find each other?"

"I'll be checking in with you regularly. Don't worry, you'll see. This will be an improvement over the way we are living now, Juanita."

An old woman wearing a beautiful crown of braided silver hair opened the door. He gave Juanita an encouraging little nudge toward her.

"This here is my daughter Rose. I give you my word she will work hard won't give you any trouble at all."

Lea Macquarrie

It began to rain but it was more like a sprinkle of mist. Morning fog remained dense and wet. He wiped some wet hair from his face. He would not cry, but he was having difficulty talking and could not say goodbye. He felt as if he might be choking. He was already backing down the stairs. The fog closed around him and absorbed him as if swallowing him. By the time he had descended to the bottom of the stairs it had enveloped him and when he looked up the stairwell it occurred to him that probably only his disembodied face was visible to his daughter in the fog. And then he felt nothing because he knew he was gone from everyone who knew him.

PALENTINE AVENUE

"DON'T JUST STAND THERE IN THE DAMP now, dear. Come in child. Come, come ..."

She wore mismatched shoes with a dress that looked as if it had been slept in. One of her nylon stockings had fallen to her ankle. Magazines, newspapers, unopened mail and accumulated debris obstructed their passage as the old woman led her down a wide hallway smelling of mold. Observing the woman's pronounced limp, Juanita saw that one of her shoes was a high heel and the other was not. She kicked both shoes off along the way. Dust motes drifted along the ceiling. Tiny microscopic particles of dust rose to her nostrils with each footstep. Juanita stifled a sneeze. The woman led her into the kitchen, a battlefield of scorched pots, blackened saucepans, and encrusted frying pans. Bags of flour, sugar, salt, and cornmeal seemed to have exploded over counters. Canned goods were strewn everywhere.

Juanita didn't know whether to be horrified or sympathetic. She touched the surface of the stove and her finger came back greasy. The woman needed help, that was for certain.

She swooned at the sight of the enormous refrigerator and imagined it to be laden with milk, peanut butter, ice cream, sausages, whatever one might want. The mere thought of it made her want to rush the refrigerator and hug it like a beloved family dog that had been lost and recovered.

Mrs. McCabe nodded toward a stool behind a counter and said, "Please dear, have a seat. I'll make us some tea."

The woman poured water in a blackened old kettle similar to the ones she had seen on the reservation at home and put it on the stove. Unlike the kettle, the teapot itself was an object of delicate Asian beauty much like one Mrs. Lee had.

"My name is Cora. You probably already know that. Walter McCabe, my grumpy husband, is mercifully away on business in San Francisco. He'll be home in a few days. He's a grumpy old man who likes to pretend he is the master of the house. He is not, but I allow him to think so."

The woman began putting herbs in the teapot. The water boiled on and on without her notice.

"What is your name again? Rose?"

"My Dad calls me that sometimes, but my birth name is Juanita Rose Vogel."

"Juanita. I like that. It's a pretty name for a pretty girl."

"It's Italian."

"Do you know how to cook, Juanita?"

"I cooked for my older brothers, father and Uncle from a very young age. My father says I am as good as anyone."

"Well, even if you are only adequate you would be far better than I. As you can see, I've let things go in this big old house. Somewhere over time I could no longer keep up with it, and by now I have just plain given up."

She half listened to the woman, her attention drawn to the tall white humming refrigerator. She imagined containers of cold milk, wedges of sharp cheese, pie. The tea kettle was whistling like mad on the stove. Didn't the old woman hear it? Apparently not.

She hurried to the stove and removed the woman's kettle and saw that the water had boiled away. She ran fresh water in it, carefully pouring water into the empty, hot pot. The pot hissed and steamed with the fresh water and steam. The odor of faintly burnt metal rushed to her nostrils. She felt the heat on her face, wiped her brow and swirled the water around a couple of times to get burn odor out, dumped the water from the kettle and refilled it. She returned it to the burner and said, "I can cook, clean, run errands, whatever is needed, Mrs. McCabe."

"Please. Call me Cora."

She poured them both teas. Juanita held the cup under her nostrils; its scent was of peppermint, spearmint, orange rind and cinnamon. She sipped it slowly and found it delicious but it seemed to awaken her hunger even more than before.

"What can you tell me about yourself, Juanita?"

"I'm from Cat Creek. It's just me and my dad. My mother is dead, my brothers are gone, and my Uncle is in the hospital. I'm hungry, Mrs. McCabe. I've had apples to eat and not much else for three days now."

* * *

McCabe returned from the King Street train station to his office on Pier 91 after five days of union negotiations with the Sailor's Union of the Pacific headquartered in San Francisco. He made coffee on the office hot plate, opened a drawer from the locked metal filing cabinet adjacent to his desk, pulled out his new fifth of Jim Beam and poured a generous amount into a water glass.

Prohibition be damned. An idiotic punitive law which never should have been passed. Damn suffrage was the cause of it. See, this was why women never should never have been given the vote. Rain pounded and rattled the windows as he stood staring down at the poor drenched homeless in the Hooverville shantytown along the docks below.

These men were camped in a sea of mud. Cardboard roofs were buckling and folding, privacy and shelter blankets becoming so heavily weighted with rainwater they were collapsing. Men were fighting the wind to get them back up. It was bad enough in relatively good weather, miserable in the rain. And there was no rain like Seattle rain; it went on and on; there was no relief. The dampness seeped into one's bones. If ever on this godforsaken earth there existed a group of men who needed a drink more than these he couldn't imagine who they might be. Damn nuisance temperance women. Their hearts were colder than the bone-chilling depths of

Puget Sound. They wouldn't so much as give a man the relief of a drink to warm his belly and his spirits. But soon implementation of the recently passed Volstead Act would end the oppressive 18th Amendment and prohibition and that was good news, though probably not for Mike Drake, Bobby Stone and others who had profited from it.

He took a swallow of Jim Beam and telephoned Cora.

She answered on the third ring and said, "If this is Mr. Walter McCabe calling, I'm angry with him and refusing his calls."

"And what may I ask might be your complaint with the gentleman?"

"Need I mention his drinking, his stinky old cigars, his reckless driving and abominable piano playing?"

"You needn't, yet do so not infrequently."

"I have a surprise waiting for you, Walter."

"You do? Oh my. Well. What is it?"

"If I told you it wouldn't be a surprise, would it?"

"No, I suppose not."

He was slightly worried; surprises from Cora were often not in his best interest. He heard footsteps on the other end of the line, then nothing. Damn, she was always doing that. Walking with the phone until the cord pulled out of the wall and then wondering what had gone wrong. He just hoped she wouldn't call the phone company for yet another expensive unnecessary service call and "repair".

"Goodbye, dear."

No one answered. She had indeed wandered off somewhere.

He hung up gently and sat at his desk behind a pile of paperwork, much of it bills of lading for the next voyage of the SS McCabe, which could not sail until repairs were completed and then he would need more cargo to warrant a profitable run. Meanwhile there were rumors of a strike when the Union contract expired. He poured more coffee but it was too strong, black and muddy. He repaired it with whiskey. The telephone on his desk rang, and he stared at it until it stopped. He opened the newspaper. Overseas there was trouble in Germany with a political movement that referred to itself as the Nazi Party, which smelled rotten like fascism. Damn Germans. You were a fool to trust them. Hadn't World War One taught the bigshots in Washington anything?

The phone began ringing again.

Frowning, he answered gruffly.

"McCabe shipping here."

"Is this McCabe shipping?"

"I just said that.

"Am I speaking to Mr. McCabe himself, or an associate?"

"I have no associate. Who the hell is this, what do you want and why shouldn't I hang up right now?"

"I am with the accounting department of the Frederick and Nelson department store, Mr. McCabe. Your business has always been and continues to be important to us. I want you to understand that."

"Fine. Goodbye."

"Please. Don't hang up. It's about your wife and our mutual agreement regarding her continued patronage."

"What about it,' McCabe harrumphed. "I presume the so-called *patronage* and mutual agreement you mention refers to her alleged shoplifting."

A year earlier he had revoked her line of credit with the Frederick and Nelson department store because the woman was buying so much art there was no place left in the house to store it. Cora, confused, when taking items to the checkout counter and informed her credit account had been cancelled, presumed it a mistake in store accounting. Later she began taking items without paying. McCabe was discreetly notified and it was agreed Frederick and Nelson would keep an accurate accounting of her thefts and bill him for property not promptly returned. By agreement items were billed as purchased merchandise, not as reparations for theft.

"This call regards delinquent payments, Mr. McCabe. It has been two months since a payment was made."

"I wasn't aware anything was even owed. Can't very well pay a debt if I don't know what it is. Send me a damn bill."

"But that's why I'm calling, sir. Our accounting department

has been sending itemized bills without even so much as an acknowledgement from you."

"Answer me this, Mr. Perkins. When was my wife last in your store?"

"It's been several months, actually."

Well, that was good news at least. Cora didn't drive but sometimes took the trolley, as often as not the wrong one, getting lost and having to call his office for help.

"You need to bill my office, not the house. And I want to be notified immediately of thefts not weeks after the fact."

"But we often don't witness the thefts, Mr. McCabe. Our house detective is instructed to monitor Mrs. McCabe and staff is to inventory merchandise after her departure and report what is unaccountably missing."

"Well then it seems you have a staff problem. Obviously one or more of them is stealing and putting the blame on my wife."

He hung up abruptly. He leaned back in the chair behind his desk, lighted a cigar and took the phone off the hook. Cora wouldn't remember the so called theft if indeed there had even been one, which he doubted because Cora could no longer find her way downtown on her own. Seattle taxi cab companies no longer complied with her telephoned requests to their Palentine Avenue address because of her history of forgetting she had called and failing to answer the door upon the driver's arrival.

No, he would go home and play the piano, his great love after Cora, though it was generally agreed among all who knew him he was probably the worst pianist on the planet, a critical assessment which, because of its indisputable accuracy, he unfortunately could not refute. But he loved the piano, played nightly at home and sometimes at parties. The response was always the same: please stop. He would not. He played to his critics in defiant, vengeful reprisal.

He took a drink straight from the bottle, no coffee this time, unplugged the hot plate and coffee pot and went for his raincoat hung to dry along with the umbrella on the clothes tree near the radiator. He buttoned the raincoat to the throat, locked up and took the aluminum stairs to his Hudson in its reserved parking place below. He inserted his key in the ignition, revved the engine and began backing out but some damn fool had unexpectedly parked a forklift behind him. He could hear his back fender crinkle with the impact. He'd examine it later. Cursing softly, he drove to the chain link fence and watchman's shack where he was waved on through.

Watchmen had been recently employed because of squatters sleeping on the docks. He was in favor of letting the squatters stay. What did it hurt? But his insurance company advised strongly against it and they were right of course. Wouldn't do to have one of them get drunk and fall off the pier and drown. Damn ambulance-chasing lawyers would love a case like that.

He no longer allowed the *Unemployed Citizen League* to use Pier 91 as a staging operation either. He'd dropped his association with them, though he still supported their cause. But it was best to disassociate himself. He wasn't afraid of confronting Robert Stone and Mike Drake if it came to it, but it was foolish to needlessly agitate them.

A group of shivering, destitute men huddled over a fire burning in a large blackened barrel. Their soot-blackened faces and haunted eyes implored him, but none actively solicited him for a handout. Many of these homeless unemployed men along the waterfront had their pride and refused to panhandle. They wanted jobs, not handouts. Of course, there were those who had given up. Men who begged for money for food and then spent it on rotgut booze.

Speaking of which. He opened the glove compartment and took a drink from a pint bottle of smuggled Canadian Club, drove on and parked on Palentine Avenue and sat behind the wheel without getting out. His three story monster loomed on the hill as if it was about to devour its neighbors. The paint was flaking so badly it looked like it had eczema, the windows needed repair, the chimney needed cleaning, the porch steps were a mess of leaves, the iron railing was wobbly and the doorbell inconsistent. Who would guess it was a house filled with exotic, valuable treasures? Even he didn't know what all he had in there. Persian rugs, vases from the Orient, frescoes taken from buildings in Italy, rare original paintings from Spain and Portugal. Cora's idea at one time had been to open a little shop selling imported arts and crafts, but she had just filled the house with his imports and forgotten about them.

Well he was procrastinating, wasn't he? He could abide the disrepair and neglect of his crumbling estate but the main trouble with his house on the hill was all those damn steps to get to it. No wonder Cora wasn't getting out much anymore. She needed a cane to get around nowadays, and rarely climbed the stairs to the third floor. Come to think of it neither did he, and he was afraid he'd buried be in an avalanche if he dared to investigate the attic. He took another drink from the bottle, put it away in the glove compartment, got out and locked up.

He hesitated at the foot of the granite and cobblestone stairs leading to the porch, staring up the winding, perilous steps while cautiously preparing himself for the slippery leaves underfoot. But leaves were absent. The wind might have swept them away but it had been raining most of the day, which normally pasted leaves to the steps. It was puzzling. There was only one explanation. Somebody must have cleared them. Maybe some tramp asking if there was any work he might do in exchange for a meal, which certainly wasn't uncommon. Cora rarely refused them, but almost never answered the door when he was not home.

He paused at the top of the steps, glancing at his Hudson below, which he could see now from the vantage point of height had been erratically parked. To descend those steps, repark the Hudson and then face those stairs yet again was not even a consideration. He fumbled for his keys and opened the front door. The foyer and hall rushed to him like a pet dog, its familiar odiferous confluence of dust and mold comingled with and largely replaced by an uncharacteristic scent of incense and scented candles that embraced him like an unfavored aunt wearing too much perfume. This was something new and it made his eyes water. The hall was clear, without so much as a single envelope littering the vestibule. Someone had swept and dusted. His usual reflexive impulse to sneeze upon entry was absent. The usual cloud of black smoke drifting down the hall from the kitchen had been replaced with a tantalizing aroma of something cooking on the stove.

A pretty young female at the kitchen stove was stirring something in a pot he couldn't see but which smelled delicious. The girl was young, with choppy raven black hair and a slim figure. She looked like some kind of foreigner. Maybe Indian.

Or something anyway.

Not white.

She bowed slightly. Cora sat at the kitchen table with two cigarettes smoldering in an ashtray, another in her hand and God only knew how many more burning a hole in a tablecloth or charring a windowsill elsewhere.

What's going on here," he inquired. "Who are you, young lady, and what are you doing here?"

"I'm preparing a pot roast for your dinner, sir. My name is Juanita Vogel. I'm pleased to meet you and I'm Italian."

Yeah, and I'm the King of Scotland, thought McCabe.

"Cora, come with me into the parlor please", said McCabe. "I believe we have something to discuss."

He watched her reach for one of the three cigarettes smoldering improperly extinguished in her ashtray. All three were wet at the ends with lipstick. She started to light another but he took it from her. Sometimes he wondered why she bothered with the cigarettes at all. She never finished them; they usually just burned out. She rose, grasped her cane and followed him down to the parlor. He passed the music room, where his grand Baldwin piano shone under the chandelier. Which of course was where he would like to be but first there was this important matter to clear up.

"Who is this woman and what is she doing in my house?"

"She told you who she was. Her name is Juanita and she is Italian."

Cora pronounced it Eye-talian.

"She is most certainly not Italian, Cora. I don't know what she is but she's not Italian. The point is, what is she doing here?"

"She lives here. She's going to be our housekeeper and cook. Don't you remember? We discussed this."

"I remember discussing it but not giving consent. I said we would discuss the matter further."

"Well, I don't remember it that way. Anyway, she is here and she is wonderful. You will love her, Walter. She's such a nice girl. So polite and helpful. Haven't you noticed how clean and uncluttered everything is? You know I have always wanted female company. Now I have it."

"Well she will mostly certainly have to go. I don't want a stranger prowling around our house and I don't think she is even white. Surely you remember why we fired the last maid. She was robbing us blind, stealing our silver and your jewelry and drinking my liquor, I'm sorry my dear, but tomorrow the girl goes."

He kissed her on her powdered cheek, turned away from her and went into the music room, where his grand piano waited under the crystal chandelier. Rain pounded the bay windows, giving a distorted view of the choppy waters of Ballard Bay and Puget Sound. He opened the piano and realized it was dust free. It gleamed under the lighting of the chandelier. He ran his finger smoothly across its surface. Someone – no doubt that girl – Juanita – had cleaned and waxed the surface. He opened the piano bench, also smoothly waxed, and reached under the Rachmaninoff score for his bottle. He held it to the light, to see if any was missing. It appeared to be as he had left it.

He took a drink and considered. He was not in a classical mood. He was in the mood for show tunes. Something he could sing along with. He rifled through some sheet music and found *You Are My Sunshine*.

Perfect.

In the kitchen, Juanita, startled, almost dropped a platter.

"What's that?"

"*That*," replied Cora, "is my husband singing and pounding on the piano."

LOST IN SEATTLE

OBSTACLES MATERIALIZED ABRUPTLY within the mist too late to be avoided. Jack tripped over curbs and walked into trees or into parked automobiles in residential driveways. He could no longer remember when he had last eaten. His stomach growled as he stumbled along without purpose or destination. He staggered into what gradually revealed itself to be a residential neighborhood. In patches where the fog and mist cleared he saw wooden picket fences enclosing yards with quenched dewy bushes and pulsating satiated flowers. People were eating in these houses. They had pantries, refrigerators. He had nothing, not even a few loose flakes of tobacco in his pockets.

A large glittering piece of orange rind winked seductively from a front porch step. The gate was locked, the chain link fence about five feet high. He tried to get the tip of his shoes into the chain link to climb but his shoe would not fit. He grasped the fence with both hands. The wire dug into his hands as he crested, gouging his stomach when he tumbled headfirst onto the front lawn. The orange rind glittered invitingly on the front porch. He would chew and suck it for its last morsel of nutrient. He frog-walked the way Frank had showed him they had done in the war, crouching low and stealthily up the porch steps. The orange rind turned out to be just a piece of broken orange glass. Alma always did say God was a practical joker.

He limped along the side of the house, then crawled on his

hands and knees under the windows to the back of the house where there was a garage and a garbage can beside it. But little of value was found in garbage cans these days. No one wasted in this economy. A man couldn't even scavenge. He lifted the garbage can lid and began rooting around for something edible. He found some damp coffee grounds and eggshells beneath a heap of wet newspapers.

He scooped the loose wet coffee grounds out of the garbage can with the eggshells. The coffee grounds speckled his teeth and tasted slightly bitter. The eggshells pierced his sore gums. He had to chew for longer than was comfortable to pulverize and swallow them. The coffee grounds stuck to the inside of his mouth and throat like they had been pasted there. He coughed repeatedly and spat. He drank deeply from a garden hose attached to a spigot by the garage.

The egg shells were disagreeable and made him spit. He remembered Elvira's eggs, farm fresh from her chickens. You could have them for breakfast, lunch or dinner, sunny side up, over easy, scrambled or in an omelet filled with vegetables, ham and cheese. You could make pancakes with eggs, French toast, griddle cakes, patties. He remembered slippery fried eggs on a platter greasy with bacon, fried potatoes and buttered wheat toast and jam. Elvira often cooked him eggs back home, fresh ones from her coop, sometimes scrambled with bits of pork and onion and green pepper. There had been plenty of eggs in Montana.

Evicted or not he should have stayed there. Elvira would have taken them in. He could have had chickens, set traps, kept rabbits, hunted. Shot geese out the sky and cooked them slow on a spit over an open fire. There was no reason to go hungry living in the country. Not like here in the city. Here he was unable to rely on his country skills. Cities turned otherwise resourceful men into garbage eating scavengers. He had heard once that starving children in faraway nations ate the bark off of trees. Some here in this country were said to eat their shoes. He could understand that. He looked down at his own as he staggered away, considering.

He had been walking for hours. It felt like years. Like a lifetime. He sloshed in his thoroughly soaked shoes with nowhere to go. It was dusk. His wet clothing clung to him; cold rainwater dripped down the back of his neck. He pulled his wet coat tightly around him and clung to it. Streetlights came on but it was still light. He stumbled weak and demoralized, on the verge of giving up, his wet heavy clothing clinging to him as if trying to pull him down. Too late he realized he was staggering into the street. He felt the impact first and then the sensation of being airborne. The driver of the Buick that had hit him slammed on his brakes and ran back to him.

The man kneeled over him and said, "I'm sorry, Mister, but you walked right into me. I tried to stop but it's slippery and there wasn't time. Are you hurt?"

"I'm fine," said Jack. "Entirely my fault."

"Are you sure?"

"Yes. Go in peace. I'm not hurt."

"Do you need help getting up?"

"I don't want to get up. I'll just rest here awhile."

"I'm going to find a phone, Mister. I'm going to call an ambulance."

He managed to crawl to a curb and sat with his feet in the cool water as if he might be fishing in the creek at home. His head throbbed and ears rang loudly. He felt the rain on his face and rain flowing in the gutter over his shoes. It would be dark soon. He couldn't stay here and would have to find a safe place to sleep. He pulled himself upright and continued walking but he didn't know where he was or where he was going. He hoped to get lucky and somehow find shelter.

Angry automobile horns cursed him as he staggered from the sidewalks into the road. He wiped the rain from his face and hair and his hand came back tinted with blood. He fell to his knees on the wet pavement. It was too much effort to stand. He crawled onto the grassy front yard of a private residence and sprawled in the wet lawn beneath a tree. Through the windows he saw a family eating dinner. He imagined himself at the table among them, clean and properly dressed in respectable clothing, with a shave and his hair combed, maybe smelling like Aqua Velva, that stuff in the gold bot-

Lea Macquarrie

tle with the white label Frank used to slap on his face after shaving. He tried it once; it stung his face and smelled like an old woman.

He looked up to the sky. The rain came down and splattered his face. It was like God was pissing on him. But God was not up there. He remembered going to church as boy. He had given it up as a man. Never as a boy had his prayers been answered. His pastors had turned out to be phonies. He let the rainwater collect in his mouth and swallowed it. He could not raise himself from the ground. He tried but kept falling to his knees.

He sprawled beneath the shelter of a tree and looked up into the canopy of dripping leaves, wet and iridescent with dappled light. Squirrels foraged in the trembling limbs. Back in Montana, he might have hunted one of these critters, shot it dead and skinned it with his knife, gutted it and cooked it over an open fire. A gust of wind shook the limbs and revealed, in the dewy shimmering foliage, the most perfect pear he had ever seen, round and glistening with rainwater. If he could just eat that pear, he would be all right. His luck would change.

Hugging the tree, he struggled to pull himself up against its trunk, but slumped back to the ground. He couldn't manage it. He lay beneath the sheltering leaves and looked up at this magnificent pear, which was so perfect but out of his reach and it seemed to him, in his hunger and delirium, the perfect epitaph. Everything he had ever wanted, which when he considered it wasn't all that goddamned much, was out of his reach.

He sat on the wet ground, his back supported by the tree, and took off his boot. Stared at it a long time, resigned to its unappetizing inevitability. He took his knife from his pocket and cut the tongue from the left boot into four pieces. It looked like a piece of flank steak, maybe torn into strips the way the Mexicans did it working the railroad. His mouth salivated. He took an initial bite. It wouldn't masticate and some kind of nasty tasting goop formed in his mouth. It tasted like old socks. He spat it out and fought the urge to vomit.

He managed to pull himself up and stagger off. There was nothing further to do but walk until he dropped. He thought if he were to die here, it wouldn't matter. Not even to him. He no longer cared what happened to him.

PALENTINE AVENUE

JUANITA CARRIED STEAMING TRAYS of roast beef and mixed broiled vegetables from the kitchen to the McCabe dining room table. The table had four eaves and could have accommodated a dozen or more easily. She wondered how they ever got it up all those steps and into the house and dining room. It would take at least four strong men to move it. The chair backs and table legs were elaborately carved with accurate representations of eagles and salmon. She had no idea what they weighed but they were heavy and had been difficult to move when setting the table. Silver cutlery reflected the sparkling light of the chandelier and gleaming silver serving trays and a coffee urn she had polished earlier in which she now saw her own reflection. Removing a polished silver lid from a platter, a mound of succulent beef so moist it was falling apart in its juices was revealed. Additional platters contained portions of stovetop asparagus, shucked corn and steaming scalloped potatoes. There were dishes of warm homemade applesauce, chilled cranberries and warm rolls with butter, jam, and apple butter.

"Well, I must say," said McCabe, "this is quite a surprise. Excellent, young lady, excellent."

"Thank you, Mister McCabe."

"Call him Walter", she said to Juanita. "You're part of the family now."

"No no," objected her husband. "Mr. McCabe will do just fine."

She bowed her head and said, "If you won't need me further, I'll take my supper in the kitchen."

Cora took her firmly by the arm.

"You'll do no such thing," she announced. "You will take your dinner with the family." Juanita thought her remark seemed directed as much to her disapproving husband as to herself.

"We will ring if we have need of you," said Mr. McCabe.

"Juanita, I insist you set a place for yourself and sit down. I'm your employer and you are to follow my instructions, not his."

Juanita served them, took a seat at the table and briefly glanced up to see Mr. McCabe frowning at her disapprovingly. The aroma from the steaming platters made her mouth water, but she had been sampling what she had cooked and the edge was gone from her hunger. She wondered what her poor father might be eating. Probably more apples. McCabe cleared his throat and began giving a benediction.

"Lord, thank you for this beautiful table, blessed life and beautiful wife. We pray for those who are hungry and out of work. We pray for this country, which has gone to hell, and for honest men who at this very moment are going hungry through no fault of their own and we pray for the sick and poor less fortunate than we are. Bless this food, amen."

Silverware clattered. Juanita did not raise her bowed head. She did not unclasp her praying hands nor open her eyes or say amen. She made no move to take any of the food from the platters. The sight of this excess and the thought of her father going hungry sickened and shamed her. She stared at the food and felt bile rise to her throat. The steaming platters made her nauseous as she breathed. Cora served her portions of roast and potatoes but she made no move to partake of any of it, nor did she look up from her plate. Rain pattered on the dining room bay windows. There were white-caps on the sea. The peaks of the Olympic Mountain Range on the other side of Puget Sound were hidden by fog. She sat silently at the table, hands in her lap, head slightly bowed, her gaze averted from Mr. McCabe who seemed to be attentively watching everything she did with disapproval. It wasn't fair. Her father had his faults and failures, but he was certainly as good if not better than this grumpy old man staring at her disapprovingly from across the table as if she was a common thief.

McCabe suddenly slammed his fist on the table with a force that made the dishware rattle.

"Waste!" he shouted. He rose from his chair and glared at her accusingly. His face was red and his fists were clenched. The bulging veins on his face were as if on the verge of exploding. He shook his fist and said, "Waste is the great sin and criminal act of our time! People with food on their plates and roofs over their heads ought to be grateful for it. People out there today are hungry and cold. I've seen them starving. The whole country is going to ruin, and when there's food on the table young lady, you damn well better eat it because it doesn't necessarily follow there will be any tomorrow."

She dared to raise her face to him and meet his eyes defiantly.

"My father is homeless and penniless without food. He's in the rain somewhere without a place to sleep and I don't know where he is or if I will ever see him again. I'm grateful for what you are trying to do for me but I would rather be with an empty stomach with my daddy than with rich people's food I don't want."

"Damn!" shouted McCabe.

He slammed his fist down on the table, this time upsetting a tea cup with a residue of coffee that stained the white lace table-cloth. His voice was thunderous. "Damn this country!"

"I'll find him," he proclaimed. "I know everybody in this town. I'll find your father, and when I do I'll give him a job."

SKID ROW

MCCABE FIRED UP HIS HUDSON and drove off in the rain to search for Jack. He went to the Mission Juanita had directed him to but no one named Vogel was registered. There were so many men without homes, men sleeping on benches or doorways or just openly on wet cardboard out on the sidewalk. How would he know Jack Vogel from the others even if he came across him? He inquired at Skid Row missions and flop houses, drove around the back streets and alleys of Pioneer Square, inquired of the men lined up for food at the Millionaire's Club and walked around the wharves asking men if they knew where a homeless man might take shelter if not in a mission or flop house and whether they might know a Jack Vogel. The answer was always the same. They knew of a Frank Vogel but not Jack.

In the morning he would look again for Jack Vogel. He would try the Missions again, the food lines and alleys around the market, the docks and piers, the day labor pools and down in Hooverville. Maybe he would take the girl with him. But this was enough for tonight.

He stopped at Harry's Skid Row speakeasy for a couple of shots and a beer. The whiskey flavored gin was bootleg rotgut and though he had better in the Hudson's glove compartment he was depressed with what he had seen and felt a need to commiserate in male company. The speakeasy was protected by the Gustafson police force, but only because Harry paid a fee to remain in operation. McCabe was known and welcome here. He sat at the bar and bought a round for a few men he knew vaguely.

Harry poured him a shot and a beer while wiping the counter excessively and regarding him with his usual poker face ravaged with damage sustained during fights when he'd had to throw rowdy drunks out of his bar. Harry's nose had been broken so many times it resembled a lumpy potato. He and McCabe were old friends from the waterfront days, when Harry worked as a longshoreman before getting hurt. He walked with a limp now, after being struck in the legs with a loaded pallet. Harry was a man of few words, but a good listener and a good friend.

McCabe slid his empty beer glass across the bar and said, "Just pour the shot in the beer next time, Harry. This bootleg gin tastes like kerosene and needs to be diluted."

"Whatever you say, Mac."

Most people down here called him just Mac. It was not a matter of disrespect. Many of his friends didn't even know his first name or had forgotten it for lack of use. Cora was the only one who ever called him Walter.

"Something wrong, Mac?"

"Why do you ask?"

"I know you have better booze at home than here."

"Well there is plenty wrong. Young kids who should be in school are out looking for work or riding rails instead, working men in bread lines, lost fathers and daughters, crooked cops and politicians. Don't get me started, Harry. Right now I happen to be looking for a man name of Jack Vogel."

"Any relation to Frank Vogel?"

" Frank might be his brother. I'm going to look into it."

Harry went on wiping the bar.

McCabe extended his glass for another boilermaker and said, "The country is going to hell, Harry. Hoover and his cronies are taking the whole damn country down."

"I agree, Mac. And the city of Seattle is going down with it. Sheriff Gustafson is dirty and everybody knows it and our chickenshit mayor is nothing but a puppet for Bobby Stone and Mike Drake and the commission. By the way, you should know that you've gotten yourself on their shit list."

McCabe wiped some beer foam off his bushy moustache and said, "I'm as much of a threat to them as they are to me. I have evidence against them that could put them in jailbird suits for a long time."

He examined his pocket watch and said, "So what do I owe you, Harry?"

"Nothing but I'd think twice about Stone and Drake and those men with the Improvement Commission. You know what they did to Frank Vogel. Be careful you don't get moved from their shit list to their hit list."

SEAMAN'S FRIEND HOSPITAL

JACK OPENED HIS EYES TO LIGHT that shone so brilliantly his attempt to visually determine his location within it hurt his brain. Light enveloped him and was everywhere and he could not separate himself from it. He watched it become softer, gradually accommodated and began to discern, in this soft new light, that he was in a room with a window. The light was not coming from the window, however. It was coming from everywhere. Its source was the room itself. He did not like it. It smelled of disinfectant and urine. It contained a sharpness that pierced him. He figured he might be dead, except for this pain. Even with his eyes closed the pain leaked in. He had thought death was darkness, but it was light. He took a deep breath but the atmosphere was redolent of lye, iodine, and disinfectant. To shield himself both from the smell and the light he pulled the sheets up over his head.

But wait. Sheets? Was he in a bed? Yes, he was sure of it now. His head was resting on something soft, like a pillow. He put his left hand behind his head and confirmed the presence of one. So he was probably dead after all. Surprised he'd gone to heaven though. Something was attached to his penis. He explored with his fingers and felt a plastic tube attached to a condom. He opened his eyes again. The light was becoming easier to bear. A small rectangular window looked out to a parking lot. Across from him a bed was occupied by a bearded man in pajamas who was staring at him intently.

"Thought you might be dead," the man said.

"That makes two of us. Where am I?"

"You're in the Seaman's Friend Hospital. They brought you in last night, but I think they may have moved you from another section."

He was in a large rectangular ward with bandaged men in double rows of hospital beds. Nurses wearing white uniforms with pointed caps moved quietly from patient to patient.

"My name's Wilson. Jimmy Wilson. Yours?"

"Vogel. Jack Vogel."

"Well, you wouldn't be kin to one Frank Vogel now, would you?"

"He's my big brother. Do you know him?"

"I do if we are talking about the soapbox socialist with early ties to the Wobblies. A man known to love women and liquor, fighting and hard work. Hell, just about everybody in Seattle knows of Frank Vogel. Used to give soapbox speeches down in Pioneer Square. Recruited for unions, organized marches, walkouts, sit downs. Stirred up trouble wherever he went."

"That sounds like my brother all right."

"Your brother is kind of famous. Was in the papers more'n once."

"Then you know he was framed for a bank robbery he didn't do."

"Somebody had it in for him, that's for sure. Enough to hire hugs to work him over and for police to look the other way. But here's the thing. I knew your brother personally because we were kind of related. He was briefly married to my sister."

"Then we must be talking about a different Frank Vogel because that can't be. My brother was married to Elvira Vogel, my sister in law back home."

"Yeah. So we found out."

Jack saw that Wilson's color was not good; his face was pale, with unnatural hues of yellow and gray. The man was so thin it was difficult to see his outline under the bed sheets. The sheet was pulled all the way up to the man's neck and Jack had the impression he was talking with a disembodied head.

"Your brother was a bigamist."

"Well, Mr. Wilson, if that's true I'm sorry for it. My brother was an unscrupulous womanizer who drank too much and made trouble, no doubt about it. But I want you to know I'm not like him."

"Oh hell, Jack, I don't care. I don't think my sister much gave a damn either. After she was done throwing the pots and pans and every dish in the pantry at him they both had a good laugh. You'd have to know my sister Mary to understand. She's not a conventional woman."

Nurses were moving carts with food trays to bedsides. Jack received his eagerly, removing the tray cover to a bland serving of macaroni and cheese, a small dish of lukewarm watery spinach, two rolls with butter and a small carton of milk. The macaroni and cheese were odorless but the spinach smelled nourishing and he scoffed it down before moving on to the macaroni and cheese. He could not under the circumstances prevent himself from devouring it gluttonously, finishing almost in seconds. Afterwards he devoured the rolls and butter and milk with equal urgency.

Wilson in the next bed said, "Been awhile, huh?"

"Since I last ate? Yeah, I can't even remember."

He felt his headache diminishing.

"You'll get one more meal before they discharge you, which will probably be today. They don't keep indigents here any longer than they have to. Medically, you get the bare minimum and you're lucky to get it. They slap a Band-Aid on you and discharge you. I have no issues with these people though. They try to help. I ought to know. I used to work here. Had a job in the kitchen until your brother tried to unionize us. Then the administration found some scabs to replace us and we were all out of a job. "

"I'm sorry Mr. Wilson."

"Not your fault and call me Jimmy. Wasn't much of a job anyway. I ended up moving down to Hooverville. I could have stayed with my sister but hell, I'm too old to take a daily scolding about my uncouth bachelor ways from a nagging woman even if that woman does happen to love me and wants to take care of me. They mind their own business and leave you alone down in Hooverville and that's the way I like it. But understand me on this Jack; I have no quarrel with your brother. He's not the one holding the working man down"

But Jack had fallen back to sleep. Sometime later he became aware of someone calling his name and lightly tugging on his arm.

"Mr. Vogel?"

He opened his eyes to a pretty young brunette woman wearing a white nurse's uniform and cap. He thought he might be dreaming because the woman was so pretty and smelled so clean and her voice was so sweet.

"We think it might be time to remove your dressing."

"Dressing?"

Confused, his mind still not working correctly and hungry once again, he thought of roasted Thanksgiving turkey stuffed with cornmeal dressing, nuts, and wild mushrooms.

"I wasn't aware I had any. Where is it?"

"Your entire head is wrapped in bandages. Didn't you know?"

He did not. He raised the fingers of his left hand to his head and touched the bandages.

"I don't see evidence of new seepage, and it is safe to remove the bandages now. With your permission, of course."

"You're the doctor, who am I to argue?"

"Thank you but I'm not a doctor, sir. I'm a nurse."

"Same thing as far as I am concerned."

"Don't let the doctors hear you saying it. They would consider it an insult and might cut off an appendage in retribution."

She removed a small pair of scissors wrapped in paper.

"You're not going to cut me with those are you?"

"Of course not, Mister Vogel. They are for the removal of your bandages."

She inserted the scissors beneath them and began cutting, disposing the bandages in a trash bag. When finished she dropped the scissors into a container of fluid.

The nurse disconnected his IV line and said, "You were severely dehydrated, but no longer."

Soon after the nurse left a female social worker introducing herself as Madeline Christopher took a chair by his bedside. She carried a clipboard, wore glasses, and held a slender pen that looked expensive.

"You're not entirely well, but we can't keep you, Mr. Vogel. I'm sorry, because you would benefit from more treatment, but we have limited indigent beds and this one is needed for triage. It's my duty to mention that you shouldn't drink to excess Mr. Vogel. We see people in your circumstances come in all the time. I know it's hard out there. But getting drunk is no solution."

"I agree, Miss Christopher. I wasn't drunk. I don't drink and don't want to and don't have money to spend for it if I did. If I was staggering around and got myself hit by a car, it wasn't because I was drunk."

"If this is so then I apologize sincerely, Mr. Vogel. In any event you could have been killed. Witnesses reported that that the automobile that hit you didn't even stop. You were thrown several feet and hit your head on a passing car while in flight. You're lucky you weren't run over. You sustained a concussion, a cerebral hematoma, and were malnourished and severely dehydrated. You've been here for three days Mr. Vogel. The good news is the bleeding has stopped and there is no evidence of an infection. We'll have you discharged and out of here in no time. We have a change of clothing for you donated by the Salvation Army."

"Thank you, but where are the clothes I was wearing when I came in?"

"We incinerated them, Mister Vogel. They were soiled, bloody and unsalvageable."

"My daughter's address was in the pocket of my pants. How am I supposed to find her again? I have no idea where she is, where I took her."

"I'm sorry, Mr. Vogel. Admittance staff meticulously inspects and records patient's personal effects. You had nothing in your pockets. But don't worry. We supplied your closet with a donated pair of wool pants, a hat, shirt and sweater and some decent shoes. We estimated your size as best as we could. We did not destroy your boots and you will find them under your bed but I hardly think they would offer protection from the rain. The soles had significant holes in them."

"Don't let them keep them," interrupted Wilson. "You can fix them soles with some glue and Hoover leather."

"Use the shower and let the nurse know when you are ready to leave Mr. Vogel. We'll give you a last meal before discharge. Good luck."

When the social worker left, Jack turned to Wilson in the next bed and said, "What's Hoover leather?"

"Cardboard," said Wilson. "Same as I got in my shoes. It's free of charge and there's an unending supply."

"Well, at least that's something I can afford. About all I can afford. So what's your story, Wilson? How did you end up here?"

Wilson's tone dropped to a whisper. He stared vacantly ahead as if, thought Jack, he might perceive a presence others did not.

"By accident," answered Wilson. "I'm not exactly sure under what circumstances. They brought me in unconscious."

"Same as me," acknowledged Jack.

"They tell me I'm pretty sick. I could tell by the way they said it that it was bad. They're going to transfer me to the Swedish Hospital for a round of tests. I'll probably go home to my sister Mary. God knows she's been pestering me about it for a year now. Doesn't understand why I would prefer Hooverville to her nagging. But I'm told I'm going to need someone to look after me, so its home to Mary. What about you?"

Jack just shook his head.

"Your lack of an answer tells me all I need to know, Jack. Tell you what. You can have my shack in Hooverville. I'll write a note explaining. You give that note to Jesse James. No, not the outlaw Jesse James, but the mayor down there. He's one of the founders. You tell him I sent you, give him the note and let him know that you're Frank Vogel's kid brother. It ain't bad down there, Jack. You'll see. It's a far sight better than the street. People help each other out and you don't owe anything to anybody or have any obligations."

Two male orderlies came for Wilson and wheeled him out for purposes unknown. Jack, wearing his hospital Johnnie, staggered to the shower stall, turned on the hot water and remained under it a long time, working up lather with the bar of soap. It felt wonderful to be clean, and he felt somewhat rejuvenated. He shaved, careful when running the hospital-provided razor over his bruised left cheek. He brushed his teeth, rinsed his mouth, brushed them again. He combed his hair back the way he like it but wished he had some tonic oil. His hair tended to sprout like prairie scrub when clean and dry. The donated clothing fit no worse than what he wore before being admitted.

"How do I look?" he asked when Wilson returned.

"Hell," said Wilson, who had returned from wherever they had taken him, "If you were running for office I'd vote for you."

"These shoes aren't fit for much, though. Hurt my feet already. Think I'll leave 'em and wear my old boots. How much of a walk is it from here to Hooverville?"

"Not too far. You head down the hill till you get to Pioneer Square and from there down to the waterfront. You'll see it. Take maybe a half hour to get there from here. Maybe a little more, but it's all downhill."

Jack removed the shoes, replaced them with his boots and said, "Nice meeting you, Wilson. They're kicking me out of here. Guess I'll head on down to Hooverville like you said."

"Bet you're strapped for cash, Jack."

"I'll get by."

"I got three fives in my billfold and you can have one of them. I'd of died a long time ago if not for the generosity and helping hands of others. You take it and don't think twice about it."

"I appreciate the gesture but I'll have to pass. I'm not the kind of man to take charity without a way to pay it back, Jimmy."

"If it's important to you to pay it back you can give it to my sister. I'll write down her address and leave it here on the nightstand."

"Well, I'm grateful to the point of tears."

"Let's not get carried away here, Jack. I don't want no fully grown man crying on me."

Jack folded a five-dollar bill and put it in his coin pocket.

"I'll take care of your house," said Jack. "And when you need it back I'll go without making any problem for you whatsoever. Do I need a key to get in?"

Wilson laughed softly and said, "I wouldn't exactly call it a house, Jack. And no you don't need a key to get in. Shack doesn't even have a real door, just a piece of plywood and a tarp. Tell you what though. You take this key here. It's to a footlocker inside the shack. You'll find some things of use inside and you're welcome to them."

"Wilson, I hope I see you again someday soon when I can return the favor."

"Good luck to you, Jack. Wish we'd met under different circumstances."

He shook Jimmy Wilson's hand vigorously and said, "That makes two of us, Jimmy. I hope we meet again under better ones."

HOOVERVILLE

SEAGULLS SWOOPED OVERHEAD, LANDED on the damp earth and strutted at his feet. It was not raining here, but the ground was mushy and there were remaining puddles. Men pushed wagons in the mud or pulled carts loaded with scrap tin, iron tubing, newspaper, wire, and broken plaster. Jack saw no women, no children. There was little chatter. The sound of men working with hand drills, saws and hammers resounded behind him as he went in search of Wilson's shack. So many looked alike. From within their epicenter it was impossible to see where Hooverville began and ended.

Men sat on junk furniture, stumps, or wooden packing crates, some silently watching him intently but most merely glancing at him without speaking or apparent interest. One or two nodded at him. His boots became caked in mud. His stockings and feet were wet with stagnant foul puddle water that leaked in through his soles, which had become soggy in the process of disintegration. Men shambled along carrying armloads of driftwood. He had in his possession the number of Wilson's shack, but the numbering system was indecipherable. Without a map to the shack's location within this maze he might never find it.

A haggard man with a shadow of rough beard watched him from a dog chewed tattered sofa supported on one end by a broken shard of concrete. He smoked a pipe under a canvass tarp and spat in the dirt. His face was smeared with dirt and ash. He wore dirty sleeveless coveralls, boots, a ragged flannel shirt and large brown glasses held together with electrical tape. Oddly, he wore a formal black stovepipe top hat. Jack would later learn the man's name was Top Hat, or just Hat, at least that was all anyone knew him by. As Jack neared, the man rose and stirred something he had cooking in a large metal cauldron.

Jack approached the man respectfully removing his own hat and said, "Excuse me. Do you think you might spare a piece of that cardboard for my boots?"

The man spat and nodded toward the pile, indicating Jack was to help himself. He did, and sat on a damp stump to remove his boots. He found a piece of dry cardboard midway in the pile but when he attempted to insert it into his boot it was too big. He kept the cardboard, figuring to cut it to size later with one of Jimmy Wilson's tools and thanked the man. The man continued stirring his pot. He could hear the pot boiling but didn't smell anything cooking. A closer look revealed the man was boiling a pile of clothing.

"I'm looking for Jimmy Wilson's place. Do you know it?"

The man looked directly into his eyes for the first time.

"Yeah, but he ain't there."

He spoke with a pronounced lazy drawl. Jack wondered where the man came from, how he ended up here and for how long, but knew better than to ask.

"I know that. I just left him in the hospital but I'm looking for his place. I'm going to be staying there a while. Name is Jack. What's your name?"

"Well, that really ain't any of your business now, is it? We aren't free with giving out information around here, Mister."

He briefly removed his stovepipe hat and scratched a scab on a bald spot on the crown of his head. He picked at something in his hair and then examined the end of his finger as if something were crawling on it.

He flicked it into the boiling water and said, "Anyway you're way the hell on the other side of where his place is. You see that two-story place with the tall smokestack?"

The man spat in the mud and said, "Well that ain't it."

Lea Macquarrie

He turned his dirty smudged face to the sky and broke into convulsions of laughter, slapping his knee as if what he had said was the funniest thing in the world. Jack felt miniscule drops of the man's spittle on his face. Most of the man's teeth were missing. The few remaining were stubby and stained brown. His laughter went on until aborted by a deep, wet loud cough that continued until Jack began to worry about the tuberculosis.

When it ended the man said, "Just head toward the waterfront. Most folks have numbers painted on the sides of their shacks."

Jack, tromping the muddy grounds, found it mostly by accident, a single-room tar paper shack made from warped ill-fitted sheets of damaged plywood. As Wilson had said, it lacked a door. There was instead only a sheet of rain-warped removable plywood covered with a tarp. The entrance into the shack was so narrow a fat man might have difficulty entering. Not that anyone he had seen in this place had been fat. Most were skinny. All were dirty. Some were skinny but with the distended stomachs he knew to be characteristic of either malnutrition or failing alcoholic livers.

There were no windows in the shack and the only light consisted of thin streams entering pinhole leaks in the tin roof. The plywood walls were unstable when he placed his palms against them and pushed against them. He heard the clatter of what he initially thought was a rat, but then heard the howl of a feral cat finding its way out of the shack. A gust of wind caused the roof to bang and clang and he made a mental note to fix the loose tin which could cause a problem with leakage and infestation.

His wooden matches in the protective wrapper were slightly damp and it took several strikes against the zipper of his pants to get one lighted. In the light the flame provided he saw a kerosene lamp on a Washington State wooden apple box serving as a table. He struck another match, lighted the lamp, and the room became illuminated with pale light.

He saw for the first time that much of the ground he stood on was covered with tarps. A small one-man pup tent had been pitched over two mattresses stacked one atop the other. Wilson probably used the oil cans with holes punched in them for small indoor fires, either for cooking or to warm his hands and feet. A bucket by the door held fishing line, tackle, and floaters. Fishing poles in various degrees of repair leaned against a wall.

He shone the lamp on the footlocker at the head of the bed and examined the rusty padlock. Groping in his trouser pocket, he found the key. The lid lifted awkwardly, one of its hinges off kilter. Jack shone the light on two shabby belted overcoats with fur collars, some sweaters, a U.S. Army issue raincoat, corduroy trousers in need of patching, and three paperback Westerns with lurid worn covers. A moth-eaten Army blanket separated these items from a layer of tools consisting of hammers, screwdrivers, knives, a nail puller, saw and hand operated drill. He felt around under the pile of tools and found a crowbar. The sight of it was like a kick to the stomach. He slammed the trunk closed and locked it, placing both the knife and key in his pocket. He removed his wet boots and entered the pup tent to lie down on the mattress, which felt slightly damp and smelled of mold. He extinguished the lamp in mind of saving valuable kerosene and closed his eyes. He was soon asleep and then he was on the train, confined within the dark boxcar. The boxcar rocked violently and Juanita swung the crowbar and the man's head exploded like a rotten pumpkin, splattering brains across the walls of the boxcar and into Jack's face. One of the man's bloody ears dangled from a strand of tissue. Juanita kept swinging the crowbar, again and again. With each blow the man's face was transfigured until Jack was no longer looking at an identifiable human face but at raw carnage.

The tent had collapsed around him and men were shouting and pulling him out from under it. A shadowed man wore a miner's helmet with an attached light which shone in Jack's eyes. Jack dimly perceived a ragged assembly of ghoulish faces. He counted three men in all. In the flickering kerosene lighting they looked spectral, as if from a bad dream. He recognized Top Hat among them and the man did not look friendly.

"That's him," said Hat.

"What's this all about, can't a man rest his head in peace?"

"This shack belongs to Jimmy Wilson, Mister. I guess you have about one minute to get the hell out, starting now. Sixty, fifty-nine, fifty-eight . . .

"Jimmy Wilson gave me permission," said Jack.

"Fifty-seven, fifty-six…"

"I got a note from Jimmy Wilson in my pocket. Here," he said, unfolding it and handing it over. " Let me show you."

But no one among them could read.

"Let's take him over to see Jesse," said the man with mining hat. "He'll straighten this out. Mister, if you are correct in this I guess we owe you an apology. If you're lying, we owe you a beating for our trouble and on behalf of our pal Jimmy Wilson."

"I'm telling the truth," said Jack. "You'll see. Take me to this Jesse person."

"He's Jesse to us, Mister. To you he's the Honorable Mayor of Hooverville. You'd best address him as either Your Honor, or Mister Mayor."

"Fair enough," said Jack. "I don't mind at all."

They marched him through a haphazard confusion of shacks that seemed made for getting lost in and came to a clearing over which planks were laid in the mud. On the other side of the muddy field were several more shacks, most of them larger than the ones he had seen earlier, some two stories high. At one of these a wooden door posted a sign announcing: *Office of the Honorable Mayor, Jesse James.*

The man with the miner's helmet knocked on the door.

Jack heard a strong baritone voice boom commandingly, "Come on in, whoever you are."

The men led him inside a large central room furnished with tattered chairs, a couch, table, and a kitchen woodstove holding pots and pans and two wash basins. Jack was surprised to see a bookcase with books and some small windows with curtains.

He figured the Mayor to be around six foot five. Clean shaven except for a bushy moustache, he wore his sandy hair longer than Jack had ever seen a man wear it, almost long as a girl's. His lace-up boots were clean, and he wore baggy trousers with suspenders, a collarless white shirt, and unbuttoned vest. He bore a slight resemblance to pictures he had seen of General George Armstrong Custer.

He took a step forward to shake the Mayor's hand and introduce himself, but the man in the mining hat pulled him back and said, "What we have here is uncertain, Jesse. Could be we have a thief, liar, and illegal squatter on someone else's property. Could be we are mistaken and owe the man an apology and helping hand. That's why we've come here. To learn the truth."

"What's your name?" asked the Mayor. His back was turned while washing his hands in a wash basin on the stove.

"Jack Vogel, Mister Mayor."

The Mayor turned as if assessing him and said, "Vogel? You any relation to Frank Vogel?"

"Yes, sir. He is my brother."

"Seems like you have some explaining to do, Jack Vogel."

"Yes sir, and I'm glad for the opportunity to do it."

"Well then," said the Mayor in his impressive baritone. "Get to it, Mr. Vogel."

Jack thrust a hand in the pocket containing the letter, which emerged from his pocket crumpled and slightly damp. He held it flat in his hand, pressing the wrinkles and dampness into his palm. Some of the ink had smeared but it was mostly still legible. He handed it to the Mayor who glanced at it and then handed it back. Jack heard the Mayor's tone shift in his favor.

"Where did you get this, Mr. Vogel?"

"Wilson was in the bed next to me in the hospital. When he learned I was going to be discharged with no place to go, he said he had a place he didn't need and offered it to me."

The Mayor gestured toward one of the chairs near the woodstove.

"Have a seat, Mr. Vogel. We apologize for testing you but these men didn't know who you were or the circumstances of your occupation of Wilson's shack. We tend to watch out for each other down here. And I'm sorry about your brother. We all are. He didn't deserve the beating he took and we don't believe he robbed any banks. He is a good friend to the working man, respected by all who know him."

"You don't owe me an apology at all," said Jack. "I bear no grudges against you, Mr. Mayor. And please just call me Jack."

Jack felt himself in the presence of a man superior to himself, someone smarter and more educated, a man confident in his decision-making and fair in his decisions and judgments. It was no wonder he was Mayor. It was impossible to think of him as anything less.

"Are you a drinking man, Jack?"

"Not really, sir. I've seen how it can change a person, and I was never much for it."

"I'm glad to hear that, Jack. Some of the men down here have a problem. Drinking is foolish and wasteful, but it's nobody's business. If men want to drink it's up to them but sometimes men who drink make trouble. Now, we have all kinds down here, and all kinds are welcome. We don't care what trouble you made before and we won't hold it against you but here in Hooverville we expect lawful behavior. We may be a city of tramps but you can't just come here and disrespect your neighbors, break laws and do whatever the hell you want with impunity. We don't have many rules down here but enforce the few we have. We have our own citizen police force and citizen court. Sometimes we have to evict a fellow. Sometimes, in the worst cases, we hold a man until the Seattle Police arrives to arrest him and take him away. We are not a lawless community."

"I'll be no trouble to you, Mister Mayor."

"I don't expect you will but I need to explain how it is. No children are allowed here, period. It's against the city ordinance allowing us to occupy this property and this is no place for children anyway. We have a sanitation code and a commission to enforce it. No public urination or defecation allowed. We have privies for that purpose, though I admit it's a bit perilous crossing those planks over the mud flats to reach them. Anyway, that about does it for rules. But know that drinking and fighting, theft and refusal to obey the rules will get you in trouble here just like anyplace else."

"Fair enough," said Jack.

They shook on it, and the Mayor said, "Welcome to Hooverville, Jack Vogel. That shack of Wilson's never was much and it's been uninhabited for weeks. Might need some sprucing up, maybe more. If you need a helping hand, let us know. We all pitch in and help each other around here."

"Would it be presumptuous to make a request Mr. Mayor?"

"Can't promise you much of anything, Jack Vogel, but you can surely ask."

"If anybody happens by here asking for me, I ain't here. You never heard of me."

"That's not a problem, Jack. A man's life is his own and we respect it if he chooses to keep it private. You're not alone in wanting anonymity and people here mostly mind their own business. We don't question a man about his past and we don't answer questions when others inquire. We mind our own business and stay out of others. You do the same and you'll get along fine."

Jack wondered what anonymity meant. Impunity too. He had heard the words before, but couldn't recall their meaning. The men shook hands again and the meeting was over. Outside it was not raining but damp and misty and he tasted salt on his lips. Clouds obscured the few visible stars. One of the men who had manhandled him earlier stepped out of the fog. It was Top Hat.

"It's easy to get lost in here till you learn your way around. Numbers painted on shack doors don't mean much at all. I'll take you back to Wilson's."

They navigated the planks the way they had come, neither man talking much. When they reached Wilson's shack he thanked Top Hat for the escort and then squeezed into the narrow entranceway and replaced the wooden plank serving as a door. The tent lay collapsed on the tarp and he went to work raising it. Afterwards he removed his boots and lay on the mattress and stared at the tent's ceiling. He had his own place to sleep now and so did Juanita. From here they could build a better life in Seattle. He fell to sleep thinking of Juanita, but dreamed again of the man they had killed.

Book Two

CAT CREEK

SPRAWLED ON HER BACK on the hard cold ground, Elvira Vogel stared up into the cloudless blue sky, adjusting her binoculars to sight yet another passage of Canadian Geese. They had been in flight all morning in noisy staggered groups, honking and making a racket heard all over the valley. Quite a conversation they seemed to be having, and she wished they would shut the hell up. She might have shot one of them for dinner but her eyesight was getting bad and she hadn't successfully bagged one in weeks.

She got up from the ground and swept a light dusting of snow from her clothing and went to sit in the porch rocking chair, her rifle across her knees, a little envious the damn geese could fly south for the winter while she had to wear multiple layers of clothing to go out and cut firewood in the freezing cold. She was wearing long johns under her faded nasty jeans, with muddy clodhopper boots and a plaid lumberjack shirt over a cotton turtleneck. For added sex appeal she also donned a black and red checked hunter's cap with earflaps. Stylish as a movie star, she thought sarcastically, staring indifferently down the length of her neglected female body slumped like a sack of potatoes in the chair.

Somewhere in all this clothing was a woman who was horny. She had been beautiful once, and was not at present without a few remaining desirable attributes a man might desire, but who would know, under all the clothing? And who would care? She got out rarely these days, hadn't been to the dance hall in, damn. Couldn't even remember last.

She adjusted her binoculars but the trail of geese was diminishing and she was catching the tail end of the group, which she remembered was called a gaggle and not for nothing. But she could barely hear them now and released her binoculars. They were good ones, expensive, her daytime entertainment and the most expensive item she owned except for her guns and chain saws and her sister Alma's guitar. Not counting Frank's old truck, of course, which no longer ran because she'd blown the clutch and maybe the engine trying to get it out of a muddy ditch. She'd pulled the clutch and hoisted the engine, presently hanging from a chain draped over a beam in the shed, but didn't have money to replace the parts and it was getting too cumbersome rebuilding the engine with gloves on and too cold without them. And even with a rebuilt engine she probably couldn't drive the damn thing. Too much else was wrong with it. Wrong like its original owner, Mr. Wrong himself, Mister Frank Wrong Vogel.

But she could do without both Frank and the truck. Doing without was pretty much what she was good at. Thank God for Gladys who came by every few days to check on her and take her into town shopping for what meager groceries she could afford and a shower in the high school gymnasium.

She had almost enough wood for the winter but it needed to be split and neatly stacked not too far from the house. She hung the binoculars on a nail driven into a nearby tree and returned to the woodpile, which measured probably three feet high and six across. She stood a log vertically on a stump and came down hard with her axe and it split neatly in two. What she really needed was kindling and cedar was the best, the hottest burning, but there wasn't much left in these parts so she had to forage mostly for oak.

Which was becoming more difficult every year. She couldn't much rely on poor old Bessie to pull the wagon deep into the forest and carry out loads of cut firewood as in previous years, the animal was too old and infirmed. Meanwhile it was getting harder to find dead wood close enough to hand carry back to the cabin. There was plenty of green wood but took a year or two to dry and cure, and she didn't feel right cutting it anyway. Who wanted to live on a bald earth?

Her isolated cabin was without plumbing. Two other ramshackle shacks were within view, but no one lived in them. Their barns had long since collapsed, and she salvaged the wood for patching her dilapidated sheds and the outhouse. Sometimes during the winter she didn't see anyone for weeks because of impassible snowdrifts. The property had a well, but its water froze solid during the coldest months of winter. She had to melt frozen snow in a pan on the woodstove to make oatmeal, which during the winter months she practically lived on.

Not that spring was any treat. That's when the flies and mosquitoes and field mice invaded. Summertime was uncomfortably hot midday but she liked her afternoons naked drinking her home brew on the porch. She was not immodest by nature but hey, if you're coming over unannounced, you take your chances. You will see a naked woman whose youth has passed her by. Good riddance to it as far as she was concerned because the voluptuous figure when she was young only brought men into her life and they were not good for much. Except sex, of course, and when was the last time she'd had a piece of that? Her affairs had been few and far between since she and Billy had broken off, one night stands mostly, alcohol fueled and best forgotten. She kind of missed Billy, but he had betrayed her. So, fuck him.

Anyway, winter was coming. The sky was utterly blue, vast, and cloudless. She knew this sky well and it was telling her the first heavy snowfall was probably going to come early this year. She'd be ready for it, though. She had her wood, canned and dry goods, rolling tobacco and kerosene, home brew and a bottle or two of smuggled Canadian whiskey. And she didn't much mind the solitude. There were snowy mornings when the deer came right up to her porch, so quiet in the snow they might have been ghost deer. Some were so pretty she was tempted to open the door and let them in to warm up by the fire. Bears were definitely uninvited, especially when in preparation for hibernation, but they were scarce. Didn't mean she didn't carry her Winchester pump action when she went deep into the forest though.

She removed her gloves, rolled a cigarette and squatted against one of the two posts holding the sagging roof of the porch overhang. Not every cigarette she smoked during the day tasted good since some were just to feed the habit, but this was a good one, and she savored it. She could hear more geese approach now, this time maybe a whole city of them because this was their loudest racket yet. She saw the lead goose, then the flanking V formation behind it, and then they were over her, a flying orchestra of wacky tone deaf saxophonists, and whatever they were saying must have been pretty damn urgent. It took about ten minutes for them to pass and their noise to diminish. When it did she heard an automobile coming over the hill and an engine sound she did not recognize. Nor did she recognize the automobile when it appeared at the crest of the hill. It wasn't Gladys, at least not her car, not her nearest neighbor who usually walked or rode a horse, and not her neighbor Marcy or heaven forbid one of her umpteen no-account delinquent kids.

She lifted her binoculars from the nail hook and sighted a luxury sedan of a kind unlike any she had seen on the rez before. She put down the binoculars and waited, not particularly giving a shit or wanting company but resigned to the inevitability of it. The unidentified car reached the bottom of the hill, bumped over her unpaved property and stopped short of the woodpile. When the passenger side door opened and she saw the cowboy boots below it she knew they belonged to the new BIA police chief and her once-upon-a-time boyfriend, Billy. The son of a bitch.

He stepped out, nodded, and said, "Vi."

"Billy."

She didn't recognize the driver, a short fellow dressed fancy in a black suit and tie with shiny black oxford shoes. He might as well have carried a sign saying, *Lawman*. Billy, lumbering forward, had recently lost some of his belly weight and kept tugging on his belt to hitch his pants.

"Vi, this here is Dexter Matthews. He's a Private Detective."

"How do you do," she said politely. "Billy, take those damn

sunglasses off. I'm not about to stand here talking to you while looking at my own reflection. What can I do for you boys?"

"Matthews here has a few questions he'd like to ask. I came because I worried if he came unescorted and uninvited you might shoot him on the doorstep."

"You're the one I'd shoot, Billy. What can I for you, Matthews?"

"I'm trying to locate a missing person."

"What's that got to do with me?"

"You're a Vogel."

"So?"

"The name Vogel is connected with this case. Specifically a certain J. Vogel. Do you know who that might refer to?"

"I don't know anyone name of Jay Vogel."

"I'm sorry. I don't mean to indicate the name Jay, but the initial J."

"Well now, that could be anybody with a first name that starts with J."

"Someone related to you?"

She disliked him on instinct. But then she disliked cops generally and P.I.'s were basically ex-cops who had either been washed out or tossed out. He stared at her with a thinly disguised smirk of disrespect. Probably thought she was a criminal. Everybody was a criminal in a cop's estimation. Well, fuck him too. Him *and* Billy.

Billy stepped up onto the porch and said, "We're looking for Jack, Elvira. Jack and Juanita."

"What's the BIA got to do with Jack? He's not even an Indian."

"Juanita is."

"But they were living in town, not on the rez."

"No one has seen them since they were evicted and sold their things at the flea market. Word around the rez is they were headed for Seattle."

"Yeah, and we all know how reliable reservation gossip is. I don't know where they are or where they might have gone. Maybe Jack went to see his brother Frank in Chicago."

Another formation of geese passed over, rendering them unable to hear one another talk. They waited and then the detective said, "By his brother you mean Frank Vogel, don't you?"

"Only brother Jack has as far as I know."

"You say Frank Vogel is in Chicago."

"That's right. He's a labor organizer."

"You were married to him, were you not?"

"Still am, as far as I know. Stupid of me yes, but not a crime."

"Frank Vogel is not in Chicago, Mrs. Vogel. He's in a penitentiary in Washington State. Have you talked with Jack Vogel since he left the area?"

"We don't have telephones out here."

"A letter maybe."

"No. Jack don't write."

Billy tipped his hat and said, "You'll let us know if you do get a letter, right Vi?"

"Billy, you know Jack don't write."

"He can get someone to write a letter on his behalf like you use to do for him, Vi."

"Well if I do get a letter from him it's personal and I ain't sharing it with you. It wouldn't be right."

"This is part of a legal investigation, Miss Vogel. If you deliberately withhold information pertaining to Jack Vogel's location you could find yourself in legal jeopardy."

"Tell you what, Matthews. Billy here can tell you I don't like cops and I won't be intimidated or threatened. Now get the hell of my property before I shoot out the windows of your fancy car."

Vi watched the two men get back into the fancy car, back up and turn around in the field and drive up the hill out of her sight. She picked up her axe, set a log upright on a stump, and came down hard. The log split in two pieces and she added them to the pile.

PALENTINE AVENUE

IT WAS INCONCEIVABLE THAT NOT ONE of the fifty-five windows in the McCabe house had ever been washed. What was the benefit of the spectacular view to Ballard Bay and Puget Sound Mr. McCabe bragged about if the windows were too smudged to see out of them? She washed them all, floor by floor. She made certain the kitchen was clean and the dining area immaculate. She waxed the piano weekly. Once she went so far as to clean the music room chandelier from a tall ladder, removing and wiping each individual prism before carefully replacing it.

She explored a maze of rooms, hideaways, snug alcoves, corner mezzanines and sitting rooms resembling little museums that seemed designed solely for the purpose of display of exotic and elaborate artifacts imported from overseas nations she could only distantly imagine. She dusted hand-painted dancing girls in native costume and exotic soldiers robed in formal native dress, jade figurines and ivory elephants and elegant vases and meticulously assembled exotic model sailing ships. There were rooms with lavish formal settings and rooms for storage of furniture. In some closets bulged with clothing not worn in decades.

She tidied dusty cobweb strewn studies with tall bookshelves and regal cushioned armchairs suitable for a monarch. She purged cluttered stairwells, swept and tidied the second and third floors, where there were rooms that seemed to have no purpose other than for storage of antique chairs, sofas, roll top desks and disassembled brass beds. She cleaned rooms with subdued velvet draperies and ornate candleholders on fireplace shelves and huge gilt-framed paintings of ships tossed in stormy seas. An attic garret with a sloped low ceiling made her stoop upon entering it. It contained an altar with cross and candles, miniature ships, and framed portrait of a handsome young Walter McCabe. There were rooms like storage bins they were so cluttered with furniture, many with bookcases so tall she couldn't reach the top shelf. She examined thick dusty books with lofty titles containing glossy illustrations and mysterious words she could not read. She opened the books, imagining the stories they contained. The books seemed to represent a world of adventure and opportunity denied to her. She longed to read them and often tried, recognizing words and trying to put sentences together.

Cora, whom Juanita had never seen without at least one lighted cigarette and often several, seemed incapable of emptying an ashtray. Cigarette butts overflowed their rims, spilling to the carpeted floor, sometimes while still burning. Carpets were riddled with cigarette burns, as was just about every windowsill on the first floor. Just about anything that might serve as an ashtray might suddenly become one. Teacups, saucers, dinner plates. Cora even sometimes removed her shoes for such a purpose.

Cora and the kitchen were an especially potent danger. When she sometimes decided to cook the kitchen became a chaotic battlefield with strewn knives and forks, cartons of milk, slabs of beef, hairpins, extinguished cigarettes, scissors, coin purses, pens, lipstick tubes, nail polish containers and numerous other items scattered over counters, stovetops and sinks as if having landed there after an explosion. A specialty was pork chops. She threw them in a pan with Crisco, turned up the flame under the pan on the gas stove and commenced to read the paper, talk on the telephone in the living room, read in the library, or sit in the backyard feeding breadcrumbs to flocks of birds while the house filled with smoke. She was allowed kitchen access only with Juanita's supervision now.

Over time the McCabe's began to mend their tendency toward disorder, or at least try. Mr. McCabe began bringing dishes to the sink and picking up after himself. Cora began to at least try to restrict her smoking to the library or den and to use ashtrays and not her shoe or window sill to extinguish them.

Cora said Juanita was her confidant and best friend. Barefoot and wearing her Florence Nightingale nightgown, Cora sometimes came to her room for what she called a "sleepover". Juanita heard the tap tap tap of her cane long before she arrived and slipped into bed with her. There was minimal room for them both in the single bed, where Juanita never failed to be astonished by how thin Cora was and shocked by her cold feet. Her breath reeked of tobacco and reminded her of her father.

"Has my father never contacted you, Cora? Not even once?"

"Never. I swear it, Juanita. Walter has looked everywhere for him in missions on Skid Row, on the docks and in the Public Market, even in Hooverville."

"I think maybe he has gone back to Cat Creek. I was a burden to him. He didn't love me anymore."

"Of course he loved you, dear. Who wouldn't? Something must have gone wrong. We have to be patient. Walter will find him."

"I said terrible things to him, Cora. I hurt him. I said he was a bad father and failed man. I told him he would never amount to anything, never succeed at anything he tried to do, that if I stayed with him I'd probably end up wasting my life taking care of him. I said I was glad to get away from him. We were both so hungry, Cora. We couldn't think straight."

Cora narrated her entire life story. How she had been kidnapped by Gypsies in Hungary, had worked as assistant to trapeze artists in big-top circuses all over Eastern Europe, had been a famous dancer and gymnast who had been married three times before Walter McCabe, to a famous matador in Madrid, to a virtuosic cellist in Hungary, an abstract expressionist painter in Paris. Cora told how she had met Walter, who had been penniless and in a sanitarium with TB at the time. She had been doing charity work and took pity on him. After they were married, she bankrolled Walter for his first business venture, which grew into the success it was now.

Juanita later learned from Walter, who spewed his drink and

almost choked to death laughing, that none of these stories from Cora were even remotely based on fact. She soon learned the truth of his assertion for herself because Cora was always changing her accounts and presenting new versions. Walter McCabe said even Cora knew they weren't true, that she just liked to talk and make things up. He said Cora, who spent hours in their library reading novels, would rather have an interesting story than a true one.

McCabe was an overgrown goat with hair all over his chest, arms and back and seemed always vaguely agitated. Cora described him as an old grump who complained about everything but he loved her with a rare and true devotion. Juanita saw for herself how he never failed to pull out a chair for Cora at the dining room table, to open the door to the Hudson for her before getting in himself, how he praised her beauty and refinement while declaring his own unworthiness.

"Walter adores you like the daughter he never had, Juanita. We both do. You have brought youth and joy into this house. But you must know, dear, it's not a betrayal of your father to love Walter."

But he drank too much, more than Uncle Frank even. He hid his bottles all over the house. He banged on the piano like it was a wild animal he was trying to kill and sang off key in a defiant whiskey voice. He smoked nasty cigars that stunk up the draperies and sofa cushions with stale smoke and made you feel you were living in a house that had been in a recent fire. He was gruff, a man with a garrulous demeanor who spoke too loud and often sounded angry when he was not. She saw through his bluff though. He would never tell her so but he was fond of her and they both knew it. He sometimes stuffed dollar bills in her apron pocket and walked away before she could thank him. They sometimes went fishing, just the two of them, in McCabe's motorized rowboat in Puget Sound. They drove out to Alkai Point, where they ate fish and chips, to Richmond Beach where they dug for clams, to the fish hatcheries in Marysville.

Chester McCabe, their son, whom they called Chettie, came home from the sea and avoided everyone. He was apparitional, a silent hallucinatory ghost ship at sea in a dense fog. Sometimes she glimpsed him in the upstairs hallway in route to his room. He rarely spoke and at mealtimes was conspicuously absent from the family table. He soon moved downtown without giving notice. He continued to go to sea. There seemed to be some rift between him and Mr. McCabe, but she never learned what it was that separated them.

McCabe notified the Interlake School department by phone that they were to receive a new student. Next he informed the management of *Fredrick and Nelson* that his wife was coming to purchase school clothing for a female student who would accompany her and to approve her purchases and bill his office. He called a cab, assuring the dispatcher he would personally watch for it at the windows. In the *Frederick and Nelson* department store, Cora guided Juanita through what seemed like a city of clothing while watched closely by a little bald man with a bushy moustache and thick round rimless glasses who wore dress slacks, a white shirt and pink bow tie.

A saleswoman fitted Juanita with a pleated blue skirt and white blouse with pretty while buttons up the front that looked like pearls. They chose saddle shoes identical to those other girls in her neighborhood wore when passing by the windows on their way to school. The man with the round glasses crouched behind a rack of men's overcoats.

Cora waved and said, "Hi Burt". He slinked off, disappearing through racks of women's dresses. "Don't mind him," said Cora. "He's Burt, the store detective, a friend of mine."

Later that night Juanita set the shoes by her bed and the skirt and blouse on a chair where she could look at them while falling asleep. She prayed the way Cora had taught her, mostly for her lost father, but also for Uncle Frank, who she knew to be in prison. She prayed for herself, but she didn't know who she was anymore.

She did not sleep well. She worried no one at school would befriend her. She worried especially it would be revealed that she couldn't read.

In the morning, dressed for school, she sat in the window seat and ran her fingers through her hair, which was finally beginning to grow out. Girls in small groups of three or four on their way to school passed by on the street below. She recognized some but only by sight. It was possible they might become her friends. There would be occasional overnights, pajama parties where secrets about boys and sex were whispered. She was curious about this.

She and her new friends would sneak Cora's cigarettes and smoke them on the porch. They might meet in the library and add a splash of Mr. McCabe's whiskey to their tea. She'd share some of Cora's books from the library and show them the brilliant colored illustrations of strange exotic locations with minarets and towers and walled desert cities. She would ask about this. Where was this? Was this illustration a city from the past or one existing now, in present time, in a part of the world unknown to her? She would show her new friends illustrations of men and women wearing fur hats and long fur coats and carrying rifles, couples kissing on snow banks while behind them a city burned. What did this mean? Was this something real, something that had actually happened, or made up? She would ask them, and if they knew they would explain this and more. And later she would be able to read the books on her own. Not right away, of course, but she would learn. How long could it take to learn to read? If you studied real hard, that is. If you read every chance you got.

Schoolgirls in the street below were looking up at her on the window seat inside the McCabe house. She was proud to live in such a castle. She hurried out the door with her lunchbox and jacket, down the winding steps to the sidewalk below where she tried to catch up. Her chest pounded and she had broken into a sweat that she worried made her forehead shiny. The girls were walking abreast and holding hands. She fell in next to them and introduced herself.

"I'm Juanita," she said. "I live in the house you were pointing at. The mansion at the top of the hill."

"It's haunted," said one of the girls. "The old woman who lives there is a witch. Her husband is a vampire."

"Yes, it's true," said another. "You had better find somewhere else to live, because they kill and eat children."

The girls ran off laughing. Juanita chose not to follow. She did not like them or find their teasing funny.

"The McCabe's are nice people," she shouted after them. "Nicer than you by far."

"Don't mind them. They think they are better than everyone else. They have their own little circle and won't let anyone else join. What's your name?"

This was spoken by a boy about her own age and height, who was suddenly matching her stride. She picked up her pace, evading him, but he kept up. She finally stopped, turned and looked at him directly. He carried an impressive number of schoolbooks under his right arm and was kind of a mess. The clothing he wore, dirty corduroy pants and an oversize faded shirt, was recognizably hand-me-down. His eyes were a peculiar shade of light brown verging on green and his sandy unkempt hair did not look clean. His shirt tail was hanging out and she noticed he had missed a belt loop on his pants, which were far too large for him.

"Do you really live in that big old house on the hill?"

She assessed his intention in asking this and took her time answering. Was he going to make fun of her too?

"Yes. It belongs to Mr. and Mrs. McCabe. They're both very nice."

"Is it true the house is haunted though?"

She reassessed him. He was a nice looking boy, kind of ragged, his sandy brown hair in need of trimming, his shoes scruffy, his clothing too big for him, but with a nice sincere politeness about him. He wore his hair long and had warm hazel eyes. She liked his voice, and the way he looked at her like he found her pretty.

"Are you teasing me?"

"Not at all. That's just the rumor, what people say. I mean you have to admit, the house looks haunted."

She couldn't entirely disagree.

"It's not. It needs some care, though, and that's for sure."

"My name is Kenny Williams," said the boy. "What's yours?"

"Juanita Vogel."

"They say Mrs. McCabe is crazy. I met her once when I was on the way to school. She asked me to throw her newspaper up the steps. She was halfway down the stairs and grasping the railing trying not slip on the wet leaves. She was wearing a skimpy wet night-shirt in the rain. She seemed okay, though. Smiled and thanked me for throwing up her paper. She invited me up for cookies, but I was afraid."

She saw the redbrick schoolhouse now, a block distant, its playground, flagpole and haphazard congregations of milling students.

"Well," she replied. "You aren't very brave then, are you? At worst you would have had to eat some of the most awful tasting cookies you ever imagined."

He hesitated a moment, his expression sincere and thoughtful. When he spoke, his tone and manner suggested the topic was of profound importance and not subject to frivolity.

"There is no such thing as an awful cookie, Juanita. Some cookies are better than others but all cookies all good."

"You haven't tasted Mrs. McCabe's."

Kenny Williams was beanpole thin but kind of cute. He kept brushing his sandy unkempt hair out of his hazel eyes, which seemed to change color with the lighting. His face was almost like a girl's but for his strong chin. He had long eyelashes and nice teeth. He kept hitching his belt and pulling up on his baggy pants, which were probably handed down from a big brother or father. The raggedy way he was dressed reminded her of stupid boys she knew in Cat Creek but when he spoke, his voice surprised her because it was a voice belonging to a much older person.

"Are you going to school? Where are your books?"

"I don't have any. It's my first day."

They approached the school itself, a red brick schoolhouse and playground comprising a full city block. They became adrift in the ocean of noisy students ascending the concrete stairs leading into the school and then she lost sight of him. She followed front steps into the interior of a vast confusing building with high ceilings, polished wooden staircases and brass banisters leading to long hallways upstairs. The main floor was so crowded she found it difficult not be jostled by students hurrying for classrooms. She followed students up the stairs to a wide hallway with doors open to mostly empty classrooms. It was quieter here but it made her feel conspicuously out of place. She had felt more comfortable downstairs amid the anonymity of the larger assembly. She fought her way down the stairs past students going to classrooms upstairs and again found herself within a stampede of noisy students.

She stood awkwardly in the hallway trying to stay out of the way as boys and girls carrying notebooks and schoolbooks hurried in a blur of motion for classrooms. Then a bell rang and the once-crammed hallways emptied and it was quiet and she was alone. Standing against a bank of lockers, she had no idea what to do. Finally she just randomly opened a classroom door and wandered inside.

A young woman wearing glasses and a pretty dress who Juanita assumed to be the teacher addressed the classroom while writing on a blackboard with a piece of chalk. Then she turned and saw Juanita standing awkwardly just inside the classroom door.

"Why, hello there," she said.

Juanita found the teacher's melodious voice reassuring.

"I'm new" she said, "This is my first day here."

"Welcome, then. I wasn't aware I was being assigned a new student. Have you checked in at administration?"

"What's administration," asked Juanita?

The teacher slapped chalk dust off her hands and said, "That's where you check in and are assigned a classroom. I'll take you there. Class, no talking. Richard, you will be in charge. I'll be right back."

In the hallway outside of the classroom the woman took her hand and said, "Are you nervous, sweetie? First day at a new school and all? It's perfectly normal. Don't worry; it's a good school with nice children. What's your name?"

"Juanita Vogel."

"My name is Miss Lipton."

Miss Lipton led her back along the hallway and down the stairs to a large busy office with and wooden desks, telephones and typewriters and tall metal filing cabinets. A tall horizontal wooden counter that bifurcated the room was piled high with pamphlets.

"New girl," Miss Lipton announced to the women working

behind the desks. "First day but she hasn't been registered or assigned a classroom."

An enormous woman with rosy fat cheeks and smudged eyeglasses replied.

"Yes, we've been expecting her. Mr. McCabe called yesterday."

"Good luck, Sweetie," said Miss Lipton upon leaving.

The other woman began asking her questions. Unlike the teacher who had escorted her, this unsmiling woman spoke in a clipped impatient voice absent of warmth.

"Name."

"Juanita Rose Vogel."

"Date of birth."

"I'm not sure exactly."

"Approximately then. Your age. Do you know that at least?"

"Fourteen."

"Nationality."

"Italian, mostly."

"Where did you last go to school?"

"Cat Creek, Montana."

"What grade level had you reached upon leaving?"

Juanita thought about it and came up blank.

"I don't understand," she replied.

"What grade were you in? Third? Fourth? Fifth?"

"I don't know. It was a school much smaller than this. There was only one classroom. The kids were all different ages and we only had one teacher."

Frowning, the woman wrote something in a ledger and said, "Follow me. I'll put you in Mrs. Henderson's s class."

"Can I be in Miss Lipton's class instead?"

"No. Come along quickly now, I don't have all day here."

Juanita followed the woman's enormous rump, which looked like a tub of laundry stirred with a canoe paddle. They climbed the stairs to the second floor and traversed yet another hallway and stopped abruptly at a classroom door.

"Straighten your skirt. Do not speak unless spoken to first by Miss Henderson."

The classroom bore no resemblance whatsoever with ones she knew in Cat Creek. There were no paper airplanes or wadded round balls of paper being tossed around, no one was passing notes or seemed to be clowning around. Here the students were orderly and seemed to be actively studying. She waited quietly while the heavy woman who had escorted her explained the new admission to the teacher, who wore round wire rimmed glasses and was pretty in a pink sweater and gray skirt.

The teacher examined the folder on her desk and said, "Come over here, dear. My name is Mrs. Henderson. Class, we have a new student. Come forward, dear, don't be shy. Please stand before the blackboard and introduce yourself to the class."

Now that she was facing the class she could not longer avoid direct eye contact. She alternated between glancing down at her new shoes and viewing the classroom and its students as a single entity without individuals.

"Hello," she said. "My name is Juanita Rose Vogel. I'm from Cat Creek, Montana and I'm Italian."

She regretted saying she was Italian but wasn't sure whether they would let Indians in the school with whites.

"Say hello to Juanita, class," instructed the teacher."

"Hello, Juanita" said twenty-five unison voices.

At the sight of them seated at their rows of wooden desks with open books on desktops she inwardly cringed. How confident and smart they looked. It seemed a certainty that they knew how to read. Fortunately, she had no book, and if there was a spare to loan her she could pretend to read along, turning pages when they did. For now at least, her shameful secret was safe.

"Juanita, please take the empty desk in the back of the room."

Juanita recognized the boy across the aisle from the empty desk. He was Kenny Williams, the nice boy who had talked to her earlier on the way to school.

Miss Henderson cleared her throat and said, "We will continue reading aloud from where we left off. Each student will read half a page. Juanita, you may read first. Now remember class, the purpose of this is not to merely improve reading skills but also to practice diction skills. Pronounce your words slowly and distinctly. Kenny, please hand your book to Juanita and show her where we left off. Go ahead, Juanita. You may begin."

In Cat Creek if you wanted help with schoolwork you asked the teacher. Not many did. The behavior inside the classroom was almost the same as on the playground. Kids there didn't care if you could read or write well and no one was interested. But she was not a kid anymore and too old for pranks and games now.

Kenny Williams handed her his book but her hands were shaking and she accidentally dropped it. He reached down and retrieved the book from the floor but she dropped it again when he handed it to her. He smiled in a friendly manner and placed the book on her desk open to the page from which she was supposed to read. The text may as well have been written in Chinese like in Mr. Lee's library. Even words that she would know easily under different circumstances seemed indecipherable.

"Please begin," said Mrs. Henderson. "We are all waiting."

She raised the book in front of her face to hide behind it and prepared to read. It was impossible. She didn't know how. She glanced over the top of the open book she held in her trembling hands and saw the full classroom of students at their desks, all of whom were focusing their attention on her expectantly. The book was slipping out of her sweaty hands.

She pushed her chair away from her desk, stood and handed the book back to the boy named Kenny Williams.

"I don't belong here," she said to the class.

She did not look back when closing the door behind her.

She was relieved upon returning to the McCabe house relieved to find Cora asleep. There would be no questions about her early return from school so at least she could cry undisturbed.

Later that afternoon Mr. McCabe arrived home early from his office on Pier 91. He removed his tweed jacket and placed it over the arm of his chair, his suspenders tightening when he sat. He smelled of strong drink, and she wrinkled her nose disapprovingly. He removed a silver flask from his jacket, unscrewed the cap and she watched him drink. He screwed the cap back on and coughed into his handkerchief long enough to worry her. When he was finished he put the flask back in the pocket and said, "Well I surmise from the amount of wadded up crying tissues it did not go well today."

"It was the worst day of my life, Mr. McCabe. They made me read aloud just like I feared. My hands shook so bad I kept dropping the book. The whole class was watching me, waiting for me to read, and I didn't know how. I hated it. I'm never going back."

"Of course you are. Don't jump to conclusions here, Juniata. You hated it *today*. Tomorrow is another day."

"I can't possibly face that classroom again. I'm too ashamed."

"You have nothing to be ashamed of, Juanita. You may be un-educated but that's not your fault and we are in the process of fixing that by enrolling you in school."

"But I'm stupid. I can't read and write."

"Because you haven't been taught. That's *why* you are in school, to learn these things. You're smart and determined. I've seen you on your own teaching yourself with Cora's books in the library."

"That's not reading. I thought it was but it's pretending like my Daddy said."

"I disagree, Juanita."

"Oh, I can recognize words and put some sentences together but no matter how hard I might try I'll never catch up to the other students."

"Don't even think about the other students and how you compare to them. Try to enjoy the experience of learning without regard to what the other students are doing. Don't worry. You'll catch up."

Someone was knocking at the front door. Mr. McCabe left the room to answer it. A moment later he returned and announced, "It's for you, Juanita. You have a visitor."

A young boy her own age lingered awkwardly behind Mr. McCabe, shuffling his feet and appearing almost white with fear, whether of her or Mr. McCabe she was not yet certain. It was Kenneth Williams.

"Have a seat," said Mr. McCabe to the young man. He gestured toward the sofa and said. "I'll leave you two to be."

"I guess he's not as mean as people say," said Kenneth after

McCabe had left. "In fact, he seemed kind of nice."

"He's going to eat you later," replied Juanita.

Kenneth Williams placed his schoolbooks on a shelf and said, "I'm sorry about what happened in school today, Juanita."

"I made a complete fool of myself. I knew this would happen if I was called on to read. I can't go back there."

He reached for a textbook on the shelf, found it and came to sit beside her on the sofa and said, "We'll practice the reading assignments together. I'll make sure you are prepared and I'll walk with your and carry your books to school. There's no pressure. You'll see. It can be fun."

Turning some pages, he began to read to her, gliding his index finger along the words as he read them. Some of the words she knew and recognized. Kenny Williams pointed to a difficult long word and broke it down into individual syllables and challenged her to identify the word the syllables belonged to. Juanita could not contain her happiness when she guessed correctly.

"But that's not a guess at all," he exclaimed. "You *recognized* the word. That's what reading is. I know you will learn to read faster than you think, Juanita. You're smart and it's not that hard. You'll see."

His warm breath smelled kind of soapy, like maybe he had been chewing the flat rectangular slabs of powdered gum found in the packets of baseball cards boys collected. She liked his voice, the way he read with feeling and the careful way he pronounced each word. When it was her turn to read he helped her pronounce the words and let her repeat them until she got them right. They did this until she saw him looking at her funny.

She closed the book and said, "What? Why are you looking at me like that?"

"Because I would like to kiss you."

"Why?"

"Because you're very pretty and I like you."

She ignored him but was pleased. And she kind of wanted him to.

"You can't kiss me," she replied. "But that was a very good answer."

NORTH SEATTLE

AFTER WEEKS OF RAIN AND DRIZZLE it was perfect Seattle weather no one had anticipated, a surprising spring day so unexpectedly sunny and warm it made Sheriff Gustafson miss the early days early in his career when he rode a Harley Davidson motorcycle instead of a desk in the precinct like now. Of course the reality for a Seattle motorcycle policeman was that it was usually raining and windy and frankly miserable, but on a sunny day like this he liked to remember otherwise.

Meanwhile, with all the rain over the past few weeks, his overgrown lawn had been too wet to mow and he knew he should get it done now, while the weather was favorable, but today was a day suitable for golf or fishing, not for yard work. Besides, Danny, his eldest, should be the one mowing the lawn anyway; what did the boy think he was getting a weekly allowance for? Maintaining his stellar C minus grade average? Well, don't get him started. He loved Danny but the boy was undisciplined and spoiled. And where *was* Danny anyway? Why was it when chores needed doing the boy never seemed to be around?

Dashing joyfully through the spray of his sprinklers his girls, five and seven years old, shrieked gleefully in decibels that made his dog Rocco howl and cover his ears. Gus Junior, three years old, was presently upstairs napping through this and how he envied the boy's ability to sleep through just about anything. He rolled his empty oil drum out of the garage, set his *Ford Picnic Kit* on top of it, lighted the charcoal and placed half dozen wieners on the grill top. Rocco, his bulldog, arrived on his stubby little legs with his tongue hanging out and mouth full of slobber. He sat on his haunches attentively below the cloud of weenie smoke.

And while on the subject of wieners, his was getting a little stiff from watching his wife in her short shorts and halter top, a bootleg gin and tonic balanced on the flat stomach on which rested her movie magazine. He often teased she must be part Egyptian because she was such a sun worshipper. Let that sun slide out behind the clouds for even ten minutes and Jen was half naked as fast as you could say oh baby oh baby.

He watched her moisten her smooth long legs with lotion. Damn. She was looking so good he would definitely do something about it if the kids weren't around. But maybe a "nap" later. Plant the kids in front of the TV, go up the stairs, lock the door.

"Down, boy."

Rocco was all over him, climbing toward the simmering wieners.

"Jenny? Be ready to eat in ten?"

"Feed the kids first, Gus. I haven't finished my drink."

"Okay. What do you say to a little nap later?"

"We'll see."

He couldn't see her eyes because she was wearing sunglasses but she was smiling, and that was promising. A benefit of marriage was supposed to be that you would get it steady, but that was a fabrication. Once the kids were born, forget about it. Maybe that's what started him patronizing Stone's clubs. Mike Drake had taken him initially, ostensibly for a nightcap. Drake said there were sexy women there for the having but he had objected, saying he was a married man of conscience who valued loyalty and truthfulness above all else.

"You don't have to do anything you don't feel right about, Gus. It's a nice place with comfortable bar stools, couches, and armchairs where you can just have some drinks and relax. There will be women who will want to take you upstairs, but you don't have to go. You can just sit back and look them over. No harm in looking, right?"

And look he did, as Drake paraded beautiful women dressed in flimsy lingerie that just begged to be removed. Stone came around and bought him numerous rounds of Canadian Whiskey he didn't even want and said, "Consider this a benefit of our trust in one another, Sheriff. You are now part of the family and that means you have VIP status here and at any of our other clubs. You are welcome to drink and enjoy what the house has to offer whenever you want and it won't cost you a cent."

No, not a cent, but maybe his career and his marriage. Anyway, that had been years ago. He was in deep now and there was no turning it around. He shifted the wieners, the meat hissing and smoking, but saw at once he had done so too early. He turned them again and scattered the charcoal bricks to adjust the flame.

"Someone is ringing in." said Jenny. "We have a telephone call."

Who but Jenny would have heard it through the shrieks and shouts of his girls in the sprinklers? Jenny had small ears hidden behind a cascade of hair, but at the sound of a telephone it was like they elongated and rose from her head like antennae. She could hear a telephone ring through the cheering of home game touchdown.

"Don't answer it. Let it ring."

Yeah, like that was even possible. He watched her rise from the recliner, showing first some cleavage and then a nice view of her rear end when ascending the porch stairs. He heard her laughter through the screen door she failed to close. He couldn't make out what was being said but it was a safe bet it was her mother calling. After all, his mother in law hadn't called in almost an hour now. Jenny's mother telephoned about nothing throughout the day. But no, it wasn't her mother on the phone because Jenny was back far too soon.

"It's for you," said Jenny. "It's Bobby Stone."

He waved both hands in front of his face. He hadn't talked privately with Stone in almost two weeks and had begun to think he was escaping his influence. He shook his head back and forth several times vigorously. He pushed against an imaginary wall with both hands, palms out. He mimed the words *no no no*.

"Tell him I'm not home."

Christ, that suntan lotion she had lathered herself in was making him crazy. He licked some off her ear, but she backed off and said, "I told him you were in the yard grilling."

He stared down into her cleavage and said, "Tell him I'll call back."

He'd procrastinated telling Jenny he didn't want Stone at the house anymore because she'd want to know why, and whatever he said in answer would get back to Stone and Drake and the others on the Commission because Jenny like most women couldn't keep her pretty mouth shut. None of the club members trusted their wives with information they wanted kept secret and all had good reason not to because they all had secrets they wanted kept from their wives.

"He said it was important. Urgent is the word he used, actually."

He sighed, handed her the spatula and barbeque brush, and went to the phone.

"Hello?"

"It's me. Bobby."

"Yeah, hello, Stony."

"We had a meeting. It was important you be there. Where the fuck were you?"

"I was busy with a case."

"You couldn't have called and let us know?"

"Things at the precinct come up unpredictably, Bobby."

"We discussed our mutual problem."

"Which problem is that, Bobby?"

"You know which problem. Don't make me say it over the phone. What we talked about before. Our obstacle."

"What exactly do you want, Bobby? Get to the point because I've got things to do here right now."

It was probably the most abrupt and dismissive tone he had ever taken with Stone and he knew he was pushing it. Bobby Stone was not someone you wanted to cross even if you were sheriff. But Stone's obsession with Walter McCabe was wearing thin.

"We want McCabe watched. We want and expect the full benefit of your investigative resources, Sheriff. You have access to information unavailable to us and the means to get it. Trained, experienced investigators with the skills and technology to secretly examine people's private lives, their backgrounds, things they might be hiding. We want to know his personal habits and weaknesses, his sexual habits, if he might be queer or solicit whores, if he has any gambling debts, whatever dirt you can dig up. "

"You're wasting your time. He's clean."

"You're a cop, Gus. You should know better. Nobody's clean."

"McCabe is."

"Based on what we know now maybe but there's more. You just haven't found it. Keep digging, Gus. If you can't find anything then make it up, throw some dirt on him. Make it something that will stick. By the way, why is it we haven't seen you in any of our nightclubs lately, Sheriff? What's the matter, Jennifer have you chained to the bedpost?"

"Been too happy at home to wander, I guess."

"Always did like Jenny. From the first time I met her I said here is a woman who is both smart and beautiful. You're a lucky man."

"I'm aware of that, Bobby, but thanks. Jenny is great."

"I'd hate to see how hurt she would be if she somehow learned you've in the past been a regular patron of our cathouses."

Gustafson well understood the implication of the remark. He hung up the phone and went back outside. The weather was the same as when he left, cloudless and bathed in sunlight with no rain in sight, as good as it gets in Seattle but the day was ruined. The warm sun shone, his gorgeous wife was sexy in short shorts and his kids cute as baby kittens, but the day was ruined because he was in it. He ruined everything, including the shriveled black wieners which were too burned to salvage. He threw them to Rocco.

"What was that about," asked Jen?

"Oh, nothing important. Bobby wants to play golf tomorrow but I told him I couldn't."

"He and Lulu and the kids are coming over for brunch on Independence Day. I invited them."

The Sheriff groaned and shook his head. Independence Day? Could she have picked a less ironic date? Of course she didn't know about the dirty work with the Commission. And didn't ask. She enjoyed the benefits of his dirty business far beyond his pay grade as much as he did but didn't want to know.

Well, at least the day couldn't get any worse.

"Mike Drake and his new girlfriend are coming too."

Wrong again.

CORA GOES SHOPPING

IN PREPARATION FOR HER SHOPPING expedition downtown Mrs. McCabe selected a spring dress a pale shade of peach like the one she had eaten earlier that morning with cream and sugar. Walter had his usual eggs and bacon only to suffocate them in black pepper. Later he complained of a stomachache and his kiss good-bye when leaving for the office tasted like alcoholic Pepto Bismal. He was so stubborn and foolish in his ways. Of course his gaseous stomach troubled him, he should eat peaches and toast in the morning like she did.

The house was quiet and she was pretty sure she had it to herself. She sat at the dresser mirror and manipulated her long silver hair expertly into a French braided roll. Surrounded by piles of clothing rejected earlier as unsatisfactory she had, again, inadvertently made extra work for poor Juanita. Try as she might to pick up after herself, it seemed sometimes beyond her capacity to comply with Juanita's supervision. But she really must try to be more helpful. Poor Juanita couldn't do everything.

She hurled a bundle of rejected garments toward the open closet but the closet floor was already piled so high with clothing it just spilled out again. She tried to push it inside with her foot and close the door but the pile obstructed its closure. The hat she wore was all wrong. She flung it toward the closet but it fluttered like a dead bird and dropped at her feet. She gave it a good kick into the closet.

She applied her favorite lipstick, some of which, because of her tremor, ended up on her teeth. She licked her teeth with her tongue, found a nice pearl necklace to pair with the peach dress and chose her comfortable flats for footwear. She wore rolled nylon stockings, twisted and knotted because their metal fasteners were uncomfortable and sometimes bruised her.

Her cat gazed at her inquisitively from the closet and meowed. She patted its head affectionately and said, "Do you know where my purse is? The white one with the glitter sewn into the fabric?"

She crawled on her hands and knees, searching the closet floor, pitching rumpled clothing behind her. She prowled through heaps of it, discovering mismatched shoes, several flattened misshaped hats and a set of keys she could not identify but which looked familiar. She found her purse buried in the pile and seized it before it could get away. She also found a lightweight brimmed garden hat to wear. She now had her purse, her keys, her money, her favorite walking cane. She scribbled a quick note for Juanita in the kitchen, locked the front door and left. Gripping her cane with one hand and the staircase railing with the other, she carefully descended the perilous stone stairs that led from her house to the street. Walter didn't like her to negotiate those stairs without his help but who was he to talk, about as steady on his feet as a one-legged drunk blind man with a noodle for a cane. Or something like that anyway, thought Cora, discarding the metaphor. I don't know.

The three laborious blocks uphill to the bus stop further reinforced her conviction that Seattle's history of earthquakes and shifting ground had somehow made the hills steeper over time. Their house was slipping down the hill. Maybe it would side down into Ballard Bay. Good riddance to it. They needed something smaller. No wonder she could never find anything. Anyway, for whatever reason, the three block trek uphill to the trolley stop was becoming more difficult each time she attempted it. She managed it, though, and collapsed onto a trolley-stop bench to catch her breath. Afterwards she began a quick inventory of her purse, finding her keys, lipstick, compact, chewing gum, Kleenex, wallet, a pen and small tablet, checkbook, cigarettes and lighter and lemon candies. Her cane rested in her lap. So nothing was missing. She saw the trolley in the distance, coming her way, its long spindly antenna attached to overhead cables sending up bright fiery sparks. She counted out fifteen pennies from her coin purse and clutched them in her moist palm in preparation to board.

She had difficulty managing her cane and keeping her balance when climbing aboard, but the nice driver left his station behind the wheel to help her up the steps. She knew this driver, a husky black man with a closely trimmed pencil-line moustache and pleasant demeanor, but failed to retrieve his name from her memory. She dropped fifteen pennies into the receptacle and began down the aisle. She recognized some of the passengers from somewhere. Perhaps they were neighbors. She smiled and nodded as she passed them. Both of her nylons slipped down her legs as she walked toward a vacant seat.

"It's twenty cents," the driver called after her. "Not fifteen."

"It is? I think you're mistaken. I've always paid fifteen."

"The rates went up over a year ago, Mrs. McCabe."

"I don't think so," she replied.

"No, honestly, Mrs. McCabe."

"Well, twenty cents is too much. Actually public transportation should be free. But I'll continue to pay fifteen cents. It's always been fifteen cents."

"Mrs. McCabe, do you see all these nice people seated behind you? Do you think it's fair for you to pay fifteen cents when they have paid twenty?"

The seated passengers watched, listening to this exchange with interest.

"No, I do not. If they paid twenty cents then I think you should return a nickel to each of them."

The driver smiled and said, "All right, Mrs. McCabe, have it your way. But next time I'm going to have to charge you full fare."

She dropped into a vacant seat and began knotting her fallen stockings.

"Such a lovely day," she announced to all. "Spring has come to Seattle."

And it was true. The sun shone for the first time all week. Woodland Park families were out strolling happily in lightweight summer clothing. High above the park several brightly colored dragon-shaped kites turned languorously in the blue sky. Girls were playing tennis when the bus passed the courts. In a residential area, boys were mowing lawns. Because of all the recent rain, the grass and shrubbery seemed to almost throb with gratitude. Across the aisle a sweet little boy with his head in his mother's lap seemed unable to contain his cough. His plump young mother, a woman with a pleasant round face who wore sandals with baggy trousers and a blouse covered by a lightweight raincoat, stroked his hair tenderly and fed him cough drops but they didn't seem to offer much relief. The boy coughed and coughed.

"Cover your mouth when you cough," said the boy's mother.

"Oh, that's all right," said Cora. "He can't help it. But I don't like the sound of that cough. He sounds very congested. How long has he had it?"

"Over a week. I'm not sure, exactly."

"What is your boy's name?"

"Oh, I'm sorry. I'm Mae Jacobson and this is my son, Calvin.."

"Hello, Calvin."

The boy buried his head deeper into his mother's lap without answering.

"He's kind of shy," explained Mae apologetically. "But he's a good boy."

The boy began coughing furiously again, his whole body convulsing with the momentum. He began crying and had trouble talking.

"It hurts, Mama. It hurts in my throat and chest."

"I know it does, son. I'm so sorry."

Cora noted the boy was dressed nicely and very clean. The boy's mother attire was less presentable and suggested a lack of resources.

"What is Calvin taking for that cough other than those cough drops?"

"I'm giving him hot tea and honey."

"No medicine for the cough?"

"We can't make a Doctor's appointment right now," she whispered confidentially. "I lost my job."

Cora rummaged in her purse and found her address book, a small tablet and pen and began writing.

"This is the address and telephone number for Doctor Mary Noonan. She's probably the only woman doctor in Seattle right now and she's very kind. She happens also to be my personal doctor. I'm writing her a note right now. Please just get a bus transfer and take this note to her office, Mrs. Jacobson. Explain that I sent you and instruct her to send the bill to Mr. Walter McCabe. I've done this before and you will have no problem. Doctor Noonan will write Eric a proper prescription."

"That's very kind of you," replied Mrs. Jacobson. But she appeared worried and sounded unrelieved. Cora instinctively understood the poor woman had no money to fill a prescription. She found a five dollar bill in her purse and squashed it into Mrs. Jacobson's hand.

"Take this too, for Calvin."

The woman began crying and said, "I wouldn't for myself, but for Calvin…"

"Don't say another word about it," insisted Cora. "I only wish I could do more."

At the next stop the woman asked the driver for a transfer and departed with her coughing son. The trolley entered heavier traffic and was soon skirting the waterfront. Cora looked out the window at men sleeping in doorways or right out on the sidewalk and shook her head. It was shameful the way the government was doing so little to help the poor. Walter was right that they were lucky to not be among them. The Depression had impacted them to a much lesser degree. Walter said they had to tighten their belts but assured her they were all right. They had a nice house to live in and ate two good meals a day.

The trolley turned uptown and soon they were amid the tall buildings of the commercial district. Cora rang the buzzer for her stop and merged with other pedestrians. Here were her favorite department stores, *The Bon Marche, Rhodes Department Store,* and of course the *Frederick and Nelson* branch of *Marshall Field,* her favorite of the three, which she entered.

The interior invited her to stroll among tables of sale items where attractive merchandise was on display everywhere she looked. Homelessness and the Depression were not in evidence here and seemed to belong to another country. Danny, the uniformed elevator operator, greeted her by name.

"Hello, Mrs. McCabe. Welcome to Frederick and Nelson."

"Hello, Danny. Is it true they are talking about making the elevators self-service?"

"Yes, there's rumors afloat, but nothing official."

"We won't shop here if they do."

The elevator stopped at house wares where she examined glassware, china, candelabras and silverware. The merchandise was of good quality but there were no sales or extraordinary bargains and nothing new she hadn't seen before.

Next stop was the dress department. What she needed was a sensible but compelling black dress that might compliment her silver hair. A young salesgirl showing just the beginning of a tummy suggestive of early pregnancy assisted her.

"Are you new here? You look familiar," said Cora, "but I don't think I've seen you in the designer dress department before."

"They transferred me from ladies hosiery and footwear."

She carried the dress into the dressing room and removed her peach dress and hung it on the door hook while changing into the black dress and examined herself in the full-length mirror. The dress was a little tight but she was slender and she liked the way she looked in it. But would it be suitable for the socials and benefits she and Walter sometimes attended? It was difficult to determine in the confining dressing room. How would it feel when dancing, for example?

She slung her purse over her shoulder, opened the dressing room door and maneuvered around the tables and hangars of clothing to get the feel of how it felt to walk in it. The salesgirl was nowhere around. Cora guessed she was in the stockroom retrieving items for other customers. No telling when she might finish in there.

She rode the elevator to the teahouse upstairs where she smoked at a table with a view to the city streets. The pastry here was baked in-house and delicious, served with English Breakfast tea delivered to her table in a silver pot and poured into delicate little ceramic cups. Her nylons had slipped again, and she knotted them before leaving. Insufficiently extinguished cigarettes smoldered in her ashtray when she rose.

"Just send the bill to my husband," said Cora. She added her signature.

"Of course, Mrs. McCabe."

She took the escalator downstairs to the second-floor cosmetics and jewelry department and she sat on a stool at a cosmetics counter to dab some rouge on her cheeks but, deciding against it, wiped it clean with a tissue. She tried several more shades before wandering off to racks of costume jewelry. What she needed was a diamond necklace to compliment the black dress. Not a real one of course, that was far too extravagant and indulgent. She found one she liked on the costume jewelry carousel and substituted her pearls on the rack. The mirror confirmed her instincts as correct. The necklace worked perfectly.

She rode the escalator to the ground floor and walked through the revolving glass doors where she was pleased to see the sun remained in evidence outside. It was pleasantly breezy, but with threatening dark rain clouds moving in from across the Sound. She was about to cross the street when she felt a man's grip on her upper arm.

"Mrs. McCabe?"

"Yes?"

The young man who addressed her was handsomely attired in a suit and tie. He wore his black hair combed straight back and had a cleft in his prominent chin. Cora thought she might have seen him earlier, when wandering about examining merchandise.

"I'm with the *Frederick and Nelson* department store. Would you come with me please? We would like a word with you."

"And who may I ask is *we?*"

"The management."

"Well, perhaps another time. I was about to have lunch."

"No. It has to be now. "

She felt his grip on her arm tighten as he tried to lead her away. She struck him hard across the knees with her wooden cane. Grimacing, he loosened his hold, but did not let go.

"Either release my arm, young man, or face the humiliation of an old lady's thrashing."

She wielded her can like a sword and waved it menacingly in his face. She became aware of a crowd of curious spectators. Among them was the saleswoman from the dress department and Mr. Reynolds, the store manager, Burt the store detective and a uniformed security guard.

"Mr. Reynolds," said Cora. "I'm so relieved you are here. This man who claims to be in your employment has been manhandling me."

Reynolds wore his light brown hair in a crew cut. He wore a tie and white shirt with an argyle sweater but no jacket. His gestures and manner of speaking had always struck Cora as moderately effeminate.

"I'm sorry, Mrs. McCabe. Why don't we all go to the security office and see if we can't sort this out."

"I would like a cigarette. Perhaps a glass of wine. I was about to have lunch. We can settle this right here."

"Very well, Mrs. McCabe. If you insist."

Cora fumbled in her purse for a Chesterfield.

Reynolds lighted it and said, "We seem to have a problem, Mrs. McCabe. Has Frederick and Nelson somehow given you the impression that our dress department is your own personal clothing rack?"

"Oh, so that's what this is about. Well of course not."

"But you're wearing one of our designer dresses without having paid for it. As much as we appreciate your past business we've had to get very serious with shoplifting, Mrs. McCabe. Do you intend to pay for this item?"

Trouble in Seattle

"I already have."

Reynolds looked askance to the saleswoman who shook her head no.

"This black dress is accounted for," said Cora. "I left the peach dress I was wearing on a hook on the dressing room door in trade. That dress, which incidentally was designer made and purchased recently, is considerably more elegant this one, which cost a fraction as much. You are lucky to have it for your inventory."

"Perhaps," Reynolds replied, "but Frederick and Nelson is not a secondhand store. Our merchandise is for sale only, not trade."

"No? Then how do you explain this necklace? I traded a genuine string of pearls for it and I might add I was cheated in the transaction. These diamonds are obviously fake."

The manager frowned and said, "We will need you to return the necklace as well, Mrs. McCabe."

"My husband will pay you. You know that."

"Yes, now that your theft has been discovered. But we have to consider how many thefts have taken place without our knowing."

"I am not a thief. I simply forgot I was wearing this dress. And why did your salesgirl let me leave with it? I'll tell you why. She wasn't present. She should have been available to complete the sale. Who knows where she was?"

"I had other customers, Mrs. McCabe."

"Then you were ignoring them as well. Mr. Reynolds, you know me. I am not a thief."

"Well, I'm afraid we will have to leave that up to the proper authorities to decide, Mrs. McCabe."

By now a substantial crowd had gathered.

Cora watched a squad car pulled up to the curb.

"I'm sorry," said Reynolds, "but we are under strict directives from the home office in Chicago to prosecute all shoplifters without exception. We had no choice but to call the police."

"I'm going to jail?"

Cora addressed the question to the policeman, who was opening the back door of the squad car to admit her.

"What about the dress she is wearing," said inquired the store manager of the policeman. "It does not belong to her. It must be either returned or paid for."

Cora lifted it over her head defiantly and handed it to the saleswoman. She stood wearing only a slip with her hat, sagging nylons and flat shoes. A murmur of shocked disbelief rose up from onlookers.

"Mail my peach dress to the address associated with my account and expect to hear from my attorneys."

Gripping her cane, she scooted into the back seat of the police car and said, "Who are you? I want your full name and badge number."

"Officer Arthur Ramos at your service, Mrs. McCabe. My badge number is 2511."

"Am I going to jail?"

"No, Mrs. McCabe. Not today you aren't. I'm taking you home."

She was certain she did not know this policeman. She'd met a few police officers when with Walter at the Policeman's Benevolence and Charity Ball, but only superficially. Walter of course knew many of the police who worked the waterfront and was friendly with Sheriff Gustafson.

"You're not under arrest Mrs. McCabe, but Frederick and Nelson, however, may see fit to file theft charges, and then you will get a summons to appear in court."

"Court? Whatever for?"

"Theft, Mrs. McCabe.'

"Hah. That's a laugh. *They* are the thieves. Did you see the *prices* in that store?"

PATROLMAN ARTHUR RAMOS

PATROLMAN ARTURO RAMOS, the newest member of the King County Seattle police department after transferring from San Pedro, California, parked his cruiser behind a late model banged up Hudson that he would learn later belonged to Walter McCabe. It began raining lightly, and the sky had turned gray.

He opened his umbrella and held it aloft for Mrs. McCabe while helping her exit the vehicle. Her hand felt soft and cool in his. He gently helped her out of the back seat and onto the pavement and placed his umbrella over her head protectively while she stabilized herself with her cane. Her thin slip, damp with mist, made visible how bone thin she was, how frail. She was a brittle skeleton wearing a slip. A fall would shatter her like an ice sculpture. He craned his neck looking up the perilous steps to the front porch and could not imagine her managing the steep winding tiers of slippery steppingstones without assistance. They had to be murder when wet.

"I'll help you up the stairs, Mrs. McCabe. Those stones have to be slippery in this rain."

"Thank you kindly, but I can manage fine."

"I'm going to have to insist, Mrs. McCabe. Please take my arm. You are under my protective custody and as such my responsibility."

"Very well then. Thank you, kind sir."

Her grip was surprisingly firm when she took his arm. He wondered how many times in her life she had made this ascent. She

232

was a damn mountain goat, this old lady, but for her own safety she needed to take his arm and let him lead. Neighbors not in evidence before were now watching from the shelter of their porches. He was used to it. Police always brought the curiosity of neighbors and Mrs. McCabe, wearing only a hat and slip and carrying her shoes, was somewhat a spectacle. Her nylons keep slipping and she stopped several times to hitch them up. At the top of the stairs he heard a piano being pounded inside. Whoever was playing it had best not quit their day job. Sounded like the keys were being struck with a ball peen hammer.

A girl probably no more than fifteen opened the door. Dark shinned with raven black hair, Indian or maybe Mexican like himself. She placed a thick brown blanket over Mrs. McCabe's bony trembling shoulders, embraced her and said, "You frightened us, Cora."

"I left you a note," Mrs. McCabe replied.

The noise from the piano stopped.

An elderly man wearing suspenders with wrinkled suit pants and an undershirt joined them under the porch roof. He was holding a stubby brown cigar in his left hand, on which a ring with a Mason's emblem shone.

To Cora he said, "Thank God you're safe. You know you're not supposed to go out without supervision. But where are your clothes, my dear?"

"Stolen, Walter my darling. But as you can see, I'm perfectly fine other than having my dress torn from my shoulders by opportunistic store managers."

"Tell me, Cora, has this police officer behaved toward you with appropriate courtesy?"

'Yes, dear. He's been a true gentleman and most helpful."

"Then thank you, officer."

Ramos accepted his firm handshake while the girl ushered Cora inside the house.

McCabe remained on the porch.

"My name is Walter McCabe. What is your name, officer?"

"I'm patrolman Arthur Ramos."

His birth name was Arturo Ramos but he gave his name as Arthur to avoid being identified as Mexican. Racial prejudice and animosity toward minorities was endemic in the Seattle police department even more so than in San Pedro. Seattle generally was a city in which races did not mix.

"Sheriff Gustafson is a personal friend of mine," said McCabe. "I'll put in a good word for you."

"Thank you but not necessary."

"Nevertheless I intend to extend my appreciation. So what's this about, officer Ramos? How did it happen my wife was brought home unclothed in a police car?"

"She was accused of shoplifting, sir."

"I see."

"The young girl who came to the door, does she live here?"

"She is our housekeeper and general helper. As you can no doubt imagine, Cora can be problematic and needs supervision."

"I'd like to ask the housekeeper a few questions for my report. It's just routine. Would you mind asking her to come out?"

"I can't imagine why that would be necessary, officer."

"Please understand we need to work together here in a co-operative spirit, Mr. McCabe. If your wife is formally charged by Fredrick and Nelson I will be called upon to testify. I would like to be able to truthfully report that your wife did not steal intentionally but accidentally, and that members of your household fully cooperated with police investigative procedure."

McCabe took the cigar out of his mouth and looked at it and said, "Is that so? Then please explain to me what information might our housekeeper have toward that end? She was not even at the scene of the alleged theft. I appreciate your escorting my wife home safely so I'll ask her, yes, but I will also inform her that she is under no obligation to comply."

McCabe went back inside the house without inviting him in. A moment later the girl opened the door and stood under the porch eave. She wore the blanket she had given earlier to Mrs. McCabe over her shoulders but her feet were bare.

The rain had intensified and rivulets of cascading rainwater poured from drainpipes and the corners of the porch overhang. The wind had picked up too. Ramos could hear the sway of trees and see a swirl of leaves loosen from lower limbs to dance briefly in the wind before falling to the wet lawn and steps.

"Cora needs help with her bath," said the girl, "so please be brief."

"Cora?"

"Yes, Mrs. Cora McCabe."

"You're on a first name basis?"

"Yes. I love her, actually. What's this about?"

"Could I have your full name please?"

"Why?"

"I need it for my report."

She did not reply. He studied her with a suspicion learned early in his career that had by now become almost automatic and involuntary. While it was normal and even expected for otherwise innocent citizens to sometimes display unwarranted nervousness or even fear when questioned by the police, this felt like something else. Past experience told him the girl was hiding something.

"I'm going to ask you again. What is your full name? Understand there is no point in refusing. I can easily obtain it by investigative means."

"It's Juanita Vogel."

"Age?"

"Fourteen."

"What's your nationality, Miss Vogel?"

"Italian."

"You're not Italian. You're either an Indian or Mexican like me. Are you a United States Citizen? Are you paid you for your services here? Do you have a work permit?"

"I am a citizen. I receive a small payment yes but the McCabe's are like family. I love them dearly."

"Where are your birth parents or legal guardians?"

"Both are dead. Why are you writing this down? Why do you even need to know?"

"It's just routine, Miss Vogel. Thank you for your cooperation."

He closed his notebook. She was hiding something, but there was nothing here of substance to pursue. The sun came out from behind the clouds and it stopped raining. People complained about the Seattle weather but it suited him. It was better than the cruel exposure of the glaring California sun that mocked him in full daylight for all to see as bill collectors and repossession teams descended on his rental, neighbors watching. They repossessed his convertible, their console radio; he'd even had to pawn Annette's wedding and engagement ring. He'd transferred to the Seattle P.D. to escape unpaid bills. To get here he'd had to borrow money from his tight fisted miserly Dad for the piece of junk he drove now, a 1928 Nash Advanced Six Coupe which seemed to have a personal grievance against him. Meanwhile the overdue bills ended up following him here anyway and he continued to be chased by collection agents who pursued him like vicious weasels. So much for a fresh start. The move had been hard on Annette and the kids too.

He tipped the wet brim of his hat in farewell and drove his patrol car to the precinct. Everyone in the department knew without exception police reports pertaining indirectly or directly to Walter McCabe were to be dispatched immediately to Sheriff Gustafson. A confidential file existed on McCabe accessible to the Sheriff only. Ramos didn't know why and it wasn't his business to. He typed up his report and forgot about it until a week later, off duty and at home working on his Nash in the driveway Annette called from their apartment doorway that he had a phone call.

She was wearing faded jeans and one of his wrinkled white shirts and her dyed hair was showing black at the roots. She needed a makeover and some new flattering clothing but he couldn't afford it. His transfer to the Seattle police department resulted in a loss of seniority and rank and a paycheck even smaller than what he had received in San Pedro. He'd only taken the Seattle post to evade the bill collectors and now the vultures were circling him again. Probably it was a bill collector on the telephone now.

"Who's it from, Annie?"

"I don't know."

"I want to finish with this clutch before it gets dark. Get a name and number and tell them I'll call back."

How he hated this damn car. In addition to the slipping clutch he was now trying now to replace, the tires were shot and the brake shoes were as bare as their cupboard. Fortunately, he had use of a squad car.

"The caller wouldn't give his name, Artie. He said it was confidential police business."

It was his day off and he was a lowly patrol cop so it didn't add up they would call him over something supposedly confidential. He worried he might be in some kind of trouble. Sighing, he dipped his greasy hands in a can of cleanser, wiping them on his pants.

"Oh no you don't, Artie. You aren't coming into my clean house with grease all over you."

He wiped his hands again, more thoroughly this time, unzipped his coveralls and stepped out of them, only then entering the house. He took the phone call in the living room. Annette had music playing on their radio and he turned down the volume. Whoever it was on the line must have heard him pick up the receiver and breath into it because he didn't even get as far as "Hello" before an unfamiliar voice said, "Patrolman Arthur Ramos?

"Speaking."

"How many people share your telephone line, Officer Ramos?"

"I don't know. It's a party line of maybe a dozen or so. Why?"

"What I have to say to you is strictly confidential is why."

"Who is this?"

"You don't know me. We've never met. I can't give you my name over the telephone. It's that confidential. Let me just say for now that I have information vital to your role as a police officer of the Seattle Police Department that is too sensitive to discuss on a party line. We need to meet where it is private and confidential as soon as possible. Now, if you're available. "

"How long is this going to take?"

"Just long enough to impart information and be on my way. Not more than an hour and probably less."

"We could meet here but I'd want to keep it short. It's a family day today."

"I understand and appreciate that, Officer Ramos. I could leave for your house immediately."

"It's an apartment complex. I'll give you the address."

"We already have it. Expect me in about 40 minutes."

Ramos hung up, puzzled. Police business would normally be conducted at the station.

Annette appeared from the kitchen, a cup of coffee in her hand, flour dusted in her messy hair, tiny beads of perspiration speckling her moist lips. Ramos found a hot pad on the kitchen counter and lifted the lid of the enamel cook pot. He took a cautious taste from a tablespoon, surprised at the proper degree of hot chili and flavor. She'd added cilantro, jalapeno, dried red chili flakes, cumin and the right amount of salt and pepper. It was an improvement over earlier versions, maybe her best so far.

"How is it, Artie?"

"I think you are finally learning to cook authentic Mexican, baby."

"Because I have a good teacher. I'm learning to make Mexican food the way you taught me."

"Where's Artie Junior?"

"Down for a nap. Who was that on the phone, honey?"

"I'm not sure. We're going to have a guest but its police business and won't take long. You don't need to serve anything but coffee."

He waited at the living room windows, surprised to see his mystery guest arrive by taxi. The man who got out was impressive in stature, easily over six foot with broad shoulders and a confident manner of carrying himself. He wore a suit that looked expensive and to Ramos he looked rich. Ramos greeted him at the door.

"I assume you are the man who called a half hour ago?"

The man smiled, extended his hand and said, "Correctly identified."

Once inside the house he said, "My name is Stone, Robert Stone. I'm an advisor to the City Council and a member of the

Seattle Waterfront Improvement Commission and the *Seattle Chamber of Commerce.*"

Ramos led him into the den and offered coffee, but Stone declined and got right down to business.

"Can you close the kitchen door, Officer Ramos? Not even your wife is to hear what I am about to confide in you. No one is to know I was even here."

Stone lighted a cigarette and offered one to Ramos, who didn't smoke.

"What I am about to tell you, Officer Ramos, is going to impact your career, your professional relations with fellow officers, your friendships, home and family and probably every aspect of your life as you now know it. But before I can tell you more I have to have your assurance of absolute confidentiality."

"I can't promise that if it involves a criminal matter. I would have to report it to Sheriff Gustafson."

"That's exactly the problem, Officer Ramos. Without your sworn promise of confidentiality, the most I can reveal is that Sheriff Gustafson and many of his deputies are about to become the subjects of a widely publicized scandal. Your Sheriff is presently being covertly investigated by Internal Affairs and I can assure you from what we have learned so far he's going to jail. So for that matter are a lot of officers under his command. It's going to be messy and we need a man we can trust inside the sheriff's department for ongoing reports pertaining to both the Sherriff and also Walter McCabe, whom we know you met recently and who is neck deep in corruption. We think you are the right man for the job but I must caution you; your life could be placed in danger by officers loyal to Gustafson if they became aware you were implicated in an investigation into his underworld network of criminal connections and activities."

"I don't get it, Mr. Stone. Why me? I have no quarrel with Sherriff Gustafson. I only recently came up from the San Pedro, California police department. I'm new to the Seattle police force. There are a lot of guys more experienced than I am and for that matter closer to the Sheriff."

"That's exactly the point. We believe as a newer officer on the force your loyalty to Gustafson is not what it is to the others. We also felt we owed you this opportunity. "

"I honestly can't imagine why, Mr. Stone."

"Had you not reported the young girl living in McCabe's house, we might never have known. Sheriff Gustafson didn't inform us and we believe he withheld the information deliberately. "

"Why would he do that?"

"We're looking into exactly that question. What we do know is that if you accept our offer and work with us on this investigation we can guarantee an expedited rise in rank and corresponding pay raise."

"I don't think that's a possibility, sir. Those kind of decisions go through a chain of command to personnel."

"I am here on behalf of the State Capital in Olympia, Officer Ramos. It is where the investigation into Sheriff Gustafson and Walter McCabe originated. You can be assured from the moment you accept your new assignment you will be promoted to Detective. The Sheriff and officers under his command will be told you are officially assigned to the McCabe investigation but not that you are also covertly investigating and reporting on Gustafson himself. Any significant information on McCabe is to be kept from Gustafson and reported confidentially to either me or my associate Michael Drake. But I must impress upon you that this matter is urgent and I need your full commitment. There's no backing out once you've signed on. We need someone we can count on."

"I'd need to talk it over with the wife before deciding."

"Of course. We understand that but you may confide only that you've been offered a promotion that will keep you away from the family more than before. Your wife is permitted to know only that you are on a confidential investigative assignment you are not allowed to discuss. No details about the assignment, now or ever. We'll need a decision soon. The State House wants swift action on this. My cab is waiting. Have your decision for me by the end of your shift next week, Officer Ramos."

Ramos stood in the littered front yard of his cramped apartment and watched the cab until it could be seen no more. He had a decision to make and not much time to make it and wasn't sure in what direction he was leaning. If he took the assignment, it would mean more money. Maybe they could move out of the low-income rental, put a down payment on a house. On the other hand, his promotion would arouse resentment and jealousy in the department. He'd be basically on his own. He turned and went back into the apartment undecided.

HOOVERVILLE

JACK WOKE TO HIS OWN SCREAMS, drenched in sweat, gasping, grinding his teeth and rubbing his eyes as if by rubbing them hard enough he might erase what he had seen. He lay on the mattress in the darkness of his windowless shack, listening to the occasional screams of other men. Hooverville at night became a nightmare factory. The camp was populated largely with veterans plagued with gruesome scenes of war in the trenches. Even those who were not veterans were afflicted with violence. They had fought scabs at picket lines, thugs at IWW rallies, had been chased by police dogs, beaten viciously by yard bulls, city police and recruited vigilantes.

Not until the murder of the man in the boxcar had he known personally the degree to which the ghosts of the dead could haunt a man. His dreams were vivid and horrifying. They attached themselves to him like bloodthirsty leeches. Even in the daylight he was not altogether free of gruesome imagery. He fought it, but his attention wandered.

He remembered nailing loose tin on the roof of his shack and becoming lost for most of the afternoon without hammering a single nail. He stared uncomprehendingly at the hammer in his fist as if uncertain how it got there or what he was doing with it. Easily distracted, he had difficulty with simple tasks. He became disoriented in a storm of imagery, hours passing before he emerged to awareness with no remembrance of where he had been and what he had been thinking. The dead man in the boxcar gently pulled on his sleeve or whispered in his ear. He would not let Jack rest. He would not let Jack forget. Jack tossed, turned, ground his teeth. He woke on his cot, shivering, drenched in cold sweat. He couldn't get dry for the sweat, couldn't get warm. Finally he ended up in the hospital with pneumonia. They put him on antibiotics. He shouted in the night. Nurses came running to his bedside.

"What's wrong, Mr. Vogel?"

He couldn't explain it.

"Nightmare," he said.

Other patients complained they couldn't rest for his screaming.

His fever subsided, and they sent him back to Hooverville with medication.

It was early morning just before daybreak. He waited for light to penetrate the shack, reluctantly parted the flap of his pup tent and removed the plywood door that leaned against the shack. Outside was the beginning of light but no sun. A dense fog hovered over the tin roofs of Hooverville. The air was damp on his skin and brought Goosebumps to his arms. The sky was heavy, weighed and pressed down by dampness.

He made a fire and boiled water in the coffee pot and washed in the enamel basin left by Wilson. He shaved in the small oval shaped cracked mirror, dressed in his raggedy wool pants, shirt, vest and necktie and took his pushcart out into the daylight for early pickings. He'd made the pushcart himself, utilizing salvaged oil drums cut lengthwise and connected with a borrowed torch to a metal pipe welded into a makeshift axle. He got the tires in trade for one of Wilson's overcoats. He used the cart to scavenge the alleys and industrial sites of the waterfront for salvageable materials to be sold for scrap or used for exchange within Hooverville's barter economy. It was awkward to maneuver and wobbled on the uneven ground.

Two days earlier outsiders had come down to Hooverville looking to hire men to break a strike by taking work as scabs. He was cautioned by more experienced men against it. A few Hooverites who either didn't know better or didn't care went ahead. Those who made it back to Hooverville were injured, filthy, bandaged and shaken by what they had seen, and swore they would never break a picket line again. Jack believed the harsh economic circumstances and lack of opportunity to be temporary. Roosevelt had been elected and was going to give them a New Deal.

He made the acquaintance of a neighbor who owned a rowboat and exchanged some carpentry work in return for its use. He paddled out into the sound and sat in the boat for hours with Wilson's fishing pole and tackle dangling in the choppy seawater, his mind drifting in unison with the movement of the fishing line while listening to the hypnotic drone of seawater sloshing against the side of his boat. He sometimes just sat there, rocking in the small rowboat, his mind equally adrift as he relived events from his past like a man who has had his memory revived after being in a coma.

He remembered in heartbreaking vivid detail his life with Alma during the years when they had been happy. He remembered how he had carried little Juanita on his shoulders into windswept fields of wildflowers, her soft little trusting arms around his neck. They'd put her on a tree branch where she would pretend she was a meadowlark and tweet into the forest. Meadowlarks answered her tweets. Juanita could imitate a meadow lark with such accuracy they sometimes flocked to her like she was their mother.

He remembered canoe trips along the Missouri River, the feel of the paddle against the current, leaves falling from the tree-lined river bank. He remembered the river stones Juanita insisted were jewels and kept in a secret outdoor location like buried treasure. He remembered afternoon picnics with Alma alone, how they'd roll entwined down grassy hills, laughing all the way. He remembered the kisses, the lovemaking in secluded woods. This was after the older kids had left but before her alcoholism got the worst of her, impairing her judgment and causing all kinds of trouble with the neuralgia and later the consumption. Even then she believed in her ability to discern omens and signals he missed. She knew she was dying long before he did, or even the doctors. He wished he had the benefit of Alma's gifts now, when it seemed like anything was possible in a future there was no way to prepare for.

Lea Macquarrie

He rocked with the boat, shamefully recalling how he had stood at the door of that enormous mansion on the hill, ringing the bell and nudging Juanita toward the wizened old lady who answered it. Giving her away to another family like a dog he could no longer keep. He meant to provide her with better life but he could not deny his relief at the time to be free of his responsibility to her. She was better off without him and he had felt an insurmountable burden of responsibility lifted from him upon releasing her. But he'd given away part of himself, part of Alma, and he had to live with the shame.

He tried to change the course of these thoughts but they were as persistent as the tide rocking his boat. He caught a Chinook salmon and cooked it slowly over a small fire in his shack. He served it with canned string beans and corn and slept well without dreaming of the man they had killed.

He was pouring a reheated pot of strong black morning coffee into a stained tin mug by the light of a kerosene lamp when a rare knock on the door caused him to accidentally spill some of the hot coffee over his fingers. He inserted the burned fingers into his mouth to wet them, reluctantly because his hands were dirty and he was sick, maybe with the flu, maybe residuals of the pneumonia, he didn't know he was no doctor but whatever it was it had him coughing his lungs out and gripped in its clutches to the point he was home in bed instead of out salvaging. It was cold and dark in the shack but then wasn't it always. He had no idea what time it was or who might be at the door. No one came here. He had no visitors. He was a known recluse. Wearing baggy denim overalls and long johns, he hobbled to the lopsided door and opened it hesitantly, anticipating trouble.

"Are you all right, Jack Vogel? You turned pale as a ghost a minute there. Don't you recognize me? We met once when you first came to the jungle and set up camp."

It was gray daylight outside, cloudy and raining lightly.

"I remember."

Jack was in no way inclined to confide in the Mayor that his first thought upon hearing a rare knock on his door was that the police had come to arrest him. Now he worried maybe the Mayor was here to warn him of their imminent arrival. Or maybe the Mayor had sprung a trap and was stalling him until the police arrived.

"Aren't you going to invite me in, Mr. Vogel?"

Jack stepped aside and said, "Ain't much to see, but watch your head Mister Mayor. This place wasn't built for giants like yourself."

"Call me Jesse," he replied, ducking his head in the entrance-way when entering.

The Mayor looked much the same as before, tall in stature, commanding in presence, handsome and bearing himself with an authority commanding respect. What was he, six two, six three? His nose appeared to have been broken more than once, at different angles, but his face was otherwise well proportioned, the features statuesque, masculine and interesting to look at. A man who had been around. A man of experience who had read many books.

Crouching because of his height and the low ceiling, the Mayor stepped further into the shack's interior. The plywood planks Jack had recently laid over the tarps on the ground gave under the Mayor's footsteps. The roof was uneven, lower in some places than others and the Mayor's head touched the rusted tin ceiling in places. He wore a rumpled pinstripe suit with a vest and a white shirt with a frayed collar, but had somehow managed to tuck his unfashion-ably long hair under his Stetson hat. Jack noticed the combat rib-bon and silver disk that the Mayor wore pinned to his suit coat. He recognized it. A *Victory Medal,* it was shaped into an angel wearing a crown and holding a sword same as his brother's. There was an-other medal next to it he did not recognize. He knew not to inquire. He knew from his brother Frank you didn't ask a man about his wartime experience unless he brought it up.

The Mayor looked around for a place to sit and spoke in the same operatic baritone he remembered from before.

"Where's your furniture, Jack?"

"I burned it for firewood Mr. Mayor. I don't have much a need for furniture. I'm out scavenging most of the day and when I get back if it's not raining I mostly sit outside on the stump until it's time to turn in."

He pointed to an empty telephone wire spool and said, "You can sit over there for now. I'll sit on this here upright Olympia Beer box."

"I can get you some furniture, Jack. The Unemployed Citizen's League delivers it regularly."

"I'd probably just burn it again. Not much room for it and not much need. Excuse me Mister Mayor, but since you have never paid me a visit in the past, I have to ask. Have I done something offensive? Broken a Hooverville rule of some kind?"

"No, you surely haven't. You've been aloof and unsociable but that's not an offense. Usually I pay honor to a man's wish for solitude and it goes against my grain to intrude, but I figured I owed it to Frank Vogel to look in on his kid brother. I know he would do the same for me. Your brother was that rare superior man who didn't always put his own wishes first. Bet he taught you good. Bet you're a lot like him in that regard."

He reached inside his suit pocket for a package of pipe tobacco and opened it, pinching clumps between his thumb and forefinger and pressing it down into the bowl of his pipe.

"Made this pipe myself," he said. "It's a sweet smoke and this is good tobacco. You want some?"

Jack accepted the pouch and measured a line of tobacco into a cigarette paper, smoothing it along the ridges and licking it closed.

"I have coffee made, Mr. Mayor. I'm sorry I can't offer you anything stronger. I don't have any liquor at all."

"No, I don't drink and I remember when we first met you said you didn't either. It's one of the things I respect about you Mister Vogel. Too many men down here have a drinking problem. But not you. "

"You can help yourself to the coffee on the stovetop, there's enough left for another cup but it's pretty strong."

The mayor lighted his pipe, held it between his fingers and puffed rapidly until it was fully combusted. He crossed his legs, emitted a huge amount of aromatic smoke and said, "Well Jack Vogel, it's not my business or nature to prod but I felt a need to see you. We only met once, and aside from my knowing you were Franks' brother I didn't know much about you. Still don't. But you don't have to tell me. Not my business as I said. But understand, Jack, you are not alone here. We are a community. Flawed and disadvantaged and politically divided yes, but a community nevertheless. It's tempting to insert political considerations into the making of our circumstances, but we're not about that. It's really about us being left to ourselves without interference at least until this cycle of bad luck passes."

The mayor rose from the spool and bent to a shelf made of loose bricks and boards and picked up a coffee cup, inspected it and poured a cup from the pot on the stove. He took a sip and made a face.

"God, Jack, this is awful."

"Well I warned you."

"You did, fair enough. I didn't come by for coffee so nothing lost. But it did feel like about time I looked in you and I was wondering why you haven't really gotten to know anybody. Not that it's any of my concern, just wondering how you're getting along and if you need anything."

"Not much time for socializing, Mr. Mayor. You know as well as anyone surviving here is a full time endeavor, Mr. Mayor."

"What I know is a man can't do it alone. Hooverville wasn't built alone, not by a single man but by several men in a cooperative spirit."

His pipe had gone out and he relighted it and said, "It's cold in here, Jack. You don't have any wood to burn?"

Jack gathered up some small pieces of driftwood and took them to the oil drum, removed the grate and deposited them inside and added some newspaper. He poured a small amount of kerosene over everything and threw in a lighted wooden kitchen match and jumped back as the flames shot up toward the tin roof with a whoosh.

The Mayor said, "You know, Jack, most of us use converted automobile gas tanks for a stove. Put some legs on it and cut away the top, you then have a nice little efficient stove. Some of the boys could help you make one if you like."

"This works for me. It was good enough for Wilson too."

"Well, up to you of course Jack. But let me ask you. Do you know why I am the appointed Mayor of Hooverville?"

"No sir, I do not but you seem like a good choice to me."

"I try, Jack, I try. But I kind of became mayor by default. You see, I was one of the first of twenty men to originally settle here. When the depression came I bummed around like everyone else, rode the rails to wherever there was rumor of work. One day I read in the newspaper a fact finding commission appointed by President Hoover advised it was not in the best interest of men to move all around the country in search of temporary work, but better for them to settle in one place. I ended up in Seattle and for a time it was hard going, sleeping in the street with newspaper for blankets, standing in food lines for watery soup, soliciting the Salvation Army or whoever might lend a helping hand or a place to flop. But you know what, Jack? Charity just kept me on the street. That's when me and about twenty other men I knew and trusted decided to build a hobo jungle here on the tide flats where there used to be a shipbuilding plant. I'm a good judge of character and when I need help I'm not too proud to ask for it."

Jack added some wood to the fire, which was quickly burning out. The inside of the shack was cloudy with smoke from the fire. He watched the Mayor remove a handkerchief from his breast pocket and wipe his eyes.

"We were said to be a vagrant mob of undesirables, bums who presented a health hazard to the city and were given seven days to get out. We ignored them. Three weeks later about two dozen men from the fire department came with torches and kerosene. By then we had about 1200 shacks in the jungle and they set it all ablaze. The fire smoldered for two days. We got out with our lives, returned for what little possessions we could salvage and rebuilt. A month or so later they were back with the torches again. This time we expected them and were prepared. We dug in with whatever tools we could get, shoveled the loose sand out of the shipyard's concrete fireproof machinery pits and covered the pits with salvaged sheet metal. They couldn't burn through concrete or metal, though they tried. Still lost most of our shacks though, and again had to rebuild.

"It was then that a man unlike any other before or since strode into our midst. He was not one of us and did not belong, drove big fancy family car, wore a nice suit and polished shoes and an expensive looking Stetson fedora. He asked if anyone was in charge and they sent him to see me, since I was the Mayor and all. The man's name was Walter McCabe and he said he wanted to lend a helping hand. Not physical labor, he was too old for heavy lifting and lacked construction skills, but help of the legal kind."

"Did you say Walter McCabe? "

"Why? Do you know him?"

"I met him once, briefly."

"McCabe is the one who brought us attorney Jeremiah Wells. It was Wells who helped us organize and sue the city for harassment, conspiracy and arson. The matter was taken up with city hall during the fall of 1932 during a city election. A new city commission was inaugurated after the election and the newly elected Seattle Health Commissioner decreed we be allowed to squat on these grounds without interference provided we met with certain health and sanitation codes. The new fire marshal swore his department would be used only to put out fires, not set them. In return all charges against the city would have to be dropped. How long you been here now, Jack?"

"Can't say for sure. I don't have a calendar and don't keep track."

The mayor tossed his mostly empty coffee from the cup to the ground and said, "How can you drink this stuff? You should come by my place for some real percolated coffee sometime and taste the difference for yourself."

"I'll do that," said Jack, but he had no such intention.

"Jack, I want to impress upon you it was men working together that made this place and men working cooperatively together who saved it. It's not always in a man's best interest to be a loner, Jack. There is no shame in asking for help. It's what we do here. Ask for help and give it. We all mostly get along here Jack. Whites, Negros, Indians, Chinese, it doesn't much matter. You may not know it, Jack, but the men around here respect you. It's true that no one here knows you much, but as a brother of Frank Vogel men will listen to you. I was hoping you might consider sitting in on some of our Council meetings. Maybe even become a member."

"I'm honored for you asking, Mr. Mayor, but I don't think I'm suited for it. I like to be by myself. It's one of the reasons I stay here. Privacy and all."

Solitary by inclination and preference, he did not solicit friendship. He bore no ill will toward men no matter what their color or inclination, but kept his distance from everyone equally and as much as possible stayed to himself. Mostly he wanted to hear more information about McCabe but wasn't sure how to go about it. He lighted his hand rolled cigarette with a wooden kitchen match, took a deep draw from it and exhaled a long trail of gray smoke. In his mind he saw through McCabe a way back to Juanita. He didn't know if he wanted it. It would better their chances of evading the law if they stay separated. And what if she wanted to come live with him in Hooverville? Children were not allowed here. How would he care for her?

"What else can you tell me about this man McCabe?"

"What do you want to know?"

"I'd like to know where he lives. Do you have his address?"

"Well, why would you even want to know that, Jack?"

"It's personal, Mister Mayor."

"I don't have his home address and wouldn't give it if I did. I suppose there's no harm in telling you where he works. He has an office on Pier 91. But I have to say, Jack, I'm a little disappointed I can't count on you for help."

"I'm sorry Mister Mayor but as I told you before, I don't like to draw notice."

The Mayor banged his head on the ceiling on the way out, dislodging a loose sheet of tin. He reached up and easily repositioned it. Jack walked him out, hacked into his fist and watched him go. He'd been suppressing that cough all during the visit. Who could say for certain the meddlesome Mayor might not suspect him of contagion and evict him? The man was getting into in his business and he didn't know whether he could trust him. And why bring up the name McCabe? Was there something more going on here than mere coincidence? Were they onto him? If only Alma were here, to interpret these signals. He stared after the Mayor, his heart pounding. For the first time since arriving he felt unsafe in Hooverville.

MAKING AMENDS

JACK DIDN'T KNOW WHAT EXACTLY he was going to say to Walter McCabe when he got to Pier 91 but here he was, walking along the waterfront intending to introduce himself as Juanita's father. It was time to make amends for having acted hastily and irresponsibly on the sole basis of a recommendation from the Unemployed Citizen's office when trusting McCabe with his daughter. He regretted the decision but what was a man to do? They had been starving at the time and without options. A man made mistakes it was part of life you couldn't avoid it but some mistakes could be corrected and should be. Turning his daughter over to the care of Walter McCabe was the worst mistake he ever made.

For a year he had isolated himself in his shack, a recluse, too ashamed to look a man in the eye and say I was not always the bum you see before you now. He could barely look into his own face in the mirror when shaving. He was too ashamed. He could not save his wife from the alcohol that was killing her and he gave his daughter to another man to raise. That was the truth, the only truth that mattered.

Men were out with their pushcarts, some nodding in greeting but most silent and grim, among them relative newcomers who did not know who he was or his brother Frank. Which was fine by him. It was daylight, but where was the light? There had been consecutive weeks when he did not see the sun and the sky and sea were the same monotonous shade of gray as the concrete under his shoes.

When he inhaled deeply it did not feel like air entering his lungs. It felt liquid, like he was breathing into gills. He could not keep from coughing. He coughed more than he talked.

It had rained heavily in the night and he had not slept well on the damp mattress where, in the shelter of his dark pup tent while listening to the rain bombard the leaking tin roof of his shack, he coughed his lungs raw.

It was not raining now, but his hair was damp and matted to his head with dew as he walked. He was sloshing through puddles that leaked into the holes in his shoes, his toes squishing in thick socks that were like wet towels on his blistered feet. Silent piers and huge inactive gray merchant ships bore witness to his passage as he walked parallel to the waterfront where cranes for loading and un-loading ships were mounted. Both the cranes and ships were inac-tive. On the hillsides were more cranes. City planners and demoli-tion crews had abandoned a project to level the steeper hills. Mean-while Puget Sound was a parking lot for barges piled high with the removed dirt, which was periodically dumped into its depths. Much of its residue floated for days before sinking to the bottom. When out fishing in the rowboat, he had often had to row through a drift-ing carpet of wet floating gravel to open waters. Once, fishing in the Sound in the afternoon, he had seen a whale. There was so much marine life here. But it was a place better suited to fish than men. He followed Railroad Avenue past Firehouse Station Number Five where its fleet of fireboats was anchored. He wondered if this was the Fire Station responsible for burning down Hooverville back in its early days.

Most of the pier entrances were chained and locked but not all. Tramps fished with crude makeshift fishing poles. There were bums everywhere. He watched a pristine white ferry glide toward shore, its contrabass foghorn reverberating over the choppy wa-ters of the sound as it approached the pier. He crossed the street and walked the railroad tracks for a while but gave up when they evoked recollections he would rather forget. He didn't know if he could ever walk railroad tracks again without conjuring a disturb-ing sequence of imagery and memories best forgotten. He passed

Lea Macquarrie

the ironically named *Millionaires Club* where tramps stood in food lines waiting to be admitted for stale bread and watery pea soup. He knew the place well, had frequented it with Juanita back when she still belonged to him.

Finally he stood at the threshold of Pier 91. It appeared to be deserted. A locked gate prevented entry to its elongated wooden dock. Behind the gate was a watchman's shack and inside of it a uniformed man could be seen reading a book while smoking a pipe. Jack stood silently watching swooping seagulls dive into the cold waters for fish. He envied the swooping gulls their freedom. They had no predators, no one wanted to capture them and lock them away in a jail. He approached the gate.

The watchman stepped outside of his shack, stood on the opposite side of the chain link fence, took the pipe out his mouth and gestured with it as if it were a baton and he was leading an orchestra.

"This is not open to the public, Mister."

"I have business with Walter McCabe. Are those his offices down at the end of the pier?"

"Yeah but he ain't here. No telling when he will be. He keeps his own irregular hours."

"What kind of man is McCabe? Do you know him?"

"Of course I know him."

"Do you think he'll eventually show up here today?"

"Always does."

"I'll wait."

"Suit yourself. He'll be along. He drives a Hudson Hornet. Banged up but a fine automobile. I warn you though, you see him coming, get out of his way. He's the worst driver you could ever imagine."

He crossed to the other side of the street, squatted, rolled a Bull Durham and smoked and waited hopefully because who could say with absolute certainty that Alma was not right in her assertion there were active spirits influencing how the dice landed? Alma's Crow spirit might somehow be weaving into the fabric of his life a reunion with their lost daughter right now. He needed only to win McCabe's sympathy and cooperation to reunite with his missing daughter. He would declare his love for her, apologize to her, promise he would never leave her again and mean it. He would wipe her tears away with kisses.

A damaged late model Hudson Hornet stopped inches short of the gate. He dashed across the street to the gate where the Hudson waited to be admitted. For a brief moment, approaching the vehicle, he saw his own reflection in the window; the unshaven dirty ghoulish face of a man wearing a torn sweat-stained fedora, his white shirt turned a pale dirty shade of gray, its frayed collar missing a neck button, the necktie soiled and askew. A bum.

He knocked resolutely on McCabe's driver's side window. Mc-Cabe slowly rolled down his window as if rolling down the reflection itself. The Hudson may have been banged up on the outside but inside it was immaculate and luxurious, doubtlessly more airtight and protected from the elements than Jimmy Wilson's shack. Mc-Cabe wore a Stetson hat and a suit with a matching vest buttoned almost to the throat of his white shirt. He was of average build but with a pot belly, his large hands on the wheel displaying long wrinkled fingers and a gold wedding band. He wore rimless round eyeglasses. Jack guessed him to be in his early sixties but it was hard to tell. His superior appearance and demeanor was somewhat diminished by the cigar clamped between his teeth and liquor on his breath but who was he to judge a fondness for cigars and strong drink? This was a man who had earned the right. A man with his own office, his own ship, or so he'd heard. Why would Juanita ever want to leave such a man for a failed tramp such as himself?

He was not one to whom good fortune was dispensed. Juanita had once said to him, in the Hotel Lee, that he was unlucky, that nothing ever seemed to work out for him. Nothing since then had changed and it was unlikely anything would. It was probable that in his attempt to reconcile with Juanita and her new family he once again was about to make an irretrievable mistake he would regret. What after all did he have to offer her? He had nothing. Even the shack in Hooverville was not his; it was owned by Jimmy Wilson.

"Mister McCabe? Mister Walter McCabe?"

McCabe regarded him with an expression of mild curiosity.

"Yes. Do I know you?"

"We met once when I was doing some work with the Unemployed Citizen's League. I recognized your car and wanted to say hello."

"Well, hello. I didn't get your name."

"Jack."

"Well, Jack, it's a pleasure to see you again but I have work to do so. Is there anything I can do for you? Do you need anything?"

"I could use a job."

"Wish I could help you out, Jack. I'm in no position to hire anyone and may be out of a job myself the way things are going."

"It's okay, Mr. McCabe. I understand."

"Well, like I said, wish I could help out."

McCabe rolled up his window, nodded farewell, passed through the gate and drove slowly to the three story aluminum building at the end of the pier. The watchman closed the gate and locked it. Jack watched from outside of the locked chain link fence as McCabe parked the Hudson and climbed the steps to his office, and then the man was gone. So too, for now, was his opportunity to be reunited with Juanita. Great was his relief. He was ashamed to admit it, but there it was. He was a man not only afraid of the law and his decisions in life, but of his own daughter.

When he heard that the Hooverville post office was holding a letter for him he became afraid all over again. No one was supposed to know he was even here. He went over to the postmaster's shack early, but nobody was home. He waited around, sitting on a stump, rolling a cigarette. It was a clear June day; it hadn't rained all week, and the mud had mostly dried. Seagulls swooped overhead in the mostly cloudless blue sky. He heard the foghorn of the Orcas Island Ferry announce its arrival, then looked out over the cold blue-green waters of Puget Sound and watched it glide into the ferry landing.

He smoked the cigarette, wondering who might have written him a letter. He figured maybe it was Vi, though she wasn't much for writing, and when he thought about it she had no way of knowing he was down in Hooverville anyway. He finished his cigarette, field stripping it and shredding the paper. After a while, far down a narrow passage between shacks, the postmaster came into view, recognizable because of the cowboy hat he always wore.

He nodded to Jack upon arrival and said, "I got a letter for you inside."

"That's what I hear."

"Been holdin' it awhile now. You're rarely home to receive a delivery and there's no way to leave it. You should check on your mail more often, Jack."

"Well, nobody much writes me so there's been no need."

"Well somebody wrote you this time. Come on inside, Jack. I'll fetch the letter."

Wheezing, the postmaster unlocked a padlock on the door to his shack, which was windowless and dark. Jack followed him inside and immediately stumbled, almost falling. When the postmaster lighted a kerosene lamp, Jack saw the place was strewn from one end to the other with piles of metal tubing, scrap metal, bricks broken and whole, bins of glass bottles, and pieces of thick chain, rope and piles of wound wire.

The postmaster lighted two more kerosene lamps. Jack noticed a claw-footed bathtub in a dark corner, but when he looked closer discovered it filled to the brim with rusty nails, screws, bottle caps and other debris. After much rummaging, the Postmaster attended to a large wooden box filled with mail. He then began looking among the envelopes for Jack's letter.

"This here is just the most recent box of mail," he said. "I get letters every day from people all over the country looking for relatives who were either never here or long gone, usually mother's looking for their lost sons. I keep most letters six months or so, then I burn them. Here's the one for you, Jack."

Jack took it from him, examining the envelope. It had a Seattle return address, but without a name identifying the sender.

"You need any help reading, Jack?"

"I can read some."

"Well, let me know if you do. A lot of men here can't read; it's nothing to be ashamed of. I read real good. It's one of the reasons they made me Postmaster. Good news?"

"I don't know exactly," said Jack.

Jack stumbled over the words as if they were dark obstacles on an ill-lighted path. The letter was written on formal stationary bearing a woman's name and address. He had been improving his reading for months, or trying to, utilizing Jimmy Wilson's paperback westerns as a study guide. He read the letter several times and believed he had the general idea of it.

> *Dear Jack,*
>
> *I don't know if this letter will get to you or if you have moved on, but I wanted to write and see how you were making out. My shack isn't much but you are welcome to it for as long as you need it and I hope it is okay for you.*
>
> *I guess I'm pretty sick.*
>
> *The Doctors say I'm going to die.*
>
> *I'm living with my sister in the Wallingford District. You'll find the address here on her stationary. She takes good care of me, and that's for sure. I told her about you and she said to invite you up for supper sometime. You should take her up on it, because she's a darn fine cook and real nice lady and it would make her happy.*
>
> *That's all for now,*
>
> *Your pal,*
>
> *Jimmy Wilson.*

Some "pal" he turned out to be. He had been derelict in his duty in not having thanked Wilson earlier. He should have gone up to the hospital from Wilson's shack the very next day to thank him. It took a man saying he was dying to get him to do the right thing. Without Wilson's offer of the shack, who could say where he might be? Nowhere good, and that was for sure. He would call on Jimmy Wilson soon. He should have done it earlier.

CAT CREEK

ELVIRA VOGEL SAT ON THE STEPS OF HER dilapidated porch, mad as hell and undecided whether the rifle balanced across her knees was intended to guard her vegetable garden, supply her pantry with venison jerky, or for stone cold personal satisfaction. Deer had jumped the five- foot protective wire fencing during the night and ravaged her vegetable garden. Not for the first time, either. She raised her rifle and sighted into the woodland where, because of drifting islands of mist tentatively enshrouding the tree line, it was impossible to see up the dirt road to the crest of the hill. She returned the rifle to her knees. Damn deer was probably watching her right now through the cover of trees and underbrush beyond the dirt road. She'd have to sit here all day and night to bag it, if even then.

It was early enough to still be chilly and she wore denim pants, work boots, a man's flannel shirt and padded vest. In another three hours the sun would be up fully. By then she'd be working in her bra and underpants with beads of sweat running down her back into the crevice of her big butt, flies buzzing in her ears and mosquitoes biting her fat ass whenever she bent over and showed some.

The garden was largely ruined and that's what she got and deserved for not having dogs like everybody else, but she'd been afraid of dogs since being mauled as a little girl. Dogs were basically wolves, in her opinion. She hated them and she hated people who loved them. Everybody that is except Billy Rasmussen, who she had to begrudgingly admit she still had feelings for but who was a low-down two-timing no-good cheating son of a bitch. She could hear Billy coming now, the sound of his truck far off. She popped the tab of her can of Canadian beer, less intoxicating than her home brew and her first of the day, swallowing half of it before Billy's truck emerged from within the mist.

Filthy with mud, dented, banged up and mistreated same as he done her, Billy's truck rattled and bumped along the dirt drive stopping short of the woodpile.

"Your truck sounds like shit," she told Billy as he stepped out. "Looks like it too."

He said something in return, but she couldn't hear him because of all the barking and growling of his damn Siberian Huskies which had leapt out of the truck bed and were now snarling and running circles around one another. She sighted her rifle in their direction and said, "Keep those damn dogs away from me, Billy, or I'll shoot them dead. You know I will."

"Hush!" shouted Billy. "Stay."

They settled immediately at his command. The dogs were well trained; she'd say that for them.

"I'm going to get me a new truck," said Billy.

"With money you're making now that you're a bigshot BIA sellout?"

"Damn it, Vi. Would you please let up on that?"

He maneuvered around the woodpile, hitching his belt as he approached the porch. Since losing twenty pounds or so he was always tugging his pants like they might fall down. Why didn't the cheapskate just break down and buy some pants that fit? He looked good though, she had to admit. Not that he didn't before. The way he had moved with the extra weight had always been endearing, but sexy as all get-out now that he had lost it. This wasn't the first time she'd noticed his butt had acquired a shape that made a girl just want to swat it.

Billy stepped up onto the porch steps, which audibly creaked. He was not in his police uniform and wore jeans with a red and black checkered lumberjack shirt and boots. She swallowed the last of her beer and tossed the empty can into the gravel behind the woodpile with the others.

Billy pointed toward the pyramid of empty beer cans and said, "You know it's only nine in the morning, right Vi? You think you might have a little problem there?"

"It may be early for you, Billy, but I get up when it's still dark. Been cutting, splitting, and stacking that wood for hours now. Not that I have to explain a goddamn thing to you."

He bounced a little on the porch floorboards, feeling where they were loose.

"This porch needs some care, Vi."

"Yeah, well, most everything around this place does."

"What you need is a man around the house."

"I need a man around the house about like I need a second nose on my face. You had breakfast yet?"

"Just coffee."

"Well, come on in. I'll fix us something."

She rose from the porch steps, gesturing for Billy to go on into the house.

"Go on in and settle yourself, Billy. I'm going to get us some eggs from the hen house."

"I intend to stand right here and enjoy looking at your rear as you go."

"Well there's damn sure more of it than when you last saw it."

When was that? You lost track of time out here where nothing changed and there were no events other than the weather.

"Go on inside now," she said. "Nothing to see here."

She walked backwards to the hen house. She wasn't ashamed of her butt, but she sure wasn't going to show it to Billy. Not that he hadn't seen it plenty of times before but that was the point. He'd lost the right to be fresh with her. It wasn't even a matter of "you can look but you can't touch". He was no longer allowed even to look. She heard the screen door close on the porch and knew Billy was inside.

In some ways the wood-frame hen house was sturdier than the one she lived in. She depended on those eggs for protein and didn't want coyotes coming out of the woods and killing her prize chickens. The habitat was protected by a tall wire fence and the coop itself was also made of wire, with a tin roof. She opened the gate and closed it behind her, entered the coop and hoisted a sack of feed. She fed the chickens first, then picked five prime brown eggs and carried them back to the house.

Billy sat on her bed though there was a chair right there next to it, and she couldn't fool herself she wasn't tempted. Which even made her madder at him than she was already. Mad at Billy but herself too, for still having feelings for him.

She put on a pot of coffee, mixed some biscuits for the wood burning oven, and scrambled the eggs. Billy was quiet. She could feel him watching her the whole time. She carried the breakfast to the small wooden table and set it down. Billy took a chair across from her and ate the eggs in less time than it had taken for her to cook them. She brought some strawberry preserves from the cupboard to the table. Billy applied it liberally to the biscuits when they were ready.

"You always did make the best jam," he said. "Biscuits too."

He was quiet after that. He seemed nervous.

"You made good love, too Vi. I think about it all the time, what we did."

"Go see one of your Cathouse Creek whores, Billy."

"I could sleep with every last one of them and all of them put together wouldn't add up to one Elvira Vogel."

"Well, that was a long time ago, Billy. Things have changed."

"Not that long ago. My feelings for you haven't changed. We could give it another try, Vi."

"Not as long as you have that damn BIA job we can't. I won't be with a man I'm ashamed to be seen with."

"Damn it, Vi, we've been over this. I needed the money, the job was offered, and if I didn't take it somebody else would."

"You made your choice, Billy. You know I hate cops."

"You have it wrong in your head, Vi. I'm more of a peacemaker than a cop. I don't go around making trouble for people. Besides, don't you think we have need of a little police intervention around here from time to time? We've got problems here with alcoholism, spouse and child abuse, bar fights in town, we even had a horse thief awhile back."

"People around here always managed to settle their differences without the police, Billy. All the police ever done around here is interfere. Why are you even here this morning instead of working?"

"Well, for two reasons. One is I came to ask you to the dance Saturday night."

"I ain't going. What's the other reason?"

Billy sighed and pushed back his chair.

"This isn't easy, Vi. You know that Detective I came here with last time?"

"The man in the suit? Yeah. I didn't like him."

"I don't like him much myself but he's in our lives whether we like him or not."

"Not in my life he ain't."

Billy drank the last of his coffee, wiped his mouth with his sleeve and scooted back his chair. He looked at Vi with a worried expression and said, "He can bring a world of trouble down on you, Vi. Federal trouble I can't protect you from. He's connected Jack and Juanita with the murder of the missing man he was hired to find. If he brings in the FBI and you aren't truthful you can be charged with aiding and abetting a criminal."

"Jack is no criminal. Whatever they think Jack did, they are wrong. "

"Probably so but here's what the investigation has uncovered so far. It seems a tramp was found murdered along the tracks in Western Idaho near the Washington state line. His head was bashed in so it took a while to identify him. Turns out the man was not your ordinary tramp. In fact, he probably wasn't a tramp at all because he was riding the rails by choice. Seems the deceased was out slumming. Turns out he had rich influential relatives. Coroner's office was able to estimate the time of death as falling within the time frame of when Jack and Juanita might have been on the train. Both Jack and Juanita are considered persons of interest if not yet actual suspects."

"Jack's damn sure no killer, Billy. He has no meanness in him.

And the so called investigation sounds phony. How would they know when Jack and Juanita were on the train? And how many others were riding the rails during the time period. Someone might have been killed, but it's got nothing to do with Jack or Juanita."

"They won't tell me what it is, but they claim to have substantial evidence placing him at the scene of the crime."

She poured him another cup of coffee from the tin pot on the woodstove and said, "Probably just talk."

Billy took a sip and blew across the surface of his cup to cool it.

"I hope you're right, Vi."

"I usually am, though I was wrong about you, Billy."

"How's that?"

"I thought you were a better man than you turned out to be."

"I wish I had been. I wanted to be."

"You didn't want it bad enough."

"I do now, Vi, and I'm trying. "

"Well I wish you luck, Billy, I really do. But if you think we can start over, it's too late. Too much damage has been done. You broke my heart."

"I'm sorry, Vi."

"I know you're sorry, Billy. It's okay. I'm over it now."

"Well, can't blame a man for trying. Let me know if you change your mind."

"You know I ain't about to, Billy."

"I think you still love me, Vi."

"You done with your breakfast, Billy?

"Looks that way."

"Then its time for you to get your ass in that junk heap truck of yours and go."

Billy slid his chair away from the table and rose, looking tall and sexy and fit as a racehorse to ride. She wondered if she would rather take him to bed or shoot him. Maybe take him to bed and then shoot him. He strode out the door, his boots sounding on the creaky porch steps, and went to his truck. He waved, a little sadly she thought, and climbed up into the truck cab and drove along the wooded dirt road out of her sight.

RAMOS

HE AND ANNIE WERE PREPARING for a dinner party when Stone called and told him they were taking him out on assignment. The timing couldn't be worse. He would not only have to leave the preparation to Annette, but it was possible he might miss the party altogether.

"What am I supposed to tell the guests, Artie?"

"Tell them I was called away on police business. It's the truth."

They came for him in a 1929 four door model J Duesenberg. Neighbors came out on their porches and front lawns to gawk at it and he couldn't blame them. They had probably never seen a luxury model Duesenberg before. Other than in the movies, neither had he. It was a car fit for a celebrity millionaire or bigshot politician, but not for a police officer. Policemen didn't drive vehicles like this; they couldn't afford them. But then, Stone had never claimed to be a police officer, only to be working on a special police investigation with political connections at the State House in Olympia.

He'd been notified that he was to wear his best suit, shirt and tie and shoes because they were to investigate an illegal gambling operation for high rollers and needed to look the part. Ramos had only his one suit and his dress shoes were unevenly worn at the heels. He felt cheap and inferior, dressed in his shabby Sears catalog mail-order suit.

Stone, leaning against the Duesenberg with the heel of one foot on the running board, wore tailored black trousers that fit him perfectly, a crisp white shirt with a matching high buttoned vest. He

266

was staring in the windows while lighting a cigarette with a golden lighter. A driver he didn't recognize occupied the driver's seat but didn't get out of the car.

"Who are those men," asked Annette. "They sure don't look like policemen to me. And why do they have that car?"

"I told you. They're part of a special investigative unit I'm not supposed to talk about. Please don't ask me again, Annie. I can't tell you more than that."

The driver honked the horn three times, long and hard. They weren't coming in. Ramos turned from the window and went for his inferior suit jacket hanging over the chair in the cramped kitchen where Annette was cooking. He smelled spices on her hair when giving her a kiss on the cheek."

"You're supposed to put the spices in the pot, Annie, not in your hair."

"Yeah? Well you better be back for our party tonight or *you* will be wearing it. And what kind of mousey kiss was that, Artie? I want a real kiss."

He kissed her firmly on the mouth but didn't enjoy it. She was still nursing and her breasts were swollen but not in a way he liked. They leaked milk and he did not want to lick or suck them though he used to, but no more. He still loved her and wanted to be with her though. He'd recently talked about it on the telephone with his former partner and best friend in San Pedro who used to ride shotgun with him on their rounds who said it was natural after the birth of a child and would pass.

He made a move toward another kiss but thought better of it and went out the front door and crossed to where the Duesenberg was parked. He knew without looking Annette was standing at the windows watching him. She was going to be angry about having been left with the responsibility of hosting a dinner party without him and he didn't blame her. It was hard enough being the wife of an ordinary police officer but worse married to one on a confidential assignment with secretive and mysterious associates she was not allowed to know anything about. He felt bad about it, but he knew his new job would be one with unpredictable hours and she would have to get used to it and try to understand.

Stone opened the back door of the Duesenberg for him, closed it and proceeded to the front seat next to the driver where he turned around, leaned over the seat and stared at him appraisingly.

"I can see we're going to have to get you a new suit, Ramos. It's important to look the part. Don't worry, we'll get you one."

Ramos frowned. He was clearly out of his league. Meanwhile the plush leather back seat responded in maximum comfort to his every slight adjustment. They rounded the corner at the end of the block and were underway, where exactly Ramos had not yet been informed. He could not help but notice the Duesenberg suspension. It was as if they were floating on air instead of driving on a road. Even on streets that were brick there was no feel of the road. Nor was there road noise. It was like they were sealed inside, impenetrable and separated from any outside interference.

The driver, watching him in the rear view mirror, made eye contact and said, 'How do you like the car?"

"Great. Let me guess. It's not from the Seattle PD motor pool."

"Ha ha no, Artie. This is my car. I'm Mike Drake. We're going to be working together."

Ramos, from his position in the back seat, saw Drake's small brown lifeless eyes in the mirror. His gold cufflinks and watch peeking out from the sleeve of his French cuffs looked expensive.

"Nice to meet you Mister Drake."

"Call me Mike."

"So what's this outing all about?"

"You'll find out soon enough", said Stone.

Stone was matinee idol handsome with a strong chin and jet back hair combed straight back. His eyes were blue in startling contrast to his black hair. His attire was impeccable without being ostentatious, his trousers creased even when seated, not a wrinkle to be seen on his white shirt. Something about him made you immediately want him to like and approve of you. He'd known guys like Stone when he had been in college and later in the police academy. Natural born leaders. You couldn't help but admire them, and if you became their friend it was like your own status was elevated by association. You became part of the club of winners and people took you more seriously.

They drove into the heart of the city, the sun low in the blue sky, its late afternoon descent replicating brilliant mirrored images reflected on the upper windows of city buildings. In another half hour the streetlights would come on. In San Pedro, from early morning until late afternoon, the sun was such an omnipresent component of the land and seascape it seemed permanently imprinted on the inside of one's eyelids. Here you were lucky to see sunshine at all and dusk was without discernible transition.

A few overly cautious drivers were already turning their headlights on. Traffic was thickening since it was 5:30 and shifts were ending for many of those lucky enough to have jobs. Stone put his hand in Ramos' jacket pocket and said, "You're part of the team now."

Ramos felt for what had been put in his pocket and retrieved it. It was a hundred dollar bill.

"This is a lot of money," he said.

Stone shrugged nonchalantly and said, "Not really."

"But where does this money come from, Mister Stone."

"Stop with the Mister Stone shit. You're supposed to be one of us. Call me Robert, or Bobby."

"But is the money you gave me a legitimate departmental expenditure? What's the purpose of it?"

"The funds are ostensibly designated as expenditures for payment to criminal informants and for narcotic and alcohol purchases made by undercover police officers. You're going to need it. We're going undercover and flashing money around is part of our act."

Ramos had never seen a hundred dollar bill before. It was so crisp it looked newly minted. He held it between his thumb and index finger and snapped it a couple of times. Of course he would not be able to keep it. Not unless it came with a paystub or official memo from the P.D. or a government office in Olympia. But he did not want to seem ungrateful to Stone, whom he admired and wanted to please, and it seemed an awkward moment in which to return it. He put it back in his jacket pocket, deciding to wait for a more appropriate opportunity.

They were travelling Railroad Avenue along the waterfront. They were flanked by railroad tracks but no trains were running. Hobos sat in the boxcars of those that were stalled. Transpacific freighters were moored at piers in the choppy sound, where small inactive fishing boats bobbed. In the distance a gigantic crane loomed over a recently forsaken construction project. Both sides of the street were populated with unemployed men standing around idly. The light changed and they drove on toward a patch of property that looked like it might be on fire because of all the smoke. A few blocks later they were skirting the nine acres of haphazardly rambling tin shacks of Hooverville.

"What do you see when you look upon this," asked Stone.

"Hooverville," said Ramos. "The poorest of the poor. The last refuge of the hopeless."

"That's what most people see, Artie. But Mike and I, we see it differently. What we see is some of the most potentially valuable property for development in Seattle. Picture it cleared of these shacks, with new hotels and restaurants and entertainment venues to replace them. Imagine the waterfront view available from one of our several new fine dining establishments. Imagine elevated cable cars taking customers from one end of an entertainment complex to the other and a fleet of water taxis to take tourists sightseeing on the Sound and through the Ballard Bay locks. Imagine company- owned fishing and whale watching boats cruising the San Juan Islands. It's all within the realm of possibility, Artie. Especially now when money is scarce and real estate is cheap. There's only one thing standing in our way, and all this could be ours. Yours too, as part of the team. Do you know who and what it standing in the way of making waterfront Seattle a vital part of the Seattle economy, Artie?"

"I probably don't, Bobby. I'm just a policeman and relatively new to the area. "

"Go ahead, Mike. You tell him."

Drake pressed the horn on the steering wheel and accelerated to terrify a raggedy limping tramp who eluded the front fender of the Duesenberg in the nick of time.

"Two words," said Drake from the wheel. "Walter Fucking McCabe. He used to support our plan for the waterfront until all the tramps moved in. Now he's protecting them."

"Drive on," said Stone. "This place is depressing me."

It was dark now with less traffic, their headlights illuminating the streets of Capitol Hill as they proceeded toward Lake Washington and the Yachtsman Country Club, an oval shaped building at the edge of the lake accessible by either boat or automobile. Drake pulled alongside the canopied entrance where an elderly parking attendant wearing a navy blue uniform with golden brocaded epaulets on the shoulders and a matching cap limped forward to open the driver's side door. Ramos was surprised when they exited the vehicle to see Drake was probably not much over five foot nine in stature. His cold brown eyes had a meanness in them that was disturbing.

He dangled the keys to the valet parking attendant and said, "You. Attendant. You see this car? You know what it is?"

"No sir, but I can see that it is a very fine automobile."

The attendant looked like he might be in his late sixties, thin and in poor health with a slight stammer. He appeared to be perspiring despite the chill off the lake.

"The best car you will park all night. Maybe all year. Maybe ever. Now, I want you to walk around it from front to back. Walk slowly and look carefully. Do it now."

The attendant slowly circled the automobile as commanded. Ramos noticed the man's limp for the first time. He figured him for a war veteran. When the attendant had circled the Duesenberg Drake said, "Did you see any dents on the car, Gimpy? Any scratches or imperfections?"

"No sir. I did not. The automobile is perfect. It looks like it has come directly from a showroom."

"Fucking right, and that's the way I expect it to look when I come back. And when I do, you and I are going to circle the car again and I hope for your sake there isn't a scratch on it, understood?"

"Yes, sir. Understood. Rest assured, sir. Your automobile will be returned to you in its exact present condition."

Drake dropped the keys in his palm and said, "For your sake, I hope so. And don't even think about taking it out for a joy ride around the lake because I've checked the mileage."

"I would never do that sir."

They followed Stone to the entrance canopy and then were inside the country club restaurant. A uniformed maitre'd, bowing repeatedly, received them.

"Good evening Mr. Stone. Greetings Mr. Drake. Welcome."

Stone and Drake exchanged puzzling looks.

"Where's the usual maitre'd?"

"I'm taking his place tonight, but rest assured he briefed me of your preferences and we are fully prepared to make your dining experience memorable and satisfying."

Tuxedoed waiters wearing ruffled shirts and bow ties hurried among tables set with lace tablecloths and sterling place settings. Ramos saw an elaborately lengthy bar made from polished dark wood that might have been mahogany. There were women seated on tall cushioned stools at the bar, the hems of their cocktail dresses showing some leg. All were elegant and out of his league.

Prohibition made it illegal to manufacture, distribute or sell alcohol, but it was not strictly illegal to possess it, or at least rarely prosecuted, so patrons often brought their own. A young man wearing a suit not much better than his own pitiful version sat at a white baby grand piano, playing softly. He recognized the song. It was Duke Ellington's *Mood Indigo,* and not a bad rendition. The kid had an empty brandy snifter on top of the piano and it was stuffed with money, but no one seemed to really be listening. There was the clatter of cutlery and cling of drinking glasses. Something smelled delicious.

The maitre'd unhinged the red velvet brocaded cord that separated the reception area from the dining room and admitted them into the plush dining area where he clasped his hands together and said, "Allow me to escort you to your usual table near the back window. It offers such a splendid view of the lake."

"That table is too close to the kitchen," said Stone.

It wasn't at all. Ramos saw waiters carrying silver platters and silver covered dishes emerge from kitchen doors located far from the lake-view table offered by the maitre'd.

"But we held that table in reserve for you at your request, Mr. Stone. I was instructed that you always choose this table."

"I want a different table tonight."

"But surely you want your usual. It's the best table in the house. We saved it for you."

"Are you trying to tell me I don't know what I want?"

"No, no of course not."

Stone gestured to a table at which a man and wife and daughter who looked to be in her early teens were in the process of dining. The father at the head of the table, oblivious, gestured with his fork and said something to his family that caused them to laugh. Ramos was unable to hear what the man said that was so funny but it must have been off color because his daughter shrieked and said, "*Daddy!*"

Ramos was acutely uncomfortable with what he hoped was not coming next.

"But as you can see, that table is taken, Mr. Stone."

"Yes, by me and Mike and our friend Arthur here. You need to clear that table to make room for us."

"Sir?"

"You heard me. Move those people to the shitty table near the back window you suggested for us."

"But sir…"

"Don't but sir me. Do you know who we are, how indebted this place is to us? Who do you think distributes the bootleg gin you serve or supplies the brand name booze locked away out of sight in cabinets behind the bar? We could bankrupt this place with a snap of the fingers. Let's get the manager down here. Maybe he can straighten you out."

"That won't be necessary sir."

Ramos watched the maitre'd sheepishly approach the dining family, his hands pressed together either in prayer or in preparation to apologize. The entire family, objecting but acquiescent, was moved to the back lakeside table while a half dozen waiters scurried to transfer their partially consumed meals, glasses, coffee cups and dinnerware. The poor maitre'd bowed so many times in apology he looked like he might be experiencing an attack of the bends.

Once seated at their freshly set table, Stone instructed the maitre'd to put the vacated family's tab on his account. He ordered glasses and soda delivered promptly. He and Drake both emptied whiskey from their flasks into the glasses.

"I'm not much of a drinker," Ramos admitted. "Beer is about as strong as I go. I think I'll just pass and let you guys enjoy it."

"Fuck that," said Drake. "You're with us now. You have to drink like everyone else or you'll arouse suspicion."

He told Ramos to extend his glass and Ramos complied. When he did, Drake added whiskey.

"This is a shitty table, Bobby. Our usual by the window is way better. Don't just sit there holding the fucking glass, Artie. Drink up."

He poured some more bourbon from his flask into Ramos' glass. Ramos chased it with a full glass of water.

"Steaks all round," said Stone to the waiter. "Rare. "

"Very good, sir."

"And fill these flasks with the good stuff you save for special customers."

"Yes sir."

"Repeat back to me," said Drake to the waiter. "How did Bobby here say to cook those steaks?"

"Rare, sir."

"That's right, and I expect to see some blood on the plate. This is a shitty table, Bobby. Our usual by the window is way better."

"Yeah, but that maitre'd pissed me off. Maybe I'll make him change us back."

Ramos left the table for the restaurant's immaculate men's room, which he found to be impeccably clean, fresh smelling and larger than his living and dining room at home combined. He admired the penny tiles on the floor, the tropical jungle wallpaper, the golden sconce lighting above a line of sinks as white as ivory. Bottles of aftershave, individually wrapped breath mints and fluffy cotton hand towels were shelved above each sink. Even combs in glasses of liquid hair tonic were provided. He faced himself in the mirror and splashed some cool water in his face. He fingered the hundred dollar bill in his pocket. Stone had shrugged it off like it was no big deal. How was it that the police department could budget for all this? Something did not fit here, did not feel right. He was thinking this when Stone came through the doors and went to the urinal. He unzipped, urinated a long while, shook it off and came to stand beside him at the adjoining sink and mirror.

Stone slapped his cheeks with some of the aftershave, ran acomb through his thick black hair and said, "So what do you think? Are you going to enjoy working with us? "

"Well, yes, sure Bobby."

"You don't show it, Artie. Are you worried about something?"

"Well," replied Arthur. "I suppose I am, a little. I don't know what I'm doing here exactly and I'm worried about the hundred dollars you gave me."

"You'll understand in time, Artie. You need to just go along and trust us. For now, just enjoy the food and drink."

They returned to their table where Ramos picked at his Caesar salad and savored his steak, which was so tender he had to wonder. If this was steak, what had Annette been masquerading as steak at home? It was nothing like this. This was tender and moist with flavor. He hardly even needed a knife to cut it.

He was disappointed when Stone rose from his chair and said, "You're right, Mike. This is a shitty table. I don't know even why we come here, Mike. They make a decent steak but the place is a bore." He threw a wad of greenbacks on the tablecloth and said, "Let's go"

Ramos stared longingly at his forsaken steak. Stone led them to the lobby and then to the circular driveway. The parking attendant brought the Duesenberg around while they waited under the canopy. The attendant opened the driver's door, bowed and silently waited for his gratuity.

Drake circled the Duesenberg and said, "What the fuck is this?"

"What, sir?"

"Come over here. Look at this."

The attendant limped around the front fender to where Drake pointed accusatorily at the passenger side chrome running board. Ramos noticed for the first time the man's limp was pronounced.

"What the fuck do you call this?"

"Sir?"

"This footprint on the running board. I told you this car was to be returned spotless."

"I believe your instruction was to return it in the exact condition in which it was received, sir."

"That's right. So where did this come from?"

"I'm sorry, sir. I don't know. I presume it was there when you gave me the keys. It appears to be left by someone's shoe when stepping out of the automobile. It's only a footprint."

"Are you arguing with me, Gimpy?"

"No, sir. Not at all. I'm sorry, sir."

"You know the manager here is a personal friend who owes me a favor. All I have to do is ask and he will fire you on the spot."

"Please sir, I have a family."

"I don't care about your family. Put your left foot up here on the running board. I want to see if it matches."

"But sir, my leg is damaged."

"So is my car. I'm getting the manager down here. Someone's going to pay for this and it's not going to be me."

The attendant dropped to his knees and began furiously wiping the running board with his sleeve.

"Sir, please. There is no damage. It's just dust. Here, I can fix this. See, I'm wiping it clean right now. See, it comes right off. There are no scratches, nothing. Please."

"I'll tell you what," said Drake. "I'll let this go if you pay me twenty five dollars."

"But sir, I don't have twenty five dollars."

The poor man appeared to be perspiring despite the chill off the lake. He looked like he might break down crying. Ramos was on the verge of intervening when to his relief Stone said, "That's enough, Mike."

Drake clapped the attendant on the back, slipped him a twenty and said, "I'm just fucking with you, Gimpy. The car is fine. We were just having some fun."

Ramos settled in the back seat again and they drove off.

When they were underway Stone said, "That was kind of harsh, Mike."

"I was just having some fun."

"You're a vicious prick, Mike."

"I know," replied Drake.

"It's why I like you, Mike. You're a fun guy."

Ramos sat silently in the back seat wondering who these people were and why he was here. He wished they would take him home. His guests were probably finished with dinner by now and chatting in the cramped living room. Annie was probably understandably mad at him. He felt the money in his jacket pocket again. He should have given the hundred dollar bill back when he and Stone were alone in the bathroom, explained he was willing to work with him in an official capacity but was uncomfortable taking money not accounted for.

"I still don't know what I am doing here, Mr. Stone."

"I can't tell you everything yet, Artie, because I lack essential information. That's what we will be doing tonight, Artie. Collecting information for our investigation. The place we are going to next is patronized by investors, gangsters and upscale politicians and they are all rich and all corrupt and don't care where a man's money comes from or if it's clean or dirty. We are going after them. We're going after big fish and need to be seen throwing money around. You need to fit in, act like you belong. It's okay to be the new guy, but you got to be rich to be accepted, so act like it. Make like you're one of them, flash some cash around, tip big and do some gambling upstairs. We need them to accept and trust you. Remember, you are with us so your credibility impacts our credibility. Spend everything I gave you and if you need more come and see me. I'll be mingling with the crowd just like you should be."

It was a cloudy moonless night penetrated by the headlights of cars in the darkness. They passed a small private airport where few cars were in the lot, only one passenger plane was on the runway in preparation for takeoff and most of the smaller private airplanes were grounded. From time to time the running lights of a small plane could be seen overhead but traffic both in the air and on the ground was sparse. Drake slowed the Duesenberg and pulled off the main road and drove along streets where they saw not a single automobile, pedestrian or so much as a stray dog. From there they entered an unlighted neighborhood of industrial red brick warehouse complexes, scrap metal junk yards and rundown vandalized buildings with broken windows and empty trash-strewn lots reminiscent of crime scenes he had known in San Pedro.

If Stone and Drake wanted to kill him this would be the perfect place to do it. It seemed possible he was being set up, but by whom and why? Was his loyalty to the Sheriff being tested because he was the new guy? Two blocks later he was surprised to see limousines and expensive late model sedans attended by uniformed drivers who looked as much like bodyguards as chauffeurs. Drake backed into a space marked *Reserved* and parked. Stone passed the flask, which was passed around.

Ramos was a little unsteady on his feet when they got out and walked. The temperature had dropped and there was a faint presence of moist wind in his face. His lightweight suit was designed for the year-round sunny weather of San Pedro, and he clung to it as if the wind might blow it away. Stone, who led the way, halted them at a redbrick building where the windows were boarded except on the fourth and fifth floors where they were painted black. A man wearing a raincoat with a sheathed shotgun stood guard. Stone greeted him by name and slipped him a twenty and they entered the building. A single hanging light shone dimly on the wire cage of a freight elevator. The cage door was secured with a combination lock and the operating panel inside required a key. Stone had both the combination and a key. They assembled inside the cage and Stone unlocked the panel and punched in the code number and the

Lea Macquarrie

groaning elevator rocked slightly to and fro during its slow ascent.

Ramos began to hear music faintly drifting down, incrementally louder as they were pulled upward in the cage toward it. When the elevator reached the fourth floor and the door opened he was facing the open interior of a full scale nightclub with two bars, tables, a dance floor, stage and nine piece band. Couples were dancing under prismatic lights thrown from a large centrally located chandelier. Groups mingled around the bar or at tables. He followed Stone into the crowd, which seemed to close around them. Everyone seemed to know Stone and want to shake his hand. Girls flocked to him. These were women like those Ramos had only seen in movies, magazines, or in his dreams, women attired in dresses Annette would have coveted, with nylon stockings, furs and jewelry. Women as exotic as tropical flowers flocked to Stone, kissing him on the cheek, rubbing up against him, whispering in his ear. Stone soon wandered off with one of them.

Drake had disappeared in the crowd and Ramos was glad to be free of him. The man was in his opinion an embarrassment at the least. Ramos rubbed his nose against the sleeve of his jacket and worried whether it might reek of perfume. Annette would sniff it out like a bloodhound and he didn't know yet how he would explain it was work related, if indeed it truthfully was, because what kind of "work" they were doing tonight he had no idea.

A patron near him said, "First time here? Impressive isn't it?"

Ramos replied, playing the role Stone wanted of him, "I've been in upscale speakeasies before of course, and this ranks with the best of them."

"It's not a speakeasy," said the stranger. "It's a nightclub."

Right, thought Ramos. A highly illegal one. Volstead Act violation, illegal gambling and prostitution more than likely because he had never before seen so many beautiful unescorted women while the men present were mostly far from their prime without desirable attributes other than apparent wealth. The band was playing *On the Sunnyside of the Street*. A woman who looked like she could pass a Hollywood screen test for a femme fatale role approached while carrying a tray of cigarettes and Havana cigars. He didn't smoke and declined but stole a look as she glided away. He was shy with women and always had been. Not that he was tempted. He was loyal to Annette. But still.

Excruciatingly out of his element, he was thankful to be a light skinned Mexican who could pass for white or he'd be even more out of place than he already was. He looked at his scruffy shoes, avoiding eye contact and conversation.

When he looked up he saw the most beautiful woman in America gracefully descending a staircase. He immediately recognized her, Jean Harlow, his favorite actress and most frequent secret fantasy. Although he was ashamed of it, he had sometimes imagined the starlet when making love to Annie. Now, to his utter shock and considerable dismay she seemed to be striding intentionally toward him, her sparkling blue eyes fixed on him. She wore a blue sequined dress that hugged her hourglass figure provocatively and which, he saw now that she was close, complimented the color of her eyes.

"You look bored," she said.

He couldn't help but steal a glance into her alluring cleavage but looked away quickly lest she catch him at it. She smelled delicious.

"Buy a girl a drink?"

She was not after all Jean Harlow, though one had to look closely to see the difference. She had the same thick platinum blonde hair in the exact same style and Jean Harlow's pearl complexion, defined thin lips, elegant long neck and cute little nose that looked like it had been sketched in with a pencil. Her eyebrows were not quite the same, not plucked and drawn with an eyebrow pencil like Harlow's but real, and there was a tiny beauty mark on her left cheek but otherwise who cared? He was certain she was not wearing a bra. Her nipples were prominent, and he could not stop looking at them despite himself.

To the bartender she said, "Two gin Martinis, dirty. I saw you come in with Bobby," she said. "I work for him as a hostess here. It's my job to stroll around and talk to the customers, make sure they are enjoying themselves and show them around if necessary."

"You work for him? I don't understand"

"It's his club. Didn't he tell you?"

"No."

If this was Stone's club, who were they investigating? How could Stone be undercover in his own club?

"Has anyone ever told you that you are the very definition of tall dark and handsome? Seriously, you should take a screen test."

Ramos hoped he was not blushing.

"What's your name?"

"Arthur but they call me Artie."

He had to keep reminding himself she was not Jean Harlow.

"Call me Jean," she said.

She winked flirtatiously and a cinematic sequence of her movie roles and his own private dirty secret fantasies played unbidden in his head. The band was playing a Latin number he did not recognize. It sounded Cuban, but inauthentic. He would dance with her, but this was not a not a Mariachi band. He debated saying so, making a joke of it, but it was not in his best interest to expose himself as Mexican. For all he knew Mexicans might not even be allowed here.

The martini, as it turned out, was delicious, not like the whiskey Drake and Stone had been forcing on him. Jean retrieved a small compact mirror from her sequined clutch purse and applied dark red lipsticks to her wet lips and took a long time doing it. The band changed tempo and mood and began playing a slow waltz. She took his hand and he let himself be led onto the dance floor, relieved they were playing a waltz at a moderate tempo because Mariachi music was basically a waltz, in three four time.

After the waltz the song was a slow version of *I'm Confessing' that I Love You* and she clung to him, her bare arms around his neck, her face nestled in the crook of his shoulder. She wore a fragrant perfume and he didn't care if Annette later smelled it on his clothing or not. The music seemed to guide them together like one person. She hummed and sang a little in a whisper as they danced, her voice seductive with melancholic longing. He was oblivious to all else. He worried maybe he was not even dancing anymore, just standing there not moving to the music, embracing her.

"You're sweet," she whispered. "I like you."

When the song ended she smiled and took a cigarette out of her purse and asked him for a light but he didn't have one and told her didn't smoke and she put the cigarette back and he resolved to start smoking and never be without a cigarette lighter again.

He cashed the hundred and threw a twenty on the bar and allowed her to lead him across the crowded ballroom to the staircase she had descended earlier. There was a view below to the bandstand, dancers and dance floor as they ascended. The martinis had gone to his head. She was a few steps ahead of him and he stole glances at her rear under the clinging blue dress. My God, he thought. Jean Harlow. No, of course not, but still.

Upstairs, she led him down a hallway along which most of the doors were closed. Some were open, the vacant rooms dimly lit by a blue light bulb. When they reached the end of the hall she knocked what sounded like a code and a sliding viewing panel opened. A guard wearing a shoulder holster admitted them into a spacious high-ceilinged room where patrons played cards at tables or tossed dice at roulette wheels. Windows ran the length of the room but were painted black. Tables were piled high with chips. Bobby Stone was at the bar under the windows and when he saw them shouldered his way toward through the crowd of gamblers and spectators.

"Hi Artie, I see you've met our hostess. Jean, I need to borrow Artie for just a moment."

He pulled Ramos aside and said, "You need any more money?"

"No, I'm good Bobby."

"Then you're not spending enough. Here's another fifty. "

"Your hostess informed me that you own this place. So how is it we are doing an undercover investigation here, Bobby?"

"It's not the club we're investigating but its patrons. You'll see. You have to trust me on this, Artie. We're just getting started. Meanwhile you need to spread money around and attract notice. If a cigarette girl shows up, tip her whether you buy any smokes or not. If some stranger talks to you, buy them a drink. And have a drink in your hands at all times whether you are actually drinking it or not. Spend heavy, talk big, and don't blow our cover. In time you will be approached by the men we are investigating. Now go back to

Jean and ask her to take you to the roulette wheel."

At the roulette wheel, he drank another martini and lost forty dollars.

"I'm not really much of a gambler," he said to Jean.

"Come with me," she replied.

She wrapped her arm in his and he felt her soft full breasts push against his arm while being escorted out of the gambling room. They were back in the long hallway again, passing green doors closed to a half dozen flanking rooms. At one she removed a key from her clutch purse and opened the door. Soothing dim blue light revealed a bed and bedside table. A throw rug was beside the bed and on the table were a clean ashtray and candelabra holding three white candles. A large mirror hung on the wall across from the bed. A small curtained area concealed a sink and towels.

She sat on the bed and said, "It's not what you think, Artie. This is my break room. Sit with me. Take off your shoes, Arthur. Make yourself comfortable."

In the soft blue lighting she was now virtually indistinguishable from Jean Harlow. He sat next to her, and she took his hand and said, "Please, sit closer and be my friend. I need company right now. It gets lonely, putting on airs with people I don't really know or especially like, trying to act the friendly hostess when I'm not in the mood."

"You don't like your job?"

"Some parts of it I do. But not all of it. There are good nights and bad nights. Bobby told me you were a policeman. That's kind of sexy, Artie. Do you find me sexy at all?"

"More than what's good for me, I'm afraid."

"Why afraid? I'm not a danger to you. I want to be your friend."

"It's complicated, Jean. I'm married."

"I know you are. I could tell right away. I don't care, Arthur. Does that make me bad? Do you think I'm a bad person because I wish you would kiss me?"

He hadn't kissed a woman other than Annie since they were married. He put his arms around her and kissed her and it was a thousand times better than he imagined it would be. He was a fool probably, but this whole night had been foolish. He drove the thought out of his mind and surrendered to the beautiful woman returning his kiss.

NORTH SEATTLE

WHAT HAD JENNY BEEN THINKING, inviting all these people? It seemed to Sheriff Gustafson that everyone in their neighborhood was here. He was tempted to take off his white shirt and wave it like a flag of surrender. They were overrun with screaming kids with dirty faces, runny noses and skinned knees shrieking through his lawn sprinklers. No one was safe from them. One pointed a gun at him right now. Fortunately for them all it was a squirt gun because had it been an actual firearm the adults would all be dead now, spread out across the front lawn like massacre victims. Teenage boys wrestled on the lawn, flattening his flower bed while showing off for an audience of gum chewing bobby-socked teenage girls with bad complexions and worse attitudes. Adults were behaving only marginally better, swilling and pillaging like barbarians dividing the spoils of victory. He was helpless to stop it.

Jenny just didn't get it sometimes. These entertainments cost money. How was he supposed to explain his ability to afford a party like this on his salary? An editorialist with the *Seattle Post Intelligencer* had recently called for an investigation into police corruption. The newspaper had since killed the story but people were losing their jobs and their homes and it didn't look good to be showing off.

Speaking of showing off, Jenny was looking good in scandalous shorts and dark glasses, drinking from a tall glass of lemonade he knew to be spiked with gin. She was a little unsteady on her feet and looked a bit tipsy. He was mildly angry with her, but not so much that he didn't intend to take her to bed and fuck her brains out first chance he got. Meanwhile, Mike, Bobby and other members of the Waterfront Improvement Commission had been shooting him peculiar glances all afternoon as if something was up.

"Let's go," said Stone. "Downstairs."

There were six of them. They marched around the back of the house and down the cellar stairs, Stone leading the way like he owned the place. This was his private office where he paid bills, made police-related confidential phone calls, and sometimes enjoyed a cigar and whiskey or two at his desk. Equipped with a large Seattle P.D. clock, typewriter and short wave radio, it was spacious, with comfortable armchairs and stools at the bar and a couch for his naps. The commission members settled themselves on his furniture and made themselves at home. Drake went to the liquor cabinet for glasses and a rare bottle of Canadian whiskey and poured shots all around like he was fucking Mister Generosity. A mahogany console with a built-in turntable and shortwave radio crackled electric static while one of the men dialed in search of a baseball game.

"Turn off the goddamn radio," commanded Stone.

"What's up, Bobby? What's this about?"

"I have news and it isn't all good. Yesterday I went on my own down to Pier 91 to talk some sense into Walter McCabe. I had hoped that he would see that the future of Hooverville and the Seattle waterfront was best left to the commission. I tried to reason with him, help him to see that our vision of the future of the waterfront was the right one for Seattle. I explained it was important the men in Hooverville were removed before they sued for squatter's rights. McCabe didn't see it that way. His take was that Hooverville was protected by city statutes and could not be removed. He even threatened the Commission with Jeremiah Wells. We went around and around and weren't getting anywhere so I made some gentle threats. He wouldn't be threatened. Stood right up to me. Fuck it, I said, we don't need you anyway. We are going to do what's best for the Commission and the waterfront. Get in our way and you will regret it. We argued and it got heated. Started pushing each other around a little. I told him we could torch his house and make it look like Cora did it. I told him we would have his wife committed to a state institution. He threatened to publicize our bootlegging operations, speakeasies, and police payoffs. He could do it too. Don't forget, McCabe was once secretary of the commission. He has notes of our meetings."

"Fuck him, Stoney. He's harmless. He drinks too much and shoots his mouth off. He loses his temper quickly but gets over it just as quick and shrugs it off and forgets about it."

"He has threatened to go to the state capital in Olympia. Don't scoff, men. I wouldn't put it past him. McCabe has always been a pain in the ass, but now he's more than that. He's standing in the way of our investments in the waterfront area of the city we love and want to protect. We're all agreed on that at least, right?"

"Damn right, Bobby."

"One hundred percent."

Stone had now become the chairman of what had without their notice evolved into an official meeting. He nodded at Gustafson and said, "Gus, what do you have for us?"

Gustafson was surprised.

Was Stone expecting some kind of report?

Everyone now stared at him in quiet expectation.

"Nothing's new. McCabe is clean like I said he would be. We've been tailing him for a month. Nothing. He drinks in working class speakeasies sometimes, but that's the extent of it."

"What about his association with The Unemployed Citizen's League."

"Not much there. Seems they used Pier 91 as a staging operation at one time, but McCabe got wind of it and put a stop to it by putting up a locking chain link fence and hiring a watchman."

"What about whorehouses," inquired Drake?

"No, he doesn't patronize them."

"Well, he must be fucking somebody other than that old hag Cora."

Drake crushed out his cigarette and added, "We know McCabe had some underage squaw living with him. If he's fucking her, that's statutory rape. A pedophilia arrest would make the papers and ruin him whether true or not."

"McCabe's got the best lawyer in Seattle," said Olafson.

"Jeremiah fucking Wells," said Drake. "He's a punk."

"He's never lost a case, Mike. Not one."

"Because he represents people who are innocent. That's easy."

Stone was now rambling on about something else. The man never tired of the pleasure of hearing his own voice, which in Gustafson's opinion was the real reason for the meeting, which was bullshit. He didn't know if he even wanted to find any "dirt" on McCabe, who he respected. Here, though, among this assembly, was plenty of dirt to go around. He wondered if he was beginning to truly hate these men or was merely resentful of their power over him.

Stone helped himself to another shot and said, "So what have you found out about the girl living in McCabe's house, Sheriff?"

"Her name is Juanita Vogel. She's estranged from her father, named Jack Vogel."

"Any relation to Frank Vogel?"

"We think so. We're looking into it."

"Officer Ramos says she identifies herself as Italian but that she looks like an Indian and he would know because he is part Indian."

"No, he's part Mexican," corrected Gustafson.

"Same difference as far as I'm concerned. Not white, anyway."

"They're all the same," said Drake. "Negros, Puerto Ricans, Mexicans, Indians, they're all basically niggers, some just have lighter skin than others. At least the slant eyes know to keep to themselves."

Gustafson sighed wearily and said, "We're running a background check on the girl now. Nothing has come back and I doubt much will. She's probably too young to have any priors but we'll keep looking. And we'll see what we can find on Jack Vogel, too."

"Keep us informed and keep digging. I want McCabe where we can control him and I want it soon."

The men joined the party upstairs but he remained behind and smoked a cigarette at the bar. He listened to his guests' voices over the sound of the upstairs phonograph while assessing his disgraced

Lea Macquarrie

career as a police officer, husband, and human being. He was a man with a secret he could not share, isolated from his wife, his kids, and many of his fellow officers. The Commission had enough verifiable information regarding his thoroughly corrupt police force and personal illegal and immoral conduct to end his career and Stone had photos to prove it. There was enough dirt on him to make headlines on the pages of the *Seattle Times* and land him in a high-publicity court case and state prison.

He poured a shot and drank it down in one swallow, crushed the cigarette in the ashtray and joined the party. Women gathered in the kitchen, ostensibly to help Jenny with the dishes. They chattered amongst themselves, laughing and talking freely until one of the men happened in for some ice for his glass, when their voices dropped to a murmur. The women had their own secrets, apparently. Drake's current girl friend was a redheaded tease with curly hair and freckles. A foot taller than Drake, she talked too loud and had sharp bird-like features enhanced by a severe short hairstyle. She wore a bandana around her head and smoked from an ostentatious cigarette holder.

Neither Drake nor Gussy Junior so much as looked up when he entered Gussy's bedroom. Drake was reading to Gussy from a Babar the Elephant book. He and Gussy seemed engrossed in the book and the scene looked innocent enough. He didn't like it though, and would question Gussy about it later.

"Time to close the book, Mike. Its way past his bedtime."

Drake tucked him in and said, "Goodnight, Gussy."

"Good night, Uncle Mike."

The party was breaking up. Jenny was at the door seeing couples off, gathering coats off the bed and following guests into the yard for goodbye hugs. He joined her there, and they embraced under the moonlight. He copped a feel but Jenny said, "I'm too tired tonight, honey. I'll make it up to you in the morning."

"I know. Its fine, Jen."

They stood together on the porch and watched the last taillights of the last car vanish into the night. In bed he lay awake, vaguely troubled.

WALLINGFORD/GREEN LAKE DISTRICT

JACK PICKED UP THREE DAYS' WORK unloading morning freight deliveries at the Public Market. Money in his pocket, he walked to a Salvation Army secondhand store on First Avenue and went through racks of clothing, choosing a suitable clean white shirt and decorative tie, gray wool trousers, black fedora hat and new stockings and underwear. He changed into the new clothes in a curtained dressing room and rolled his old blue jeans, longshoreman's cap and work shirt into a newspaper wrapped with twine. His grimy underwear and socks were fit only for the trash bin out back.

He paid fifteen cents for a shower at the public bathhouse where he lingered longer than he needed under the cascade of warm water, reluctant to leave. It had been far too long since he was truly clean. He had forgotten how grimy he was, how tired, how much his shoulders and back ached and how his head had felt burdensome, as if his neck were perpetually engaged in a struggle to support it. He surrendered to the warm water running from his head down his back and shoulders and felt his nostrils and sinuses loosening until his fifteen minutes were up and the water shut off. He stood a moment longer, inhaling the residual steam and then sat on the bench near his locker.

He took a trolley out of the waterfront area of downtown Seattle, transferred and got off at the stop the driver said was closest on the route to the address written on his envelope. From there he walked through a quiet suburban neighborhood with a small park with picnic benches for adults and monkey-bars for climbing children. The sun was out and women hung laundry on porches. Boys mowed green lawns or shot hoops in driveways.

Later he began to pass houses with posted eviction notices nailed to the doors, some with furniture out on the street. On every block at least one was boarded up and vacant, with *Foreclosed* and *Keep Out* signs posted in their yards and entrance ways.

The Wilson house was near, a large two and a half story craftsman with attic windows facing the front yard, which had mostly gone to weed. The upstairs windows of the house were boarded up. An old Ford was parked in a driveway that ended at a two story garage with a peaked attic room upstairs. A front porch tentatively supported by a sagging roof ran the width of the front of the house. The porch held an old Sears's model washing machine not attached to a visible water source. He felt the wooden planks give slightly under his weight when he ascended the creaky wooden steps. He hesitated at the front door, straightening his tie and shirt collar before striking the brass knocker. He heard footsteps creak on wooden stairs and then locks on the door opened. He presumed the woman who answered to be Jimmy Wilson's sister. He removed his hat respectfully.

"I hope I'm not disturbing you, Miss Wilson. I'm Jack Vogel, here to see Jimmy Wilson. He wrote me a letter and said it was okay."

Wilson's sister wore her dark brown hair cut to the shoulder and showing streaks of gray. She was pretty, wearing sandals and a brown cotton shapeless dress with a plain white apron around her waist. He believed her smile warm enough to melt the snows on Mt. Rainier.

"Yes, of course. Jimmy told me about you. You're Frank's brother. Please, come in, Jack. Thank you so much for coming. Jimmy will be so happy to see you."

He stepped into the foyer, his attention diverted to whatever was cooking on the stove. It smelled delicious. His stomach rumbled reactively as he breathed it in. His mouth and throat flooded with salivation. He hoped Wilson's sister did not hear his stomach, which sounded vicious.

Miss Wilson gestured toward a narrow hallway, signaling for him to follow. He did so, led by his nostrils toward what had smelled so good while he had been in the foyer. She led him into a large, brightly lighted kitchen with windows facing a back yard and large garden.

"Jimmy is with his nurse," she said. "She'll have him ready shortly. Please, have a seat here at the kitchen table and we'll chat."

He saw again that she was pretty, with auburn hair streaked in places with gray, eyes that changed color in the light and a face probably younger than her years. She stirred the pot of whatever it was on the stove and he heard his stomach growl like a rabid dog was trapped inside of it. He listened with disbelief as it all but barked. If she heard it, she didn't show it.

"I do hope you can eat with us, Mr. Vogel. Jimmy eats hardly at all and I hate waste. Especially in these times."

"I agree, Miss Wilson. These are hard times for most. And thank you. I'd be honored to sit with you and Jimmy."

Jack heard his stomach shout back at her angrily.

Wilson's sister regarded him curiously without a word of acknowledgement and went to the pantry and emerged with a loaf of thick home baked bread, a jar of jam, a stick of butter and a knife.

"We're going to have vegetable soup with Puget Sound clams," she said, "but I'm afraid it won't be ready for a while yet. Meanwhile why don't we have a little snack?"

She cut a generous slice of bread, gave it to him on a small plate and took some for herself. They spread the bread with jam and ate in silence. As much as he wanted to he couldn't stop himself from eating faster than was proper. But at least then his stomach stopped growling angrily.

"Did you bake this bread, Miss Wilson?"

"Yes, and please call me Mary. The jam is from our own strawberries. Almost all of our fruits and vegetables are grown in the garden in back. Would you like to see?"

She turned down the heat on the stove, added some sliced

potatoes and chopped carrots to the pot, wiped her hands on her apron and said, "Follow me."

Clinging to what remained of his thick slice of bread, he followed her out a kitchen door leading into a small porch pantry and then outdoors to the driveway and garage. A Ford sedan was parked in the driveway in front of the garage where a steep wooden staircase led to a second-floor attic room. Its windows were encrusted with dirt and the room did not appear to be in use but he learned later it was being rented to a widowed war veteran.

"We don't see him much," Mary Wilson explained. "He's kind of odd, keeps to himself like a lot of veterans. The rent money helps with maintenance and payment of taxes on the property."

A spacious fenced vegetable garden was behind the garage. Wilson's sister walked him between rows of vegetables, pointing out carrots, beans, cucumbers, snap peas, and peppers. Tall wooden stakes bore clinging green vines from which large red tomatoes were hung She picked a pea pod hanging from a wire between two poles, snapped it open and ate it shell and all.

"Go ahead," she said. "Pick one."

He had been eating out of a can so long he had forgotten how fresh vegetables tasted. He felt like he could eat the whole garden. When they returned to the kitchen Mary Wilson stirred the pot on the stove and opened the oven door. He saw two pies baking, their crusts turning golden, the scent of baked apple so tantalizing he thought he might faint.

"Your brother and I were sort of married," she announced suddenly.

He knew this from Jimmy Wilson, but it seemed to him overly personal. He hardly knew her, and Frank in his letters had never mentioned her.

"It lasted less than a month. It turned out the marriage wasn't legal because he was already married. I kicked him out but let him stay sometimes in the room over the garage. That's his Ford in the driveway."

"He was legally married to my wife's sister, Elvira Vogel."

"You seem different from him."

"Frank was my big brother. I looked up to him, but not for the way he was with women. And I'm sorry he lied to you."

"Oh, I don't care, Jack. He didn't break my heart or anything like that. I was sorry to hear he was sent to prison."

"Frank is why I came to Seattle. If I'd have known he was in prison, I don't know if I would have left Cat Creek. He was going to find work for us."

"He wanted to, Jack. He talked about it all the time, how you and he would work together, save some money, and build a big house for the rest of the family here in Seattle. It was his dream."

"Mine too."

"I'm sorry about your wife. Frank told me how she died."

"It was a long time ago."

"Where is your youngest child now, Jack? I remember Frank saying your kids were grown and far from the nest but that you still had a young daughter at home."

"Her name is Juanita. She's here in Seattle but I don't know where exactly."

"I don't understand. You lost her?"

Jack thought the question impertinent but she was clearly waiting for and expected a reply. She seemed to him the kind of woman who pried for information in a way that was tricky because you ended up giving away more than you wanted.

"What happened is, I couldn't find work and times got really hard for us, Juanita and me. We didn't have a penny between us and no place to go. An agency found placement for Juanita as a domestic in a house in another part of the city. I took her there myself but could never find that house again. I only remember it was near Woodlawn Park. I don't remember the name of the people who lived there. Mac something or other is best I can come up with."

"You didn't inquire with the agency that placed her?"

"I did, but everyone I knew there was long gone and there were no records."

But this was none of her business. No wonder Jimmy had chosen to live down in Hooverville.

"It's probably just as well. I'm kind of relieved to tell the truth.

I don't know if would want Juanita to see me living the way I do now."

"I don't understand."

"You know. Like a bum, down in Hooverville."

She went to the pot again, opened it and added some string beans. When she sat down again her face was faintly beaded with steam from the open pot. She wiped her brow and said, "You needn't be ashamed for that, Jack. Hooverville is Seattle's shame, not yours. Money doesn't make the man, Jack. It's clear you are well mannered, polite and clean and know how to behave like a gentleman."

This woman did not understand. Men didn't estimate their value by what women thought of them. Men were judged by other men, and it was by the opinions of other men they judged themselves.

"Well, you are seeing me at my best. Down home in Hooverville, it's mostly all men. You don't have to watch your manners so much down there. I don't normally dress like you see me now, either. I usually have an unshaven dirty face and greasy cut hands and wear ragged sour clothing that smells like it should be put in a pile for burning. In fact I bought the clothes I am wearing now just before coming here. The old ones were so soiled I left them bundled on the porch before I came in."

"There's no shame in getting dirty from working hard, Jack. You should see me when I come out of the garden or out from under that Ford in the driveway."

"Is it just you and Jimmy in this big old house?"

"We have a student nurse staying here temporarily, but otherwise yes. In the past I've had people renting a room here, but not since I began renting the attic room over the garage. Your brother Frank stayed there when he wasn't on the road. As you know, he was a union man, mostly on the road, organizing, engineering strikes, marching in picket lines or fighting scabs trying to break them. He was in some ways my best friend."

She opened the oven door and said, "These pies are ready. We just need to let them cool. We'll have them for dessert."

She removed them with oven mitts to a shelf on the enclosed

porch off the kitchen. While she was away a young, blue-eyed, fair skinned woman in a white cotton nurse's dress entered from the hallway.

"Oh," she said. "I didn't know Mary had company."

"I'm here to see Mr. Wilson," said Jack.

"Well, I've bathed him and given him his medicine but he's fallen asleep. He tends to sleep in brief intervals, though." She nodded toward the room down the hall and said, "It shouldn't be long before you can go in. I'm Rebecca, his nurse. Well, not a real nurse yet, I'm still in school."

"I'm Jack Vogel."

Miss Wilson returned from the mud room and said, "Oh, hi Becky. Is Jimmy all cleaned up now?"

"Sleeping, bathed and shaved, teeth brushed, bed linens changed."

"Jack will be having dinner with us."

"Lucky him", said Nurse Becky. "I smelled those apple pies all the way down the hall. Mary makes great pies," she said to Jack.

Mary Wilson turned her back and reached high for three large bowls in the cupboard. Jack thought she had a pretty rear end but would rather die than be caught looking. He quickly averted his gaze. She set the table, cut more bread and ladled generous servings of vegetable and clam soup into the bowls. Jack took a deep breath, his olfactory senses altered to the hearty fragrance of clams simmering in savory broth.

"I'll say the grace," said Mary Wilson. This is Jimmy's prayer. I'm an atheist, but am in the habit of reciting it in his honor."

She cleared her throat and said, "We thank you for these blessings we are about to receive. Please bring justice to the workers of the world and punish those who oppress them. Amen."

She smiled at him from across the table and said, "Let's eat, Jack. It's nice not to eat alone."

Jack reminded himself began to eat slowly without slurping but he wanted to pick the bowl up, drink it down like a glass of beer and ask for more. He grabbed a thick piece of bread and sopped up some broth. Juice ran from the bread to his fingers. He wiped them with a cloth napkin, ashamed but helpless to control his urgent hunger or unmannerly behavior. He had been living amongst men too long, eating out of blackened cans with an old spoon, either in his shack or from communal pots with bums like himself. He didn't know how to behave any more with decent people, and especially not with women. Don't slurp, he reminded himself, don't talk with your mouth full, keep your elbows off the table.

Miss Wilson announced there would be pie and coffee later. Jack offered to help with the dishes but Nurse Becky said she would do them. They heard Jimmy calling from down the hall.

"He's awake," said Nurse Becky. "What did I tell you? He mostly sleeps in little cat naps, until his pain wakes him. Then I give him medication. He's dying, but he's not suffering. Jimmy will be happy to see you. He almost never gets company unless it's a Doctor, druggist, or nurse."

Jack followed them down the hall, again noting Miss Wilson's appealing figure and the womanly way she walked. In his opinion she had a perfect pear-shaped figure. During the year he had been living in Hooverville he had not felt desire, and to feel it stir now surprised him. He wondered if Mary Wilson was a good dancer. He remembered his own agility on a dance floor, back in the day when he and Alma had been courting. They could have won a contest they danced so well together. Later when Alma had been too sick to stand for an extended period of time he'd lift her emaciated wasted body and support it, her legs dragging on the floor while dancing to the music on the radio. Later still she became too sick even for that. Then she was gone.

Jimmy Wilson looked as if he had lost maybe half his weight, most of his hair gone, skin a pale shade of yellow not normal for a human being. Wilson looked like he'd long been dead and buried but dug up special for this occasion. But you had to hand it to him, he managed a smile, nevertheless.

"Jack," he said. "Goddamn. It's good to see you."

"Same here. How are you, Jimmy?"

"They tell me I'm dying but I ain't licked yet."

"Well I have to honestly say, Jimmy, I've seen you looking better but its good see you." After a brief awkward pause he added, "I hope they're wrong about you dying, Jimmy."

"Well, they've been wrong before. Take this hospital I was in after I saw you last for instance, Jack. They cut the wrong leg off a man. Hey, that reminds me, Jack. You heard the one about the guy the doctor says probably won't make it through the night? So, the guy says to his wife, 'Honey, you heard what the doctor said. This is gonna be it, I'm gonna be dead by morning. I just want to have sex one last time before I die so how about it?' So the wife says, *What? Are you kidding?* I have to get up early for work tomorrow morning and you don't."

"JIMMY!" shouted Miss Wilson.

But neither she nor Jack could altogether stifle their laughter.

"I owe you an apology," said Jack. "I feel bad I haven't gotten up here earlier. For one thing, I didn't know how sick you were."

"Hell, Jack, that's okay. Nobody knew."

"Yeah but I shoulda come even if you was well. The offer of your place in Hooverville saved my ass excuse my French, Miss Wilson. No telling what would have happened to me if not for your generosity."

"Well you're welcome to it. It's yours to keep for as long as you want it. When you don't need it anymore, pass it on to someone who does. So how is it down in Hooverville these days, anyway? Jesse still the Mayor?"

"That's right."

"I guess they still have their Postmaster, considering you got my letter and all. The truth is, I kind of miss the place."

"Yes, you probably do," scolded Mary. "That's what made you sick, eating out of cans and sleeping in the cold when you could have been eating nourishing home-cooked meals and sleeping here in a warm comfortable bed."

Jack noted her admonishing tone and suspected a less pleasant side to Wilson's sister thus far held in reserve.

"Yeah," said Jimmy, coughing, "but down in Hooverville we didn't have a bunch of meddling women nagging and bossing us around."

But Jimmy Wilson's face, already white and pale as spilled milk, turned an even whiter shade.

"I think I'm going to be sick again," he said.

Nurse Becky arrived with a basin, bedpan and washcloth and told them to leave.

"Jimmy has his pride," she explained. "And he needs his rest."

Miss Wilson and Jack returned to the kitchen table. Miss Wilson poured coffee and cut slices of pie but Jack, thinking of his sick friend down the hall, had lost his appetite for pie or anything else. Out the kitchen windows it was turning dark.

"I should probably be getting back," he said. "The trolley doesn't go as far as Hooverville and I'm not ever sure how late it runs."

Mary Wilson emptied the remains of her coffee in the sink and said, "You can stay here tonight if you like, Jack. I can make up a bed in the spare room."

"I don't think that would be proper, Miss Wilson. I mean, to be taking advantage of your kind hospitality and all."

"At least let me give you ride back. In fact, I insist."

"Well since you put it that way, I'd be grateful, Miss Wilson."

"Just let me get changed."

She whipped off her apron, called down the hall to the nurse of her intention to give him a ride home, and hurried upstairs. He was surprised when she returned to see she had changed into jeans and a sweater, a brown leather bomber jacket with a fur collar, a scarf and high leather lace-up boots. She led him through the mud room and pantry to the yard outside the house where they immediately became aware of the scent of apple blossoms. The night was clear and fresh, filled with brilliant stars. Moonlight shone through the leaves of apple trees as she led him toward the driveway, garage and parked Ford. It was the gentleman's way to first open the door for the lady. He did so and waited for her to slip into the front seat.

"It doesn't run," said Miss Wilson. "Frank taught me a bit about auto mechanics but nothing I've tried to get it running has worked and I'm running out of ideas."

She opened the garage and turned on the overhead light. Jack saw a 1929 Harley Davidson motorcycle. He was familiar with them. The vehicle had a 45 cubic-inch flathead engine capable of speeds up to a hundred miles per hour. Its sidecar lay unattached in two pieces in a tight corner of the garage.

"It was your brother's. When Frank was staying upstairs in the garage he was always down here tinkering with it. He taught me how to ride and some basic repairs."

She kick-started it and banged it out of the garage and shouted at him over the engine's roar.

"Climb on back and hang on tight."

The bike had no sissy bar to hold onto and he hesitated. Would it be disrespectful to put his arms around her waist? He lifted himself over the seat and situated himself behind her, holding her as gentlemanly as possible without falling off. She rode slowly on the street outside the house but later when leaving the neighborhood opened it up hard and then they were streaking through the night at a high rate of speed, leaning low on the corners.

Mary Wilson turned her head, smiled back at him and shouted, "You all right back there?"

He could barely hear her. The wind whistled in his ears and the engine's roar necessitated he put his mouth almost in her ear to be heard when answering.

"You're frightening me," he replied. He was no longer reticent to hold his arms around her. He hung on for dear life.

Her hair was like something alive as they accelerated into the wind. They crossed Aurora Avenue, rode up to Greenwood and crossed the Freemont Bridge over Union Bay. He turned his face to the wind and took a deep breath, grateful for the female company. It had been a good night, a good day. She decelerated when they reached First Avenue and turned at Pioneer Square for the steep wooden steps that led down to Hooverville. From here he would walk.

"Thanks for the ride," he said. "Thanks for dinner. Thanks for everything."

His legs were wobbly and equilibrium disturbed. He felt unsteady on his feet, as if returning to land after months at sea.

"You left your hat and shopping bag of old clothes on the porch," she replied.

"I'm sorry about that, Miss Wilson. It wasn't intentional."

"It was intentional on my part to not remind you. Now you have to come back."

She gave him a wink and sped off and then he watched the path of the motorcycle until he could no longer see its taillight or hear the roar of its engine.

ESCAPE FROM PALENTINE AVENUE

AFTER INTERVIEWING SEVERAL satisfactory young men, Walter McCabe decided on a University of Washington sophomore English major to tutor Juanita. His name was Tom Payton. The boy was highly recommended by University professors and other University sources and met with Juanita privately three days a week. The young man dressed collegiate in style, usually wearing clean pressed white pants, a white shirt and his University of Washington letter sweater. What this boy might have been awarded a letter for was anyone's guess but McCabe was willing to bet it wasn't for athletics. Debate team maybe, or chess. Meanwhile that scruffy Kenny Williams kid continued to come sniffing around like someone's underfed whippet. Cora often burned the boy a plate of scorched leftovers. The boy was scarecrow ragged and skinny as a broom handle and always hungry. If anyone needed a free meal it was poor Kenny Williams. The Williams boy had his belt cinched so tight it dangled halfway to floor. He was smart, though, you had to give him that. He always seemed to be reading a different library book and Cora, also a book lover, was fond of the boy and made a big fuss over him.

But life with these women had made of him a fugitive in his own house. They ganged up on him, scolded and shamed him, saying it was for his own good, to eat more vegetables and less meat, exercise and give up his cigars and refrain from alcohol. They had formed an alliance against his drinking especially, and he despaired he couldn't treat himself to the hard-earned working man's right to a drink or two without being reprimanded, scolded, nagged, and lectured. Sometimes they even robbed him of his carefully hidden bottles of expensive scotch and bourbon whiskey smuggled in from Canada and hid it from him. Was he expected to acquiesce quietly to this injustice?

Making his escape down the wet front steps to his parked Hudson, he raised his eyes to the heavens in thanks he was getting away from his house, which had been taken over by fussing, intrusive women. The Hudson was both his refuge where he was free of them and his means of deliverance. Settled behind the wheel, he breathed a sigh of relief and turned the key but when the engine started and he pressed his foot on the accelerator to pull out the Hudson backed into a Plymouth coupe. Apparently he had been in reverse. He opened the door and stepped out to examine the Plymouth for damage, but other than a shattered headlight which was probably broken prior to its kiss from the Hudson, he saw no damage. He got back behind the wheel, making certain he was in the right gear.

The Hudson was the safest most reliable car on the road but it could probably use some new points and plugs. Engine felt like it was missing a little as it sputtered to the light at top of the hill. He waited at the light and pulled out into traffic when it turned green. A symphony of angry automobile horns and screeching brakes acknowledged him immediately. Someone yelled at him out the window. People were passing him and shaking their fists. It was possible the light had not turned green after all. Maybe he had run it. Well, give him a break. How was a man to keep his mind on traffic when his whole world was in chaos? Hoover's Depression was dragging the whole country down into shame and misery. Not to mention the damn Germans up to their old tricks, militarizing and saber rattling. And then of course there were his own problems, both with Cora at home and with his failing shipping business. It was no wonder he ran a light now and then. He turned the corner wide, pedestrians miraculously spreading like the Red Sea to get out of his way as he drove through them, dozens of automobile horns shouting at him from all directions.

He drove on without further incident except for some damn fools blowing their horns and signaling him with an obscene gesture for no discernible reason. People were just rude and pissed off and there was nothing you could do about it except try not to join them in their futile misdirected anger at the whole damn world and the fact that people had no safe place in it.

He missed the brake pedal at the chain-link fence at Pier 91 and ran into the gate. The fence wobbled back and forth audibly, but no harm done and where in hell was the security guard who should have opened it for him? Fortunately he had a key in his watch pocket, so he got out and unlocked the gate, which seemed a little bent from the impact of the Hudson and which upon opening resisted and made a scraping noise against the concrete not previously present. It closed with difficulty and they were probably going to blame him for this just like they did for the stack of barrels for which he had been unfairly billed after knocking them into the sea with the front end of the Hudson, where they floated around the bow of a ship a half hour before sinking. The incident had not been his fault because the barrels had been stacked improperly and should have been contained within a wire cage. Nor should he bear any responsibility for damage to the gate since the gatekeeper should have been there to open it for him.

He drove to the end of the pier and parked alongside the three story aluminum building that housed his office on the third floor, climbed the aluminum stairs and sat behind his desk savoring his first drink of the day, which was overdue, and felt much better for it. The next hour involved itemizing inventory and paying past due bills. His ship, a leased rust bucket owned by a shadowy company of dubious reputation and obscure foreign registry, was in for minor repairs. Not that it could sail anyway, not until the strike was settled. Meanwhile it was his conviction the company from which it was leased should be held responsible for the repairs, not himself, but a notice of overdue payment on his desk greeted him like an obscene gesture. A telephone number to the leasing company's billing office was infuriating. Good luck trying to get someone there to answer. The phone just rang and rang. He shoved this and several other

Lea Macquarrie

papers in the top drawer of his desk. When he looked up he saw a police car pull in and park next to his Hudson. Just his luck someone took his plate number and reported him as a reckless driver. Wouldn't be the first time.

But it turned out to be Sheriff Gustafson. He stood on the pier hitching his trousers and situating the shoulder holster under his jacket. His hat was close to blowing off in the cold Puget Sound wind sweeping the pier. He clomped up the metal stairs and walked in without knocking like he owned the place and pulled a up a chair facing him from across the desk.

He removed his hat, shook it free of some rainwater and said, "Hello, Mac."

"Gus."

"I have something here you more than most might appreciate. Thought maybe you and I could share it."

He reached into a paper bag, withdrew a fifth of Johnny Walker Black and placed it on the desk.

"Where'd you get this?"

"Confiscated."

McCabe rose and withdrew two glasses from a cabinet.

"We'll have to drink it neat," he said. "I don't have any ice."

"That's the best way, Mac. This isn't the usual bootleg crap. It goes down nice and smooth."

Both men took an initial swallow and smacked their lips in appreciation. Gustafson swirled it in his mouth a little and made an appreciative kissing sound with his lips.

"Prohibition ends this December, Mac, and then we can buy this legal. Right now, it's a treat."

"The end of prohibition just in time for Christmas and the New Year," said McCabe. "'Tis the season to be jolly ho ho ho and all that. So what brings you here, Gus? Why are you sharing this bounty with me instead of Drake, Stone, and the rest of those sons of bitches on the *Waterfront Redevelopment Commission?*"

Gustafson sighed and placed his empty glass on the desk and said, "When prohibition ends it's going to be a whole other ballgame Mac. Bobby Stone and Mike Drake are going to lose their speakeasies and that's going to hurt them financially."

"Good. Their talk of burning the men out of Hooverville was the last straw."

"Well, that's just it, Mac. That's one of the reasons I'm here. Stone, Drake, and the others are looking to go legal and go big. They want to open high-end entertainment venues on the Hooverville property and land adjacent to it. Clubs, upscale restaurants and ballrooms, all legal and legit and highly profitable."

"Yes, I know, I've heard all about it. Who will patronize them? No one has any money, Gus. We're in the grips of a nationwide depression here, or haven't you noticed?"

"Sure, I've noticed, and so have they. They see it as an opportunity. They don't think it will last and can turn it to their advantage by buying waterfront property from the city at rock bottom prices that won't be available when the depression ends."

Both men took a drink, and McCabe offered cigars. The men lighted up.

"Well," McCabe inquired, "how are they going to negotiate that purchase, Gus? The city has given the men of Hooverville legal occupancy rights."

"Yes, because of your attorney, Mac."

"That's right. Jeremiah Wells. Best damn attorney in Seattle."

"They're determined, Mac. They're not used to not getting their way and they see you as the as the primary impediment to their investments."

McCabe took a deep puff from his cigar, leaned back in his chair and attempted a smoke ring. Gustafson refilled their glasses.

"I'll be straight with you, Gus. If Hooverville is set afire or the men are driven out by thugs, I'm going to the newspaper and to the county seat in Olympia. I've got enough dirt on them to ruin them financially if not put them behind bars. All of them. That includes you, Gus. Sorry but that's the way it is."

The Sheriff rose from his chair and stood at the window, with its view to Hooverville in the distance.

"I don't get it, Mac. I thought we all agreed we had a mutual interest in waterfront development."

"We do, but not until the depression ends and the population of Hooverville has somewhere to go, either to sponsored public housing or assimilation into a workforce. Frankly, I'm disappointed in you, Gus. You're picking the wrong side. That settlement you see out the window was built from scratch with nothing but primitive hand tools and a lot of hope. I'm proud of them for what they have done without help from the city and nothing to sustain them but a lot of hard work and determination."

"You never protested the first time we burned them out."

"Well if you remember correctly nobody gave me notice but you're right. It was sitting up here watching them rebuild that changed my mind. And my mind is set, Gus. You aren't going to change it."

"Well I'm sorry to hear that. Maybe you'll think differently when you hear what I have to tell you. But listen, Mac, this is confidential, okay?"

"I'm not promising anything, Gus. If you want to tell me something, it will have to be without conditions."

"Damn it, Mac. You know what? You are the most stubborn, difficult, cantankerous old coot I have ever met."

"So they tell me."

"Hear me out on this, Mac. It's important you understand. Stone, Drake, and the others won't be stopped. They see you as the one remaining obstacle standing in their way. I can't protect you from what they might do."

"What, are they going to hire some thugs to beat me up the way they did to Frank Vogel? I'm not afraid of them, Gus"

"Well you should be. It's not in my control anymore, Mac. They're working as we speak to dig up any dirt on you they can find."

"Well they won't find any."

"They'll make it up. You know how unscrupulous these men can be. I'm not here to threaten you, Mac, but to warn you."

"Fine. You've done your duty."

"And you might want to get yourself a gun."

"I already have one. I keep it right here in my desk drawer."

He took it out and placed it on the desk where Gustafson could see it.

"Jesus, Mac, where did you get that cannon? What is it, a Colt 45?"

"Hell, I don't know. I've never fired it."

"Well my advice is don't. Probably has a kick that will knock you on your ass."

"Well, I have this one too."

"Now that's a good gun, Mac. Colt 1903 semi-automatic same as I carry. Do you know how to use it?"

"Damn right, I do."

"Well, maybe you ought to carry it, Mac."

"Is that a threat or a warning or both?"

"I'm looking after you, Mac. I wish this conversation had gone better, but I guess I knew you wouldn't listen."

"I did listen, Gus. I'm not moving on my position. The depression will end of its own accord, and then the commission can do whatever it likes with Hooverville. Meanwhile, Drake, Stone, Olafson and those other sons of bitches on the commission can damn well find some other community to plunder. You can tell them that. And tell them if anything happens to my wife or Juanita, I'm off to the *Seattle Post Intelligencer* and the state house in Olympia."

"I can't tell them something like that, Mac. It would only provoke them. No, this meeting was private. I came to you as a friend, not as a representative of the commission. You can keep the scotch."

"Well, I accept your friendship and the Scotch but not any offer of cooperation with the commission. You go back and tell them I said they can all go to hell."

Gustafson paused at the door before leaving, turned and said, "You're a tough old son of a bitch, McCabe. You would have made a good cop."

"Naw," answered McCabe. "I'm too honest."

DOWNTOWN PRECINCT

DETECTIVE ARTHUR RAMOS SAT IN at the kitchen table and watched his wife nurse their infant son. It was a moment so beautiful and precious to him that it bordered on holiness. The Catholicism of his boyhood and the maternal devotion of his own mother flooded his memory. Ann placed Artie Jr. gently in his bassinet and looked up to meet his eyes and it was more than he could bear. She did not deserve the life he had given her. She was a loyal, good woman who deserved so much more. He took a sip of coffee and fought back tears. He was a lousy husband and dishonest human being. At moments like this, he felt so ashamed he could not meet her eyes.

"Honey," she said. "You're crying."

She hurried to him and knelt beside him, pressing her cheek against his leg and taking his hands.

"What is it, honey? What's wrong?"

She was a perfect mother and wife with a sweet disposition and cheerful non-complaining manner. She was pretty too, not glamorous perhaps but pretty, with a figure other women in the complex envied. She was everything he should want and didn't. Not anymore. His heart had been stolen and was being held for ransom in a little blue room in an upstairs nightclub.

"It's not something I can talk about, Annette. Mostly pressure I'm feeling at work."

"You need to get it off your chest, Artie. You need to talk it through. It's hurting you all bottled up inside."

"Yeah, but its official police business I'm not allowed to discuss. You know that."

"Isn't there someone within the department you can talk to? A counselor or someone?"

"Maybe. I don't know. I'll look into it."

She sat on his lap and kissed him on the cheek and said, "Please, honey. I've been worried about you. You seem so distant these days. Silent and brooding, looking out the window, lost in your thoughts and not really here. And you're always working. This new job has you out at all hours of the night."

Jean understood things about a man his wife never would and he didn't have to explain what he needed from her. She gave him her body to explore, her secrets about herself and her work. How she was more than a hostess, how she took other men upstairs the same way she did him. She hated it but did it for the money. It was different with him, she said. But she had to work and couldn't always be available to him. She was the most requested girl in the club and Stone expected a return on his investment in her.

Cop falls in love with a prostitute. It was a cliché but it was his life now. He didn't want it, and he didn't know how it had happened.

It tormented him to imagine what took place in the blue room when he was not there. His jealousy was an open wound. Jean was the focus and source of his anguish but also the balm that gave comfort from it. His heart told him he belonged with her, that the happiness he felt when they were together was meant to be and not to be passed over. Men might go their entire lives in search of the pleasure he found with Jean and never discover it. At such times he knew he wanted more. He wanted all it could give. He wanted a new life with Jean. But then he'd come home from the blue room to his wife and son and he was in love with Annette again, a woman he knew he *should* want, a wholesome, faithful woman who loved and trusted him. The mother of his child. Why would he not honor this gift of marriage, fatherhood and family? Why would he risk it?

He was a man in love with two women. He cursed himself for being such a fool. On and on it went.

"I've got to go to work," he said. "I'm running late."

"Will you be all right, Artie? I'm worried about you. See if you can talk to someone there. Some kind of police counselor or someone."

"I will."

He finished his coffee and gave her a quick kiss.

"Hey, come back here. That's not a real kiss, Artie."

He kissed her genuinely on the mouth. He knew this mouth, its taste, its smell, the texture of her lips and tongue. There was comfort in it, but not excitement. Not like with Jean.

"I know it's been a long time since we had sex together, Artie, and I'm sorry. I'll try to do better, but with Artie Junior and all I'm so tired and it seems like whenever we have some free time to mess around Artie wakes up or needs something."

"I understand, it's okay."

It was raining lightly when he drove to the precinct. As usual no one acknowledged him when he parked and entered the building. He had his own cubicle and assignment now, but his recent promotion to Detective provoked widespread departmental enmity since other officers rightly believed, because of their seniority and service records, to be more deserving. He was the most hated guy in the downtown precinct and reminded of it every day. No one so much as greeted him upon arrival and no one took up conversation with him whether about a case, sporting event, or newspaper article. He was excluded from office birthday celebrations. If he entered the break room for a coffee or snack, it went silent.

He wore expensive suits to work now instead of a uniform, drove a late unmarked sedan from the motor pool instead of a police cruiser. Annie knew of his basic pay raise, but not its amount. He explained the suits, watches, cufflinks and rings as undercover attire on loan from the police department. Envelopes of cash were kept hidden in a safe deposit box. Much of his money ended up going to Jean for gifts or services.

He sat behind his desk and removed a package of Chesterfields from his desk drawer. He'd picked up the smoking habit from Jean. Annette had smelled it on him and mentioned it. Better the odor of tobacco than the scent of Jean's perfume.

The Sheriff was staring at him from behind the windows of his office, his expression suggesting less inquisitiveness than suspicion, as if he knew it was himself and not McCabe exclusively being investigated. He seemed to not want to discuss the McCabe file at all.

Ramos learned early in his career from his more experienced partner when he first joined the force in San Pedro that everybody to some degree was hiding something and everyone was guilty of something, it was just a matter of finding it. But he was hard pressed to find it on McCabe. The man had no gambling debts, no criminal associates, did not belong to a Communist or Socialist organization nor attend their meetings He'd investigated McCabe's legitimate shipping business, made the rounds of his favorite pool halls, speak-easies and poker rooms, but everyone he talked to liked McCabe and agreed he was a rare, honest, decent man worthy of their trust.

Which of course was bullshit. Bullshit like this so called "case" he was assigned to, an investigation into a crime that probably did not exist.

The phone rang on his desk and he picked up. It was Stone and as usual he got right to the point, no hello it's me Stone, no hello how are you, no hello thought I'd give you a call how's the new job working out.

"So what dirt have you found on McCabe, Ramos?"

"None yet, Bobby"

"I made a mistake when I picked you for this, Ramos. You're the worst investigator in the history of the department. You're just not up to the task. It's because you're stupid, isn't it? All you can say for an excuse is McCabe is clean. That's not even important. If you can't hook him up with one of our girls then get him into one of my gaming rooms where he might run up a debt he can't repay. Set him up, Ramos. Whatever it takes to bring him under my influence and control. What have you got on Gustafson?"

"He's disloyal, Bobby. I know that he has met with McCabe at least once in secrecy without notifying you. I'm trying to find a way to implicate him in a graft and corruption scandal without involving you or the Commission."

"I don't know what happened to the Sheriff but he's changed. He's sympathetic to McCabe and I don't trust him anymore. Maybe next election we'll run you for Sheriff."

"I'm hardly qualified, Bobby."

"Your qualification is that you are loyal to me. Your value to me is that you are outside of the influence of Gustafson or anyone else in the department. You're on the payroll not for what you are contributing now, but for what I expect of you in the future."

"Yeah but everyone in the department hates me and bad-eyes me and gives me the cold shoulder."

"Ida can warm you up. I think she's kind of fallen for you."

"Who is Ida?"

"Jean. It's her real name."

"I didn't know that."

"There's a lot you don't know."

"Well since you mentioned her I was going to ask you. Is there any way I could buy her from you?"

"What the fuck are you talking about, Ramos? She's a whore, not a slave. She works for me voluntarily."

"I'd like to have her exclusively. I want to be her only client. I'm saving money to pay for her freedom."

"Stop thinking about your dick and start thinking about Mc-Cabe, Art. I expect results. You had better come up with some information I can use against Gustafson and McCabe or your wife is liable to find some very interesting photographs in her mailbox."

Stone was always threatening him with this, holding his relations with Jean over his head like the blade of guillotine, but what Stone didn't know was that it wasn't going to work. He was going to outplay Stone, beat him to it. He was going to tell Annette about Jean himself. And he didn't give a damn about becoming Sheriff or rising in the ranks of the Seattle P.D. because he planned to take the money from his safe deposit box and drive off into the sunshine of San Diego and take Jean with him. He hadn't told her about it yet, but she'd been telling him how much she hated Stone and working the blue room and how she wanted to get away to a warmer, dryer climate. She'd jump at the chance to get away. They'd get a motel, lie on the beach and get all horny from the hot sun, drink rum tonics and swim in the ocean and fuck in the Jacuzzi.

He hung up and left his cubicle for the break room coffee pot which, considering the icy silence and cold stares he received, was something like walking into a refrigerated meat locker. Later Stone called back, not exactly apologizing, but softening his tone.

KISSING LESSONS

JUANITA LEARNED DURING ONE OF their tutoring sessions that the letter on the sleeve of her tutor's university sweater had been awarded for fencing. She had no idea what fencing was and imagined men lined up in a field competing to see who could hammer in the most fence posts. She later found out it was like sword fighting, which she knew about because kids in Cat Creek had played it with sharpened tree branches. Mr. Payton, her tutor, explained that fencing was not solely a contest of force or who was stronger, but of agility and grace. He said it was in some ways like dancing and mostly a matter of footwork, anticipating one's opponent's moves, and of skillful manipulation of the foil. The foil was the name of the sword they used. He explained that although he enjoyed the sport, he did not consider himself an athlete and did not otherwise follow team sports such as football, a game she did not understand but which seemed so important to all the boys. All except Kenny, who loved baseball. Poor skinny Kenny who would probably break in two if he were tackled playing sandlot football with the other boys.

Her tutoring completed for the afternoon, she watched Mr. Payton get into his funny little foreign car and drive off. Kenny was coming and she didn't want him to know that she had a private tutor. Poor Kenny thought her greatly improved literacy was due to his own efforts, and she intended to keep it that way. He was proud of her and of himself for teaching her to read and she didn't want to hurt his feelings by taking credit for it away from him. Meanwhile

315

she had been investigating the McCabe library shelves in search of books with lurid covers and titles like *This Side of Paradise*, which she had found disappointing and *The Bridge of Desire*, with some good descriptions of kissing and petting, and *Lady Chatterley's Lover*, which excited her so much she sometimes touched herself when reading certain parts.

She began straightening up the parlor, removing the two teacups and plate of her baked oatmeal cookies. Mr. Payton, during their lesson, had only eaten one between sips of tea, holding his cup between his thumb and index finger, his little finger held aloft, with long pauses between tiny bites. Kenny would have swallowed the whole cookie like an aspirin tablet and only gulp down the tea as an afterthought after picking all the crumbs of his lap and eating them.

She caught a glimpse of herself in the parlor mirror and turned sideways to scrutinize her profile. She was happy she had breasts now. She remembered when she didn't even want them. Kenny was even happier about it. He couldn't seem to keep his hands off them. It was nice that Kenny liked them but she did wish sometimes when they were talking he looked at her face and and not her breasts, but all the boys did that. That was just how they were.

Juanita sometimes imagined what it might be like to be kissed by Tommy Payton. She thought him probably more experienced than Kenny, who pawed at her like a drowning kitten and who was sloppy in his kisses. At school she'd had boys suddenly push her against the lockers in the hallway and try to kiss her. The more she squirmed and tried to get away, the more they seemed to like it. They ground their hips and wiggled against her and tried to put their tongues in her mouth. Once she got sent to the principal's office for biting George Miller's tongue. The Miller boy was the school bully who in the past had beaten Kenny Williams for trying to protect her. Administrators called the McCabe's for a meeting with the vice principal over the tongue-biting incident resulting in a month long after after-school detention washing blackboards and cleaning the lavatories, but it had been worth it because it stopped further aggression toward both her and Kenny Williams. That was another new word, and she was proud of it. Aggression.

Lea Macquarrie

Kenny arrived hungry as usual and asking for a snack. His shoes were scruffy, his shirt half tucked in and half out. His pretty light brown hair had a cowlick in back she wanted to wet and pat down. His hand-me-down trousers were way too big for him. Even with the cuffs rolled up he kept stepping on them. She fixed him a bologna and cheese sandwich he devoured in three bites.

"Thith thith good," he said.

"Don't talk with your mouth full."

Sometimes she wondered what she saw in Kenny and why on earth she would let a boy like Kenny kiss her, but when he smiled sweetly she knew why. He was so cute. And he liked her so very much.

They soon sequestered to one of the many neglected little upstairs rooms they considered safe from intrusion by Cora who, searching for mislaid articles, tended to unpredictably wander the halls, opening doors without knocking and then stand around as if trying to remember why she had come. He sat on an immense regal armchair making him look like he had shrunken. She read aloud, pretending to stumble over passages while Kenny, following in his own copy, corrected her "mistakes".

"Good," said Kenny. "You're becoming a good reader, Juanita."

"And you're a good kisser. Come here, Kenny."

He moved next to her on the love seat and kissed her, which she liked, but his hands went immediately to her breasts, which seemed to give him much more pleasure than it did her. He fumbled with her bra but couldn't manage to unhinge it, so he lifted it until her breasts were exposed and his fingers became busy with her nipples. This seemed to make him very happy. Juanita thought if Kenny were a housecat, he would probably be purring by now. He kissed them, but he was kind of drooling and it was kind of a turnoff.

"That's enough," said Juanita.

They went back downstairs to the kitchen, surprised to see Cora drinking tea and stirring a pot of what resembled some kind of hot cereal. It was hard to tell because it had boiled to unidentifiable congealed mush. Whatever it might be, it smelled like burning rubber. The pan was scorched and the kitchen smoky.

"Kenny," said Cora, "You're in luck. Just in time for some nice hot cereal."

Kenny took a chair at the kitchen table while Cora served up a huge gob of a glue-like substance which adhered to her wooden serving spoon. She held the spoon over Kenny's bowl but the goop hung from the spoon without dislodging and was like the thick white paste they used for crafts at school. Cora shook the spoon vigorously until the cereal plopped into the bowl. Ashes from her cigarette fell into the mush.

She smiled sweetly and patted Kenny on the head.

"There you go," she said. "Just for you."

Lea Macquarrie

KENNY MOWS THE LAWN

KENNY WILLIAMS WADED WITH MR. MCCABE through the tall grass of the overgrown back yard of the Palentine Avenue estate, McCabe gesturing toward the dilapidated rusty tool shed. Squirrels darted across its tin roof, scampering over the litter of broken limbs fallen from surrounding trees. An apple suddenly dropped from a high limb and crashed to the tin roof and made a sound like someone hammering.

"Please Mr. McCabe. There must be something I can do around here to make some extra money. My family needs it bad. I'm doing all I can to help out with a paper route and everything, but it's not enough."

"Well Kenny I wish I could help but there's really nothing much to do. Everything around here is beyond fixing."

"I could pick you a bushel of apples from that tree," suggested Kenny.

"You could, but then Cora would make her catastrophic version of apple crisp, and we'd have to eat it so as to not hurt her feelings."

Kenny couldn't even fake a laugh. Nor was he certain the comment was even a joke. At home he'd awakened late in the night when everyone was supposed to be sleeping and heard his parents whispering downstairs. He'd tiptoed in his pajamas from his upstairs bedroom and down the stairwell, a feeling inside him that something was wrong. His parents didn't see him. They were seated at the kitchen table. The tabletop had notices and bills all over it, and his Dad was crying with his face in his hands. Mother kept trying to comfort Dad, stroking his face and saying over and over again it's all right it's all right we'll think of something.

"Anything that needs done around here, Mr. McCabe, I'll do it."

"Well, son, I honestly don't know what that would be. Maybe you could set the house on fire so I can collect the insurance money."

"How much would you be willing to pay me for that, Mr. McCabe?"

"Easy, boy. I'm only kidding."

"I could mow this lawn," suggested Kenny. They were standing in it, moist from a rainfall earlier that morning, and it almost reached his knees. The weather had since cleared and now the sun had arrived. Beads of rainwater shone like baby diamonds on quenched blades of grass and trembling leaves of green shrubbery. A choir of grateful Robins sang their happy thanks.

"Do you have a lawn mower, Mr. McCabe?"

"We used to, in the shed, but I don't know if it's still there or if it works. The shed leaks and just about everything in there is rusted and useless."

"I'll clean the shed *and* mow the lawn, Mr. McCabe."

"I have no objection to you trying, Kenny, but I think the lawn and mower are a lost cause."

Kenny waded through the tall grass to the rusty shed. The shed door hung lopsided on its rusted hinges and opened with a violent shriek; it probably hadn't been opened in years. Inside it smelled like it also hadn't had any fresh air in years and was so dusty he sneezed upon entering. He had to fight his way through a network of cobwebs occupied by large brown spiders, trapped flies, and insects. He stumbled over piles of trash to reach the lawnmower, which was all but hidden behind an accumulation of wooden storage boxes, paint cans and glass canning supplies, stacks of burlap, rakes, shovels and a disassembled motor and transmission.

Above the lawnmower's worn wooden handles an enormous

hornet's nest hung from an eave and there was no way he might remove the lawn mower without disturbing the nest. But he saw no wasps and the nest was probably dead because nothing could live for long in this lifeless dark crypt. He found an old shovel, held in a deep breath and knocked down the nest with one hard swing of the shovel. He was immediately swarmed. He fled for the open shed door but there were so many obstacles and so much underfoot that he stumbled and tripped and briefly fell to the dirty flooring where he was stung innumerable times before crashing through the shed door for open air. Even then, out in the yard where he ran in what he hoped were evasive circles, he was stung several times by angry hornets pursuing him. Clouds of them were evacuating the shed.

Juanita must have heard him screaming from inside the house because she ran out into the yard to see what was wrong. By then most of the hornets had gone off somewhere, but his face was a mess of red blotches. Juanita understood instinctively and ran back into the house for the calamine lotion on the bathroom shelf.

Kenny was crying when she returned and applied the lotion.

She applied calamine lotion to balls of cotton and dabbed at his wounds.

"I'm not crying because of the bee stings," he said.

"Doesn't it hurt?"

"Yes, but that's not why I'm crying."

"What is it, Kenny?" She kissed each bee sting and said, "Tell me."

"Last night I heard mom and dad talking when they didn't think I could hear them. We're going to lose our house. Dad says there's nothing we can do. We're way behind on the rent and the landlord is going to evict us. Dad says we're going to have to move to Hooverville. I might not even be allowed to join them. He says no kids are allowed there. I might have to go to an orphanage."

"But you can't! I won't let you. You're my best friend. Will we even go to the same school?"

"Dad says I may have to leave school to get a job and help with the finances. I heard him talking about it with Mama. He says even in Hooverville nothing is free."

"But Kenny, that's terrible. How much time do you have before you have to pay the rent?"

"I don't know. I keep thinking I'm going to come home from school one day and see our furniture in the street and not have a house anymore. That's why I'm trying to get extra work, like mowing your dad's lawn."

"How are your stings, Kenny? Better?"

"A little, but they still hurt. I'm going to have to go back into that shed though if I'm going to make any extra money."

Even from outside the door he could hear the buzzing of remaining angry hornets as they circled inside the shed. He entered bravely and fought the lawnmower over the debris and out the door, his legs stung multiple times during the removal.

There were welts on his arms and on his face. He lifted his pants legs and saw more stings. He was beginning to feel a little bit sick and thought he might vomit and was becoming so sleepy he wanted to lie in the grass. He ran the hose and cold water over his head and felt less drowsy. He knelt to examine the lawnmower blades, which were orange with rust and which would not revolve when he tried to spin them. He made a mudpack from wet dirt from the garden and applied it to his wounds, and then tried to mow. The blades were dull and the lawnmower only flattened the grass without cutting it. He entered the shed again and was stung twice more before finding and lifting a toolbox and scythe. The toolbox rewarded his efforts with a file, sharpening stone and can of lubricating oil. He sharpened the blades the best he could and oiled the joints where the wheels met the body of the lawnmower. The tires were low but not entirely flat. Juanita brought him her bicycle pump from the porch and he inflated the tires.

He sharpened the scythe and began swinging it, cutting the grass down to ankle length. Juanita brought glasses of lemonade and watched from the front porch as he fought the mower, pushing it over the tall grass. The newly sharpened lawnmower blades were cutting now but quickly became so clogged with clumps of mowed grass they could not revolve. He had to stop after every few pushes to remove the clumps from between the immobilized blades.

Lea Macquarrie

He removed his shirt and worked all afternoon, able to execute no more than three pushes of the lawnmower before having to remove the accumulation of cut grass from the blades. Juanita brought him sandwiches he ate while resting under the shade of an apple tree. An apple fell on his head and he ate that too and then went back to work. He stopped only to drink from the hose. Grass stuck to his bare back and chest and he periodically washed it off with the hose. He worked all day, from morning into the late afternoon when the sky began to change to a darker shade and the mosquitoes started biting. His hands were blistered and hurting to the degree that he had forgotten all about the bee stings. It was getting dark when he finished raking and piling the last of the cut grass and called for Mr. McCabe. He waited, staring across the lawn he had just cut while wondering how he would be paid. How much was the job worth? Should he just leave it up to Mr. McCabe and take whatever he offered? What if Mr. McCabe asked him directly how much money he expected for the job? What would he say?

Not only Mister McCabe came out, but Cora as well. Mister McCabe whistled approvingly and shook his head in amazement. Cora roamed the cleared yard with her arms spread like a ballerina. McCabe reached in his back pocket for his wallet.

"Good job, Kenny. We haven't had a yard in years and I like it very much. I think we'll move some of the porch furniture out here when it's not raining and maybe string a hammock."

He held his open wallet and said, "How much do I owe you, Kenny?"

"Would five dollars be unreasonable?"

"It would," replied Mr. McCabe. "It would indeed."

He handed Kenny a fifty-dollar bill.

Kenny glanced at it briefly and handed it back.

"You've made a mistake, Mr. McCabe. This isn't a five, it's a fifty."

"I know that, Kenny. Take it. You've earned it."

Kenny accepted it with tears in his eyes.

"Really?"

"Yes. Give it to your family. Juanita told me about your trouble with the landlord. I can't pay you this much again, Kenny, but you can mow once every two weeks and I'll pay you fairly. Now that the grass is finally cut to a manageable length, the job should be much easier next time. Maybe we can find some other things for you do as well. Clean the shed, maybe clear the trash out of the basement, we'll see."

He put his arm around Cora and guided her up the side porch stairs into the house.

Cora whispered, "Fifty dollars, Walter?"

"I know," he replied, "but it was money well spent."

MISS WILSON

WHEN NOT SCAVENGING FOR SCRAP along the waterfront or fishing from the rented rowboat in Puget Sound, Jack helped with household repairs at the Wilson house. He found it satisfying to be working with the tools Frank had left in the garage and took pride in being able to apply his skills and be of use to someone again. He repaired the steps to the Wilson's porch, nailed shingles on the roof, replaced rotted planks on the porch and reinforced structural beams in the basement. He measured and cut sheets of glass for window replacement, welded the sidecar to the motorcycle, replaced the elements in the hot water heater and serviced the washing machine on the porch. Miss Wilson fed him, did his laundry, and encouraged his use of their bath. She tried to pay him for his work but he knew she couldn't afford it and always refused the money. Her home cooked meals and the fresh fruit and vegetables she packed for him to take back to Hooverville were payment enough.

He was still looking for work but mostly going through the motions without expectation. Bethlehem Steel was shut down, there were no ships to at the docks to be unloaded, and fishing boats were idle. The Weyerhaeuser Lumber Mill was open but working with a skeleton crew and the men working the saws held onto their jobs until their fingers were amputated in sufficient number to cause their dismissal. Some ended up down in Hooverville,

One day a drifter came into the settlement who told Jack he knew Frank in prison. According to this fellow, Frank was caught trying to escape and ended up with time added onto his sentence. Jack wasn't sure and hoped the man was wrong. He wanted to write Frank and ask about this but the postmaster was away to visit a sister in Oregon. He was due back soon, so maybe then. He was embarrassed to ask Miss Wilson for help writing.

When he wasn't working on the house he sat in a chair by Jimmy Wilson's bedside. Jimmy was already mostly gone. He lay immobile in bed soaked in perspiration despite multiple changes of linen and was hardly eating at all. He tried to prop Jimmy against the bed's headboard and feed him broth from a spoon but Jimmy only managed a few sips before collapsing like a man just gunshot. Jack could neither wake him nor see much point in it.

As it turned out, Mary Wilson was educated. She had graduated from high school and had taken correspondence courses from an ad clipped out of a magazine. She owned a set of encyclopedias and was always reading. Jack was ashamed he still couldn't read properly or intelligently discuss much with her. She figured it out, smart woman that she was, and said illiteracy was a condition easily remedied and insisted on teaching him. He tried but he was a slow learner and she was sometimes impatient and cross with him.

Miss Wilson could be a nag sometimes, pushy, stubborn, and bossy. She pried into his private life as if she had every right, and it seemed whatever he said in answer to her inquiries wasn't enough to satisfy her. She obstinately fished for more personal information than she had any business asking for and more than he was willing to give. He'd never been one to share his personal history, but especially not now, when a man was dead because of him and it was likely one day he would be taken to prison because of it.

One night after dinner she asked him to dance to a live music broadcast on the radio. He obliged, leading her to the center of the living room where there was ample space for dancing. He pressed his left hand firmly on her back and led her through the foxtrot, waltz and rumba the way he had done when single in the local beer halls and later under the low lights of their little kitchen with Alma. Mary said she would never have guessed him to be so clearly experienced and confident on a dance floor and he enjoyed the moment too, until he felt activity in his pants that embarrassed him. He had not held a woman other than his daughter in well over a decade. He was relieved when the broadcast went off the air and he could get away to the couch.

She sat beside him and said, "Why didn't you ever marry again, Jack?"

More prying. He ignored it. There had been a time when he had wondered about this himself but what woman was going to take in a man with hungry children to raise? Of course, his children were long gone, but he was well past the marrying stage in life. Mary Wilson had no children. He often wondered why, but it was not his business to inquire.

"When do you intend to see Juanita again," she asked.

She wouldn't let up on the subject. He'd explained many times his less than truthful account of how he'd taken her to live and work somewhere near Woodland Park but was unable to find the house again and knew the owners only as Mac something. He did not mention the name Cora or Walter McCabe.

"I think you're just afraid," she said.

She was right about that, but she didn't know the circumstances. Juanita was right when she had said in the Hotel Lee that she would end up having to take care of him instead of the other way around like it should be. She said nothing ever worked out for him and it hurt him at the time to hear it but he saw the truth in it even then. Maybe someday his life would be different and he would have something to offer his daughter other than the burden of responsibility to him but he doubted it. His daughter had a better life now, better than he would ever be able to provide for her. Meanwhile at the very least he didn't want to risk breaking Juanita's heart by reentering her life only to abandon her again for a bum's life in Hooverville. Of course he couldn't say any of this to Miss Wilson, who would surely argue the point.

Miss Wilson often talked about the importance of what she termed "relationships", a word spoken with a reverent tone more suitable for matters Biblical and Holy than the subject at hand. She didn't seem to get it when he said what he needed now more than anything was a job, not a relationship, which he understood to be mostly someone meddling in his private business. Mary Wilson said there were no jobs and he wasn't likely to get one if there was, and if he wasn't so stubborn and headstrong he'd take an honest long look at his life and come to his senses and realize he already had a relationship. What exactly she meant and why it made her so angry he had yet to figure.

"I've got to be getting back to Hooverville," he said. "I have a job helping a guy build a shack and have to be up and ready early."

It was a lie and he figured she probably knew it but Miss Wilson seemed to be in one of her prying moods and he didn't like it and she should know better. He went home to Hooverville and stayed away for seven days. When he saw her next she was angry and asked where the hell he had been as if he owed her an explanation or anything else. He wanted to tell her maybe this was one of the reasons he never married again but didn't dare.

When she asked him to drive he said no, he didn't want to be responsible for someone else's car if he wrecked it but she argued it was he who had gotten the Ford up and running again after her own failed multiple attempts so he had earned the right to drive it. He didn't mind making plumbing or electrical repairs or carpentry or working on her car, but he drew the line at being her damn chauffer. Next thing you knew, she'd have him wearing an apron and wiping down furniture with a feather duster. He reminded her he didn't have a driver's license and she replied she didn't either.

"No one should have to purchase a license for permission to drive," she declared. "No one should pay road taxes either, except maybe the automobile manufacturers who are raking in money from people for whom ownership becomes a burden keeping them in debt. The oligarchs *need* us driving, Jack. They want to bleed us of what little money we have in exchange for their gasoline and oil when in fact they are the ones that need us, not the other way around. Capitalist plutocrats intend for us to drive their automobiles to their unsafe underpaid jobs in their sweatshops and factories and make us pay at the gas pump and license bureau for doing so."

God she could be tiresome sometimes. What a plutocrat was

she didn't explain and he didn't ask. He had become so weary of these editorial rants from Mary Wilson he didn't much bother to reply he would be more than happy with one of the "sweatshop" factory jobs she so summarily dismissed as exploitative. Not that it mattered since there were none to be had.

"I'm not driving and that's final, Miss Wilson."

She glared at him when he settled into the passenger side seat and said, "My name is Mary, and I expect to be addressed as Mary. Not Mary Wilson, not Miss Wilson but just Mary. If I hear you refer to me as Miss Wilson one more time I'm going beat you with a claw hammer."

A shudder went through him at the mention of it. Miss Wilson saw it.

"Is something wrong?"

He tasted bile in his constricted throat and managed only to reply, "Nothing."

He had forgotten. That was one of things he liked about being with Mary Wilson. In her company he felt normal. At the mention of a claw hammer the masquerade had ended and he was made to face who he really was, a liar and a fake who out of necessity would never be honest, not with Mary Wilson, not with himself. He was a fugitive and a liar who had buried bloody clothing and a murder weapon somewhere in the woods off the tracks near Everett, Washington.

She turned the key in the ignition and said, "Sometimes I wonder if you even like me, Jack Vogel."

He stared through the windshield into the gray Seattle day without answering.

"Well?"

"Well what?"

"Do you?"

"Do I what?"

"Do you like me? God but you can be exasperating."

"Of course, I like you. You and your brother are my best friends."

"You don't always act like it."

"You have a way of getting under my skin, Mary. I guess I just have been away from women too long. And I ain't been with all that many to begin with."

"Haven't."

"What?"

"You haven't been with that many women to begin with."

"That's what I said."

"No, you said ain't."

"Well, you see now? That's what I mean. You're always correcting me and trying to change me from what I am."

"Well honestly, Jack, you could use a little changing. Some educating too. You're a well-mannered decent man, but I saw the same thing in my brother when he came back from Hooverville. Something about living with all those men."

"I suppose there's some truth in that. I used to talk more civilized when I was raising my daughters. I don't know exactly how to talk to a woman of your education."

"Education isn't everything, Jack. It doesn't make a person any better than next. You're a good man, Jack. Don't ever think otherwise. You're the only man I would let live in my house and you won't do it."

"I'd rent, but not freeload. When I get a job and have something to bring to the table we'll see."

She smiled sweetly, her face happily aglow, and he could see he had somehow pleased her, which made him happy, but he wished he knew how he had done it. She drove up 45th Street and passed a public school, crossed Highway 99 and then uphill to Woodland Park. They passed the first park entrance but at the second she turned left, proceeding down a steep hill toward Ballard Bay. She parked on a quiet residential street and pointed to a massive three and a half story Queen Victorian house perched above them.

A gust of wind shook trees along the curb. Shivering robins perched on quivering bare limbs, their wings tucked beneath them as if huddled for warmth. Why they chose to stay in Seattle and not migrate south for the winter like more sensible birds he did not understand. Maybe they were incapable of such a long flight. It was not raining, but the air was damp and cold. She turned on the heater but the windows fogged up so she turned it off. The gray sky threatened rain.

"Does that mansion on the hill look familiar, Jack?"

It was the kind of mansion his brother Frank always said after the revolution would be assimilated to house as many as three or four otherwise homeless families. It had three floors and an attic and two rounded turrets.

"We're on Palentine Avenue, Jack. This is the home of Mr. and Mrs. Walter McCabe. It's where Juanita lives. Look at the beautiful chandeliers in the windows, Jack. They have furniture on their porch better than anything in my house and look; I see a baby grand piano through the bay windows on the far right."

It had been enshrouded in fog when he had first seen it but it was the same house, with the same granite path up the steps to the front porch. In the daylight, without the concealment of fog, the house evidenced both neglect and disrepair. Much of the paint had bubbled and chipped, the railing up the staircase was askew in places, and the pillars that supported the roof over the porch looked in need of stabilizing. His mouth had gone dry and he worked up some saliva and swallowed. It seemed to stick in his throat. He could feel his heartbeat pound. His hands and forehead were sweaty and he thought he might be sick. Miss Wilson was still talking and he wished she would stop. He mumbled a pathetic failed attempt to change the subject.

"Someone needs to trim the shrubbery along the walkway," he said. "They're overgrowing the steps and narrowing the path. As steep as that pathway is, those bushes should be cut back. It looks like an accident waiting to happen. It doesn't look like any one has bothered to pick the apples from that tree either."

"Jack, get it through your thick head."

She punched him on the shoulder. She had a good punch for a woman. Jack felt it.

"This is not the same house, Miss Wilson. I don't know why you would say otherwise."

"Because it is, Jack. This beautiful old house is where Juanita lives. You'll see."

"I don't know why you are so insistent on thinking this, Miss Wilson."

"Then I'll tell you why. You once mentioned the house was down the hill from Woodlawn Park. You said the house was owned by Mac something, you couldn't remember exactly. So I went through the telephone book and looked up the Mac listings near Woodland Park until I found an address for a Walter McCabe on Palentine Avenue. I don't understand, Jack. You could have found the address as easy as me if you tried. You could have seen your daughter any time."

"Miss Wilson, you're right I could have found it easy. I've known for some time the address and the names of the people who live here. This is the house where I left her. I'm sorry but I can't do this right now, Miss Wilson. Please, let's leave. I'll explain everything later. We can come back another time."

He did not initially see the three teenaged schoolgirls and one boy down the block, but something drew his attention to them. They were in no hurry, and their faces were indistinct, but there was no mistaking Juanita's way of walking the way he remembered, a stride not quite a skip, like her feet did not lift entirely off the ground. He remembered how she wore through shoes with that manner of walking, how he had tried to correct it.

It was her same way of walking but she was not the same girl. This girl was better, not a Cat Creek waif, not a tomboy ruffian, not a Crow Indian breed. She was a smart teen schoolgirl dressed in a school jacket and pleated skirt and clean white blouse, a little older, taller, with her hair lightly curled and cut in the popular style of the day. She looked much less like an Indian girl now with her new hair style. She had a figure now too. She was a pretty teenage girl and she was going to be beautiful as a woman.

He would not again attempt to play the part he never got right, the part of a father. He slumped down in his seat, closed the car door and pulled his hat down to the bridge of his nose. This girl who had once been his daughter was not anymore. She was Juanita, but not a version he knew. She was not the little girl he rocked to sleep as a baby, not the smiling gurgling toddler who had wobbled on infant feet, arms spread wide for a hug. She was not the girl he had taught to ride bareback and to fish with a spear and shoot a rife. She bore no resemblance to the girl in pigtails and torn jeans who loved horses, who loved to climb trees and imitate forest birds, nor the tomboy who loved to wrestle and fire rocks from her slingshot, not the girl he had brought to Seattle in pursuit of a foolish doomed dream. Like Alma, that girl was gone. This one belonged to the McCabe's now. He was crying, and it made him ashamed for Miss Wilson to witness it. It was not manly.

ALKAI POINT

ON THE AFTERNOON OF JIMMY WILSON'S death they were on the beach at Alkai Point. It was late afternoon and brisk, white-caps distant across the sound. The odor of the sea was strong in the wind, the water cold beyond endurance. Mary hitched her dress and waded barefoot into the sound. She smiled at him and dared him to join her.

"I'm cold just sitting here watching you, Miss Wilson."

He sat on a large piece of driftwood, a bucket of clams in the sand at his feet.

"Come on, sissy. I dare you."

"Only fools act on a dare."

"Always the practical man."

Clutching her dress above her knees with one fist she waded in the surf. The mirrored sunlight on the water sent shafts of light across the sound behind her. She returned to the rocky shell-strewn shore and sat beside him on the large stump of driftwood and lifted her dress to wipe her legs free of sand and cold salty sea water. In Jack's opinion you had to be a seal to stay long in salty Puget Sound. It was too cold. They both stared out to sea at the incoming frothy tide and quietly listened to the sounds the sea made crashing on the rocks.

"What are you thinking, Jack?"

She was always asking him this. He didn't know what he was thinking and didn't know if he would want to tell her if he did. A man had need of his privacy. She either didn't understand this or wouldn't accept it, and continued to prod at every opportunity for personal information she was not entitled to. She reached into the sand at her feet, gathered a handful and let it slowly trickle between her fingers like sand in an hourglass.

"Why have you never kissed me, Jack?"

"It wouldn't be right, Miss Wilson. You were married to my brother."

"The marriage was a mistake and not even legal, Jack. Frank and I were lovers less than a month before the bogus marriage, which lasted about the same length of time. When I learned of Elvira and all the other women it ended it between us. But you couldn't help but like Frank. We eventually became friends who could laugh about it. You know how he was. He was fun to be around, and I liked having him near, but that was as far as it went."

This was already more information than he asked for or wanted to hear. He remained silent, brooding as they strolled back to the car. They drove over the Freemont Bridge to Greenwood and from there to her Wallingford neighborhood on the outskirts of Green Lake. When they pulled into the driveway nurse Rebecca came out to greet them on the front porch. He knew immediately Jimmy Wilson had died.

The next morning he dug Jimmy Wilson's grave under a pear tree forty feet behind the garden. Notices of Wilson's memorial were distributed by the Hooverville Postmaster. It was a hardship for the shabby group of Jimmy Wilson's Hooverville friends to come to the Wilson house to pay their last respects, but many came. They limped in quietly, heads bowed, haggard and scruffy, with broken ruddy noses and red faces weathered with hard times and plans that never worked out, but clean shaven and quietly respectful. Most had made the effort to dress respectfully, wearing Salvation Army suits and ties for the ceremony.

Jimmy Wilson was buried in his going-to-church suit and best shoes. Wrapped in a bed sheet tied on both ends, Jack and three others carried him in the sheet from the house down the steps and into the garden area as best as they could manage, though Jack thought he might have heard Wilson's head strike a step when they came off the porch. He felt bad about it, and whispered Wilson an apology. Mary spoke to the assembly gathered at his resting place.

"I'm an atheist and my brother and I used to argue about it. He was a Bible reading man and a Christian. I guess to Jimmy his faith was a comfort. There isn't any heaven, no Jesus at the gates like my brother expected, but he's dead and doesn't know it. We all die, the good and the bad alike, and my brother was better than most."

Jack admired how she spoke these words without so much as a tremor. He had not seen her cry but knew she would, frequently and without warning, same as him after Alma died. He waited for her to finish and cleared his throat to speak next. It was not expected of him but he wanted to.

"This was a good man. He is now free from suffering and hardship. Jimmy helped me in this life with my own hardships. When Jimmy gave me his house in Hooverville, it saved my life. I am grateful for it, and for his friendship. I'm also grateful for his sister Mary Wilson who like her brother is another fine person, better than most of us standing here while Jimmy awaits his burial. If there were more like the Wilson's here this earth would be a better place and maybe we wouldn't have a need of heaven at all. A-men."

There were few tears. Most of the men present had seen far too much death for that. He returned with them to Hooverville and stayed away because it was different now. In the past he had called on the Wilsons ostensibly out of friendship to Jimmy, but to do so now would make evident his intention to seek the company of Mary Wilson specifically. He thought it over for five days and finally concluded he owed it to his Jimmy to look in on her.

Mary acted like he had never been gone. Started bossing him around right away. Had him make a cross to put over Jimmy's resting place, had him planting flowers around it, made him clean out Jimmy's closet for clothing to take back to the men in Hooverville. She was alternately crying and bossy and he didn't know how to act around her or comfort her.

Three weeks later they were dancing in the soft light of the living room to a sad instrumental. She began crying, her face on his shoulder as they danced. He felt the wetness of her tears on his neck, her quivering chest against his. He figured she had earned a good cry and had it coming and it wasn't his business to take it away from her. They remained holding one another while the music played on the radio but were no longer dancing.

"It's about time you had a good cry," he said. "Jimmy was a good man. Everyone liked and respected him. It's no wonder you're sad."

"I don't know if I'm crying because I'm sad or if it's because I'm angry," she said. "I suppose both."

"Angry at Jimmy?"

"Yes. If he hadn't chosen to live down in Hooverville he might be alive today. Eating canned food, shivering in that shack, it's no wonder he got sick. I told him and told him but he wouldn't listen. And now you're the same way, Jack. I'm angry at you too. You won't accept the comforts and safety life has to offer you. Too darn proud."

"I do the best I can, Mary. Or at least try."

"No, Jack, you don't. You may think you do but you don't. If you did you would move in here with me and live with me."

"Is that what you want?"

"It's what you want. You know you want it and I do too."

Her feminine bedroom was furnished with a large mirrored dresser, lace curtains and pretty stained glass lamps. The brass bed was spread with quilts. Fluffy female pillows rested at the headboard. He saw himself in the large mirror on the bureau against the wall and did not know who this man was, this man in the mirror who was being kissed by Mary Wilson. Could it really be himself, after all these years, kissing a woman who was not Alma?

She gathered some night things that looked like lingerie, bundled it in her arms and said, "I'll be right back. Go ahead and get into bed."

"Are you certain? You have recently lost your brother and you've been acting oddly ever since, not that I blame you. I don't want you to do anything you'll regret in the morning."

"Of course I won't regret it in the morning. I'll make you pancakes."

She lighted candles on the dresser. Pinpoints of reflected light danced in the mirror. She closed the bathroom door and left him wondering whether she meant for him get in the bed or just sit or lie on it, and what was he supposed to wear? He had no pajamas and if he didn't think of something quick he would end up having to undress in front of her. He worried at the edge of the bed, quickly removing his boots, then his outer clothing. He pulled back the covers and felt the softness and warmth of the bedding and mattress but couldn't relax.

Suppose Alma was looking down from where the dead go. What if she saw him with Mary Wilson? Would she be hurt by it? Would sleeping with Mary Wilson be a betrayal of what they had been together? Would it be a final, irretrievable separation from Alma? He didn't know if he wanted that. He didn't want to lose his memory of her.

He could hear water running in the bathroom, Mary Wilson washing up. He smelled his armpits and wrinkled his nose. How could it be possible a woman like Mary Wilson would want him? What did women with their smooth beautiful bodies find desirable in ugly men who were like hairy monkeys or in his case a gorilla.

Mary Wilson was floating toward him without a sound. It was as if he was dreaming this. He could not hear her footsteps. He could see her thighs and the shape of her breasts under the silk in the candlelight. Breasts with a sway to them when she floated toward him. He was embarrassed to look but couldn't stop. He remembered Alma's breasts, hard and swollen, how they became engorged and how she wanted him to pinch them. Mary Wilson slipped the nightgown over her head. Naked, she presented herself to him and said, "I think it's possible I might love you, Jack Vogel."

They were married six weeks later. He wore his only suit with a white shirt and tie and his shoes shined to a high gloss. Mary wore a pretty white cotton dress extending pioneer style to her ankles but went barefoot. She wore her hair with yellow flowers fixed into a tiara on top of her head like a crown. The Honorable Mayor of Hooverville stood as Jack's best man and presented the ring, a plain silver band Jack had traded for in a pawn shop on 2nd Avenue.

Lea Macquarrie

Music from the radio played in the background as they said their vows. It was Mary's first legal marriage, Jack's second. Mary learned soon after that Jack was a man who sometimes woke screaming in the night but not why.

INTERLAKE SCHOOLHOUSE

JUANITA HIT ORVIN NORDSTROM ON THE HEAD with a textbook so Miss Chambers held her in detention and assigned her to clean all the blackboards and erasers on the third floor of the Interlake schoolhouse. It wasn't fair. Orvin had started it by making a spectacle of her by standing in the classroom and announcing that in his opinion she should not be in this school at all on account of she was not Italian but a squaw who didn't belong in a white school, and Orvin wasn't punished at all. Not that her heritage wasn't suspect and a subject of speculation of the school administration, who had sent to the Cat Creek, Montana county seat of Winnnett for her birth certificate. It turned out she had been delivered at home by Aunt Vi and there was no record of her birth to be had.

The blackboards should have presented little problem because it was a simple matter of erasing what had been written on them but the erasure marks were themselves thick with chalk and she was supposed to clean those as well. She had to repeatedly take the erasers and bang them together, which sent up clouds of chalk dust that made her sneeze. She was almost finished though, having worked her way to the last classroom on the third floor, which happened to be her home room, presided over by her home room teacher, Miss Gertrude Chambers, who was nowhere near as good a teacher as Tommy Payton and not even as good as Kenny Williams because she made reading an act of drudgery when it should be fun.

Earlier in the week Miss Chambers had written in the comments section of her report card *Juanita has made great strides in her reading and writing and is progressing at a rate that is far beyond what we might have expected under the circumstances, but she is still behind the rest of the class. She is, however, progressing at a rate that gives promise she will catch up soon, possibly even by the end of the school year. She is a diligent and studious pupil but unruly, a discipline problem with aggressive outbursts of temper in the playground, and disobedient classroom behavior."*

She liked learning, but not school. She thought it would be different in Seattle than in Cat Creek. It was, but she wasn't sure she liked school here any better. Rows of desks were lined before her like obedient dutiful students. The entire east wall of the classroom was windowed with a view to the concrete playground's basketball hoops for the boys and hopscotch lanes for the girls. It was far too nice a day to be unfairly cooped up and it wasn't fair. Afternoon light cascaded into the classroom. Angrily, she banged the last two erasures together and spat the ensuing chalk dust from her lips.

She picked up a piece of chalk and wrote: *Miss Chambers, as you can see I cleaned this blackboard and all the others on this floor. I should not have had to do this alone. Orvin should have done it with me and it's not fair. I can't wait until next year when I might move on and get a better teacher.*

She replaced the chalk and wiped her hands and went into the hallway to the girl's bathroom but when she opened the door to its glaring row of porcelain sinks and bank of mirrors she saw a ghost staring back at her. Chalk dust coated her hair and her face was white as a pillowcase. She ran water in the sink, washed her face and removed her blouse, shaking it up and down to free it of chalk dust. Her arms were coated and she washed them clean. Her blue skirt had also turned white and she shook that out as well. The room filled with billowing clouds of chalk dust and made her sneeze repeatedly. Finally, unknowingly leaving a trail of chalk-outlined footprints all the way down the hallway behind her, she reached the double doors to sunshine and Kenny Williams. He had a book open on his lap and smiled, closing the book.

"I'm sorry it took so long. You didn't have to wait, Kenny."

"I wanted to. We always walk home together. It's my favorite part of the day."

"You are so sweet, Kenny."

"It's because I love you."

They were often teased about this. Earlier in the semester she had found her locker door papered head to foot with notebook paper on which was written *Juanita loves Kenny* hundreds of times in different handwriting. It was supposed to embarrass her but it didn't because she did love Kenny Williams and she didn't care who knew it. She told Kenny often that she loved him.

"Cora says its puppy love," said Kenny.

"It's still love though."

"I think you probably shouldn't have hit Orvin. At least not as hard as you did. That was a big book and he was crying it hurt so much."

"I hate our school. No one likes me there. Other than you I don't have a single friend."

"The girls are jealous because you are the prettiest girl in the school. The boys tease you because they can't kiss you."

A black four door sedan pulled to the curb at the end of the block. When they were abreast of it a man wearing a black suit and fedora hat stepped into their pathway, took Juanita's arm and began forcing her toward the sedan's open back door. She swung her lunch bucket and struck him across the face, cutting his lip and eliciting a curse of surprise. He ripped the lunchbox from her hand, threw it to the ground and maneuvered her into a hammerlock. He slammed her down hard on the hood of the sedan. Kenny Williams tried to pull her loose. Another man, unseen until now, leapt out of the car and showed a badge.

"Back off, kid. Right now. I'm with the Seattle Police Department and this is police business."

Juanita managed to scream but the man who held her down on the hood of the car clamped his hand over her mouth. She hung on with her teeth until he pulled her hair so hard she thought her head would snap and had to release him. Handcuffs were locked behind her back then she was pushed into the back seat of the sedan. Kenny was pounding on the window but the sedan was pulling away and then she was watching him recede from view in the back window. He was chasing the car, running as fast as he could, and then he was gone.

Her abductor sat wiping his injured hand with a white handkerchief. She could see the indentations of her teeth marks and wished she had rabies and he would die from them. He wore dark glasses and did not speak, acknowledge or as much as glance at her. It was as if she were not even sitting beside him in the back seat. She, worked at freeing her handcuffs until her wrists were raw with the effort.

"I want to see your badge" she said. "I want your badge number."

He removed his dark glasses, looked at her directly for the first time, his cold blue eyes utterly without a trace of sympathy.

"You're not exactly in a position to be making demands, young lady. "

His voice lacked cadence or nuance; it was what she had once heard Walt McCabe describe as monotonic, another new word. He did not speak to her again. It was raining again now, and she did not recognize anything out the steamy window. She sat as far away from her captor as possible. She tried to turn the locked door handle with her bound hands, but was unable. The view out the window was to drab factories and silent industrial warehouses. She had no idea where they were.

She began crying but became angry with herself for doing so and cut it off. The driver turned around and said, "You *should* cry." It was the first sentence he had spoken to her. "You are in a lot of trouble."

The sky had turned dark gray and she could hear rain striking the sedan's roof and sloshing under their tires. They crossed a steel bridge into a redbrick industrial area where they parked. A three story concrete building with a Washington State flag took up most of a city block. Her captors, gripping each arm, led up the wet front steps.

They entered a spacious, busy, brightly lighted receiving area noisy with the clank of typewriters, ringing telephones and police radios. Uniformed police were everywhere she looked, some behind their desks talking on telephones, others afoot with handcuffed civilians in their charge. At one station a man was being fingerprinted. She was cold and soaking wet but no longer crying. She wondered if they had her father here somewhere too. The enormous room was a maze of desks and cubicles. She heard the persistent ring of telephones, the knocking of radiators and clattering busy typewriters echoing off the walls, windows, and linoleum flooring. Police came and went with handcuffed detainees in custody; some arrestees had bruised faces and had been obviously beaten.

"I want to call Walter McCabe," she said. "He's my guardian."

No one so much as acknowledged her request.

Two uniformed policewomen bullied her down a steep flight of steps into a windowless basement hallway flanked by rooms with steel doors and small wire-meshed windows. At the threshold of one such room her handcuffs were released and she was pushed inside. She heard the door lock behind her and then she was alone in a stark windowless concrete room. Except for a desk, telephone, and two wooden chairs, the room was empty. She picked up the phone to call Mr. McCabe but was unable to get an outside line. Apparently some kind of code was needed. She stood on tiptoes to view through the small rectangular window high in the door but saw only a small part of the hallway. She wondered if she could break the window and if so whether she might be able to slither out. She pounded on it with her fists until they were swollen.

The corner radiator was turned off and she was shivering. She had been soaking wet when they brought her in. She turned the handle on the radiator but nothing happened and there was no heat. She figured it was deliberate. The radiators upstairs had been working. She was hungry and had to go to the bathroom. She sat on one of the wooden chairs and rested her face on the desk but the chair had brass rollers and kept sliding away. She turned the chair upside down and pulled away two of the brass rollers and rolled them up in her fists in simulation of brass knuckles. Her need to urinate became pervasive. She pounded on the door and small window but no one who might escort her to a bathroom was in sight. She shouted but no one came. She listened to her stomach and prowled the desk drawers. One was locked and the others empty. She had no idea where she was or whether anyone knew she was here or would come for her. She had not seen another human being, prisoner or otherwise since having been brought downstairs. She was hungry, and her pervasive need to urinate had become profound.

She heard footsteps in the hall again and then keys jangling in the door. A plainclothesman entered, not one of the men who had accosted her earlier. He had a sharp chin and pronounced cheekbones. His dark brown eyes, pencil-line moustache and dark olive complexion suggested a non-white ancestry, not Indian but maybe Mexican or Cuban. She recognized him now. He was the policeman who had questioned her on the McCabe's porch when Cora had been brought home in a police car after shoplifting. He had been wearing a police uniform then. He wore a suit and tie now.

He placed a legal notebook, pen and package of life savers on the desk between them and said "Hello, Miss Vogel. I'm Detective Ramos and I'm here to help you. You are in serious trouble. I suggest you return those brass rollers to the chair. They are hollow, lightweight and for use as brass knuckles ineffective."

"I want to call Mr. Walter McCabe."

"And I want to see if I can save you from a life in prison. Can I get you something? Would you like a coke or a sandwich or something?"

"Right now I just want to go to the bathroom. I need to go bad."

"All right, Juanita. We're not here to bully or shame you. We aren't like that here. We treat offenders with dignity and respect. Leave the rollers on the desktop. I'll replace them while a matron takes you to a bathroom."

A plump uniformed policewoman who might have been mistaken for a crossing guard at school if not for the gun strapped to her side escorted her down the hall to a foul-smelling closet-sized bathroom and locked her in. She sat on the toilet after urinating and wondered how long they would hold her. She had not been charged with a crime or even accused of one specifically. She wondered again about her Dad, whether they had him locked up in here somewhere.

The matron pounded on the cubicle door.

"Are you about finished in there?"

Then it was back to the room with the desk and two chairs. Detective Ramos had a file with her name on it visible on the desk. He motioned her to the chair across from him and said, "Are you any relation to Frank Vogel?"

"He's my Uncle."

"He was famous around here. From what I hear a trouble-maker, rabble rouser, and general pain in the ass."

Juanita shrugged and said, "Good for him.'"

"Fortunately for the state of Washington he is now locked up in the state penitentiary where he belongs. I don't want to see the same fate for you, Juanita. I don't want to see your young life ruined and misspent behind bars. That's why I want to help you. It's why I've brought you here to a West Seattle precinct instead of booking you downtown. They aren't as nice there as we are here."

"I still want to call Mr. McCabe."

"We've already done that for you, Juanita. He says you are on your own. He's not going to help you. Only I can do that."

Ramos unlocked the desk drawer and removed a large manila envelope. He placed a black and white photograph on the table between them where she could see it and said, "Do you recognize this, Juanita?"

She did. The photo was of her locket.

"It's inscribed to J. Vogel. That's you isn't it, Juanita? And I don't have to tell you where the locket was found, do I? I'm sorry, I really am. I want to help you, but you're going to have to face what you have done. Murder is not something you can walk away from free of charge. In return for your full cooperation however, we can offer you the lightest sentence possible under the circumstances. But we are going to want something from you in return."

He pushed the notebook paper and pen across the table and said, "We want you to write a statement stating that from the age fifteen, from the time you first arrived in McCabe's house, he has been molesting you."

THE LAW

WALTER MCCABE, AFTER HEARING FROM Kenny Williams how Juanita had been abducted by men with police badges, immediately called Jeremiah Wells from the phone in the downstairs parlor. He next telephoned Gus Gustafson. Furious, he found himself all but spitting his words accusatorily into the receiver.

"Is it within your normal course of business to abduct and terrify young children, Sheriff?"

"Whatever are you talking about, Mac?"

"You know damn well what I am talking about. I am referring to the girl staying in my house. Juanita Vogel. One of your officers picked her up on the way home from school."

"Mac, believe me, I wasn't aware of it."

"Well damn it, Gus, are you the Sheriff or not? Shouldn't you know what goes on in your own precinct?"

"If one of my officers has picked her up he's done so without my authorization, consent or knowledge."

"Sounds to me like you've lost control of your own police department, Gus."

"You let me worry about that."

"Fair enough Gus but I've already called Jeremiah Wells. You better worry about an illegal arrest and detainment suit if I don't have Juanita back within the next hour."

"I'll find out what's going on and get back to you right away, Mac. I promise."

McCabe hung up abruptly, poured a whisky and drank it while waiting by the telephone.

"I'm sorry this happened," he said to Kenny Williams. "You must have been very frightened."

They were both in the parlor with a view out the water-streaked windows. A hard rain ran down the glass surface in rivulets, giving the outdoors the wavering appearance of liquidity.

"I can't offer you what I'm drinking," said Jack, "but go to the kitchen and help yourself to anything you can find to eat or drink in the refrigerator."

Kenny Williams shook his head.

"No thanks," he said. "I'm not hungry."

He could hardly believe his ears. It was the first time the boy had ever refused an offer of food. In the past the Williams boy had even enthusiastically eaten Cora's burned mush. McCabe considered the boy's present dismissal to be commensurate with his fear.

McCabe, upon hearing back from the Sheriff, met with Jeremiah Wells at the West Seattle precinct where Juanita was being held. Sherriff Gustafson and Attorney Alan Parson were also there. Wells, well known in Seattle for twenty years of success litigating difficult and highly publicized criminal trials, demanded to see a warrant for Juanita. None existed. Juanita had been picked up and detained unlawfully.

Silver-haired and unselfconsciously handsome, Wells was a friend of the family. Though he and McCabe were the same age, Wells was in top physical condition. He had in the past been a crewman on the University of Washington rowing team and was known to presently haunt the tennis courts. McCabe trusted him implicitly. Parsons, a stocky man with the build of a wrestler, was mostly a business lawyer who in the past had successfully represented McCabe shipping interests.

Wells summarily dismissed the evidence of Juanita's locket as circumstantial and notified Sheriff Gustafson that unless Juanita was released immediately they would bring an unlawful internment suit against the Seattle Police Department and kidnapping charges against Detective Ramos, who had given the order to pick her up independently without a warrant. Juanita was subsequently released in Walter McCabe's custody but informed she remained a person of interest in a murder investigation and as such was forbidden to leave the state.

McCabe guided her out of the precinct to the Hudson and shook his head in disbelief to see a wet parking ticket placed under the windshield wiper. He tore it into several small pieces and let them float in a puddle and got behind the wheel. He looked over his shoulder before backing out of his parking place and drove home without incident in the pounding rain to Palentine Avenue where a drenched and soaked Kenny Williams stood dripping on the windblown porch. When Juanita got out of the car the Williams boy galloped down the steps to embrace her. Whether his face was wet from the rain or tears McCabe could not discern.

SUSPICION

RAMOS WAS ABOUT TO GET IN HIS CAR and leave when Sheriff Gustafson shouted in the wind for him to stay put. It was raining and both men wore wide brimmed hats and raincoats. The rain was cold and wet but failed to dampen the Sheriff's temper. Ramos, his back turned to him, stood at the partially open driver's side door of his unmarked police car.

"Turn around and look at me, Ramos. Don't turn your back. You had no authority to pick up that girl and I'm going to recommend disciplinary action."

Ramos, about to get in his car, complied, turning around to face him. His expression was contemptuous but otherwise absent of concern.

"The authority came from Bobby Stone. He ordered it."

Raindrops pattered on the brim of his hat.

"I am your commanding officer not Stone, Drake or anyone else. You're a pitiful excuse for a police officer, Ramos."

"I'm not a police officer. I'm an Investigative Detective and you interfered with an ongoing criminal investigation."

"Yes, an unauthorized investigation of an illegally unrepresented underage girl."

Ramos spat into a shallow puddle and leaned against his police car with a smug expression that made Gustafson's fists clench as he fought the urge to replace Ramos' disrespectful smirk with a bloody mouthful of broken teeth.

"You're an embarrassment to the King County Police Department and the city of Seattle, Ramos. I'm going to recommend the review board bust you back down to street patrol."

"Yeah," replied Ramos. "Like you can do that."

"I can and will," replied Gustafson.

But he knew he could not. Any official personnel action whether a demotion in rank or mere written reprimand was beyond his jurisdiction and had to go through the chain of command and be approved by the police commissioner.

"Stone will have any disciplinary report you submit rescinded. We almost had a morals charge on McCabe and you blew it so I suspect you're kind of on his shit list right now, Gustafson."

"That's *Sheriff* Gustafson to you. You can kiss your promotion goodbye Officer Ramos. I'm going to have you demoted."

"You can't do shit to me without their approval and you're not going to get it, *Sheriff*. Ramos almost spat the word Sheriff. "You know it as well as I do."

Ramos got in his car, slammed the driver's side door and drove off, splattering Gustafson's legs with dirty puddle water. Oblivious to the rain that ran down his face and the back of his neck in rivulets, Gustafson shook with rage. He felt his fists tighten as if he had Ramos' throat in his hands. He watched until Ramos' car could be seen no more, got in his car and drove to an anonymous waterfront dive.

He ordered a drink and it was cheap foul tasting stuff he slammed down quickly. He ordered two more. He remembered coming to this place only once before, early in his career, to arrest a wife-beating pickpocket and shortchange artist. There was no circulation and the room reeked of stale beer and cigarettes, cheap aftershave and urine. No one knew him here and that was the way he liked it. It was preferable to one of Stone's comfortable lounges where he could get free shots of Canadian Club or Seagram's. He was done with that. Their so called perks had ended up costing him his integrity, self-respect and at the rate things were going probably his marriage, career, pension and personal freedom.

Ramos was right. He had no power or independence as Sheriff. Stone and the rest of them on the *Waterfront Improvement Commission* were holding all the cards and he was one of the cards they played. They had merely complied with his wishes, his greed, his lust for money, status, and power. They'd probably done the same thing with Ramos, who didn't even know yet he was a patsy. That's how they operated. They didn't bring disgrace on a man; they let the man do it to himself. They merely identified and made available what a man coveted and then watched him bring down his own ruin.

He tossed some cash on the bar without counting it and walked out, swaying slightly when he met the windy street. He staggered to his car, slumped behind the wheel and watched beaded rivulets of rain run down the windshield and thought about resigning from the force. Maybe move out of state, draw on his pension, get a fishing boat and take tourists out deep sea fishing. But as long as he was of use to them Stone, Drake and the other members of the commission would never let him go. He turned the key in the ignition and pulled into traffic, home for Jen and the kids. If not for them, he would have eaten his gun long ago.

Rain cavalcaded down his windshield. He glanced repeatedly from the road to the speedometer. How many drinks had he consumed? He knew he shouldn't be driving in his condition. He'd disciplined cops under his command for exactly this type of offense, busted them down to making the rounds on foot in Niggertown.

Much of the tension in his shoulders and arms released when he drove into his own neighborhood. He rolled down the window and inhaled the bracing chill and dampness in the whoosh of air passing by the window. It was good to be home, but he didn't recognize the Buick parked in his driveway.

He parked adjacent to it and took the garage door entrance into the kitchen. Lucy ran to him, her long blonde hair twisted into two cute little braids that looked like rabbit ears. She was carrying her stuffed kangaroo, Kiki, which she referred to as her lovey and which was always with her. She was gently chewing on one of its ears. She wrapped her little arms around both of his legs without dropping her precious Kiki and buried her face in his knees. He lifted her and gave her a kiss. She giggled and he returned her to Jen.

Jen wore a pair of pedal pusher pants and an old sweatshirt with an apron around her slim waist and still looked sexier and prettier than the women working Stone's best cathouses, which he regretted ever having been so foolish to have in the past frequented. He took her in his arms and hugged her. Stone came into the kitchen and interrupted.

"We need to talk".

Where the fuck did he come from?

Stone had a lighted cigar going but the smoke might have been coming off Stone himself because it was clear he was fuming with anger. He was close to biting the cigar in two.

"Now?"

"Yes, now. Downstairs, your office."

They descended the stairs to his office. Stone slammed the door and grabbed him by the collar and pushed him against a wall.

"Goddamn you," Stone hissed. Spittle flew from his mouth. Gustafson felt its spray on his face. "We had McCabe and you lost him. We were on the verge of getting the Vogel girl to sign a statement he had molested her. Then you showed up and ruined it."

"I had nothing to do with any of it. You and Ramos were acting on your own without my knowledge. Ramos picked the girl up illegally and he even screwed that up by doing it in front of a witness, that Williams kid. Now take your fucking dirty hands off me, Bobby. I swear to God you put your hands on me again I will personally give you a beating you will never forget."

Stone released and straightened the collar he had clutched and rubbed it with his palm as if ironing the wrinkles out and said, "I was out of line there, Gus. I shouldn't have handled you like that and for that I apologize. But I'm still pissed at you. We used to be friends. I don't know if I can trust you anymore."

"I don't intend to help you railroad McCabe with a phony molestation charge if that's what you're asking."

"Well, that seems to me a change of loyalty. You always went along with us before. What the fuck's happened to you, Gus? You don't socialize anymore. You don't come out to the club."

"I've told you before, I prefer it at home."

"Well then what more can I do for you? Do you want more money?"

"You can stay out of my way and let me run the investigation. I'm taking Arthur Ramos off the case and busting him down to patrolman."

"No. You are not. He's remaining as Chief Detective on the McCabe case."

"He's looking at a suspension right now."

"I'd think twice, Sheriff. There's an election coming up. The day might come when you're not Sheriff any longer and find yourself working under a Ramos command."

"Well in the meantime you have to deal with the present Sheriff. And don't forget, the voters elect and decide, not you."

" Gus, we can get you replaced easily. Maybe the *Seattle Times* would like to see some interesting photographs of their upstanding sheriff taken at illegal card games, taking bribes from known gangsters and in bed with whores."

"You can't incriminate me without incriminating yourself."

"You surprise me, Gus. You still have no accurate grasp of what we can and cannot do."

Stone removed the cigar from his mouth and looked at it. The end was wet with his spittle and coming unraveled. He spat a small spec of tobacco from the tip of his tongue and said, "You will work for us and follow our orders as long as we want under whatever circumstances we choose. Otherwise we'll reserve a nice retirement spot for you with Frank Vogel in the State Penitentiary in Walla Walla."

Stone returned upstairs without giving notice. The downstairs bathroom door opened in the hallway and Gussy Junior stepped out, zipping his fly. Mike Drake was with him.

"What the *hell?*" said Gustafson. "Gussy go upstairs. Right now. Not you, Mike. You stay."

"What's up," asked Drake.

"What were you doing in there with my son, Mike?"

"Helping him pee. He said he had to go."

"So what's that got to do with you? Jen could help him with that."

"Jen was busy. She's the one who asked me to help."

"Jen doesn't know about your priors, Mike."

"Is that what you think of me, Gus? That I would molest a little three year old boy?"

"Probably not Mike, but in the future I don't want you and Gussy alone together in a bathroom, understood?"

"Whatever you say, Gus, though I'm a little hurt. Gussy is like a godson to me."

Drake could charm a rattlesnake. He was a man who took pride in his ability to deceive, who had in the past demonstrated and boasted of his ability to beat a lie detector. But three year old Gussy? He didn't think so. Not even Drake would stoop that low. Later that night, unable to sleep, he figured he probably owed Drake an apology.

WALLINGFORD

JACK BECAME A BEWILDERED PARTNER in a marital dance in which he had forgotten the steps. He had been a bachelor far too long with only Juanita and Elvira for female company. Recently he had lived a solitary life in Hooverville. Now he had to learn how to live with a woman again. He was awkward and shy. He made it a habit to rise from bed in the morning before first light to dress behind the closed bathroom door out of her sight. She insisted he sleep naked and kiss her first thing in the morning. He worried his breath was bad because of his neglected teeth. He was private about his bodily functions in a way she wasn't. He found himself going into the bathroom to fart, closing the door and running water in the sink so she wouldn't hear. Sometimes when he was on the toilet she just came barging into the bathroom as if a party were going on in there to which she had been invited. When he asked her to please respect his privacy she just scoffed.

But late at night, in bed after making love, they became whispering confidents sharing the stories of their lives. Jack began to open up to her, disclosing the facts of how he came to love Alma and how she had died from alcoholism and related complications of pneumonia. They discussed his brother Frank with praise and regret. Jack told Mary how as a young man he had once admired his older brother to the degree of hero-worship and had wanted to be like him, but how his brother had come back changed after the war.

Mary said his brother was a flawed hero, both as a soldier in the war and to the working class to whom he had given his life in the fight for worker's rights. She told of her father, a railroad brakeman killed on the job and of her mother's second husband, who had owned the Wallingford house until both her stepfather and mother were killed in a drowning accident. She and Jimmy had inherited the house, which they had always intended to hold on to despite the difficulty of rising tax rates.

Jack told Mary about his lumberjack father, a man who smelled of pine pitch, pipe tobacco and beer, how he just disappeared one day and no one ever knew what happened to him. He related how his mother killed herself six months later, how he and his brothers and sisters were sent to foster homes and orphanages. His sister Hannah was killed in a motorcycle accident. She always was a wild one, said Jack. The rest of his siblings had scattered. His own kids were long gone, where he couldn't even guess. Other than Frank and Elvira, Juanita was the only family he had left. Elvira was alive and well back home in Cat Creek. She had been his best friend and was like a sister to him.

They took quiet midday lunches in the back yard on a folding table set with a white linen tablecloth and embroidered cloth napkins. They swam in Green Lake, tossed breadcrumbs to the ducks, rented canoes and watched lazy fish and slumbering turtles.

They drove to Deception Pass and sat high at the edge of the cliffside facing the sea. The taste of salt lingered on their tongues; their faces were wet with spray. They stared out far to sea beyond the whitecaps where the seawater turned a darker shade of blue. They watched passing ships while imagining their possible destinations, Mary naming exotic locations he could not pronounce and had never heard of.

They loved to dance in candlelight to music on the radio. They danced so late into the night they all but had to hold each other up and said it was like sleepwalking and named it sleep dancing.

They took ferry crossings to the San Juan Islands, picnicked in the Olympic Rain Forest, fished for trout in Green River and foraged for mushrooms on Mt. Rainier. Mary made wine and taught Jack, a teetotaler, how to drink it.

Lea Macquarrie

His dreams became less troublesome, diminishing both in frequency and vividness. McLane's ghost still sometimes unexpectedly appeared, but as a vague insubstantial shadow cast from a far distant place. He rarely thought about the murder on the train anymore and eventually accepted his past was past. The challenge now was to accept that he was free of it.

He worked on the Ford and Harley Davidson in the garage, organized tools in the shed and reinforced the chicken coop. He repaired or replaced rotten window frames and re-shingled the roof. He thought back on his life in Hooverville and pondered the future of Jesse the Mayor, the Postmaster, Top Hat, Long Underwear and other men he had known there. The time would hopefully soon come, as it had come for him, when they would not need Hooverville any longer and move to a new chapter in their lives. Better times were coming. President Roosevelt was going to change America.

He thought often about Juanita, how pretty and happy she had appeared when he had briefly seen her coming home from school to the Palentine Avenue house. He took assurance in this memory of her. He had made the right decision in taking her to the McCabe's. Someday he would knock on their door and politely introduce himself. He would thank them, but he would not take her from them.

There were nights when he looked into the stars and wondered if Jimmy Wilson's spirit was out there, looking down on them. He believed Jimmy Wilson would understand and bless their marriage. He sometimes tried to talk to Alma but she didn't seem to be listening and had presumably moved on.

Mary sometimes read to him at night. His favorites were Jack London, Frank Norris and Sinclair Lewis. When she sometimes read Marx, he fell asleep. Sometimes Mary hit him on the head with Freud and told him to wake up.

Spring rains pattered around them as they worked in the garden. She found a rotten tomato and tossed it at his head but he felt it coming and ducked. It splattered against the side of the garage, reminding him of what had been done to a man's face with a crowbar. He pushed the thought away easily. Such images were brief and rare now.

They washed their hands with water from the garden hose and carried the vegetables in a wicker basket to the mudroom. Mary turned on the water at the sink and began cleaning lettuce, carrots, tomatoes, and peppers to pack in wooden crates. The radio played *April in Paris*.

"My brother was there," said Jack.

"Where?"

"In Paris, after the war."

"The war to end all wars," said Mary. "Why we got involved I'll never know. We have battles to fight right here at home. Your brother always did say we were fighting the wrong war."

"I wish Frank was free to see what President Roosevelt is doing. This New Deal is going to save America, Mary. The Conservation Corps he's begun has already gotten thousands of young men off the streets into productive jobs and it's only just begun."

"We'll see."

The radio played the Lucky Strike Orchestra version of *Singing in the Rain*.

"That's a song about Seattle," said Jack.

"Not today it isn't. The weather has turned lovely today."

And so it was. Shafts of sunlight were breaking through the clearing clouds. Watched by an assembly of birds, Jack and Mary finished loading the Ford. The day warmed to the degree they were both perspiring lightly. Jack hosed off in the yard but Mary went in the house to change into jeans and a man's white shirt with the sleeves partly rolled up and a red bandana tied around her head. The red bandana emphasized her pale green eyes and auburn hair. She smiled, tossed him a clean shirt and got behind the driver's seat. The rumble seat was loaded with carrots, cucumbers, tomatoes and greens. The back seat was loaded with apples, cherries, and pears.

She backed out of the driveway and headed the loaded Ford toward downtown. There was a view to the triangular rooftop of Seattle's tallest building, the thirty-eight story Smith Tower. Mt. Rainier was enshrouded with mist, but its snowcapped peak became visible as they drove. Mary turned the radio up loud and rolled down her window.

"You ever been up there," asked Jack?

"Mount Rainier? Of course. And so have you. We were there together, don't you remember?"

"No, I mean the tall building you call the Smith Tower."

"Oh. Yes, Jack, once. With Jimmy. It was a long time ago, before he moved down to Hooverville. He had some kind of veteran's business there. Afterwards we took the elevator up to the rooftop where they had an observation deck. It was windy as heck up there, but it was a clear day and you could see all out across the sound to Mt. Baker. The entire city skyline was below. It was strange to be so high, looking down on the city as if with the perspective of a seagull. I got kind of woozy looking down. I'm probably a little afraid of heights. Are you?"

"I've never been above the second floor of a house. There were a couple of shacks in Hooverville that had second stories but there were no windows and they weren't all that high. I've never been in a building like the Smith Tower, never been in an elevator or anything. I've been in the mountains though, so I know what it feels like to be on top on the world with a view to all that's below."

"We'll have to get you up there, Jack. Get you your first elevator ride."

Top Hat greeted them at the Hooverville steps. Skinny as a pencil, he wore coveralls with no undershirt and smelled of hard labor and a poor diet. Jack thought he didn't look so good but then when had he? It was difficult to discern whether the men who arrived to unload the fruit and vegetables had always looked this unhealthy, or if his own improved circumstances had altered his perspective.

Hat picked a carrot from a crate and said, "Well, they are gonna love these fresh crispy carrots. I would too if I had the teeth to eat them." He smiled, his missing teeth evident, and spoke with a slight whistle between his missing teeth.

Men from below were already descending the stairs with the produce. Jack didn't know most of them but knew well from past experience how the men of Hooverville, limited mostly to eating out of cans, had an appreciation of fresh fruit and vegetables.

They drove from there to the Smith Tower where he experienced his first elevator ride. The view was all Mary promised it to be despite the initial vertigo when standing at the edge of the observation platform. Diamonds of dancing sunlight sparked on the sound. He loved it here in Seattle now, loved it as much as his beautiful home state of Montana. He loved looking out across Puget Sound to Mt. Baker and the San Juan Islands and the sight of Mount Rainer behind the city skyline. Sometimes he saw an Orca whale surface. It was a spectacular sight beyond his imagination. He didn't miss Montana at all anymore. Seattle was his home now, where he wanted to be.

They drove to the Pike Place Market and ate Chinese Food, which Mary said she liked because it was the only food she couldn't make at home. He remembered Juanita's fondness for it when they had been in the Hotel Lee.

They danced to the radio in their kitchen while making dinner and later by the window in the spacious living room where they drank Mary's wine and humorously agreed they had the best nightclub and dance floor in Seattle.

In the bedroom upstairs they lay side by side, Mary with a library copy of *Lost Horizons*, which she had almost finished and said was frivolous but entertaining. To save on electricity, the only lighting was from a kerosene lamp on the nightstand by Mary's side of the bed.

"Juanita wanted to read more than anything she could name. I wonder if she knows how by now. I mean, she's in school, right? I'll bet she can read."

Mary set the book down on the nightstand, turned to him with a serious expression and said, "I've been thinking about that, Jack."

"About what, exactly?"

"Well, since we're both settled and happy now, why don't we have Juanita over here? In fact, why don't we have her move in with us? We have plenty of room."

"I might like that, Mary. Don't think I haven't thought about it. I always did plan to bring her home to me once I had steady work and could make a life for her, but she has a life of her own now."

"You aren't likely to get any steady work and don't need it, Jack. All the new jobs are going to young people in Roosevelt's Conservation Core. We're fine here the way things are and Juanita is old enough to decide for herself."

"Well, I suppose there would be no harm in having her over for supper one night. You're right it's probably about time we saw each other again."

"Of course it is, Jack. No matter what kind of life the McCabe's have to offer, you're still her father. I want to see you two together one way or another. We could have her over this weekend."

"Is that what you want?"

"What do you want, Jack?"

"If you are willing to have her with us and that's something she wants, I'd be happy for it."

Headlights arched through the bedroom windows and slanted across the bedroom walls. He heard the tires of what sounded like numerous automobiles on the gravel in front of their house.

Mary said, "Somebody's here."

Beams of light played across the walls and ceiling. Dressed in his pajamas, he went slowly down the stairs in his slippers while Mary followed a few cautious steps behind. When he opened the door he was blinded by the flashing lights of a half dozen police cars.

PALENTINE AVENUE

JUANITA MISTAKENLY THOUGHT THE WOMAN pounding the front door so early in the morning might have been a hobo looking for work in return for a meal. At first glance the woman resembled one, wearing a man's white shirt with the sleeves rolled up, overalls and heavy laced work boots, but she was too clean to be a tramp. Her eyes were warm but she looked frightened. Some of the woman's braids had come undone, which somehow only seemed to make her even prettier. She wore silver earrings and a ring on her wedding finger but was otherwise plain with no lipstick, jewelry or other adornments. Her eyes were sometimes green and sometimes hazel depending on the lighting on the porch. She spoke in a pleasant, friendly tone as if they were acquainted.

"You don't know me," she began. "My name is Mary Wilson. Or was until three months ago. It's Mary Vogel now."

"Vogel? I don't understand. That's my name. Are we related?"

"Your father is my husband, Juanita."

Cora hesitated at the top of the staircase, her liver spotted hands alternating between clutching her cane and closing the unclasped chenille robe long overdue for the good will bin. She grasped the staircase railing during her cautiously slow descent. Pale and thin, she had lately not been well. At the bottom of the stairwell, she called for her husband. McCabe, in his blue silk pajamas, appeared from the hallway off the kitchen, the little remaining hair he had left on his head standing straight up as if by electrocution. He had lost weight over the months and looked diminished in the ridiculous overly large pajamas decorated with cigar-smoking poker-playing hunting dogs.

He cleared his throat and said, "What's going on here?" His whiskey voice contained a morning croak. He coughed into his fist, cleared his throat, and said. "Who's here? Who is this?"

"I'm Mary Vogel," the woman replied.

"Vogel?"

McCabe looked to Juanita as if for explanation and said, "Is she family?"

They gathered in the parlor facing the bay window as Mary Wilson related how she had met Jack through her brother Jimmy, who had been in the hospital with Jack. Jack, she explained, had spent well over a year in Hooverville when he had first come to her house to visit her sick brother.

"I looked for Jack Vogel in Hooverville," said McCabe. "I was there two or three times but no one there would give me any information."

"That's how they are down there," said Mary. "They're protective of one another and suspicious of outsiders."

"Did you live there too?"

"No, but my brother Jimmy did. He actually liked it down there, don't ask me why. Later he got sick and had to come home. Jack took up residence in his shack."

She described how the police had come in the night, charged Jack with murder and taken him away.

"It all happened so fast. Jack didn't protest, didn't ask a single question. He just extended both arms for handcuffs as if he had been expecting it. He left me with no parting words, not even a glance back. I'm told that he has confessed to killing a man. I don't know more than that," she said, her voice breaking. She blinked away a tear and added, "I didn't even know he was in trouble."

"He confessed to protect me," said Juanita. "A hobo on the train tried to rape me. I hit him with a crowbar but I didn't mean to kill him. Just to stop him. But the man died. We threw him off the train and never told anyone of it."

"I don't believe you", interjected McCabe. "You're obviously protecting your father. You're smart and I'm sure you know the law will go light on a juvenile. Where is Jack now Mrs. Vogel? Do you know where they took him?"

"King County jail. I spent most of the night there hoping they'd let me see him."

McCabe rose from his armchair and said, "Cora my dear, would you please thoroughly extinguish two or three of those cigarettes you have smoldering? This woman is not shedding tears so much as her eyes are watering from the excess of smoke."

He called Jeremiah Wells from the hallway phone. The news was not good. Jack had confessed and signed a court transcript witnessed by a police official, clerk and an assistant state prosecutor.

"So what do we do now," asked McCabe of Wells.

"We get the charges dropped at the preliminary hearing for lack of evidence. If the preliminary hearing rules for a trial our first motion will be for a change of venue from Idaho to Washington State."

"What's Idaho's business with it?"

"The victim's body was found in Washington State but the time of death puts him in Eastern Idaho, which has jurisdiction. We'll plead not guilty and cite the evidence as circumstantial and inconclusive, which it in fact it is. A self-defense plea would be difficult to substantiate. The other recourse would be to plead no contest and cite extenuating circumstances. Submit a motion to get the charges dropped to third degree involuntary manslaughter. He'd end up going to prison, but not for murder. Sentencing could be negotiated to five years with parole eligibility in three but based on what we know so far I'm in favor of a not guilty plea. There are no witnesses to testify to having seen the crime other than Juanita, and as his daughter and a juvenile she cannot be called to testify against him against her will."

"I know you will do your best by him," said McCabe into the telephone, "but I want you to know this is important to me. I couldn't stand to see the young girl's heart broken again. Bad enough losing a father once, but twice…."

RAMOS AT HOME

DRIVING HOME FROM THE PRECINCT, Ramos wiped tears of happiness from his eyes. He was going to be an honest, principled man again. He was going to be the exemplary man he was meant to be, the superior man he knew he could be. Love was always the right decision, no matter how difficult.

He slowed the Nash when turning onto his street, shutting off the headlights and parking. The neighborhood was ugly and low class, its streets littered with broken bottles, beat-up malfunctioning cars not worth stealing, dog shit, tricycles, filthy broken dolls, dog bones, broken bottles and other trash. It was low rent, largely populated with divorcees with noisy unsupervised children and dirty-faced toddlers with shitty diapers. Dogs barked day and night and everyone who lived here seemed to have a loud radio turned up as high as it could go. The police were called in once a week at the least, usually for domestic violence. He himself had once been dispatched to a dispute just three doors down.

Their shitty apartment had a cramped galley kitchen and there was barely enough room inside for a dinner table. He'd only rented it because it was immediately available, furnished and all he could afford at the time. He'd remained here after his promotion because it was cheap and he had other uses for his money. Annie didn't complain but he knew she hated it. She had not wanted to leave San Pedro. She came because of him. Because she loved him and was loyal to him. She had said what mattered most was they were together and free to make their own lives.

She had sat beside him in the cramped front seat of the Nash, her swollen pregnant belly straining against the dashboard as he drove Highway 101 from San Pedro to Seattle, her having to stop to pee every ten miles. You had to give her credit, she didn't complain during the drive or about their new life in Seattle. Her parents, who had never liked him and who wept when he took her away, had since moved to Tucson, Arizona. She had made few friends since moving here from San Pedro, and those she had were not close, mostly just housing complex acquaintances she barely knew. He was basically her only friend up here.

He shut off the motor and sat in the car without getting out. The night was crisp and beautiful with scattered stars. He opened the car door and stepped outside and stood looking up at the moon. He lighted a cigarette and smoked it down to the nub, procrastinating. He finished the cigarette and ground it out with the heel of his shoe and walked across the dying lawn to the front door and unlocked it with his key.

Annie was so happy to see him come in the door she clapped her hands in a display of joy that embarrassed him.

"Artie," she said, rushing to him, "You're home early."

She clung to him, holding him longer than he wanted.

"I'm so glad you're home," she said. "You've looked so tired and troubled lately I've felt sorry for you. You work too many hours, Artie. You can't keep it up indefinitely. You're going to make yourself sick."

"I haven't been working nights, Annie."

"What? What do you mean? Of course you have."

She was wearing one of several frumpy secondhand housedresses he had seen far too often since putting on weight during the pregnancy. She deserved better, but he had not given her spending money except for groceries and basic needs. She was pretty, but not like Jean. Not sexy. She seemed to always be wearing an apron, and her hair needed a cut and color and styling. She was a young woman and he was already seeing traces of gray. She always looked tired and sleep deprived. Artie Junior fussy with the colic, waking all hours of the night, it showed. The dark circles under her eyes were not there before they were married, when he had been dating her. She had great tits, small but perky, but he hadn't tasted them since she had started nursing. Otherwise, if she lost fifteen to twenty pounds, her body would rival Jean's. But Jean knew how to use her body for pleasure, both her own and his, and was always available and open to his sexual needs while Annie often said she was too tired and when she did make love didn't exhibit her pleasure or talk dirty to him the way Jean did.

"I'm sorry, but I've been lying to you about working nights. I met someone, Annie. "

"Artie, I don't understand."

"Yes, you do. I just told you."

"Artie, please. You're scaring me."

He saw the worry distort her face and discerned for the first time in his memory traces of frown lines on her mouth. She wrung her small, delicate hands. Her fingernails were painted but chipped. They'd been that way as long as he could remember.

"I'm sorry, Annie. I'm as surprised by this as you. I don't know how it happened, just that it did. I've been seeing her every night when I told you I was working."

She was crying, but softly and it seemed to him without anger.

"Are you in love with her?"

"Yes. Her name is Jean. I'm sorry but I've just come home to pack and then I'm leaving."

"But why, Artie? Why? What did I do wrong?"

"Nothing but I can't keep living a lie. I don't love you anymore. I love Jean."

She was sobbing now, wringing her hands and backing away from him. He moved to console her but she pushed him away and said, "Don't you dare touch me."

He turned and went to the bedroom closet for his suitcase, put it on the bed and began packing. He could hear her anguished cries in the next room. He packed his suits, white shirts, shoes, socks and underwear and toiletries. Annie came into the bedroom while he was packing, her eyes red from crying.

"What about Artie Junior?"

"I haven't figured that out yet. I'm moving to San Diego and maybe when I'm settled and he's older he can come down for a visit."

"Fuck that," she said. "Fuck you too, Artie."

He had never heard her utter profanity before. It was a side of her she had kept hidden from him. He rather liked it.

"You will never see Artie again. I'll make sure of it. I'll tell him you're dead and you were a disgrace. I'll sue for as much alimony as the law allows. That and child support and anything of value you own and if you don't pay it no matter what the reason you will go to jail."

"Fair enough," he replied. "I expected that. Someday you will understand, Annie."

He closed the suitcase and snapped the locks, zipped up his clothes carrier containing his suits and strode for the door. She followed him onto the front parking area.

"We don't have to do this, Artie. Tell me what she was giving you I didn't. I'll make it up to you. Tell me, what did she do to make you love her this much?"

"You really don't want to hear it, Annie."

He locked his suitcase and clothes carrier in the trunk of the Nash and got in behind the wheel. Driving away, he fought back tears again because he had hurt Annie, a good woman who didn't deserve it, but she would get over it in time. She'd probably get married again and he hoped she would, that she might find the happiness in love he had found with Jean. Maybe then she would understand. It hurt him to think Artie Junior might grow to maturity calling another man father but that was the way life played out sometimes.

FREEMONT POOL HALL

WHEN BOBBY STONE AND MIKE DRAKE entered Big Lou's *Freemont Pool Parlor* wearing polished black dress shoes and tailored black suits with clean white shirts and neckties, most of the regulars took one look at them, figured they were the law, laid down their pool sticks and left. Stone, who had arranged the meeting, brought Drake along for backup, cautioning Drake to keep his revolver at the ready and his mouth shut.

"Don't say any stupid shit that's going to embarrass me, Mike."

Five pool tables occupied a dark cavernous section toward a divided rear section of the large front room that faced the street. You needed to know someone to be admitted to the private area upstairs. Lou's was a legitimate pool hall but also a haven for illegal gambling, numbers running, and a meeting place for smalltime dealers in sales of heroin and marijuana. The pool hall windows faced the street in front but had not been cleaned in so long the view was distorted. Inside it was kept purposefully dark but for the hanging lamps over the pool tables. The stench of nicotine failed to altogether mask the odor of stale beer. What sounded like burlesque music for strippers with a hard backbeat and prominent raunchy saxophone blared from a juke box.

They had come specifically to meet Willie the Fixer and had to go through Big Lou to do it. They found Lou at his usual place behind the front counter, ostensibly in charge of renting racks and sticks. Lou ran the downstairs and communicated with the upstairs by written message delivered by his limping longtime assistant and former cellmate who destroyed them afterward. Lou wasn't exactly a deal maker himself, but had far ranging contacts. In return for a commission he put people together with mutual interests and needs. Stone had used Lou's services before, back when he contracted to have Frank Vogel beaten by thugs.

"Thanks for running off my customers," said a deadpan Lou. "Come in here wearing suits looking like the law. What were you thinking?"

Lou was a veteran and ex con who had once played football for the Washington Huskies before flunking out. He wore his dark hair combed straight back and maintained a bushy western moustache. He wore loose cotton dress pants with a white short sleeved shirt unbuttoned almost to the naval. Tattoos of naked women were exhibited on his chest and there were tattoos up and down his arms. Because of his warm brown eyes and youthful coffee and cream complexion, he appeared to Drake less tough than his reputation suggested, more like an actor playing the part of a gangster than the real deal.

In this he was wrong.

Lou nodded toward Drake and said, "Who is this?"

"Friend of mine," said Stone.   .

"My name is Mike," said Drake. "Mike Drake."

He extended his hand, which Big Lou took. Drake was surprised the man's grip was soft. The man's fingers briefly tickled his inner palm and Drake recognized the look of mildly interested appraisal in the man's eyes. Drake knew well the handshake and the look he was getting. The guy knew him for a Queer and didn't mind.

In fact, he was interested.

Stone said, "Is my contact here?"

"Yeah. Upstairs. I'll let him know you're here. He has some peculiar ways. He may take one look at you from the stairwell and decide he doesn't want anything to do with you. I collect my introduction fee either way. Make it look real. Rent some balls, rack them up on the back table and shoot some pool."

To Drake he said, "You a player?"

It took Drake a moment to be certain of his meaning.

Lea Macquarrie

"I played some pool in college if that's what you mean. I was pretty good but it's been awhile."

"Stone here," said Lou, "don't play for shit. The pussy can't even break the balls."

"You're breaking mine now," Stone replied.

Drake recognized the banter as friendly.

"Stone and I go back a long way," said Big Lou to Drake. "You on the other hand I don't know."

"He's okay," said Stone. "You don't have to worry."

"I'm not worried. You are the ones who should worry. This guy you are about to meet? He's a professional and it works both for and against you. Something goes wrong, he fucks up in his work and gets pinched, he won't even know you. Your name will never come up. And that's how it should be. On the other hand, if you fuck up make problems for him, you and your families will wish you never were born. Especially if you sing to the cops."

"Hey," said Stone. "No need. You know I'm solid."

"I'm just saying. No offense."

He pushed the rack forward and said, "You men going to shoot some pool or not?"

They wandered off, carrying the rack to the back table.

"I hate that guy," whispered Stone. "Hate to do business with him."

"I thought he was okay," replied Drake.

"Yeah, I noticed."

"What's that supposed to mean?"

"You really want me to explain?"

Drake set up the balls, and Stone broke, but only a few of the balls loosened from within their triangular shape.

Drake summarily ran the table.

"Jesus," said Stone. "You can really play."

"I worked my way through college playing pool," said Drake. "The trick is in setting up your shots. It's all about ball control."

The man who appeared at the top of the stairs probably weighed 300 pounds easily, maybe more. He wore pleated blue trousers held by suspenders and a white shirt come partly un-tucked. He stood on the top step, staring down at them. He was so bloated and rotund it seemed unlikely he would be able to navigate the narrow stairway. Each step creaked as he descended, his enormous belly undulating independently of the rest of his body. When he reached the end of the stairs and was free of the confining staircase however, the effortless gracefulness of his stride surprised them.

The man didn't speak to them. He looked them over silently for a length of time that made Drake uncomfortable. Drake was about to introduce himself when the man said, "You guys up for a game of pool? Dollar a game?"

"My partner here will play you," said Stone, racking the balls. "I doubt if I'd be much of a match."

Drake broke and began picking his shots. He ran half the table before missing a shot. Then it was the Fixer's turn. He ran the rest of the table but missed the 8-ball shot. Drake was left uncertain how to handle it. The 8 ball was a shot he could make and win the game, but should he? They hadn't come to play pool but to do business, and it was important not to offend the man who was their real purpose in coming here. In the end he decided to sink the 8 ball, which he did, in the corner pocket.

"You just passed," said The Fixer. "If you had missed, I'd have known it was on purpose and I would have taken it as an insult and you as fools who think you are smart when you are not. Let's rack up and talk business."

Stone did the talking, while Mike and the Fixer shot pool.

"Do you know who Walter McCabe is?"

"Never heard of him."

"Well, he's the guy we need your help with."

"Understand something. I personally don't do the kind of work you are contracting me for. I subcontract it out. The people I get to do the work won't know who you are or that you have any involvement. It's safer that way for both of us."

"Understood," said Stone. "That's not a problem at all."

"Hey, I know it's not a problem. I'm not asking permission here. I'm explaining how it works."

"Whatever you say."

"So tell me about this guy McCabe. Is he tough? Does he carry?"

"He carries a briefcase sometimes," said Drake. "Sometimes a lunchbox."

Stone grimaced and said, "Shut up, Mike. That's not what he means at all."

Stone apologized and said, "Mike here has a habit of saying stupid shit at the wrong time, but he's okay."

"It's all right," said the Fixer. "I understand you're not acquainted with the terminology, Mister Drake. I don't want you pretending you're something you're not. If you're honest about what you don't know it helps eliminate mistakes."

"I don't know if McCabe carries or not," said Stone. "I'd be surprised if he did though. Here's what I do know. He has an office on Pier 91. He's the worst fucking driver in Seattle and everyone who knows him knows it. It would surprise to no one to find him in a fatal accident."

"Big Lou told you how it works, right? Regarding my fee? When you pay Lou for the pool table rentals you will also pay a deposit for my referral and an advance on the contract. You pay the full amount when the contract has been fulfilled and it won't be cheap. Lou will write down the amount, show it to you and then destroy the paper it's written on. After you pay the deposit you wait patiently for results. These things sometimes take planning and time to carry out."

"Any idea how long that might be?"

"Is there a hurry? Because this is something that needs to be done right. Sometimes the men contracted for the job want to do prior research. It could go down in a few days or weeks from now. I'll request they prioritize the contract but that is not up to me. They will act when the time is right. Now, if that's not all right with you, if it's imperative it's done quickly, then you go to someone else."

"No, no problem so long as it's done."

"I guarantee it will be done and done correctly at the right time in the right way by the right people. That's why people who are smart come to me instead of some flunkey who doesn't know what he's doing. But understand this. Once I have paid the men who will perform the contract, all communication with them is suspended until the contract is carried out. I might not even be able to contact them until it's done, and then they will contact me. Main thing for you to understand is once this ball gets rolling there is no stopping it. There's no coming back from this decision. When it's over they contact me for final payment."

"We definitely want this done. We should have come to you a long time ago."

"Then you can consider this guy McCabe already dead. He just doesn't know it yet. From here on, you don't talk to me. I don't know you. You want to message me, you go to Lou. Fuck," said the Fixer to Drake, who just ran the table. "You're kicking my ass here."

"Sorry, sir. I'm just having a lucky day."

"Hey, no problem at all. You ever want to play pro, I'll stake you."

Later, walking out of the Freemont pool hall to their car, Drake was surprised when Stone stopped midstride to wrap his arms around him and briefly kiss him on the lips. Stone had never done this before and he was astonished to experience it now. Stone hugged him like a long lost brother, then held him by the shoulders with both hands, looked deeply into his eyes and said, "I'm proud of you, Mike. Proud of what you did in there. How you handled yourself. I had no idea you could play pool like that. I don't think the Fixer even liked me. It was you who won him over. I saw it happen. I didn't expect it. So now thanks to you we don't need to dig for dirt on McCabe anymore. That's over. Now we just wait. McCabe is finished and I'll finally be able to give that asshole Ramos back to Gustafson to fire or bust down to patrol cop or whatever he wants. We don't need him anymore and he turned out to be a wasted investment of time and money. Not only money out of the commission treasury, but money I lost personally during his time spent freeloading with Jean."

Drake understood. Jean was one of Stone's top earners and it was reasonable he would want to take her off the Ramos account and put her back to work soliciting wealthier clients.

Lea Macquarrie

DOWNTOWN SEATTLE

RAMOS, WHO FOR TWO WEEKS NOW had been staying in a cheap North Seattle motel, strode across the Olympic Hotel's polished granite and marble lobby floor, trying not to look impressed by the gilt framed vaulted ceiling and Renaissance style elliptical staircase, oak paneled telegraph rooms and phone booths and exclusive storefronts displaying expensive merchandise for sale. The Olympia Hotel had a nationwide reputation for opulence, exclusiveness and excess with expenses to match. Movie stars, politicians and celebrities stayed here, even Herbert Hoover once. He had a reservation for the night, both for dinner in the hotel restaurant and for a room on the 12th floor featuring a spectacular view of the Seattle skyline. He confirmed his room reservation at the check in desk and asked for the restaurant location and made arrangements to have a bucket of Champagne on ice delivered to the room at 9 o'clock.

There were three restaurants in the hotel, and he didn't know which had his reservation. The desk clerk checked while he waited. Finally he was directed down a long marble hallway to its location. Arriving, he slipped a twenty to the restaurant maitre'd and said, "The actress Jean Harlow will be my dinner companion this evening. I want a table with a view."

"Certainly, Mr. Ramos. Jean Harlow, my goodness. What an honor."

"We don't want to be disturbed by intrusive photographers. No photographs and no autograph seekers, please."

"Of course, sir."

He poured vodka from his flask into the empty glass at his table. Through Jean, he had developed a taste for it and drank it almost nightly. He'd taken up smoking at well, much to Annie's disfavor. He'd told her he'd picked up the habit at the precinct, where everybody smoked.

It was such a relief he didn't have to lie anymore. Annie knew everything now; there was no need to hide or sneak around. He was ready to bring his love affair with Jean out into the open and he believed Jean was too. No more confining their love affair to the hideaway blue room in Stone's nightclub. No more hiding and no more lying. He wanted everyone to know. He was proud of them.

He heard murmurs of surprised recognition from diners in the mezzanine and knew Jean had arrived. He thought she looked even better than Jean Harlow. She wore white gloves and a white off the shoulder cocktail dress showing just a tasteful tease of cleavage. She carried a clutch purse with sequins and wore a gold necklace set with numerous small glistening diamonds complimenting her long graceful neck. She was more Jean Harlow than Jean Harlow.

But en route to his table, amid the whispers of spellbound voyeuristic diners, she stopped and made an unnecessary announcement he regretted.

"Sorry to disappoint you, but I am not Jean Harlow, though I have on occasion worked as her understudy."

She glided to his table and he rose and pulled out her chair, he hoped with the gentlemanly chivalry befitting a woman of her status but also to show himself off as her escort. Men stared openly, he thought enviously, and it made him proud. She sat and removed her gloves and he poured vodka from his flash into their water glasses and they clinked glasses.

"To our being together in public for the first time," he said. "The first of many, I hope. I have a room for us on the 12th floor. You look splendid, by the way. Jean Harlow would be envious."

"Silly boy," she replied. "She's prettier than me, but thank you. I must say, Arthur, you are looking devastatingly handsome. Is that a new suit?"

"It's not new but I don't think you've seen it before."

"Well, usually we remove your clothing pretty quickly, don't we? Oh, Arthur, you dear. You're near to blushing."

She laughed and removed a cigarette from a silver case and he hurried to light it for her. A pianist was playing *Moon Indigo*. He remembered it from when he first met Jean at Bobby's club. Or was it somewhere else? At the yacht club that first night with Bobby and Mike Drake maybe. This pianist was more appropriately attired, wearing a neatly pressed tuxedo, but his music was less inspired.

Their waiter arrived, bowing obsequiously, citing specials as if he might be reciting poetry. He ordered a steak and she the salmon. Afterward there was a moment of awkward silence as if, thought Ramos, they didn't know quite how to behave or what to say to one another in public with their clothes on. Naked there had been little need for talk. She reached across the table and placed her cigarette between his lips, and he took a puff and then she took it back and took another puff and then a sip of her vodka.

"I like sharing cigarettes with you, Arthur. Have you ever smoked marijuana?"

"No. Have you?"

"Of course. It's quite lovely. Very nice for sex. We should try it sometime."

"It's against the law. I'm a policeman, Jean."

She laughed and said, "I'm sorry, Artie. I don't mean to laugh at you but you're so cute. Bobby smokes it frequently."

"Have you smoked it with him?"

"Do you really want to know?"

"No. I have enough trouble thinking of you with customers at the club without thinking about you and Bobby."

"Let's talk about something else then, Arthur. Let's not ruin this. This is nice. Is there any more vodka?"

He reached for her cigarette, took a drag, and handed it back to her. She took it between her middle and index finger, took a drag and exhaled. He studied her mouth and lips and the slow indulgent way she drew in smoke and exhaled it and she saw him watching and winked at him.

Who could not want her?

He poured some vodka and said, "You ever been to San Diego, Jean?"

"No. I was in LA once, but only for a weekend during a Jean Harlow shoot."

"You should see the people who live there, how happy they are. Everyone looks healthy and tanned from the sun because it's sunny almost every day. People smile at you as if they can't believe their good fortune to be living where they do. The ocean is warm enough for swimming all year round and the beaches are clean and the water clear as glass. Everyone you see is tan and healthy. On the other hand if you get want to get away and get crazy for some dancing or gambling action it's a short drive to Tijuana. Do you like Mexican food, Jean?"

She wrinkled her nose and said, "Ugh. I would never eat anything that looked like that. It's nasty. Mashed disgusting beans. Who could put something like that in their mouth? Mexicans, I guess. It has to taste hideous. That's probably why Mexicans hide the taste in all that hot sauce. I mean, its okay for Mexicans who don't know any better but yuk."

"You'd be surprised, Jean. It's not all rice and beans. There are a number of upscale gourmet Mexican restaurants featuring fine dining and fresh seafood. I know several in San Diego. But I know other good restaurants there too, French and Italian for example. We should go there together sometime, Jean. You would love it. We could even fly down this weekend."

"You know I can't, Arthur. Bobby would never let me. He doesn't even know I'm here. You don't know him like I do. If you did you wouldn't even ask me this. He's dangerous. Sometimes I hate him."

She was cross with him. He heard it in her voice.

"Then why do you stay with him?"

"I have my reasons. It's complicated."

"Then explain. I'm trying to understand."

"It has nothing do with you and I don't want to talk about it."

"It's important to me."

"Why?"

"It's important to me because I'm in love with you, Jean."

"You love Jean Harlow. I'm Ida Fitzgerald not Jean Harlow and frankly I'm sick to death of the whole Jean Harlow shtick. If it weren't for Bobby who started it I'd be someone else. Myself I guess, though I sometimes think I don't know who I am anymore."

"You don't like being compared to the most beautiful woman in Hollywood?"

"I hate it. It was Bobby's idea. He said I would be able to pull in extra money as Jean Harlow. What's so bad about Ida Fitzgerald?"

"Nothing,"

"Then I want you to call me Ida. Drop the whole Jean bit."

"That's fine, I don't mind."

But he was disappointed.

The servers appeared with their meals at an inopportune time, balancing silver platters of salmon and steak. When the platters were placed on their table she smiled and said, "This smells delicious." She took a small, delicate bite of salmon and said, "This tastes so fresh it's like it was just caught."

"It probably was. But didn't you hear what I said to you, Jean? I said I love you and you said nothing. I think some kind of response is warranted."

"Honestly I don't even know for certain what love is. Frankly, from what I have seen from the girls at work who say they are in love, I don't even know if it's necessarily a positive condition. If they are in love, it doesn't seem to make them happy, usually the opposite. But I will say this, Arthur. You were a surprise. When Bobby first approached me and told me I was to start working as your escort I told him I didn't want to do it. I looked at you and saw a common Mexican in a cheap mail-order rumpled suit and I don't do cheap and I don't do Mexicans, Jews or niggers. I refused him. It was one of the few times I said no to Bobby."

"What changed your mind?"

"Bobby offered me twice the amount of my normal rate to hook you. Of course it was a bonus you were light skinned and didn't have an accent. In the dim lighting of the blue room, I could almost forget you were Mexican."

"What's wrong with Mexicans?"

"Nothing really. They aren't white is all. I may be a prostitute but I have my standards. I said before no Negroes, no Jews, no Mexicans. But if all Mexicans are like you, I may become less racially exclusive. Charge them a little more of course but not automatically refuse them."

"But wait a minute, Jean. Back up. Bobby was paying you all those times we were together in the Blue Room?"

"Of course, silly, do think I would give myself away for free? But you surprised me, Artie. I ended up enjoying my time with you. So much so that Bobby caught on and cut my pay. I ended up making less money with you than with the others. Bobby resented you but needed you in his control and used me to bring it about. But you surprised me, Artie. You turned out to be the most kind, gentle, sweet man I have ever had the pleasure of knowing."

She finished the vodka in her glass, grasped her clutch purse and rose from the table.

"I have to go to the lady's room, Arthur."

"Okay but hold that thought."

He watched her stride toward the rest rooms. So did every other man in the restaurant. He poured more vodka for them both and waited.

Once she had left their table and he was alone he began to have second thoughts. Bobby had been paying her for her time with him? This was the first he knew of it, and he didn't know if it was opportunism on her part, because she was taking money from him as well. Did Bobby even know this? Had she been taking advantage of them both?

It hurt him what she had said about Mexicans, saying she was relieved his skin been a shade light enough to pass and that he had not spoken with an accent. And then there was her disdain for Mexican food, not that it in itself mattered but it was the way she said it, like it was beneath her to even try it. This was all a surprise to him. He had planned and expected a much different night, the perfect meal, the perfect hotel and perfect room for lovemaking. His plan was to ask her to go with him to San Diego for a weekend get-away; maybe three or four days. If she liked it, maybe they'd come back, pack her things and move down there permanently. Now he wasn't sure of anything, not of what was to come, not even of what they had been to one another in the blue room. Had he made a mistake, leaving Anne for this woman, who he thought he knew?

But when she returned, fresh lipstick and cologne applied, he rose and pulled out her chair and when she sat and smiled at him across the table all his doubts and fears melted away. The problem was not with Jean, but with his own suspicious mind. If she had had a prejudicial notion of Mexican men, had she not overcome it by her mere presence with him? Wasn't that what really mattered?

"You've always said you wanted to stop working for Bobby and get away. We could both move to San Diego. I'd get a job with the police department there. We'd rent a bungalow on the beach and swim every day. We might not have much money and have to scrimp a little, but you wouldn't have to work and we'd be happy and I'll take care of you."

"You're married, Artie."

"I haven't told you this before because I've been saving the news for tonight. I told Annie everything, Jean. I've already left her. It's over between us now. I left her two weeks ago. I told her I had been seeing you for months and was in love with you."

"That was cruel and unnecessary, Artie. Why did you do that? Aren't you satisfied with what we have now? Why complicate it?"

"Because I'm tired of hiding my feelings. I love you, and I can't pretend at home anymore. I'm through hiding, Jean. No more dishonesty and lies. You've made an honest man of me."

"Artie, you're a nice guy and all, but do you really think for one moment I would go down to San Diego with an ordinary policeman and try to live on his salary? Can you honestly see me living in some squalid little beachside motel shack like one of those Oakie dustbowl refugees? No, Artie. That's not anything I want."

"That's not what you led me to believe, Jean. You've told me time and again how much you wanted to escape your life working for Stone, how you hate the work and hate him. You said you hated Seattle because it rained too much and the beach was useless because there was no sun and the water was too cold for swimming. You said when having a bad night at work just seeing me lifted your spirits. You said the other men meant nothing to you."

"Well that may have been true, Artie, I do like you but it's not enough. Do you have any idea how much *money* I make working for Bobby? I've got plenty of money saved and the work I do I can do anywhere. I could easily go on my own to San Diego or anywhere else on what I make. I could go to Paris or London, live in first class hotels and dine exclusively in top rated restaurants. You want me to live in a trailer court surrounded by a lot of greasy Mexicans and eat mashed beans? Why would I want to do that? For love? Not a chance. Artie. I never said I loved you and much of what I did say to you in the blue room was pillow talk, though you were one of my favorite clients and I may have enjoyed being with you more than the others. But I'm not going to change my whole life and take a vow of poverty because of it."

"You're calling me a *client*? Is that all I was to you? A fucking *client*?"

"That's exactly what you were."

"But I thought you loved me. You made me believe that. And I think you are lying, both to me and to yourself. I think you love me now but are just afraid of it."

"I don't love you, Arthur. I didn't then and I don't now."

"I've left my family for you Jean, probably lost my job, all that I had, my whole life as I have known it."

"I'm sorry about that, Artie. You should not have done that."

She finished the vodka in her glass and rose with her clutch purse and said, "You have ruined everything, Artie. Don't come to the club anymore. I don't want to see you, and if I do, I'll have Bobby throw you out."

He sat at the table long after she had left, not touching his steak. Finally the waiter came, motioned toward his plate and said, dubiously, "Was everything not satisfactory sir? The steak not cooked properly perhaps?"

"No, its fine," he replied. "Charge it to my room.'

The ice had melted in the champagne bucket when he entered his room on the twelfth floor. His took off his jacket, threw it on the bed and removed his gun from its shoulder holster. He opened the champagne and drank it straight from the bottle while staring at the gun on his lap while wondering what had happened. By the time he finished the Champagne, he had it figured out. He'd been played, and it was Stone who played him.

CAT CREEK

ELVIRA WOKE IN URGENT NEED of the outhouse. It was dark in the cabin but traces of light through the windows gave a glimpse of dawn. She guessed it to be around six in the morning. The fire in the woodstove had burned out, its residual stale odor of ash and charcoal that was a daily component of her morning life remaining. Every winter night she made a fire before getting into bed, only to wake in the middle of the night shivering under the huddle of blankets and too cold to get up and start the fire again. Wearing her long johns, she slid out from beneath her pile of warm blankets, her bare feet cold on the frigid pine flooring. She had removed her socks from her ankles during the night because of poor circulation. Debating whether to get dressed first or start a fire, she stepped into her jeans, found her socks, pulled a hooded sweatshirt over her head and stumbled like a drunkard when trying to put on her mud boots while standing. Once she had fallen over doing just this.

All this trouble just to take a shit. Life out here looked basic and simple to those who didn't know better, but was complicated. Well, what was a lady to do, move into an apartment in Cat Creek? She'd tried that once. Big mistake.

She found her barn jacket on its hook by the door, grabbed her Winchester pump action and stepped onto the porch. The gray sky threatened a light snow but it was too early yet for snow and except for some light dustings that melted quickly none had yet come.

Three weeks earlier one of her goats had been killed by a

mountain lion. It happened in broad daylight. She'd heard the goat's horrific bleating, ran onto the porch firing this very Winchester, but too late. The goat was already down, the wildcat ripping out its intestines. The cat looked up and made eye contact with her, its mouth foamy with the goat's blood, and she fired again and missed. It vanished into the tree line so quickly the entire incident might have been a dream except for her poor quivering goat dying in its own shit and entrails at her feet. There was no saving it, and she'd had to shoot it. Meanwhile the mountain lion was on the loose and had been recently seen by others.

She carried the rifle under her arm as she hiked to the outhouse, the ice crystals on the tall frosted grass dampening her clothing. She'd built the outhouse years earlier in a huddle of tall bushes. It was some 30 yards away and faced away from the cabin toward the forest.

The urgency had abandoned her and now she didn't know if she had to go anymore but if she went back into the house the urge would probably just come over her again. That damn seat was going to be cold, too. She crossed the frozen ground and sat in the outhouse with the door open for the fresh air and panoramic view to the distant mountains. She peed and frowned at the same time. She could have peed off the damn porch. The seat was damp and cold on her bare bottom and she finished, wiped quickly and stepped out. Morning light was spilling across the plain as if washing it clean. Where the mountains began, a line of tall trees swayed.

She first heard the movement of brush being disturbed in the woods, then saw a full grown black bear. It was still, and watching her. She was as much astonished as afraid. She had never seen a bear around here before though she knew others who had. Bears were known to sometimes come down into the plains from the mountains in search of food. This one should be hibernating by now and was probably hungry. She carefully cocked her Winchester.

The bear rose to a standing position on its hind legs and she raised her rifle, hoping she wouldn't have to pull the trigger, but it dropped to all fours and went scampering off into the cover of woods. She lowered her rifle. Her sister would have said it was an omen, that the bear was someone's spirit animal come bearing a message.

She shook her head as if shaking off such nonsense and went back into the house and made a fire in the woodstove and put on the morning coffee, but she couldn't stop thinking about the bear. It made her think of Jack and she couldn't exactly say why. Something about the way the bear had lumbered off as if ashamed or guilty of something. Jack was mixed up with the bear in her mind there was no getting away from it. It was more Alma's way of thinking than hers and she wished her sister were here to interpret what she was sensing.

She boiled water in large pan on the woodstove, poured it in an enamel basin and washed her face and hands. She dropped her jeans to her ankles and unfastened her long johns and pulled them down to her knees. She soaped the washcloth and scrubbed between her legs and wrung out the washcloth. She stared at the washcloth suspiciously, then sniffed it. The rag was nasty and needed washing. Washing herself with it probably only made her stink more than she did already. She really needed to somehow get a load of laundry into town.

Later when the sun was out, sitting on the porch drinking some of her home brewed beer, she saw Billy Rasmussen babying his fancy new truck along the deeply rutted dirt road to her house. She hadn't heard him coming because the engine was so quiet and he drove so damn slow. Billy was driving probably not much over five miles an hour, easing the truck over potholes as if they might break it in two. What was the point of having a truck if you were afraid to use it or get it dirty? He drove to where the dirt road ended some thirty yards from the porch, where he shut off the engine. He used to drive his old truck off the road onto the field and park right in front of the woodpile but not this one. If Billy had treated her as well as he did his new truck they'd still be together. He was slow getting out from behind the wheel. Six foot three inches tall, he wore jeans, a red snap-button shirt, denim vest and cowboy boots. He moved like a lemur, tall and languid, but without its effortless liquidity and grace, more like he might have been screwed together and the screws were loosening and he was coming apart. Everything Billy did was in slow motion. He'd been roughed up in bar fights and banged up in alcoholic car crashes so many times he was a bag of broken bones. It probably hurt him all over just to walk the thirty yards to her porch but he hid it well.

He was out of uniform but wore his BIA badge on his vest. She'd heard he recently had to break up a vicious fight in a dance hall. It was hard to imagine. Seemed like his punches would be delivered in slow motion. His opponent could probably hit him five times before he got in a blow. He was big, though, with big hands and long arms and broad hard shoulders. Probably only needed to land one good punch to bring a man to his knees and end it.

As usual he wasn't much for making conversation but the big palooka sure looked good, damn him to hell. He was looking better while she was getting fatter and uglier in her baggy jeans and oversized tee shirt that could no longer hide her extra pounds. It wasn't fair.

On the other hand, an advantage was when she did dress up, say for a dance at the Eagles or VFW in town, the contrast from trash-picker to beauty queen was such a surprise men normally indifferent fawned over her, especially if they had not seen her dolled up before. Not that anyone lately was asking her to any dances. It had been so long she didn't know if she even remembered how to dance. But it was supposed to be like riding a bicycle, which they said once learned you never forgot. Or like fucking, which to her occasional regret, she had also mostly forgotten.

Billy wore clean clothing because he lived in town and had a washing machine in his house. He wore his glistening black hair long and clean, braided with black and red ribbons. She wore a sweat stained tee shirt. She hadn't washed her hair in so long she didn't even bother to brush it and just wore a rag on her head. She washed her body every morning upon arising and before going to bed at night but her last real bath had been weeks earlier, taken in her friend Marge's house in town. She figured she was about as unglamorous as a girl could get. On the other hand Billy was taking a good long look at her tits, which showed her nipples under her bra-less tee shirt, and she knew her tits were good ones. The low-down cheating lying son of a bitch used to love to fondle and suck them. Too bad for him.

He sat beside her on the porch and she offered him a beer.

"You know I quit. I haven't had a drop in two years and if I was inclined to start again it sure wouldn't be with your nasty tasting ginger beer."

"Yeah, the whole damn Crow Nation has heard you brag about your sobriety ever since you quit. I remember when you guzzled my brew like a man dying of thirst. But good for you, I won't hold it against you. You seem to be dropping by here more frequently lately, Billy. Why is that?"

"I can't stay away from you, Vi. It comes over me like a spell. I've got to see Elvira or I will surely die."

"And you're a sweet-talking liar who hasn't changed a bit."

"What hasn't changed is that I'm still in love with you, Vi. I've loved you from the moment I saw you and never stopped loving you."

"I think you just want in my pants."

"That too, but I'd take you however I could get you."

"You had your chance."

"I want another."

"Right. One more chance. How many times did I hear that?"

"I was drinking back then. I'm different now, Vi. I've changed."

"You're still a man."

"You'd rather have a woman?"

"I'm happy with my goats, chickens, and tired old horse, which is on its last legs, by the way. But this isn't why you have come to see me, is it now?"

"I wish it was, but it's not."

A pair of hawks glided overhead, circling closer to the fenced area where her chickens and roosters roamed. She retrieved her rifle from where it leaned against the porch rail, stood and fired into the sky. The rifle shot echoed in the hills. There was the smell of gun powder and then silence.

"Missed by a mile," said Billy.

"My eyes are getting bad. Maybe that's why you look so good to me. You came because of Jack, didn't you Billy?"

"How did you know, Vi?"

"Woman's intuition. Same way I knew you were cheating on me. Jack is innocent and that detective is full of shit. I know Jack. He ain't got it in him."

"What makes you think so?"

"A bear told me."

"Well, a lawman told me Jack's signed a confession back in Seattle."

"If he confessed they must have beat it out of him. I know damn well he didn't do it."

"They have some pretty convincing evidence, Vi. I'm not saying I think Jack is guilty but it turns out the dead man was found with Juanita's locket."

"I'll bet they have it in for him because he's Frank's brother. You know as well as I do Jack couldn't kill anybody."

"I'm just bringing the information, Vi. I'm not judging one way or the other."

"Well I'm not going to stand by while Jack takes punishment for something he didn't do."

"Not much you can do about it, Vi. "

"The hell there ain't. I'll go to Seattle and talk some damn horse sense into him. Make him detract that phony confession they forced out of him."

"And how do you intend to get there? On that old horse of yours? He can hardly stand."

"I'll hop a damn freight if I have to."

"Yeah, you would, too."

"Damn right I would."

"That's what I'm afraid of. You got no sense sometimes, Vi."

"Yeah, I demonstrated that when I let you in my pants."

"That was one of the more sensible thing you done."

"Ha. That's a laugh."

"We had plenty of laughs."

"What I mostly remember is the tears, Billy."

"I'm sorry about that, Vi. I truly am. I been tryin' to make it up to you."

"You been trying to get back in my pants is what you've been tryin'."

"Well, that's a fact I can't argue but I can deal with just being your friend if that's the way it's got to be, Vi."

"Well, Billy, I may be mad at you but I do consider you a friend. I like you plenty, and that's for sure."

She opened another mason jar of brew and took a long drink and wiped her mouth. Billy, frowning, said, "Kind of early in the morning for beer, isn't it?"

"Breakfast of champions, Billy."

"Not in my experience. You should give it up like me. Remember what happened to your sister."

"I ain't my sister."

Billy's dogs, puppies but bigger than she liked with large sharp teeth and an agitated manner of circling around each other, began growling and jumping on one another.

"Get control of your dogs, Billy."

"They're just playing, Vi."

"Well I'm not."

She picked up her rifle and Billy quieted the dogs.

"Stay," he said. "Sit."

Damned if they didn't do what he said. Billy had a way with them, maybe because he was a dog himself. When they'd lived together he'd sometimes talked about raising Huskies and selling them, another point of contention they disagreed on.

"I can't let you hop no freight train, Vi. It's too dangerous. You don't believe me, go talk to the Paulson's across the way. They rode the rails plenty. They'll tell you same as me."

"You want some coffee?"

"No, I have to be going. I just wanted you to know about Jack."

. She walked him to the truck, following him through years of accumulated rusted tools, scrap metal, bed springs, discarded appliances and automobile parts scattered on the grounds around them.

"You think I could maybe sell some of this stuff, Billy?"

"You could try."

The huskies were sniffing her now and rubbing up against her.

"Keep those mutts away from me, Billy. I told you."

"They like you, Vi. Something about the way you smell."

"You saying I smell like a damn dog?"

"No, Vi, that's not what I'm saying at all."

"Well, I probably do at that. I ain't petting them though they do seem to kind of like me."

Billy climbed up into the cab of the truck and the dogs jumped in back and settled down.

"Anyway, Billy, the point is I need to come up with money for a train ticket somehow if I'm going to Seattle. Otherwise I have no choice but to hop a freight."

Billy spoke to her through the window, which he had rolled down for that purpose.

"Damn it, Vi, I told you. You're not hopping no damn freight." He gestured toward the scrap strewn around the cabin and said, "I'll come by next Friday and we'll load the truck for the Saturday flea market."

"Thank you, Billy."

"It'll be our date," he said, winking.

She gave him the finger.

He smiled and said, "Is that an invitation, Vi?"

She didn't tell him so, but had to admit she'd been thinking about it.

"To be honest," she replied, "I ain't sure."

Later she rode her horse over to the Paulson's to learn how to hop a freight train to Seattle. The Paulson's were her closest neighbors and the ones who had given Jack the tips on train locations and schedules. Turned out old man Paulson near to scared her to death with stories about train rapes. There was no way she could pass as a boy. Not with her tits.

Friday afternoon she sat on the back porch drinking black coffee wondering why Billy was late. She had been staring for an hour across the patch of overgrown yard to the scatter of tools, winches, engine parts and cookware she had assembled for sale at the flea market.

Jack's confession didn't make sense. It wasn't in him to kill a man. Jack Vogel was the sweetest man she had ever known. More than once she had considered the fact she had married the wrong Vogel. Not that she had feelings for him in that regard; he was more like a brother to her but Jack had been there for her after his no-account rambling-man brother ran off like a dog chasing a scent and later, when Alma died, she helped with the kids and did some cooking and wash for the family and had been kind of like a wife to him. Minus the sex of course, which had never been an issue. Jack would have run like a skittish deer from that idea.

She caught a flash of Billy's new truck through the trees. His old truck you could hear coming from far off. This one she hadn't heard at all until seeing a flash of red through the tree lined road. If the sun was shining directly on it, it blinded you to look at it. Candy apple red and way above what he could afford new job or not, it was about as embarrassing a display of one-upmanship, whoredom, and shameless flaunting as she had ever seen. She watched it approach, slower than her old horse. God but it was ridiculous how Billy babied that truck.

He was a big stupid strutting peacock now, a bigshot B.I.A. dick and not unemployed like everybody else. He paraded around the rez in a vehicle he was afraid to drive for fear of it getting dirty. What the hell had become of him? He'd changed. Maybe he never should have quit drinking. But she didn't mean that. She just hated his job.

She'd told him straight out. "I don't like cops and I don't like the BIA."

"That's because you don't understand what it is exactly I do," he had replied. "I don't bother people; I mostly leave them alone except to make myself available when they need me. You should ride with me sometime and see for yourself. I take old folks to the clinic, make safety checks on the infirmed and shut-ins, give rides to folks too drunk to safely drive or ride a horse home. Sometimes I might have to break up a squabble, but rarely need to lock anyone up except for their own protection."

She watched his truck slowly make its way to her porch, heard the quiet purr of the engine, and then nothing, not a single sputter from the tailpipe. Billy stepped down from the truck cab and tipped the brim of his hat. He wore a pair of work jeans, a T-shirt and unbuttoned flannel shirt with workman's boots. In his hands were thick workman's gloves. She saw him look her up and down but couldn't quite read his expression; it was like he was hiding his thoughts. Like Billy, she too wore jeans with boots, but with a tee shirt she had slept in.

Billy looked like he had just got out of bed after a sleepless night. He'd probably been with some floozy in town. They didn't call the place Cathouse Creek for nothing. He hadn't bothered to tie back his hair, his unbuttoned shirttail was out, and his fly was unzipped. Had he even brushed his teeth? It was damn sure obvious he hadn't gone to any trouble fixing himself on her account. But then, who was she to talk? More importantly, what did she care?

Billy yawned and stretched, his shirt riding above his naval.

The cheating son of a bitch.

"You look like shit, Billy. Your eyes are all bloodshot like you been drinking again."

"Well I haven't. I couldn't sleep for tossing and turning. Up half the night worrying about you and your hair-brained scheme to hop a freight to Seattle."

"Well maybe I won't have to. Depends on how much we make at the flea market."

Alma's guitar leaned against a porch rail. Billy picked it up and strummed it, his playing as awful as she remembered.

"I'll buy this myself," he said. "How much you asking for it?"

He was holding it up by the neck like it was duck he had just shot out of the sky. The talentless big galoot thought he could play and sing just because some hussies at a party who wanted to fuck him told him so. He could hardly play the guitar at all and when he sang he sounded like a heifer birthing a breeched calf.

"It's not for sale, Billy. It belonged to Alma and I intend to keep it as a memento. Besides, what would you do with it? You can't play."

"I thought to serenade you with it, Vi."

He meandered through the conglomeration of rakes, shovels, axes, hoes, functioning and non-functioning chain saws, gasoline cans, coils of rope, pots and pans and utensils. He knelt among this debris examining individual items and when he looked up at her she didn't like what she saw.

"There's more in the sheds," said Elvira. "A lot of Frank's things."

The chain saws had to be at least some value even if only for parts. And she had Frank's old truck, which had to be worth something. Of course it was dead as a doornail, rusted out and probably worthless except for parts, the transmission slipping the last time she had driven it, the throw-out bearing on the clutch making a terrible racket and the engine probably seized since last started two hard winters ago. A truck engine good for parts and a transmission that might or might not belong to Frank's truck was in one of her three sheds.

Billy strode back and forth through the merchandise, sometimes kneeling to inspect a motor part or examine an assortment of saws and axes.

"What else you got, Vi?"

She pointed to a dilapidated tin shed the same rusty color as Frank's old truck. He disappeared inside and was in there awhile. She could hear him banging and crashing around in there like maybe the bear was in there and he was having to fight his way out. He came out carrying some of Frank's toolboxes which he set on the ground. Kneeling, he opened one and looked up at her and frowned.

"These tools have mostly gone to rust, Vi."

"That old shed is like a bucket with holes in it, Billy. I kept meaning to fix it, but never found the time or inclination."

"I know Frank took better care of his tools than this."

He began unrolling a tarp and laid it out in the truck bed to protect it from possible scratches and said, "Help me spread some of this stuff across the bed of the truck. Do it real gentle. I don't want to scratch any paint."

"What in hell do you have a truck for if you are afraid to use it for what it was intended, Billy?"

"Is this all you have to sell, Vi? Because it's not worth much at all."

"I have this firewood." She nodded at the truck bed and said, "There's room back here for at least half of it."

"No, we'll have to make a for sale sign on the flea market table saying it's available for pickup. You have about two cords here."

"I can sell my horse and wagon, the goats and chickens."

The wagon for collecting firewood was in fair condition, but the horse was getting too old to pull it. The goats and chickens were producing milk and eggs and should sell.

"I've got six cases of my brew in the shed."

"You don't actually think you can sell that nasty concoction, do you, Vi?"

"Well, the mason jars ought to be worth something at least. They're good for canning."

"I doubt it. Too stinky from your nasty brew. Good for target practice is about all. Anyway, you can't sell beer at the flea market, Vi. It's against the law."

"Yeah and you're a bigshot lawman."

She sat on the top rickety step of her porch and stared at a lifetime's accumulation not worth enough even to pay for a train ticket to Seattle. She was near to feeling sorry for herself.

Billy removed his gloves, threw them on the ground as if they were something he hated and said, "Vi, how do you expect to get through the winter here without wood, axes or your chain saws?"

"Maybe you ought to move into town where there's electric heat and hot and cold running water."

"I love the quiet here. I'll always be a country girl."

"Vi, I don't know what you think you can accomplish in Seattle, but if you really have to go I don't want you hopping a freight train to get there. I guess I'm going to have to buy you a ticket. I'll feed the animals and watch the place for you while you're gone, get your wood together for winter and do what's needed for you to come back."

Vi found herself confused about why exactly she was crying softly.

He took her hands and said, "There's just one condition, Vi."

"You want to fuck me, right?"

"I do, but that's not it. I want you to give serious thought to marrying me. I know I hurt you in the past, but I'm different now. I don't drink anymore and I love you, Vi. I've always loved you. I'm on my knees now, asking you to marry me."

"This ain't the place to discuss it, Billy. Come to bed, Billy. Let's find out if we still got the feelings in us."

They were married three days later. Billy asked where she wanted to honeymoon and she said why, Seattle, Washington, honey. A week later the newlyweds were taking meals in the Northern Pacific Railroad's formal dining car with a view to countryside neither had seen before. They made honeymoon love in their sleeper car. In Seattle, despite Vi's insistent intractable demands, Jack stubbornly refused to withdraw his confession. She cussed him up and down for his stubbornness. He eventually had her stricken from the jailhouse approved visit list.

Lea Macquarrie

PIER 91

MCCABE DIDN'T RECOGNIZE THE WATCHMAN in the Pier 91 gate shed. He eased the Hudson to a stop while the new watchman ran out to unlock the gate. The gatekeeper, opening the chain link fence, had to fight it a little, grimacing when it resisted and audibly scraped against the pavement. McCabe rolled down his window, the salt air permeating the Hudson interior when the watchman spoke to him.

"There's a couple of union men waiting for you," he said. "I hope you don't mind my admitting them. They had union I.D."

"And who are you? I've never seen you here before."

"Name is Fitzgerald, sir."

"Where's Al this morning? Is he sick?"

"Search me. Company calls me to sub, I don't ask why. I take the work offered with gratitude and thanks to the Lord."

"I hear that," said McCabe.

He drove slowly down the pier alongside numerous pallets bearing crates scheduled to be crane lifted and eased down into the ship's holds. Grey swollen rainclouds hovered over the sound where rain threatened but had as yet not begun.

The two men waiting for him waved when they saw him coming in the Hudson. He had no love for the union right now and thought about running the men off the pier into the Sound. They were standing in the center of a flock of pestering seagulls where one of the two men was engaged in kicking the gulls away from his legs and feet. McCabe didn't hold it against him. The birds were thieves and a damn nuisance. Why, he'd seen them steal a man's salmon before he could get off his hook and into his tackle box. Sometimes they ganged up and dive bombed. He'd once seen a seagull swoop down and take a hotdog from a boy's grip.

He watched the union men stomp their feet on the pier to scatter the birds, which rose in a flock, shrieking their indecipherable curses, some taking occupancy on nearby pilings. Some circled around and defiantly returned to strut around the men's feet again. The damn birds were defecating bombardiers splattering whatever unfortunate human target might inadvertently be below. Even the sustained Seattle rain could not entirely wash their defecations away. The planks on the pier were white with their scat. Until recently they had been gathering mostly near the canning factory but for reasons known only to their species they had recently returned to Pier 91. They'd soon be shitting on the men's shoes, McCabe knew.

He drove through their assembly without adjusting his speed and they scattered as he knew they would, most simply taking a few hops out of his way, a few taking flight. Years of this and he had not hit one yet. He slowed when approaching the two men waiting for him. He tapped the brim of his hat in acknowledgment but passed them by and drove down to the end of the pier without stopping. He parked and got out and leaned against the Hudson's front fender and took a mouthful of whisky from his flask and watched them walk toward him on the pier. They were men unaccustomed to the brisk, damp Seattle wind, both wearing suits and ties and shoes inappropriate for the weather. They were without the raincoats or overcoats Seattleites wore this time of year. The collars of their skimpy suit coats were turned up against their bare necks. They were modern company men, sissified and bureaucratic. Whatever happened to real union men, like Frank Vogel? Was even one left?

A tall thin man with a neatly trimmed moustache who introduced himself as Augustus Knight handed him a business card. He wore large frame glasses, black gloves and carried a leather briefcase.

The other man introduced himself as Sean Sullivan. He carried a copy of the *Sailor's Union of the Pacific* monthly newspaper under his arm. The men's cards identified them as not exactly union men but attorneys representing the Union, which was worse. He took their cards and put them in his vest pocket and asked himself why they were here if they represented the union? Arbitration was finalized. Ships were already sailing. It would soon be time to finish loading his own with cargo and get it underway.

"Is there someplace we can talk, Mister McCabe?"

"We're talking now."

"We have documents to be signed and it's windy out here."

"We can do it in my office but be quick about it."

McCabe was pleased to see birdshit on the man's fancy shoes. He ushered them up the aluminum steps to his third floor office and sat behind his desk, deliberately giving the attorneys no choice but to sit in the smaller inferior chairs giving him the advantage of height from which he could enjoy their discomfort. His massive desk, a fortress of oak thick as the hull of a ship, created a barrier between him and the union men. He reached in a side drawer and took a drink from a bottle in plain view without offering any.

"What can I do for you men," he asked?

"Well now, Mister McCabe, that depends."

"Depends on what?"

"On whether or not what we hear is factual or just talk."

"I have a ship behind schedule," said McCabe. "Let's get to the point."

"That *is* the point," said Sullivan. "We hear you intend to break the strike and sail before arbitration is finalized."

Judging by the expression on the man's face, he seemed to have only now noticed the gob of damp white birdshit on his left shoe. He began furiously wiping it against the back of his pants cuff.

"You were one of the last holdouts during the San Francisco negotiations, Mr. McCabe. Our information is you are unwilling to wait for a settlement and plan to sail without one."

"I was informed the negotiations have been settled and the contract signed." said McCabe.

"Yes, and so were we, but there has been a postponement of the final signing,"

"Why haven't I been notified of it?"

"You're being notified now."

He leaned back in his chair, put his arms behind his head and interlocked his fingers.

"That's an unusual means of notification. I know damn well ships are sailing again. I saw a tanker sail out of here yesterday and a Liberty ship the day before."

"Scabs," said Knight. "It's another reason we are here in Seattle."

"Well I'm not going to risk my ship, its cargo, and customer trust by sailing with a crew of scabs. That's for damn sure."

"Then this has all been a misunderstanding and we apologize for your inconvenience, Mr. McCabe. We just need you to sign a 2933 and we'll let you get back to work."

"What in god's name is a 2933?"

"A solidarity oath with the union stating your intention to wait until the strike is successfully arbitrated and the contract signed by all parties before sailing."

McCabe took another drink, wiped his mouth and shook his head in dismay. He capped the bottle and put it in his pocket.

"What the hell has happened to the Sailor's Union? I don't even recognize you anymore. You have nothing in common with the hard fighting working men who started the union movement. I admired those men. All they wanted was an honest day's work under safe conditions with a decent wage. You guys with the Union today are paper shuffling bureaucrats who don't understand the waterfront. Well, let's get it done."

Knight set his briefcase on McCabe's desk and snapped it open. McCabe rummaged through his desk for his favorite fountain pen. When he looked up Knight was holding a gun.

"Well this takes the cake," said McCabe. "Union officials may in the past have employed strong-arm tactics to get their way but as far I know did not arbitrate at gun point. The safe is empty," he said dryly to Knight. "There's nothing of value here. Take whatever it is you want and leave."

The blow to the back of his head had to have been struck with a blackjack. A human fist couldn't do this. He slumped forward with his face on the desk and blacked out. He was face down on the desk's surface, which was sticky with his blood. It hurt to open his eyes and there was pain everywhere inside his head, not just where he had been struck. He could see through the blood but not know with certainty what had happened. The lighting was dense but not clear. It separated him from what he saw. He was unable to lift his head. The fake union officials were arguing about how to dispose of his body.

"We make it look like an accident. Put him in his car, ram it into a tree or a light pole. We'll have to smash his face in, make it look like it hit the windshield or steering wheel."

"So who is gonna drive the car into it? You thought about that dimwit?"

"You. I'll tie you in the seat."

"Fuck that, Sean. I'm not driving into any fucking light pole. Why don't we just load him in the fucking car and push it into the Sound?"

He closed his eyes and played dead. It was difficult to focus and excruciating not to succumb to the urge to pass out again. He fought a wave of nausea that he knew was caused by fear. His hands shook slightly. The uppermost desk drawer in the column tended to stick and make a squeaking sound when pulled. His damp fingers slipped off the desk knob. He wiped the blood off his fingers on his pants and gave it a slow gentle tug and probed around inside. The Colt .32 semiautomatic pistol was where he remembered it to be, buried under some papers. He held it in his right fist with his index finger through the trigger mechanism. He was uncertain whether it was even loaded. It probably hadn't been cleaned and oiled in years, if ever. He made himself still, his face on the desk, the gun in his hand concealed below the desk. He tried to quiet his breathing. His vision was blurry. Blood from his wound trickled down the back of his neck. He fought the urge to wipe it off. The men continued to discuss how to kill him and dispose of his body. Their voices seemed to travel a long distance through an echo chamber. He couldn't be sure of what he was hearing.

His first shot was wild but lucky. The impact flung the man backward into the wall, leaving a smear of blood on the wall behind him as he sunk to the floor and returned fire. McCabe crouched behind his desk, heard bullets streak over it, then leaned out from behind it for two more shots. Both rounds went wild, one shattering a glass framed painting of his ship when he had first commissioned it. It pissed him off. The man he had shot made a break for the door but didn't make it. McCabe shot him again. He fell and slithered in a pool of blood and lay blocking the door, twitching.

The remaining assassin toppled two metal firing cabinets and took cover behind them. All this happened in what seemed like seconds. More rounds were fired; windows shattered. McCabe felt a searing pain in his shoulder making it difficult to hold on to his weapon. He wiped the sweat out of his eyes, drew a bead and fired. He round came nowhere close. The man behind the filing cabinet was firing his pistol and charging across the broken glass toward him. McCabe shot him in the throat and the man fell to his knees and tried to speak but the sound that came out of his mouth was a gurgle and blood came gushing out of the hole in his neck. He was crawling away, and no longer had possession of his weapon. He lay in a puddle of blood and looked up at McCabe. He seemed to be trying to say something but no words came out of his mouth, only blood. McCabe, gun drawn, approached him. The man's gun was out of reach but still he grasped for it. McCabe kicked it away. The dying man twitched at his feet. It looked like a bullet passed all the way through his throat. He sat on his desk waiting for the man to die and not until then did he pick up the phone to dial the police.

Lea Macquarrie

HIGHWAY 99

SHERIFF GUSTAFSON WAS ON HIGHWAY 99 when he heard static come across the police radio and then the incoming call. He gunned his police sedan, siren wailing, passing everyone on the highway. He flew over Seattle's steep hills, barely tapping the brakes when descending. At the crest of the last hill he glimpsed the aquamarine sheen of choppy Puget Sound below and then he was on Railroad Avenue making his way along the waterfront. The gate to Pier 91 was open and there was no watchman in the cage. Two police cars were already on the scene. He drove along the pier, pulled alongside the office building and ran the metal steps.

McCabe's office on the third floor was riddled with bullet holes. Broken glass was strewn across the width of the room and a ceiling light fixture was down. Wind and a light rain entered shattered windows. Two bodies were face down in pools of blood. Officers took photographs of the crime scene. A police dispatched medic was busy applying a tourniquet to where McCabe had been shot in the shoulder and arm. Mac sat on the edge of his bullet riddled desk with his feet hanging over, a bottle between his legs and a cigar clamped in his mouth. His leg had been grazed and his pants leg was torn. An ace bandage had been applied to his leg, where blood showed through.

McCabe removed the cigar, spat a fleck of tobacco and said, "You want a drink, Gus?"

"I'm on duty and it looks like you need it more than me."

"Shook up is all. You going to charge me, Gus?"

"Should I?"

"If you are asking whether I killed these two men the answer is yes but they fired first."

"Do you know these men?"

"Never seen them before. I thought they were from the union, which is what they said."

"Why you, Mac?"

"Search me."

"There had to be a motive."

"I would think robbery but there's no payroll here, no safe and no cash other than what's in my wallet. Maybe they were misinformed."

McCabe took a deep drink from his bottle and wiped his mouth. Blood dripped from his elbow to the surface of the desk. There was blood on the whisky bottle and on his hand.

Gustafson said, "No witnesses, two dead men, one wounded survivor who happens to be a friend of mine. It puts me in an awkward position, Mac. I may have to take you in. We'll get you to the hospital first. Let's have a look at the deceased, officers. Finish with your photographs."

Gustafson saw one of the men had been shot in the throat and had probably died drowning in his own blood. The other victim had been shot three times. Gustafson recognized him. His body was positioned in a manner suggesting he had been trying to crawl out the door.

"It looks like someone has it in for you, Mac. At least one of the deceased is a known contract killer. Let's get you to the Seaman's Hospital, Mac."

"I'm not going to any damn hospital. Your men can patch me up right here."

"You'll either go to the Seaman's Hospital or I'll arrest you and take you to the police infirmary. Believe me, Mac, you don't want that. Those nurses are sadists. I'll drop by the house and explain the situation to Cora."

"Don't do it, Gus. I don't want to worry her thinking someone wants to kill me. I'll call her and tell her I was in an auto accident."

"I'm sure she'll have no trouble believing that one Mac."

Gustafson put a cigarette in his mouth. He struck a match but gusts of wind rushed through the broken windows and extinguish the flame. He threw the match to the floor and tried again with the same result. He gave up and put the cigarette back in the pack.

McCabe slid to his feet from the desk and said, "Maybe I should go to the hospital after all. I'm starting to feel a woozy and I'm in pain."

"Make the call," said Gus to the medic.

"I already did. The ambulance just pulled in."

"What about my office, Gus?"

"I'll take care of it, Mac. I'll call a glazier to replace the windows, lock up and post an officer here until it's done."

Two ambulance attendants dressed in whites wheeled in a gurney and explained to McCabe that they would carry him downstairs to the ambulance. McCabe grabbed his cane from the floor beside the desk and hobbled to the hat rack, which had overturned during the fighting. He inserted his cane under his hat and flipped it into the air, catching it in flight, just to make a point. Tiny particles of glass were stuck to the felt and he picked at them before slapping the hat against his thigh to remove dust and whatever remaining glass particles he could. He punched it's interior with his fist, shaped it the way he like it with the brim turned slightly upward and put it on his head. Holding his cane in his right hand he hobbled past the two attendants and said, "Nobody is carrying me down any damn stairs. I'll walk, goddamn it."

A DIFFICULT CLIENT

DEFENSE ATTORNEY JEREMIAH WELLS chanced upon county prosecuting attorney William Cummings in the bar of the exclusive Seattle Golf and Country Club to which they both belonged. The meeting was unplanned but since both men were members who frequented the club not a surprise. Professionally, they shared cautious, adversarial respect. Outside of the courtroom they were cordial, though they were not friends. The country club's lounge provided a gathering place for professional men who mostly knew each other to congregate and discuss business, sports and politics. Framed photographs of former University of Washington rowing crews were displayed on the walls behind the bar. Bartenders provided glasses, ice and mixtures. Men here carried flasks and sometimes drank more than they should, but knew how to behave with civility in public. They were prominent successful men of the public who knew the importance of maintaining an unblemished reputation.

Wells sat on a cushioned leather barstool nursing a scotch and soda while listening to the radio broadcast of the Huskies playing Stanford. The Huskies were behind by a touchdown and loosing yardage through penalties but here in the fourth quarter they had come alive and had the ball near Stanford's end zone. He did not welcome Attorney Cumming's interruption. Cummings carried a prominent belly and looked older than his thirty-eight years. He was known to be intensely competitive, with a reputation for being vicious on the golf course. Friendly games were known to turn ugly. He could be ruthless with defense witnesses, causing some to leave the stand sobbing. The most adroit criminal liars were known to sometimes wither under his brutal cross examinations. Wells sometimes admired the prosecuting attorney's skills but disapproved of tactics he considered to be bullying.

Hoping to avoid legal shoptalk and wanting to return to the Huskies game, Wells avoided mention of the Jack Vogel case. The freshman UW quarterback threw an interception causing an outburst of profanity from the crowded men's club bar, words not to be spoken in female company, though any female who might enter here did not belong and had no right to take offense. None were present.

Cummings lighted a cigarette and said, "Vogel is guilty, you know. He's going to have to pay."

"This shouldn't even go to trial, Bill. You have no witnesses and the evidence you have is entirely circumstantial."

"We have a signed confession."

"Given without the presence of an attorney. Your so called evidence is a bucket full of holes."

"If you're looking for a dismissal it's not going to happen. We have the body, the coroner's estimate of the time of death and freight train schedules from Helena. But most importantly we have the locket which was found on the victim's person and we have Vogel's own confession. The best you can negotiate is a guilty plea to a lesser charge, maybe manslaughter. We want Vogel to have a fair trial if it comes to it but bear in mind a man has been killed and justice has to be done."

The two men came to no agreement. The Huskies lost the game and he lost fifty bucks. He met with Vogel for the first time the following morning and learned that he had what is called in the trade a difficult client. Wells identified himself as his defense attorney and explained Walter McCabe had hired him. Vogel seemed to not understand this. He seemed to be distracted and to not fully understand the gravity of the charge against him. When explained his defense options, he seemed impatient.

"The arraignment is tomorrow, Mr. Vogel. You have the right to wear civilian clothing and I strongly advise you do so."

"I don't even know what an arraignment is."

"I'm sorry, Mr. Vogel. I should have explained. It is where the prosecution makes a case in pursuance of formal charges. There's a chance the matter will be dropped altogether for lack of evidence. Otherwise we will enter a not guilty plea. Do you have any questions regarding this?"

"My daughter is not being charged, right? Because she had nothing to do with it. If she says otherwise, it's only to protect me."

"Yes, of course. The prosecution understands this."

Vogel breathed a sigh of relief and leaned back on his stool.

"Who is paying my bill, Mister Wells?"

"Walter McCabe."

Someone was yelling a few cells down. Two uniformed policemen hurried past in the corridor outside the room. Their shouted voices diminished down the corridor.

"Let me ask you this, Mr. Wells. My brother Frank once told me if you are ever tried for a crime and found not guilty they can't try you for that crime again."

"Your brother is correct."

"If I'm found not guilty in a court of law it's still an open, unsolved case, right?"

"I'm not sure I understand what you're getting at Mr. Vogel."

"If I'm found not guilty they might come after Juanita. I'm told they have a signed confession from her. They framed my brother, you know."

"If a confession from your daughter even exists it was coerced from a minor without the presence of an attorney. It's doubtful it would be admissible. Anyway no one believes your daughter is the perpetrator or even a direct accomplice. If anything she is a victim of the incident. We have been over this."

"Say I plead guilty and am convicted of the crime. Does that get my daughter off the hook?"

"There is no hook, Mr. Vogel. Your daughter has not been charged, nor do I expect her to be."

Vogel lighted a hand rolled cigarette and said, "I want to get this over with as quickly as possible with as little expense to McCabe as possible. I intend to put myself at the mercy of the judge."

"You won't find much mercy there, Mr. Vogel. This is the same judge who sentenced your brother to the maximum penalty his charge would permit. As your attorney I strongly advise you to plead not guilty. I'd be surprised if this even goes to trial but based on the evidence the prosecution has to offer, I don't believe a jury exists that would convict you."

Wells went to lunch at a nearby diner and contemplated the odd behavior of his client, who had not exhibited the requisite commitment to his own defense. Vogel had been only mildly inquisitive regarding the evidence against him, nor had he inquired as to possible sentencing repercussions if the case went to trail and ended in a conviction. The sole exception to this centered on his daughter, who was not a suspect. Did the man not understand the seriousness of the charges against him? They were talking a possible life sentence here. What was wrong with this man? Did he not care what happened to him?

JUSTICE

GUSTAFSON SUSPECTED HE MIGHT be coming down with a virus or the flu. His oldest boy had contracted a mild case two weeks earlier and it had been going around. Even Jen, usually a dynamo of busy housekeeping and shopping, had been complaining of not feeling up to par, while he had been to the precinct toilet three times in the last forty minutes. His fellow officers, sharing the common facilities, hastily evacuated its chambers with wrinkled noses and grimaces, sticking their tongues out and making satirical gagging noises while clutching their throats like World War I soldiers amidst a poisonous gas attack. One of his wise-ass junior officers sealed the men's john with yellow crime-scene tape.

His bowels rumbled, his stomach churned and he had a case of the nerves, unusual for him. He felt jittery inside. Even after the bottle of Pepto Bismal had somewhat settled his stomach and his headache began to dissipate he found himself vaguely confused and easily distracted. He was having difficulty applying himself to the impending budget proposal for which he was responsible, a tedious undertaking due in the state capital in a month and the part of his job he liked least.

He drove to a downtown Seattle crime scene primarily as an excuse to get out of the precinct. A stabbing had taken place in a small Chinese restaurant during a robbery. Gustafson knew the place. A smalltime numbers racket had been running out of it for over a year. A poker room operating out of the back, since shut down, had been the source of previous trouble. Two of his attending officers informed him upon arrival the victim had been taken to General Hospital. He interviewed restaurant staff and customers who had witnessed the stabbing, then drove to the hospital to interview the victim, a skinny smalltime criminal called Stretch, a known pool hustler with priors who had done time in Walla Walla and who when interviewed exhibited reluctance to describe or otherwise give information regarding his assailant. Gustafson doubted there had been a robbery at all and figured the altercation had been personal, having to do with a woman, gambling debts, or both. He assigned the case to Detective McAllister but doubted much would come of it.

An as yet unidentified aggravation continued to nag him as he drove back to the precinct and the unfinished budget proposal. He worked his desk for an hour but couldn't concentrate or get anything done and after an hour went to lunch. Reading the newspaper at the luncheonette counter while eating a hamburger sandwich and coffee, mental provocations persisted. He ate half the sandwich, set it down on the plate and stared into his coffee cup as if reading coffee grounds the way fortune tellers were said to sometimes read tea leaves.

Back at his desk in the precinct his gastrointestinal symptoms returned. He found himself spending as much time on the toilet in the bathroom as in his office. At 2:30 that afternoon he clocked out early and drove directly home and parked in the driveway with a sigh, anticipating the comfort of his bed. His girls were playing hopscotch with some neighbor kids next door. He waved at them when getting out of his car but they didn't wave back. His oldest boy had not yet come home from school.

He found Jen in the kitchen.

"You're home early," she said. She gave him a little kiss.

"Yeah, I wasn't feeling well. I think I'm coming down with something. Where's Gussy, napping?"

"Yes. A long one today."

"Good for him. That's where I'm heading. Upstairs to lie down. I feel terrible."

He padded up the carpeted stairwell, locked his gun and shoulder holster in the top dresser drawer in the bedroom he shared with Jen, and stretched out on the bed. He adjusted his pillow and got comfortable, but the provocations persisted. He knew he would not sleep and finally gave up and went to lie beside Gussy.

Gussy's room had been recently wallpapered with dancing yellow ducks and red bouncing balls. A model airplane both he and Gussy had been working on perched unfinished on a table. Toys spilled from a wire bin by the open closet. Gussy, barefoot and wearing denim overall shorts over a tee shirt curled into a tight fetal ball taking up only the smallest possible area of his bed. His messy blonde hair in need of cutting did not altogether conceal the sweet expression on his soft young face. All kids his age were probably angelic in appearance when asleep but Gussy, because of his startling big blue eyes and sweet smile, maintained his expression of angelic purity even when awake. He was not the only person who thought so, either. Complete strangers made a fuss over him, commented on how good looking and sweet he was, and were rewarded with Gussy's winning smile, which could melt hearts. The boy was well behaved too, never giving them a moment's trouble. Almost from birth he had slept through the night, rarely fussing. Often during his infancy he and Jen, alarmed to see it was morning and Gussy had not wakened hurried into his room fearing the worst to find him in his bassinette fully awake, cooing and staring with his sparkling blue eyes at the birds and airplanes on his mobile. He was goodness itself, innocence more precious than anything he could name.

In his early career as a police officer he had sometimes come home defiled by his intimacy with brutality. His work exposed him to murder, rape, sexploitation, wife beating, drugs, child abuse, hatred and the full spectrum of criminal behavior. But when Gussy smiled at him he knew there was love in the world.

Such deep breaths for a little boy. Gussy did not stir but something about the way he breathed suggested that even asleep he knew his father was here. Even asleep the boy loved him. That's who Gussy was. He was love. He was the personification of love in his life and in his house. He could understand why Christ implored us to be as little children.

His thoughts tossed and turned. The usual, reliable peace when he rested beside his son was not there. It had been stolen. He startled to see Gussy's big blue eyes looking at him curiously. Gussy smiled, his little white teeth wet and glistening.

"Hi, Daddy."

"Hello, Gussy. Did you have sweet dreams?"

"I don't remember. I was looking at the pictures in my Babar book."

Gussy retrieved the book from the bedside table and handed it to him. Gustafson read to him, pausing at pictures Gussy wanted to study along the way. It was Gussy who turned the pages. Finished, he closed the book and put it aside.

Gussy said, "Thank you, Daddy."

That's the way the boy was. He appreciated and gave thanks for small favors. He always had and it wasn't because it was expected. It just came natural to him.

"Gussy, do you remember when you and Uncle Mike were in the downstairs bathroom during mommy and daddy's party and I got mad and told you to go upstairs?"

"He was helping me pee-pee."

"Yes, I know, but *how* was he helping you pee-pee?"

"He helps me to unbutton and stand close to the toilet so I don't miss. He told me I did a good job and kissed my wee wee. Uncle Mike needs help going pee-pee too. I hold his wee wee for him while he goes. His pee is yucky. He made me promise I'd never tell."

"I'm sorry, Gussy. I promise you this will never happen again."

He patted Gussy on the head and hurried into the bathroom and vomited.

He looked in the mirror and did not recognize himself. His face was drenched in perspiration and there were flecks of vomit around his mouth. He washed his face and returned to the bedroom and strapped his shoulder holster and gun under his jacket and went downstairs to Jennifer. Jennifer regarded him curiously as he stood by the door dangling his son's car keys. Danny's car would be less conspicuous and not as recognizable.

"Where are you off to, honey? I thought you were feeling sick?"

"I do feel sick, Jenny. Sick of just about everything except you and the kids."

"But why are you taking Danny's car."

"Too many questions, Jenny. This is police business."

Jenny followed him out to the driveway, shouted over the engine noise as he started his son's car.

"Gus, what's wrong. Talk to me."

He pulled out and left her standing there.

Drake's American Craftsman house was located on a dead-end street in a Richmond Beach neighborhood still in development. A neighborhood in which, Gustafson knew, Drake had a lot at stake. Drake's dirty money and loans siphoned from the Waterfront Development Commission treasury were fueling the project. His was only one of two houses on his street that were finished. Others under construction were in various stages of completion. Drake's was flanked by skeletal projects on each side. Both were presently empty of workmen. The gravel road to Drake's house was about thirty yards from the driveway and front windows. He pulled off to the side of the road and adjusted the lens of his binoculars and focused. Stone was standing at the window.

It was a development he had not anticipated. Drake would be easy but not Stone, who was ruthless, vicious, cunning and far more dangerous. Stone, who had contracted the assault on Frank Vogel and most likely the failed hit on Walt McCabe. Stone who had had his fingers in every development project and speculation on waterfront Seattle. It was rumored he was being primed as a possible candidate for state congress.

But he was the Sheriff. He had the authority to knock on the door and arrest Mike Drake on charges of pedophilia and there was nothing Stone could do about it. He'd have to take Mike to court. There was no way he was putting Gussy through a court proceeding in which he might have to relive the filth that pervert Drake had made him participate in.

It was impossible to approach Drake's house from the bull-dozed front yard without being seen but behind the house was un-obstructed woodland. He pulled off and crouched low when running across the road that flanked Drake's house. In an unfinished project three houses down from Drake's, he stepped over strewn pieces of lumber, nails and joists and passed through the construction site's skeletal rooms, leaving footprints in the sawdust. From the unfinished house he dashed across the back lot and vanished into the shaded concealment of a wooded trail and followed its narrow path into the dark interior. He could no longer see the Drake house because of the thick trees and underbrush overgrowing the path. Broken twigs cracking under his boots, he lost the path, parted tree branches and found it again. He was directly across from Drake's elevated back porch. He slumped to the pine-needled forest floor and sobbed at the thought of what Drake had done to his son.

The sky began to cloud over and it began to drizzle lightly. He waited until it turned dark and then waited some more. The light on Drake's back porch came on but no one came out. He sprinted across the field behind the house, dropped to a crawling position and quietly ascended the stairs to the back porch. He knelt below the small rectangular window in the back door, listening for voices inside. There were none. He tried the doorknob and it turned slightly. It was unlocked, but he did not open it.

The window in the door showed a sink piled with dirty dishes, empty bottles of beer on a countertop and an overflowing trash container beside the stove. He heard footsteps and caught a glimpse of someone entering the kitchen. It was Mike. He leapt over the back porch railing and crawled away into the darkness beyond. Drake came down the steps, a large trash bag in his arms as he sauntered unaware to the garbage cans behind the garage.

Gustafson watched, hidden in the darkness beyond the field of porch light.

"Hold it right there," he said.

Drake, holding the garbage bag, squinted in the darkness and said, "Who is it? Who's there?"

Gustafson stepped into the light.

"What's going on, Gus? Why are you out here hiding in the dark?"

Gustafson wished he could take a picture of Drake's expression. It could go into a dictionary beside the word coward. Drake was not looking at him. Instead his eyes were fixed on the .38 police special pointed at his heart.

Mike looked at him and said, simply, "Gus."

And in that one solitary whispered syllable Gustafson knew Drake understood he was about to die and why. He was already on the run when Gustafson fired his weapon. Shot in the leg, Drake whirled and fell to the ground and limped toward the porch. He fired again and Drake fell and slithered on his belly up the porch steps, his blood trail illuminated under the porch lights. Gustafson shot him again and then Drake was quiet and not moving anymore.

Bobby Stone came bounding out, already firing his weapon when crashing to the porch. Gustafson felt a round from his gun impact his shoulder and twirl him around. He rolled out of the path of the porch lights into the darkness. Stone paced the porch, cursing and pointing in all directions with his pistol. He presented a perfectly illuminated target under the bright porch light. Gustafson shot him three times. He heard screaming inside the house. In the distance, he could already hear approaching sirens. He put the barrel of his revolver in his mouth and pulled the trigger.

STATE OF WASHINGTON TRANSPORT

THE YAKIMA VALLEY IS A DRY, monotonous landscape hemmed in by what is known to locals as Rattlesnake Ridge. Jack viewed it from the wire meshed windows of the bus that ascended it. The Yakima River far below dispatched glittering flashpoints of dancing silver light over the sky blue river. The sun, a fierce presence that seemed to alternately shadow and illuminate the landscape, ignited and set aglow hillsides and ridges on the distant horizon, which pulsated as if the sun was inside of them.

Alma would have found a message in the way the land seemed to slowly open and close its eyes. She might have said it was winking because life in the end was a practical joke. He remembered this place from before, when he had traveled to Walla Walla to visit his brother Frank. This time around the dead man's ghost did not whisper to him or otherwise make his presence known. He watched a hawk slowly glide along elevated wind currents, a predatory thing of beauty circling high and wide in the cloudless blue sky. He may have dozed. There was little traffic on the two lane road. An hour later they were in a combination of woodland and farm country. It was a sunny afternoon but the seasons were on the verge of transitioning. It was growing colder by the day, and winter came to this side of the Cascade Range more quickly than along Puget Sound where the Japanese gulf current provided relative temperance.

He felt the vertiginous motion of the bus as it rumbled along interminable steep hills and turns. The landscape out the window was a glorious thing to behold. He'd been away too long from scenes such as this. The bus stopped at a railroad crossing but there was no train, the stop probably a state mandated precautionary. He drifted with the motion of the bus as it continued beyond the railroad crossing, remembering the life he had left behind. He had tried to be a good man. A working man, a family man. It hadn't worked out.

He remembered fishing, walking in the woods, searching out quail eggs, picking blackberries and huckleberries, foraging for edible mushrooms and finding honeycombs and bringing them home to Juanita who would mine the honey inside and spread it on fresh baked bread still warm from the woodstove oven. Some of his life had been good at least. Much of it, when he thought about it.

He had been husband to Alma Vogel, brother to Frank Vogel, and father to Juanita Vogel, Willie Vogel, Matthew Vogel, Francine Vogel, Dianne Vogel and Jack Junior. All gone now, scattered like the leaves he saw swirling out the window. He remembered laying track across Montana and Idaho, sleeping in the worker's barracks or sometimes a tent, his legs and shoulder muscles aching. It was maybe six hundred miles to Montana from here.

Yellow orange leaves somersaulted from the limbs of silver maples. Caught in wind drifts, they swirled midair like weightless ballet dancers. Picturesque farmhouses with barns and grain silos were visible on green hills. The cloudless sky was the color of Mary Wilson's eyes in the sunshine. Mary Wilson, whom he had loved. With whom he had danced, laughed, and drank sweet wine she brewed herself, who teased him and tousled his hair and kissed him at the most unexpected moments. They had shared a house, a life. He remembered working in their garden, her bright smile, her cheerful but sensible disposition so different from Alma's.

How clear were these memories! How astonishing and precious when memory was all that remained. Odd the moments that returned to his mind, insignificant at the time, but now transformed by what he had lost. The bright summer day on Alkai Point when Mary had waded in the frigid seawater, her skirt hiked above her knees, her sandy feet and the sweetness of her breath when she sat with him on a piece of driftwood and spoke to him. He even remembered the driftwood, how it had turned blonde with age and tidal seawater, the feel of its smooth surface speckled with wood knots as he ran his hands over it. It was where Mary Wilson had asked him to kiss her and he did, for the first time.

A hawk swooped down and glided to the weathered roof of a barn. Elvira would have tried to shoot it. She would have missed. Was there a worse shot on this earth than Elvira Vogel? Elvira Rasmussen now that she had married, not Vogel.

Men wearing denim overalls and straw hats knelt in brown dirt fields between long green rows picking strawberries like red jewels. He had worked as a field hand, remembered working in the dirt with his hands, picking berries, pulling long damp carrots from the earth. He'd worked side by side with the Colored, Mexicans, Indians and Breeds. He couldn't keep up, couldn't make half the money they did at the end of the day even though they tried to teach him. Little kids were making more than him. He'd gone back home to Montana. Sometimes he wished he had never left, except then he would never have met and married Mary Wilson.

They drove through a succession of quiet townships with barber shops, post offices, and mercantile establishments. In the nearby hills, the uppermost points of white church steeples could be seen. The land was blessed with shaded Silver Maples, White Birch and Flowering Dogwood. It was enough to make a man believe in God. He'd never been a church going man and maybe that was the problem right there.

Fields of hops flashed by the window as the bus rumbled along a dirt road along which farmhouses were interspersed. The bus passed a slow moving tractor on the two lane road. The farmer who drove it sat high on his seat and waved his hat farewell. Jack stretched his legs into the isle, the heavy chains that bound them rattling. He stood awkwardly spreading his legs as widely as the chain would allow and reached for the window levers over his seat, the chains around his waist answering his leg chains when he lowered the thickly screened window as far as it would go, about a quarter of the way down.

They drove over a bridge under which blue herons floated on a shimmering lake reflecting the blue sky. He saw fish leap and then the spread of ripples in the crystal blue water.

It seemed there was nothing a man could do to save himself from his life. You could dig in your heels like a stubborn mule but the past and future would eventually meet and require an accounting and in the end maybe it was as it should be because there was no other way it could be. Life was bigger than a man's wishes no matter how well intended or unselfish.

Alma would have said it was written in the land itself. Alma talked with the spirits. Mary talked common sense, except when she got off on her political jags. They lived in different worlds, but both had loved him and he had loved them in return. He still loved them. That would not change. He stared out across the golden fields and silent emerald trees of earth, breathing deeply of the restorative sweet breeze, savoring the beauty of nature he would not see again for years. The bus rumbled through the prison gates, which closed behind them, and then he was behind the walls and his mission was accomplished. He had saved Juanita from prison and life as a fugitive.

A BIG HOUSE

WASHINGTON STATE INMATE JV11778 SQUATTED in the yard, his back against the concrete wall, knees bent, feet planted flat on the ground, elbows on his knees and buttocks on his heels. It was his usual yard squat and yard location, chosen mostly from habit since the view was the same no matter where he chose to position himself, a view only to more concrete walls, gun towers, and a patch of open sky above. There was nothing more to see. Only more of the same.

In the summer, through the rectangular view of sky available from behind the walls, he had been able to trace the flight of migrating birds but this time of year there were few birds remaining to be seen, whether in flight or perched on the walls. He watched one strut back and forth along the ledge of a gun tower, a local robin probably, and it seemed to be watching him as well, but the moment he thought this it flew off. He briefly wondered if it was Alma. Alma always did say her sprit animal was a bird.

The sky today threatened snow, but for now the ground was dry. The usual card games were in progress in the yard, men were sitting on the cold ground, a basketball game was in process at the hoop near the north wall, men lingered, smoked and talked. This time of year the gray sky in combination with the gray concrete walls of the prison and state-issued gray uniforms of the inmates contributed to the absolute absence of color. He looked up into the sky hoping to see a patch of blue but all was grayness, as if the sky itself was a slab of concrete, amplifying his sense of confinement. Only the guard's uniforms were not gray, and they were a shade of blue almost gray.

Sometimes he had trouble remembering what a certain color even looked like because he couldn't see it in his mind clearly. It helped to fix on certain objects in his memory. Alma's red bandana for example, the way it contrasted with her black hair and silver jewelry. If he wanted to evoke the color blue he would remember Mary's eyes, but they were sometimes green and sometimes hazel and the memory in turn led to a whole progression of other memories, and with those memories a deeper sense of loss.

Mary visited when she could and sometimes brought Juanita. She wrote to him weekly. Elvira had come once, but had been denied further visitation after barging into the administrative office uninvited, demanding to see the warden, making a ruckus and spewing accusations. Mary's Ford was unreliable and it was too cold for the motorcycle so she had not visited the prison in months. Elvira wrote from Montana and said she was happy and she and her husband were getting along just fine. Juanita wrote him too, and he was proud she could read and write.

Once a week he was tutored by a representative from Literacy Volunteers, not always by the same tutor, and there was a prison reading program he took advantage of. Otherwise there was no activity here, no rehabilitation, just the slow passing of time. He passed his time in the yard, or in the prison library. He was reading *Call of the Wild* by Jack London and had it with him, but could not concentrate and gave it up for now. He glanced across the drab concrete yard to where groups of inmates gathered and recognized the singular bearing of the inmate who now approached him.

Funny how from a distance, wearing identical drab prison issued clothing, everyone looked at first glance more or less alike. But not his brother. Even from across the wide expanse of concrete there was no mistaking him. Frank strode across the yard, shaking hands with inmates along the way, everyone here liking and admiring him just as most had done on the outside. He had all his teeth, all his hair, and kept himself in shape by working out every day. As always, he did not measure up to his brother Frank in this and in so many other respects.

Frank plopped beside him on the cold ground and warmed him with his smile, which was maybe the warmest thing about this cold winter day. His brother always seemed to be in good spirits, with a generally optimistic outlook even when in prison, while he on the other hand was subject to dark foreboding and brooding. Frank's breath smelled like tobacco combined with alcohol and sure enough, he reached in his prison issued denim jacket and offered him a forbidden flask.

"Want a warm nip, brother?"

Jack declined. He would never forget, even now, the damage alcohol had caused Alma, and by association, his own decline into depression after it had killed her. Frank unscrewed the flask, took a nip and returned it to his pocket.

"Guards see you with that hooch they'll put you in solitary again, Frank."

"Frank tapped the cover of *The Call of the Wild* and said, "Jack London. A good writer and a good man. Try *People of the Abyss* sometime."

Jack groped in his pocket for a small bag of his tobacco, loosened the string holding the flakes within the pouch and poured a trail into a cigarette paper without spilling so much as a fleck. Frank slapped it out his hands and offered a commercially rolled Chesterfield.

"Have one of these, Jack. In fact take the whole pack. I don't want to see you smoking that shit tobacco. If you need hand rolled cigarettes or brand name quality tobacco to roll you let me know."

He lighted his brother's cigarette and said, "You know you shouldn't be here and don't have to be, Jack. Wells says he would represent you in an appeal and you won't let him. Question is, why did you ever plead guilty in the first place."

Jack was doing time for involuntary manslaughter.

"You know why, and I don't regret it."

"Well I for one am ready to move on, Jack. I have an escape plan in the works that can't miss. I have it all set up. A driver waiting outside the walls will take us as far as Bellingham, Washington. From there we get a private boat through the San Juan Islands into Canadian waters and from there along the Aleutian Straight all the way to Alaska. Beautiful sights, brother, two hundred Aleutian Islands floating in ice blue cold crystal waters. In Alaska we'll live on the bounty of the land. You can catch a salmon with your bare hands there are so many. Great hunting, too"

"Why would you even consider that, Frank? You're up for parole in six months. You'd be out on parole by now if you hadn't had time added for the escape attempt last year."

"I don't want parole, brother. That's not freedom. You have to report in, they can put you back behind the walls with the slightest infraction and they control you with all kinds of rules and regulations I can't live with. No, it's either do my time, all of it without parole, or keep trying to escape till I make it. So are you with me, little brother?"

"No. I'm up for parole in nine months and I can make it easy. But you know what, Frank? When Juanita and I were down and out in Seattle she said that all that had gone wrong in her life was because of listening to her father and crediting him for knowing what he was doing and trusting his judgment instead of her own. She said she had to stop letting me make decisions for her solely on the basis of me being her father. It hurt me at the time, and now it hurts me to say the same to you. Frank, I have always looked up to you, but I can't keep going along with you just because you are my big brother. It's different for me than it is for you, Frank. I only have another year until I'm eligible for parole. It would make no sense for me to try to escape. If caught I'd be sentenced all over again. I love and admire you, but I don't know if I want to be like you anymore."

Frank nodded as if he understood and said, "Hell, that's all right little brother. I'm not hurt by it. But I am sorry about how all this turned out."

"Look, Jack. On the North Wall. Just landed."

"It's a red tailed Hawk," said Jack.

"You know, Jackie, they breed in Alaska. Alma would have said it was a sign."

Jack felt his brother's muscular arm go around his shoulders, felt his strength, his brotherly love. The hawk flew off majestically; both men watching silently as it glided in wind currents. There were only gray skies again.

Frank nodded in the direction of the walls that confined them and said, "Well Jackie, not exactly what I had in mind when I said you should come west and we'd live together in a big house, but here we are."

EPILOGUE

WHEN WALTER MCCABE DIED in his sleep at age 69, Cora seemed not to understand. She kept looking for him, wandering the halls, calling his name. She sometimes became agitated when she couldn't find him, but Juanita had a way of calming her. Cora continued throughout her life to have moments of lucidity during which she sometimes told Juanita she missed her husband, and once went as far as to say she longed to hear his piano play in the front parlor. She occasionally engaged in lengthy conversations with Walter during imaginary exchanges she seemed to greatly enjoy, since there was usually much laughter present during the discourse.

McCabe had long suspected he was not well, but failed to understand the severity of his condition. Near the end he could not ascend the Palentine Avenue steps without running out of wind and doubling up in excruciating pain, and there were days, coming home from work, when he sat in his car for an hour or more staring up at those formidable steps before attempting them. The effort was exhausting and he usually went to bed upon completion of them. He found himself frequently falling asleep behind his desk at work, at home in his easy chair, at the dining room table, and once, briefly, in his car, which resulted in an accident. He stopped driving altogether after the accident and took a trolley or cab to work, often arriving late or not at all. Even playing the piano exhausted him.

Cora rediscovered her house, its many rooms and invisible inhabitants as if in a museum she was visiting for the first time. She wandered the halls and rooms at all hours, took languorous baths in candlelight, and acquired her deceased husband's fondness for strong drink. As her mental faculties deteriorated further she was known to put her clothing on backwards, inside out, or both. She became intermittently incontinent. Juanita took over the task of dressing her in the morning, fixing her hair, preparing her meals and changing her when soiled or wet.

Cora continued to smoke, but lightly. Juanita rationed her cigarettes and supervised her smoking, which was restricted to the outside porch and a designated parlor area that became a formal smoking room. Juanita also dispensed Cora's evening whiskey, giving her enough to calm her and help her sleep, but not so much as to threaten her declining equilibrium. Juanita became her caretaker, surrogate daughter, and best friend until the day she died, which broke Juanita's heart.

Billy Rasmussen kept his house in Cat Creek after they were married, but he and Elvira used it mostly to shower and to cozy up during the worst part of winter. During the time of year when the weather was kind, they stayed in Elvira's shack in the woods.

Cora and Walter McCabe were buried side by side in the Aurora Cemetery. Their estate was sold and probated and the house on Palentine Avenue sold, the proceeds divided between Juanita and the McCabe's son Chester, who seemed estranged from the family for reasons she did never understood.

Juanita moved in with Mary. She used much of the McCabe inheritance toward repair of leaky plumbing and unsafe wiring and put a new roof on the house. She and Mary whenever possible visited Jack in Walla Walla and continued when possible to bring produce to Hooverville.

Juanita kept in touch with Kenny Williams, who joined the navy as soon as he was of legal age. He later died in the Battle of Midway.

In prison Jack began to look his age, his hair having turned completely gray, but to Mary he seemed less troubled. Jack said a weight had been lifted from him. Jack told Mary for years he believed himself to be haunted by the killing. He said his punishment and imprisonment seemed to ease intrusive memories that had haunted him since arriving in Seattle. He had not had a nightmare since being jailed. She assured him she was still his wife and would wait for him faithfully, which she did.

Jack in turn was thankful his daughter Juanita was never accused and had grown into a fine young woman. It pleased him that she and Mary had become friends.

Frank, meanwhile, walls or no walls, continued to stir up trouble like a pot of mulligan stew. Because of prison violations, his sentence kept getting longer instead of shorter. On his third attempt, he finally managed to escape. Jack, much later, long after having been released from the walls, received a mysterious postcard from Alaska with no information or writing, just a picture of fishing boats tied at a pier.

Arthur Ramos was forgiven by his wife, with whom he moved back to San Pedro. She left him three months later, moved in with her parents in Tuscon, and filed for divorce.

Jack was paroled in 1937 and met outside the prison gates by Mary, Juanita, and the Rasmussen's, who had come west for the event. They drove to the Wallingford house where he was led to a table set with chicken and dumplings where he ate his first of many good home cooked meals to come.

The three of them, he, Mary, and Juanita, lived together in the Wallingford house for nineteen years. Jack had no more nightmares. He died in 1961 of a cerebral aneurysm at the age of seventy three. Mary predeceased him by one year.

Juanita lives in the house to this day, but is disabled with multiple sclerosis, and survives against all expectations.

Hooverville was bulldozed in 1940, but no one moved in to rebuild it. What happened to the men after Hooverville is another story. Most of the men had already left for manufacturing jobs created by The New Deal and the war in the Pacific and Europe.

— The End —

Acknowledgments

THE STORY LINE OF THIS NOVEL regarding the King County Police Department and other events was entirely fictitious, but the author otherwise endeavored to remain true to historical fact. For more information on Hooverville and *The Unemployed Citizen's League* the author directs the reader to University of Washington archives online, specifically *Seattle/Hooverville*, and also *Civil Rights and Labor History Consortium*. Also utilized was *From Boom to Bust, Seattle Volume Two 1921-1940*, Richard C. Berner *Charles Press*.

The author would like to express his gratitude to several early readers of this novel.

Thanks to Mark Leeder who read two different versions of this novel.

Thanks to Sandy Hutchins for her encouragement and early reading.

Thanks to Dan Lehman for his support, and to Carol Lee Lorenzo.

Thanks to Marilyn Macquarrie for her meticulous proof reading and editorial observations.

Thanks to Kathy Raines for her artwork which graces the book cover, and to book designer Gary Broughman of CHB Media.

About the Author

A NATIVE OF SEATTLE, Lea (pronounced Lee) Macquarrie has lived in Mexico City, New York City, San Francisco, the mountains of New Mexico, and the Greek islands. He has worked too many jobs to list or even remember, including employment as a merchant seaman, dishwasher, janitor, pharmacy technician, psychiatric assistant and musician. In addition to *Trouble in Seattle* he is the author of *A Holy Ghost in Mexico City*, available in paperback or Kindle through Amazon. He is currently working on what he calls his "definitive jazz novel."

Made in United States
North Haven, CT
12 January 2023